THIS
DAMNATION

Associated with sharing the experience of watching Chelsea
Football Club, Mark Worrall has broadened the scope of his
writing to embrace fiction, screenplays and journalism. *This
Damnation* is his second novel.

ALSO BY MARK WORRALL

FICTION
Blue Murder, Chelsea till I Die

FOOTBALL
Over Land and Sea
One Man Went to Mow
Chelsea Chronicles (five volume series)

COLLABORATIONS
(with Kelvin Barker and David Johnstone)
Chelsea Here Chelsea There
Making History, Not Reliving It
Chelsea Football Fanzine, the best of cfcuk volume one

THIS DAMNATION

MARK WORRALL

Gate 17
9 Priory Business Park,
Wistow Road, Kibworth Beauchamp,
Leicestershire. LE8 0RX
Tel: 0116 279 2299
Email: enquiries@gate17.co.uk
Web: www.gate17.co.uk
Twitter: @gate17marco
Cover Design: Jennifer Parker

ISBN 978 0955745 966

British Library Cataloguing in Publication Data.
A catalogue record for this book is available from the British Library.

Printed and bound in the UK by TJ International, Padstow, Cornwall

Typeset in 11pt Aldine401 BT by Troubador Publishing Ltd, Leicester, UK

Gate 17 is an imprint of Troubador Publishing

Thank you: Russell De Rozario, Oskar de Rozario, Tony Hood, Keith Sanford, John King, Paula Harding, JoJo Gorman, Peter Coyne, The Godfathers, Colin Hillier, Mark Parry, Tom Cox, Kenny Mackin, Cheam Sports Club, Rob Harverson, David Johnstone, cfcuk, Al Gregg, Terry Goodwin, Private John Samuel Goodwin (1896–1982).

This Damnation is dedicated to the men and women who have served and continue to serve Crown and Country. We owe our freedom to their dedication and selflessness. Lest we forget those who have fallen, and those whose lives have been shattered by injury and stress.

For my daughter Misty Blue

THIS DAMNATION

PROLOGUE

31 May 2007

Kennedy held the vodka bottle at arm's length in front of him, sinewy fingers wrapped tightly around the glass ensuring there could be no spillage as his cold, clammy hands trembled from the illness that wracked his body and had ruined his mind. Beside him, head tilted back, eyes scrutinising his every move, sat a short-haired, muscular Staffordshire bull terrier. Faithful and obedient, the dog had been his constant companion for the past six months. Indifferent to being ignored, attentive when shown affection, in a judgmental world man's best friend had offered no opinion on the trials and tribulations of the life that his master had shared with him.

'Vodka, vodka, vodka.' The clear liquid swirled as Kennedy swayed unsteadily on his feet. Was the bottle half full or half empty? It was hard to tell… the dank, damp, piss-stinking room he was standing in the middle of was enveloped in darkness and blanketed by a brooding, pessimistic gloominess that matched his mood of despondency and despair. Right now, nothing mattered anymore… except getting the job done. Finishing things off… once and for all.

Outside, driving rain rat-a-tat-tatted machine gun-like against the naked window he was staring at, water cascading down the pane blurring a hi-rise tower block vista of familiar London landmarks that skirted the River Thames and beyond.

A bolt of lightning zigzagged across the night sky illuminating his craggy face… sallow, scarred, stubbly skin stretched taut as a drum across chiselled, once-handsome features... dilated pupils constricting to pin pricks, bloodshot eyes widening... betraying the all-embracing horror of living life beyond the edge.

Kennedy's grip on the bottle tightened as he drew it slowly towards his mouth, knuckles whitening, biceps flexing as if battling against some hitherto unseen force. Good versus evil, God against the Devil... angels and demons... heaven and hell.

The sound of thunder cannoned into the room, ricocheting off the bare walls, assaulting his ears as he pursed his cracked lips and then bared his yellowed rotting teeth. He grimaced as he repeated the process several times... outwardly readying himself for what he'd planned would follow.

'My grandfather was a drunk.' Rasping words hacksawed through the sound of the storm. 'My father was a drunk.' Profound phrases punctuated by throat-searing swigs from the bottle. 'I am a drunk.' The last of the vodka consumed. 'I drink to forget the pain of life.'

Sensing imminent danger, the bull terrier began barking loudly. Kennedy rocked back on his heels. 'CHAAAAAAARGE!' he bellowed, hurling the empty bottle grenade-style at the window which shattered explosively on impact as he lunged towards it. Shards of glass caught by the wind now gusting into the room lacerated his face and hands drawing blood, its dark crimson hue thinned instantly by the lashing rain. He clambered onto the windowsill and crouched on his haunches. Seventeen storeys high, fifty metres down to the ground, the sudden impact would kill him instantly. In his forty-four years he'd been beaten, stabbed and shot and lived to tell the tale, but the bone-shattering, tissue-pulping, multiple injuries consistent with a fall of this magnitude were unsurvivable. Game over, problems solved. The dog whimpered and mewled as it jumped repeatedly at the wall, trying to join him on the sill, claws scrabbling in vain... again and again and again.

Kennedy sucked his lips into his mouth, ferrous-tasting blood congealed on his dry tongue. Heart racing, head pumping, adrenalin and alcohol coursed through his body as he momentarily surveyed the scene before him. Blinking deliberately to clear rain and bitter tears from his hollow eyes, his vacant gaze meandered from the chimney stacks of Battersea Power Station to the east, along the southern bank of the dirty old river to the nearby spire of St Mary's Church. The church bells were tolling loudly, but for whom? St Mary's congregation had long been lost to apathy, ignorance and vast self-interest.

'Nothing will ever fill the void Kennedy's tragic death has left in all of our lives. We can only pray that one day we can come to terms with his passing.' Father Slattery stood at the pulpit and spoke solemnly, his hushed tones addressing row after row of empty pews... empty save for one. 'Kennedy was a kind, sensitive and hard-working man. He was a grandfather, husband, father, brother, uncle, friend and loving son who served his country in time of need, a man to be proud of.'

An old woman sat at the first pew swathed funereally in black fidgeted with a Rosary necklace as she listened to the priest. The committal would soon follow, and then it would be over. She stared at the coffin laid at the altar steps, eyes focusing on the maroon beret placed neatly in the centre of the red, white and blue Union Flag that was draped across the casket. 'For Queen and Country,' she whispered, stifling an anguished sob. 'Why? Where is everyone? Where is the gratitude? You took my father, my husband and my son.'

Kennedy's body arched forward involuntarily. The vodka soaking through his nervous system dulled the pain in his slashed hands that continued to grip the window frame and prevent him falling. Swallowing hard, he felt the coarseness of the surface of his tongue sticking against the roof of his mouth that was wide open. He wanted to scream again.

'MOTHER!' Was this it? His miserable life flashing before his eyes? Memories of the why's and the wherefores? Of how it had all come down to this? Yes, this. The end.

He looked up at the sky. A dark, turbulent, stormy void showering him with water, baptising him with resentment. Thunder, lightning, the devil riding out on his chariot across the clouds looking for the souls of the damned. 'MOTHER!' An anguished scream. 'MOTHERRRR!' Standing up, hands instinctively reaching out for the support afforded by the frame of the window, he lapped at the rain. 'Please! Mother! I'm still here.'

★ ★ ★

Vera Jones leaned forward in the rocking chair she was sitting on, right hand clutching a remote control pointed at the television in front of her, left hand resting on the silver crucifix attached to the emerald-beaded Rosary necklace nestling in her lap. There was something comforting about the creaking noise her gentle motion initiated. The hand-me-down heirloom had been her mother's and her grandmother's before that.

Generations of women from her family had sat in the chair down the years and pondered the meaning of life and she was no different. An old woman coming to terms with the passage of time, remembering departed relatives that were dear to her heart and the ebb and flow of conversations that had once coloured her days as brightly as the fresh roses beautifully arranged in the flared crystal vase sitting on the pine cabinet alongside the television set.

The soporific tick-tock of the ornate brass carriage clock on the mantelpiece had eased her to sleep a couple of hours earlier, however the sound of rolling thunder and the violent storm outside had disturbed her. An instinctive motherly concern overwhelmed normally peaceful waking thoughts.

She thought she'd heard a voice, a cry for help. Her mind playing tricks again. Was it time for her tablets?

Vera shrugged her shoulders and flicked from channel to channel. Modern television was rubbish. Too many stations, not enough quality. She always ended up with the BBC, and it was just the same with the wireless. The British Broadcasting Corporation was, well just that… British, and, most of the time, there was something very reassuring about that.

BBC2. An over-made-up, corset-wearing, whorish-looking woman with copper-coloured hair discussing sexual deviancy with a middle-aged man who appeared intimidated by her presence. No thanks!

BBC1. "And now we present a feature-length documentary about the Falklands War which commenced twenty-five years ago this week".

As the continuity announcer spoke, Vera gasped, rocking the chair forward sharply, her sudden movement causing the remote control to slip from her grasp and fall onto the parquet floor where it split open spilling out the batteries that powered it.

"This programme contains strong language and scenes some viewers may find upsetting".

'Oh dear! Well I'll have to watch it now,' Vera muttered, pressing her feet against the floor to stop the motion of the chair and gazing at the television screen as she listened to the narrator.

"In 1982, when Britain went to war with Argentina over the ownership of the Falklands, a group of bleak South Atlantic islands that few people had ever heard of, critics questioned the logic of the governments of both nations, indeed one prominent Argentine writer described the conflict as two bald men fighting over a comb. But the war was anything but pointless to the men who fought in it, many of whom still carry visible and mental scars of bloody battle".

As grainy images of tired-looking young soldiers filled the screen, Vera shook her head and began to weep.

THE BATTLE

Argentina! Argenfuckingtina! The 1978 World Cup winners. Chain-smoking manager, Cesar Luis Menotti. Captain, Daniel Passarella. Two-goal final hero Mario 'the matador' Kempes. Osvaldo Ardiles… even if he was a Spurs player now. Footballers not warmongers. The 1982 tournament was just about to start in sunny Spain so why the fuck had the Argies decided to kick off in the Falkland Islands, a British overseas territory whose capital Port Stanley was almost eight thousand miles from London?

Kennedy knew the score but still struggled to get his head around it. Even now, listening to the Battalion Battle Plan being explained in detail, being told that in a few hours he was going to be engaged in trench warfare, hand-to-hand combat, a real fire fight, one he might not survive… it was difficult to comprehend. Why Argentina? Don't fucking cry for me Argentina. *'Evita.'* Julie Covington, Elaine Paige. Mum loved it, but not now.

Life in the Parachute Regiment had been what he'd expected. Join the Army. Be the best. Private Kennedy Jones, Private Paul 'Fletch' Fletcher and Private Brian 'Bertie' Bassett, the three inseparable friends from Battersea were the best. 'Utrinque Paratus', the Para motto, 'Ready for Anything'. Anything? Yes! The Falklands Conflict, their first experience of active duty.

Having spent their initial year in the Regiment training with the Junior Parachute Company, Kennedy, Fletch and

Bertie had an expectation that once they'd won their wings and been sent to 3 Para, the battalion they'd requested to join, they would be deployed to Northern Ireland on the next scheduled tour of duty. 3 Para left for the Province in December 1980 for a four-month tour but Kennedy, Fletch and Bertie weren't with them. Yet to reach their eighteenth birthdays, they were too young.

In 1971, three off-duty soldiers, two of them teenage brothers, the youngest just seventeen years old, had been lured from a bar in Belfast and driven to a remote location where they were shot dead by members of the Provisional Irish Republican Army. As a result of the atrocity, the British Army raised the minimum age for serving in Northern Ireland to eighteen.

Kennedy had felt frustrated. It didn't make sense that at seventeen years of age he could have been sent to fight on the front line in a war, and yet couldn't go to Ulster. He'd wanted to immerse himself totally in the hostile world his father Alec, who'd served in the Province with the Parachute Regiment, had described. Demonstrations, rioting mobs, car bombs, shootings, ignorance, hate. He wanted to understand why his father had been murdered there and by whom? If he got the chance, he'd find the perpetrators. If he didn't, so be it. His was an intense and personal agenda that he'd shared partly with his friends but with no one else.

Schooling in urban warfare had taken place in a replica environment. The Ministry of Defence national training estate at Hythe and Lydd in Kent included a perfect recreation of a Northern Irish village. The level of detail from the ground up was exceptional. From the bricks and mortar, graffiti, unseen snipers, gunfire and explosions, to the antagonistic dummies that yelled abuse. Without ever having been to Ulster, the words of those with experience had to be taken at face value every second of every minute of every day. Well-drilled foot patrols. Looking, listening, making notes, making mistakes, doing it all again. The atmosphere had crackled with an intensity that permeated Kennedy's senses. He'd thrived on it. Mentally, he was prepared for the streets of Belfast, the Falklands though? That was different, an unknown quantity, an unwelcome intrusion. It wasn't part of the plan. His plan.

At the time news broke that on 19 March a group of scrap metal merchants had raised the Argentine flag on South Georgia, 3 Para, stationed at Kandahar Barracks, Tidworth, Wiltshire, was the UK Spearhead battalion on standby to be deployed anywhere in the world within forty-eight hours.

Fletch had joked about the Argentinian equivalent of Steptoe and Son being responsible for the occupation, but regular intelligence briefings suggested otherwise, creating an expectation in the camp that deployment to the South Atlantic to deal with the invaders was imminent. Up until recently, only the politically informed had known about Argentina's longstanding dispute with the United Kingdom over the sovereignty of the Falklands. Now however, the papers and television news bulletins were full of stories about the islands and how Argentina's latest military dictatorship headed by General Leopoldo Galtieri was deflecting the attention of the nation's citizens away from the dire economic situation they faced at home by appealing to their patriotic fervour.

Following on from the civilian occupation of South Georgia, on Friday 2 April, Argentine armed forces mounted amphibious landings on the Falkland Islands. "Las Malvinas son Argentinas", Galtieri had proclaimed.

The next day, an emergency meeting at the House of Commons was convened and Prime Minister Margaret Thatcher presided over the decision to form a task force to retake the islands. "Defeat? I do not recognise the meaning of the word", she'd declared.

Immediately, 3 Para's Commanding Officer informed the

battalion that they were going to the Falklands. "Let's fucking have it". Kennedy, Fletch and Bertie had hollered exultantly.

It wasn't the only tumultuous piece of information Kennedy received that day. In the evening, he'd telephoned his wife Nicky from a public callbox to inform her of the news, and was left speechless when she'd advised him she was pregnant with their first child. A rapid succession of pips had followed and, as he'd jammed a ten pence piece into the coin mechanism to extend the call, he'd finally found his voice. 'I love you babe.' He couldn't think of anything else to say as he'd listened to Nicky sobbing as she spoke on the other end of the line.

"Come home safe to us. Please come home safe".

"*Us*". It was a lot to take in. A few hours earlier his only concern had been finding out how Chelsea had got on against Oldham Athletic. Now, not only was he going off to fight for Queen and Country, he was going to be a father as well. 'Fucking hell!'

A boot planted squarely on the kiosk door distracted him. He turned, waving the telephone receiver irately, to see Fletch stood outside holding a beer can aloft, mouth wide open, pulling a face. 'Oi oi! We drew two each,' he shouted. 'Alan Mayes got 'em both.'

Kennedy grinned. 'Good old Chelsea.'

'We're the Boys in Blue Division Two.' Fletch started singing. Kennedy didn't join in… his mind was already eight thousand miles from Stamford Bridge.

★ ★ ★

Mount Longdon, four miles west of Port Stanley, provided the high ground requisite for Argentine forces to make maximum use of artillery bombardments against British troops seeking to reclaim the Falklands capital. Minefields, machine gun bunkers, mortars and anti-tank weaponry were already in place to support Longdon's defence by the Argentine 7th Infantry who were augmented by two Marine Infantry platoons and several Special Forces units. Militarily, its occupation was essential. On 10 June, 3 Para, the Spearhead element of 3 Commando Brigade located on nearby Mount Estancia, received orders to take it. The attack was planned for the following night.

It was almost three weeks since the battalion had come ashore at Sandy Bay on the northwest coast of East Falkland and just over two months since they had set sail from Southampton aboard the SS Canberra, a P&O cruise liner requisitioned by the Ministry of Defence for use as a troopship.

At sea, the daily regime had consisted of physical training and weaponry drills. Arduous and tedious, the activities felt pointless. When docking en-route at Freetown, Sierra Leone, to take on provisions and refuel, the general consensus among the men had been that Argentina would give up the Malvinas cause long before they arrived. The belief remained as the Canberra sailed south and anchored at Ascension Island where beach landings had been practiced in readiness for an assault on the Falklands.

On 4 May however, the real gravity of the situation hit home. The previous day, British nuclear submarine HMS Conqueror had sunk the Argentine battlecruiser General Belgrano with the loss of 368 lives. The Argentine Navy retaliated by striking British destroyer HMS Sheffield with an Exocet air-launched missile. The warhead failed to detonate, but the impact tore a hole in the Sheffield's hull and burning missile fuel ignited the diesel supplies aboard the ship causing a raging inferno. Twenty men were killed in the attack.

Suddenly, everything felt serious, real and deadly. There would be no going back until the job was done. Argentina was clearly not going to give up the Falklands without a fight.

Two days later, escorted by two Royal Navy battleships, HMS Ardent and HMS Argonaut, SS Canberra set sail on the final 3,800-mile leg of its journey to the Islands.

'Look after yourself.' It had been easy to say, and good to hear. But the words had a new meaning. His father had always said the same when leaving home to return to barracks. The sentiment had a matter-of-fact quality to it. "Look after yourself son". Kennedy shivered. 'Look after yourself mate.' He glanced at Fletch and Bertie. His friends were glassy-eyed, freezing in the bitter cold, staring at the Landing Craft Vehicle Personnel carrier they were about to board.

On 18 May the SS Canberra had sailed into the 200-mile Total Exclusion Zone around the Islands. The following day, 3 Para moved from the SS Canberra to HMS Intrepid, and final preparations were made for a beach assault on the northwest coast of East Falkland scheduled for 21 May.

'BEACH!' The command sounded like 'Bitch!' 'Fucking bitch!' Kennedy lifted his Self-Loading Rifle and stepped over the LCVP's ramp into the icy San Carlos Water breakers. To the left of him Bertie, just ahead Fletch, all of them laden with almost 130lbs of equipment comprising a fully loaded SLR, ammunition, grenades, mortar rounds and webbing carrying the essentials for survival. The large 'Bergen' rucksack on Fletch's back looked unwieldy, he was carrying one too. They all were. Not sitting ducks, but moving. Easy targets, like the allied forces storming the beaches of Normandy. Step-by-step, and still the enemy gunfire didn't come. Pumped with adrenalin and motivated by fear, Kennedy gulped in lungfuls of air as he splashed through the grey-green water and made it to the stone covered beach.

Momentarily, he turned to look out to sea. As he did so the sound of his heart beating and blood pounding in his ears ebbed like the water retreating from the shore. Suddenly, as he tuned in and registered what he was seeing, the crackle of radio transmissions and men shouting grew louder. He picked out HMS Intrepid and scanned the horizon rapidly round to landfall at Fanning Head where automatic gunfire, tracer rounds, explosions and thunderflashes immediately enveloped his aural and visual senses. It was like watching an uncoordinated 5 November firework display. The experience felt surreal, slow motion, compelling… almost filmic. But this was no 'lights, camera, action' scenario. The director wasn't going to yell, 'CUT!' There were no fluffy blondes on set, no tea breaks to re-read lines. This was is it! This was war!

★ ★ ★

Kennedy's platoon had been briefed. The battle plan to take Mount Longdon, the primary objective, sounded simple. The mission statement code words for each sub-objective were related to the game of rugby. Advance up the mountain from the Start Line, codenamed 'Free Kick'. Capture and clear 'Fly Half'. Advance again. Clear and hold 'Full Back'. Rugby eh… a gentleman's game played by hooligans. Hooligans they may be, but this was no game. Intelligence indicated the Argentine Army were armed to the teeth and lying in wait for them.

Tabbing across the coarse, frost-covered tussock grass that flecked the craggy terrain between Mount Estancia and Mount Longdon was energy-sapping. The grass was slippy and buffeted collective ankles afforded little support by regulation issue DMS boots clearly unsuitable for sustained use in such trying conditions. Insufficiently waterproofed, the boots were easily saturated. Kennedy's feet ached. Sore, chafed, blistered and almost permanently damp, he was fortunate not to have succumbed to the perils of trench foot that had already affected many of the men.

Napoleon Bonaparte once said, "An army marches on

its stomach". Bollocks to Napoleon! He would have said that, greedy bastard! Kennedy humoured himself. 'An army marches on its feet. Feet are precious. Feet need to be cosseted and loved. Feet need to be kept warm and dry.' But here, at the end of the earth, in this Godforsaken place, it was hopeless, an impossible challenge. From the minute he'd stepped off the LCVP into the sea at Port San Carlos, his feet had been wet. The four-mile uphill hike through bracken-covered marshland to Windy Gap... wet. The twenty-seven-mile squelching, sweaty slog through sleet and snow to Teal Inlet... wet. The eighteen-mile unforgiving trudge across the boulder-strewn, pothole-riddled peat bogs to Mount Estancia ... wet. There was no escape from the water. It lashed down from the sky, it was whipped by the wicked wind, it rose from the ground... it permeated every last stitch of clothing. And then there was the cold. Sub-zero temperatures exacerbated by the wind increased the chill factor. Frostbite was an evocative word, icy teeth biting the skin. Here on this non-existent road to perdition, those fangs bit deep. Surely walking through the raging fires of hell would feel like heaven in comparison.

Crouched in position on the Battalion Start Line facing the west slope of Longdon, Kennedy could make out the shadowy figures of Fletch and Bertie and wondered what they were thinking. They had to be thinking something. Thinking time during the ten-mile tab from Estancia. Thinking time now. Waiting for the command to move forward.

Like him, Fletch had always been up for joining the Paras, but Bertie was different. He had a more philosophical approach to life. Bright in school, he'd passed his CSEs and should have stayed on and furthered his education... but he didn't want to be left out. It wasn't a case of peer group pressure, as an adopted kid who'd been in and out of care homes he wasn't part of a close-knit family. To him, the trio were like brothers. Enlisting together represented an opportunity to strengthen their kinship. It removed the need to think about what to do next.

Now though, Kennedy wasn't convinced Bertie had done the right thing. If his friend could have changed things or maybe turned the clock back, he reckoned he would have done so. It had been etched on his grimy, sweaty, wide-eyed, 'wish I was anywhere else but here' face as they'd attempted to dig trenches the first day they'd come ashore at East Falkland. The discordant cacophony of Argentine Pucara fighter aircraft engines whining overhead, gunfire from British Navy ships anchored in San Carlos Water, missiles exploding, machinery grinding, and men shouting had been an unnerving soundtrack for all of them. He pictured Fletch standing ankle-deep in water in the pit he'd dug brandishing his trench tool at Bertie.

"I wouldn't want to be in your shoes later mate", he'd hollered, the grin on his face appearing maniacal because of the way he'd applied his camouflage cream.

"Why's… Why's that?" had been Bertie's stammered reply.

"Cos they wouldn't fit me". Everyone looking on had laughed. Bertie however failed to appreciate the joke.

"Fuck right off", he'd retorted bluntly, turning to glare at Fletch.

"You'd have laughed at that back home".

"Yeah! Well we're not back home. We're fucking here".

Gallows humour wasn't for Bertie, it made his spirit sag just like the damp cigarette wilting at the corner of his mouth. Fletch on the other hand gave the impression he didn't give a fuck. He was a joker, the platoon comedian, good to have around, great for morale. But like all clowns he had a serious side, and happy face was stern tonight. Gritty, determined… but was he ready for anything? Maybe. Kennedy wasn't one hundred percent convinced. He recalled the look in his mother's eyes when he'd said the same. 'Utrinque Paratus'. She'd shaken her head.

'Fuck it!' Kennedy cursed inwardly. He felt responsibility for the wellbeing of both his friends. They were here because of him. He looked up at the hulking, brooding, malevolent mountain that was eerily illuminated by the moon and shivered. Tonight, of all nights, there was a cloudless starry sky. Momentarily, he imagined Nicky looking out of her bedroom window, into the same night sky, seeing the same moon and the same stars, rubbing her hands gently across her stomach, feeling the little kicks inside her, pleading for his safe return. "Come home safely my love. Please, please come home".

Shortly before they had left Estancia, the Company Sergeant Major had addressed the platoon about the forthcoming attack on Longdon. CSM Stan Roper, known as Stan the Man, was well respected for his tactical knowledge and admired for his indefatigable appetite for soldiering. Everyone feared the consequences of letting him down, and a respectful silence had greeted his words. He'd spoke sanguinely about hand-to-hand combat, about trench warfare, about winning the fire fight, about battling on when friends were wounded, about the possibility of not coming back.

That was the chilling reality of the situation. Not coming back. Stan the Man advised prayer. Prayer! God help us! As Kennedy looked across at Bertie and Fletch his mind grappled with feelings of guilt and fear. Not coming back. That wasn't a part of the script, but who was writing it? God? His mother would say so. Religion, she was full of it. Forever quoting from the Bible. *"For God so loved the world, that he gave his only begotten Son, that whosoever believeth in him should not perish, but have everlasting life"*. (John 3:16) Everlasting life? What about Dad? Fuck it! If your number was up, there was little you could do about it… or was there? Not being here. That would have dramatically altered the probability of being killed. His father could have gone to work for Uncle Manny's security firm and be living to tell the tale. Manny had offered to take him on when he'd left school and Fletch... and Bertie. Why not? Fuck it! It was too late now.

Kennedy mentally mapped out the possibilities of his future. Death on the mountain. A sniper's bullet to the head. Being blown to smithereens. At least that way he wouldn't know a thing. "I'm sorry to have to tell you Mrs Jones..." Getting home safe and sound. Pacing the corridor outside the maternity ward at St Thomas's. "Ten little fingers and ten little toes. Your wife has given birth to a healthy baby boy Mr Jones, come this way". Fuck it! Fuck it! Fuck it! He had to stay alive tonight and get off the mountain in one piece, if only to be able to tell his first born not to follow in his footsteps as he had followed in his father's. The poor kid might think it was family tradition. He needed to know the facts. Fact one. You could die fighting for Queen and Country. Fact two didn't matter.

'Fix bayonets!' The terse command being passed along the company line sliced through Kennedy's thoughts as he instinctively pulled the cold steel blade from its scabbard and clipped it into place. The clunking sound of every man simultaneously following the order added to the tension. In training, Stan the Man had brought home the personal nature of hand-to-hand combat that was symbolised by the bayonet.

"What if it breaks Sergeant Major?"

"If your bayonet breaks, strike with the stock; if the stock gives way, hit with your fists; if your fists are hurt, bite with your teeth. Not my words, but the words of a Russian General, Mikhail Dragomirov. Only he wins who fights desperately, to the death. Do you understand?"

Stepping forward over the Start Line that had been demarcated with white tape Kennedy felt bile rising in his gullet as his stomach knotted. Slay... or be slayed. "Only he wins who fights desperately, to the death". He muttered the words slowly, gripping his SLR and contemplating what the next few hours might bring. Would he really get to see the whites of the eyes of an unseen enemy? Where were they? Were they blind to the advancing figures of the platoon? Ghostly heaving breaths vaporising in the freezing air, body shapes silhouetted by the moon. Were they deaf? The sound of motion... of boots scrunching across the ground, of ammunition and equipment being carried... it was loud. Maybe the Argentinians, knowing what was coming, had walked away. Given up Longdon without a fight. It was only twelve miles to Port Stanley. Victory. Maybe...

The explosion was cataclysmic, an anti-personnel mine detonating. Kennedy's train of thought juddered to a halt as he dropped to his haunches in the cold, damp grass. The flash of light, the percussive sound, the shock wave, the shock. The harrowing screams of a wounded man wailing in agonising pain. Men shouting. A terrifying echo. 'Man down! Man down! Man down! Man down!' In an instant, machine gun tracer rounds zipped through the air and smashed into the ground like a plague of steroidal green and orange kamikaze fireflies. A flare lit up the position. Kennedy felt naked. The enemy were here all right... and he was in their sights.

'Fucking go! Go. Let's fucking move.' British voices barked out orders, Spanish voices melded into the commotion. The silhouettes of soldiers resembled manic marionettes. Friend or foe? Automatic gunfire, muzzle flashes. Foe! Take aim, fire. 'Move forward!' It felt chaotic. It felt blind. But at least there was no time to think. Firing his SLR at the muzzle flashes above, Kennedy scrambled across the ground towards the comparative safety afforded by a rocky outcrop. Three metres to his left he could make out a prone figure lying motionless on smouldering ground. 'Help me.' The voice sounded familiar. 'Please.' Feeble and fading, then replaced by groans that were masked by the repetitive thudding sound of heavy artillery.

'Bertie!' Kennedy called out, but there was no reply. A sixth sense and instinct told him it was his friend. He began crawling across the grass, but as he moved out from the cover of the rocks a volley of automatic gunfire peppered the area missing him by inches. Rolling over as he retreated back behind the outcrop he caught sight of muzzle flashes from the side of a large boulder five metres up the slope. The Argentinian sniper knew his position. He probably thought Bertie was dead. If he moved again to his left he might suspect differently and fire at both of them. He edged to his right and braced himself in a crouching position.

'CHARGE!' The order from further along the slope ripped through the deafening noise of battle. Unexpected, but impeccable timing. The mountainside became animated with shouting scurrying figures advancing up the hill. The sound of machine gunfire, grenades exploding and men swearing and screaming curdled his blood but Kennedy was focussed. Clutching his SLR he sprang forward and dashed towards the boulder, firing as he went. For once, perfect purchase enabled him to cover the ground quickly.

'CAAAAAHNT!' His battle cry was drawn out, unrehearsed and terrifying. The last word he ever said? No. As if propelled by an unseen force, Kennedy reached the boulder, rounded it, and lunged at the shape rolling to face him. A flare lit up the sky just as he bayoneted the Argentine who howled as he was impaled by the cold steel. The soldier dropped his weapon and fell back screaming in Spanish, legs kicking, arms flailing trying to protect himself from the brute force of the attack. Kennedy could see terror in the man's face.

'Never take your eyes off your opponent.' Again and again he thrust forward. 'CAAAAAHNT!' Heart racing, blood coursing through his veins. 'CAAAAAHNT!' Flooded with adrenalin, drenched in sweat. 'CAAAAAHNT!' The Argentine fell silent. Bloodied, battered and beaten. Dead!

There. It was done. Kennedy gasped for air and crouched down as the light from the flare flickered as it drifted and then expired. Darkness... but there was no rest in peace. Despite the cacophonous sound of the battle raging on unabated, pummelling his eardrums, he could still hear the last words of the man he had just killed. "Madre de Dios! Yo no quiero morir por esto".

Kennedy slithered down the slope to where Bertie was lying. 'Fuck!' The lower parts of both his friend's legs were missing, all that remained were two stumps of bloody flesh... gristle and bone tangled with charred, frayed material and matted with mud. His right arm was a mutilated mess of shredded, sinewy skin and minced muscle... the hand was gone. He had two choices, to try and dress his wounds in the open and risk them both being shot, or drag him to the comparative safety of the rocky outcrop.

Bertie, his breath shallow, raised his left hand and grabbed at Kennedy's webbing. 'D, don't... le, le, leave me here,' he croaked, shivering as he spoke.

'Never.' Kennedy snatched at Bertie's dog tags, freeing the Syrette of morphine that was taped to the cord he swiftly injected him with the anaesthetic. The fire fight further up the slope intensifying provided him with the opportunity to grapple Bertie into a position whereby he was able to hook his arms under his chest and half carry, half drag him back to the outcrop. As he shuffled behind the rocks, a hail of machine gun fire splattered across the ground they had just covered.

'Medic!' Kennedy called out as Bertie whimpered in pain. 'Medic!' He took his own Syrette of morphine and administered it to his friend. It was a selfless thing to do, done without thinking of the consequences of also being wounded. Of being alone, in pain... with nobody to help. 'Medic!' Kennedy elevated Bertie's legs resting them on a clump of earth before applying shell dressings to his wounds to try and staunch the flow of blood.

'What's his name?'

Kennedy turned to see two dark shapes crouching over him. 'Private Bassett... Bertie.' Dazzled momentarily by a red torchlight shining down, he leaned back against the cold hard stone as one of the men knelt down next to Bertie and assessed his injuries.

'He needs to be moved to the RAP immediately,' said the second man authoritatively. Kennedy recognised the voice of CSM Roper, and as his eyesight regained its night focus he heaved a sigh of relief. Three more members of the platoon arrived and began preparing Bertie's evacuation to the improvised Regimental Aid Post set up thirty metres further down the mountainside in a narrow rocky gully that afforded reasonable shelter from incoming fire.

Kennedy looked on as Bertie, who had lost consciousness, was lifted onto a makeshift stretcher. He wanted to scream, to call out... to cry at the injustice of it all. "Madre de Dios! Yo no quiero morir por esto". Mother of God! He guessed that, but what did the rest mean? That soldier. That bloody mask of death. Somebody's son, somebody's husband, a father. 'It could have been me.'

'You okay?' CSM Roper tapped Kennedy on the shoulder. 'You did well.'

Kennedy shrugged is shoulders. The CSM's voice sounded muffled. He pinched his nose and blew until his ears popped and he could hear more clearly.

'That machine gun bunker on the right of the cliff face has to be cleared before we can make any further progress.'

'Yes Sergeant Major.' Kennedy considered the prospect of being cut down by a hail of bullets. Surely death would come quickly, his morphine was gone. Bertie was gravely wounded, so who would save him should he fall? Fletch? Where was Fletch? 'Fletch!' he called out, not thinking.

'Fletch?' enquired CSM Roper.

'Private Paul Fletcher.'

'Nothing too serious. Shrapnel wound. Being patched up at the RAP.'

Kennedy's eyes welled up as he stared straight ahead. 'Fletch as well. For fucks sake!'

CSM Roper grimaced and signalled the attention of a sergeant from a different platoon who was scrambling past the soldiers preparing to move Bertie. As the sergeant backed into the outcrop, another flare burst overhead heralding a fresh spate of heavy artillery bombardment and exchange of gunfire.

'Sergeant Prime. You know what to do.' As CSM Roper spoke, the sound of Spanish voices shouting nearby highlighted their proximity to the fire fight. Kennedy swung his SLR round and crawled to a gravestone-shaped wedge of granite jutting from the ground at the edge of their cover. As he reached it, a volley of bullets smashed into the rock splitting it in two thereby permitting a brief glimpse of green muzzle flash from the enemy bunker. 'Gotcha!' He shuffled back to his previous position and sat up.

'Are you ready?' Sergeant Prime was holding a grenade and bracing himself to toss it towards the bunker.

There was nobody else behind the outcrop now. As the flare began to flicker and drift, Kennedy could see CSM Roper moving down the slope to where another fallen soldier lay.

'When this goes. We go.' Sergeant Prime arched his right arm back. 'The boys back there will lay down covering fire. We go in from the right.'

No time to think. No time to wonder. No time to ask. Who was this man? Sergeant Prime. 'Prime'. That name rang a bell.

Kennedy crawled to the edge of the outcrop once more and eased himself up against the rock so his cheek was resting against its cold, abrasive surface. 'Never take your eyes off your opponent.' He smiled at his personal mantra but knew he shouldn't have. 'What if I can't see my opponent?'

'MOVE!' Sergeant Prime roared.

As he lobbed the grenade, pandemonium ensued. Leaping from his position, Kennedy heard the resounding thud of the explosion. Red, green and orange tracer rounds cut through the air to the left. The decoy was working. It was less than ten metres to the bunker, but as he skirted across the ground firing his SLR he saw two figures running down the hill just above it. Enemy reinforcements? Silhouetted by the light from another flare bursting higher up the slope, he pointed his weapon in their direction. 'Fuck!' The shockwave from four successive blasts knocked him over. A round he had fired had struck a grenade one of the soldiers was carrying in his webbing setting off a chain reaction, detonating all the grenades both soldiers were armed with. A colossal cloud of white phosphorus smoke marked the point of their demise. 'Fuck that!'

'Down! Down!'

Kennedy buried his face in the frozen peat as Sergeant Prime ran past him tossing another grenade that was pitched perfectly at a green muzzle flash. Hysterical screaming followed the thud of the explosion. Kennedy began crawling towards the bunker from which white smoke was billowing. The pained shrieking and howling was intensifying. As he raised his SLR, the horrific sounds were silenced by repeated gunfire. Crack! Crack! Crack! Crack! Crack! Simultaneously, mortar rounds began pounding an area several metres further up the slope showering shards of rock and clumps of earth downwards. Instinctively, to avoid being hit, Kennedy stood up and bundled himself into the bunker. Landing hard on the ground winded him and, as he gasped for air, the stench of sweat, shit and burning flesh pervaded his nostrils causing him to retch.

'Position cleared. We got the cunts!'

As he lay on his side vomiting uncontrollably, Kennedy could make out the dark shape of Sergeant Prime. There was a sinister quality to his voice that added to the horror of the vision of hell in front of him now being eerily illuminated by another flare. Amid the dust and debris he could see pulped, smouldering bodies. Severed lifeless limbs of mangled crimson tissue and bone. Spilled guts, bloody brains, faces blown away. Two men? Three men? Four men? More? Lying amidst the carnage it was impossible to tell. He eased himself up against the side of bunker, wiped his mouth and picked up a packet of cigarettes that was on the floor next to him.

'You wanna give that up it's bad for your health.' Sergeant Prime drawled.

'So's getting shot.' Kennedy placed the packet on the floor.

'What's your name Private?'

'Jones… Kennedy Jones.'

'Kennedy eh.'

'Yes Sergeant.'

'Alec Jones' boy?'

'Yes Sergeant.'

'I served with your father in Northern Ireland.'

The sound of groaning from the far side of the bunker distracted them both. Kennedy looked across and saw an Argentine sitting in what appeared to be a cross-legged position pointing his rifle at them. The soldier had been blown in half and his upper body, speared by smouldering shrapnel, was an oozing mass of scarlet entrails. Face scorched, eyes blinded, mouth moving spluttering spittle, he spoke with foaming bloodied words. 'Madre de Dios! Yo no quiero morir por esto.'

'Mother of God!' There it was again. As Kennedy puzzled over the meaning of the rest of the dying man's words, he thought he heard him mumble 'I surrender' in faltering English.

Sergeant Prime raised his rifle and squeezed the trigger.

"By 11 a.m. on the morning of 12th June 1982, the battle for Mount Longdon had been won by the British. Twenty-three paratroopers lost their lives in the bloody and bitter conquest and upturned rifles standing in the peaty soil marked the spot where they had fallen".

Vera glanced up from the television screen and sighed as she dabbed her eyes with a handkerchief. As the narrator continued to relay the human cost of the Falklands War, she turned her attention to the four head-and-shoulder colour photographs mounted in highly polished brass frames hanging side-by-side in a neat row above the fireplace. Each photo portrayed a man dressed in military uniform. From left to right, grandson Jack, son Kennedy, husband Alec and father Jimmy. The drabness of the faded orange flock papered wall that had once brightened the room enhanced their lifelike quality. Rocking her chair back and forth, as she looked at each photograph in turn, tresses of long hair, white from years of worry, tumbled across the porcelain skin of her face which had yet to succumb to the ravages of aging. She'd been beautiful once. Blessed with silver screen goddess looks that had attracted a host of wannabe matinee idols. But there had only ever been one man for Vera Coyne… Alec Jones. 'Alec.' Her green eyes moistened again as she called his name, blurring the vividness of his image.

'Alec. Dear Alec.' Tears welled as her heart ached with sadness. As she wept, she began to sing.

'I vow to thee, my country, all earthly things above, Entire and whole and perfect, the service of my love; The love that asks no question, the love that stands the test, That lays upon the altar the dearest and the best; The love that never falters,

the love that pays the price, The love that makes undaunted the final sacrifice.'

The hymn comforted her. The words were personal to her. Her meaning. Her faith. Absolute, undeniable, just like her love. As if to prove a point to the four men looking down on her, she gripped the silver crucifix at the end of the Rosary necklace tightly, crying out in pain as the points spiked her skin and drew blood. Sobs stifled by the sudden discomfort, she opened her hand and stared at the crimson-stained sculpture of Christ on the cross. Now was the time to remind herself that the period for self-pity had long since passed. Jesus had died for her, for everybody. His suffering, death and resurrection had been foretold in the scriptures of the Old Testament. A life preordained. The only begotten Son of the Father. But how could any father allow such a thing to happen to his son? How? Why?

Men. What was is it about them? She'd never met her father, but Alec, Manny, Kennedy, Fletch, Bertie and Jack all subscribed to the same hand-me-down philosophy nurtured in youth and later propagated by a common-or-garden, alcohol-infused stubbornness that influenced their actions as adults. Born into a generation where women were seen, but seldom heard, just like her heroine the Virgin Mary, Vera had been powerless to do anything about these self-fulfilling, self-destructive prophecies but she'd declared herself guilty by association and was forever remorseful for their legacy.

Could it have been different? Choice. What did the Bible say? *"A man's heart deviseth his way: but the Lord directeth his steps".* (Proverbs 16:9) What about a woman's heart? What about cause and effect? What about her life? The consequences of choice were obvious to her. Were the lives of Alec, Manny, Kennedy, Fletch, Bertie, Jack and all the rest of the people in her world influenced by her choices? What had been the catalyst, the pivotal event? Vera rocked the chair back and forth and closed her eyes. The answer lay somewhere in the past.

PART ONE

PART ONE

HAPPY ST GEORGE'S DAY

23 April 1955

Caius House on Holman Street had always been an integral part of Vera's life. Architecturally, with its tall imposing red brick walls and narrow stone-arched stained glass windows, the building resembled a chapel, and it was her understanding that its origins lay in a partnership that had been established between nearby St Mary's Church and Caius College Cambridge which lent its name to the place.

Towards the end of the nineteenth century, a group of undergraduates from the university had come to Battersea, established a mission, and taken it upon themselves to improve the quality of life of the desperately poor slum kids by setting up clubs and societies, the most notable of which was Caius Amateur Boxing Club. Having survived the bombing blitz of the Second World War that had reduced much of the area to rubble, Caius did an outstanding job of keeping local war babies, many of whom had been orphaned by the conflict, off the streets.

Vera's mother Doreen had taken to religion after her husband Jimmy had been killed in action on 10 June 1944 while serving with No.4 Commando part of the 1st Special Service Brigade. The D-Day Invasion of Normandy had seen Corporal James Coyne land at Sword Beach on 6 June and march on to join the defence of a strategically important bridgehead to the east of the River Orne. Following a period of sustained artillery and mortar bombardment, Jimmy had led

3

his section in what proved to be a successful bayonet counter-attack on German infantry but he'd been fatally wounded engaging in hand-to-hand combat during the short and brutal battle.

Posthumously awarded the Military Medal, Jimmy Coyne had been honoured along with other casualties of war in a special commemorative service at St Mary's during which Doreen read a short passage from the Bible containing a verse that had insightful meaning for her. *"For God so loved the world, that he gave his only begotten Son, that whosoever believeth in him should not perish, but have everlasting life"*. (John 3:16)

Grief at God-fearing Jimmy's death was counterbalanced by joy from this newfound knowledge of the possibility they might be reunited in heaven. It was a simple question of faith. Consequently, Widow Doreen began devoting all her free time to church activities. These included assisting with the Sunday School Bible classes at Caius House that Vera had attended from an early age.

Doreen was beautiful, and Vera possessed her striking looks. Sharing the same flawless complexion, fine-boned sculpted features, flowing mane of russet hair and green eyes guaranteed mother and daughter plenty of attention. Attention of the wrong sort in Doreen's opinion. She was well aware of the dishonourable intentions of the feral boys who were members of Caius, in particular the Jones' brothers, Alec and Manny, who were smitten by Vera's innocence and beauty. She didn't approve of their interest, or the fact that they were about to fight each other in the boxing ring in front of her. Their father Fred, who'd made a point of standing next to her, was a lecherous type and she suspected his sons were cut from the same flash-Harry cloth.

Looking around it seemed that everyone she knew had turned out to witness this pugilistic rite of passage. She'd listened as Fred had explained that the winner of the bout would be acknowledged as the finest junior boxer at the club. He'd told her the fight had to be sanctioned by the Amateur Boxing Association as his boys were both below the age of seventeen with less than twelve months between their birthdates. It all sounded contrived. How could a father look on as his sons beat each other with their fists? Men! Having said that, the sibling factor was compelling and had garnered interest right across the area with fishwife tittle-tattle suggesting there was more than one trophy at stake. Doreen had heard the tongue wagging and initially protested at Vera's insistence to attend, but religion-influenced morals were soon overcome by a deep-seated romantic curiosity. A close knit family, two brothers, one girl... her girl. It had all the ingredients of a Hollywood epic, and the escapist aspect this represented distracted her from the kitchen sink drudgery of day-to-day life. A nudge from Fred brought her back to reality.

'There's Don Cockell, the Battersea Blacksmith. British and Commonwealth Heavyweight Champion. He's a member here.' As he spoke, Fred combed back his slick blonde hair that was fashionably styled into a quiff with a greased-back duck's arse.

Doreen frowned as Fred pointed Cockell out and waved enthusiastically at him. 'I don't care much for boxing,' she replied nonchalantly, reaching out to her daughter who was staring at a group of boys stood at the far side of the hall.

Fred puffed out his chest with pride as Cockell raised his hand in acknowledgement. 'Next month he goes to San Francisco to fight Rocky Marciano at the Kezar Stadium for the world title.' Unperturbed by Doreen's obvious lack of interest, he continued the lop-sided discussion. 'I thought he boxed better at light-heavyweight. Struggled to make it on the scales though... and that's why Randolph Turpin did him for the belts in that division.'

Doreen tilted her head back slightly and rolled her eyes. She wanted to say, 'Give it up. I don't know what you are talking about.' But there was no point.

'Do you think he has a chance against Marciano?' Fred nudged Doreen again. He wasn't expecting her to say anything. Ignorantly, he was ready with his own answer. 'I think he's got a fighter's chance. Don's got guts, but Rocky's a noble artist all right and unbeaten at that. I think he'll knock our Don out.'

Pleased with his summation of Cockell's prospects, Fred thrust his hands into his trousers. Doreen glanced sideways at him, making sure to avoid eye contact. His sartorial appearance wasn't lost on her. She'd always admired smartly dressed men. There was something familiar and peacockish about the silk-patterned navy blue brocade waistcoat he wore over a white shirt that had a blue cravat tied at the collar. What was it? And then there were the high-waisted, narrow-legged black trousers with a pleated front. They looked an absolute nightmare to press. Who did his ironing? It was a strange thought to cross her mind and she banished it quickly, scowling as she glimpsed the blue box jacket carefully folded over the chair behind him. Teddy Boy! That was it. Now she remembered. The clothes and attendant hairstyle used to be known as the Edwardian look until a couple of years ago when the 'Daily Express' had shortened Edwardian to Teddy. Fred the Ted, that's what everyone called him. Now it made sense.

Doreen frowned, she knew the story about how he'd raised his boys on his own since his had wife died, but initial sympathy she'd felt for him had been diluted by local gossips who'd told her he was all too handy with his fists when he had a drink inside him. Punch first. Ask questions later. That Teddy Boy look was all a part of the act, inviting attention. Satisfying a need. Look at me. No. Don't look at me, or my girl. "Who are you looking at?" SMACK! A few too many drinks and it might be his girl that got a black eye. That's what they said about Fred.

It was an all too common trait in men. Jimmy had never laid a finger on her, just the curled ball of a hardened fist in the face of any man who was forward or flattering. She'd got used to it, but it wasn't an experience she was keen to repeat, and besides her Jimmy was irreplaceable. Doreen had made a pact with God to do his work on earth. In return she would be reunited with her husband once more in heaven. It was written in the Bible. 'Amen to that!'

'You what love?' Fred turned to her, wondering perhaps if after some careful deliberation maybe she was agreeing with him about Cockell's chances against Marciano, but before he could say anything he was distracted by the sound of his name being called.

'Oi Fred! FRED! We done it! We done it.'

Fred looked across to the boxing ring and saw Nick Hill waving at him. The sharp-dressed, barrel-chested leader of a motley assortment of flick knife-toting villains, card sharps and snooker players that went by the collective name of the Latchmere Lot, Hill, who made his living as an illegal bookmaker, wasn't a man it was wise to ignore, especially if you owed him money.

With an, 'I might have known' expression written on her face, Doreen shook her head in dismay as Hill made his way over.

'Happy Saint George's Day! Three cheers for the Blues,' he bellowed, rheumy eyes twinkling with alcohol-imbued enthusiasm as bystanders parted to let him through. Like the majority of people who lived in the area, Nick Hill was a fervent supporter of the local football team Chelsea who had just secured the League Division One Championship, the club's first major trophy in their fifty-year history, with a 3-0 victory over Sheffield Wednesday.

'Thanks for coming down.' Fred beamed with self-importance as he grasped Nick's outstretched hand and shook it vigorously.

'I said I'd be here, and here I am.'

'I bet it was good at Stamford Bridge today.'

'Not half! There must have been over fifty thousand of us. Parsons the rabbit bobbed up with a brace and Sillett got a penalty.'

'Champions eh! Who'd have thought it?'

'I wasn't too sure about Ted Drake when he got the manager's job, but he's finally shut up the music-hall jokers. That Norman Long for a start.'

Fred nodded approvingly. In all fairness, Long had long since deserved a slap, but there was something amusing about his piano-led ditty which chronicled a series of improbable events, including the sun coming out in Manchester, that occurred when he'd dreamt that Chelsea won the cup. Long was referring to the FA Cup, but winning the League was a far greater achievement. The hoary old joke was over, and match-going supporters like Nick Hill were entitled to be in their element.

'I remember when Drake started he'd said, "Let's have people eating, sleeping and drinking Chelsea". Bubbling with excitement, Hill grabbed Fred by the shoulders. 'And that's what's 'appened ain't it. You wouldn't believe it!' He paused to catch his breath intermittently as he spoke. 'Thirty of us from the Latchmere... together with the Plough Boys... and the cosh boys and the creepers from Brixton... and the Elephant. On any Friday night at the Locarno it would end up in bloody murder... but not at the Bridge.'

Fred shrugged his shoulders. He'd have loved to be a part of it all. As a kid he'd regularly gone to watch Chelsea with his father Chapman. He could remember his first game like it was yesterday. 20 April 1925. Thirty years ago. South Shields visited the Bridge. Football League Division Two. The game itself was unremarkable, a 1-1 draw in which Andy Wilson equalised an early South Shields goal. What had stayed with him though was the memory of the crowd. Always positive, always expectant... never chiding. Born optimists all of them, none more so than his father.

For Chapman Jones, hope had continued to spring eternal right up to the minute he was electrocuted in an accident at Battersea Power Station where he worked as a foreman. Suddenly, and not for the first time, a fog of bitter memories shrouded Fred's mind. 11 a.m. 3 September 1939. His wife Avis was in painful labour, about to give birth to their second child, and British Prime Minister Neville Chamberlain was addressing the nation in a speech being broadcast live on the wireless. *"This morning the British Ambassador in Berlin handed the German Government a final note stating that, unless we heard from them by eleven o'clock that they were prepared at once to withdraw their troops from Poland, a state of war would exist between us"*. As a sign perhaps of the horror to come, Avis began to scream... a prophetic accompaniment to the grave conclusion of Chamberlain's statement. *"I have to tell you now that no such undertaking has been received, and that consequently this country is at war with Germany"*.

Less than thirty minutes later, air-raid sirens began to screech for the first time, their undulating wail jarring with the sound of his wife's continued distress... the discord enough to start his infant son Alec crying. Fred winced as he gently rocked Alec's pram. He thought about putting a gas mask on. What about Alec? There wasn't one for him, so he'd do without as well.

There was no air-raid. Soon the sirens fell silent and Alec fell asleep. There was silence from upstairs as well. Fred lit a cigarette and went out into the street. The sun was shining... the sky was blue. 'Perfect! How could you start a war on a day like this?' He looked up at his bedroom window and saw the midwife beckoning him. As he turned to go inside, he heard his name being called by a man who was running along the pavement.

'Fred… Fred… You'd better come quick. It's your dad, he's been involved in an accident.'

'Oi Freddy… Are you listening to me? FREDDY!'

Fred blinked and shivered, his spine tingling as he shook his head and saw Nick Hill's beery face in front of his own.

'What's the matter? You look like you've see a ghost.' Nick pulled a hip flask from his jacket and unscrewed the cap. 'Here, have some of this VSOP.'

Fred grabbed the flask and took a slug. The brandy warmed him. It tasted expensive. Knowing Nick it probably was.

'Go on. Have another tot.'

Fred needed no encouragement. He enjoyed the taste and aroma of the burned wine and the glowing sensation he felt as he swallowed the liquid. There was something comforting about drinking spirits as opposed to beer and he often resorted to a few drops of the hard stuff when the past came calling as it always did. In lonely moments he found himself wishing he had someone to speak with, but then he might get an opinion he didn't want to hear. At least the bottle never answered back. He glanced at Doreen. He could talk to her, but she wasn't interested. He knew that. He should have spoken to her earlier. Much earlier. A ready-made family, it would have been nice.

'Go on… Have some more.'

Fred put the hipflask to his lips again. Out of the corner of his eye he could see Doreen talking to Vera. She was pointing at his sons who were clambering into the ring. He'd wanted to have a quick word with them, and Danny Prime who ran the boxing club and organised training, but Nick Hill had sidetracked him.

'What time does the fight start?' Nick cocked his head to one side as he looked at the black hands on the large white-faced clock. It was a couple of minutes past 8 p.m.

'It starts when, they're ready to start.' Fred raised his hand trying to attract Prime's attention.

'Maybe they can wait a while longer.'

Nick winked at him and patted the breast pocket of his jacket. It was no secret he was running a book on the outcome of the fight, and Fred had expected the conversation that followed to have taken place beforehand. Right on cue, Nick put his arm around him and whispered in his ear. 'Now if there's one person in here who knows these boys better than anyone else it's you.'

Fred laughed. There was no way Alec or Manny could be persuaded to throw the fight. They were too young to understand the concept of taking a fall and there was too much at stake for both of them. 'Ha ha… I don't know. No idea. Honest.'

'If Manny wins, it will be good for business. Good for you as well. Do you understand?' Nick narrowed his eyes and gripped Fred's shoulder tightly.

'You know I like a bet the same as the next man Nick, but the boys won't do nothing.'

'I happen to know you like a bet *more* than the next man, so perhaps the boys *do* need to do something.'

'They can't. But he can.' Fred pointed at Prime.

'Who? Lilywhite Dan the Tottenham fan?'

'Yeah! He can stop the fight at anytime.'

Nick nodded in approval and, as he walked off towards the ring, Fred turned to Doreen and tapped her on the shoulder. 'I'm just going to have a word with my lads. I don't want them hurting each other. I'm sure you understand.'

★ ★ ★

Vera had felt embarrassed for her mother at the attention Fred Jones was paying her. She may only have celebrated her fifteenth birthday the previous day, but she had an intuitive understanding of the order of things. Of right and wrong. Of morals… and the sexual tension a woman could create just by saying, 'No!'

'No!' That's why Alec and Manny wanted her. Manny, who was slightly older than her, and the younger of the two brothers by eleven months, was constantly trying to woo her. Heartthrob looks, chiselled features, blonde swept back hair, slim physique and a confident demeanour suggested he could have any girl he wanted if he put his mind to it, but she found him awkward. There was something about him that unsettled her. He'd pressured her into a date before Christmas and tried to kiss her, touch her. 'No! No! No!' Undeterred. She found he'd always be there wherever she went. At the school gates, on the street corner, here at Caius. Her mother said she'd speak to his father about it, but it was obvious that no discussion had taken place.

Alec was different. With his close-cropped mousy hair, freckled face and boxer's nose he wasn't exactly an oil painting, but maybe that wasn't a bad thing. He was also far more straight-laced than his brother who was turning into a dandy like his father. What she liked about Alec was his maturity, kind smile and polite manner when he was in her company. Of course, when they stole a few moments together away from Manny's prying eyes, he'd also tried it on. A peck on the cheek, a hand brushing against her legs. Seeing how far he could go. It was okay, she felt more relaxed, less pressured. A squeeze of her breasts. A slap! Alec understood what 'No!' meant.

She often wondered if the brothers spoke about her behind her back? Told tales about what they'd done to her or what they'd like to do? There was a cockiness inherent in all the local boys that she found off-putting, even Alec was prone to being a braggart when he was with his friends. Her mother said all men were the same and only after one thing. In order to retain her Godliness, until she married she must remain

12

faithful to the Lord, sincere, pure and above all chaste. *"Flee fornication. Every sin that a man doeth is without the body; but he that committeth fornication sinneth against his own body"*. (Corinthians 6:18) Her mother made her read that verse of the Bible daily so she fully comprehended its meaning. Sexual immorality was a sin not only against God but also ones self.

They both knew Alec was joining the Army soon. "To fight for Queen and Country", as he always put it, and her mother had once recalled the memory and 'shame' of falling pregnant to her father before he went off soldiering. Understandably, it influenced her viewpoint. They'd married the first time he returned home on leave but that was all Vera knew. It didn't seem right to ask. Maybe one day, but not now.

She looked at Alec and Manny squaring up to each other in the ring. Why did men always want to fight? The type of fighting Alec was talking about had taken her father before she had been old enough to really know him. Every time it crossed her mind, a profound feeling of sorrow overwhelmed her. What if it happened again? At present, there was no battle to be fought for 'Queen and Country'. Hopefully it would remain that way.

'What's the matter love?' Sensing her daughter's unease, Doreen put her arm around Vera. 'Would you rather we went home?'

Vera smiled as she shook her head, vision blurred slightly by teary eyes. 'I'm okay,' she said with a deep sigh. 'I was just thinking about Dad. Imagining if he were alive we would all be here together.'

Doreen flinched at her words. Even after all these years, scarcely an hour passed when she didn't think about Jimmy. She looked over to the near corner of the boxing ring where Fred was standing deep in discussion with Danny Prime and Nick Hill. No one could ever take her Jimmy's place, certainly not Fred Jones. A bell rang to signal the start of the fight and as Alec and Manny came together the crowd began to cheer. Doreen grabbed Vera's hand and squeezed it tightly. 'The Bible tells us, *"there is no fear in love"*, (John 4:18) so do not feel afraid.'

★ ★ ★

Boxing. Alec Jones versus Manny Jones. The Noble Art at ten stones and seven pounds. Clenched fists and clean punching. Ducking and weaving... weaving and slipping. Left-hand, right-hand, jab, jab, block, move. A shiny gold-plated trophy and the right to represent the club at junior level at the National Championships... all of this and more immediately forgotten from the first minute of the first round. This wasn't about pride and glory... this was a brawl between two brothers scrapping over the same girl. An in-your-face, claustrophobic, crouching, mauling, win-at-all-costs street fight that could have drawn a large crowd at the Royal Albert Hall or even nearby Nine Elms Baths where a lot of bouts were held.

Plumes of acrid cigarette smoke billowed above the canvass on which Alec and Manny were jabbing and countering with a ferocious velocity that suggested the fight would be over in a matter of seconds. Doreen was transfixed, lost for words. There was no passage from the Bible she could quote to stifle the sudden surge of excitement that was making her body tingle. Vera noticed the expression on her mother's face and frowned. For her it was all too close, all too real. She couldn't bear to look. Tilting her head down, she clasped her hands together, rested them on her lap and stared at the delicate embroidery of the pristine white blouse she was wearing. Doves of peace... woven together in unity, in hope. One, two, three, four, five. Silently she counted them.

In the ring, Manny began to get the better of Alec, pummelling his brother's sides with a flurry of punches that had visibly reddened the skin.

'Go on my son!' Fred roared, losing himself in the moment.

The irony of his words wasn't lost on Nick Hill who was stood beside him. 'Which one?' he quipped, but Fred didn't hear him.

Who was going to win the bout? Manny was the underdog with the slighter build, but it wasn't the size of the man in the fight that mattered, it was the size of the fight in the man. Everyone knew that, but some, especially Fred, who appreciated the concept fully, knew more than others. Nevertheless, Alec could fight back. Prime might throw in the towel, or the referee stop the contest on a technicality. In truth, as far as the audience were concerned, anything could happen. The only certainty was that one of his boys would win. Which one hadn't been a care or consideration until Hill had got involved, but now it was serious. 'Go on my sons!' he shouted, laughing at the embellishment, joyful he had prior knowledge of the outcome of the fight. Hill's money would be useful. He could buy Doreen flowers. Good idea! A present... maybe some jewellery. Take her to dinner... Manny and Vera could come too. They'd all say "Yes!" to the ready-made-family... even Alec. He'd soon get over it. All he wanted to do was join the Army and that was happening next month. "Queen and Country". Good luck to him. Good luck to them both. 'GO ON MY SONS!'

Fred's shouting and the whistles and cheers of the crowd drew Vera's attention back to the action in the boxing ring. The sight of Alec backing up against the ropes in front of her taking a savage beating from his brother was enough to provoke a reaction. 'Stop it Manny!' she screamed, jumping to her feet and raising her hands, but her words were lost in the general uproar as spectators edged towards the canvass.

'Manny!' she cried out again, grabbing her mother's arm. 'MANNY!'

Doreen, spellbound, was blind to her daughter's concern.

Manny heard Vera call out his name. He looked up and over Alec's shoulder and caught sight of her.

'MANNY!'

She wanted him. For one split second… what he thought was a precious moment, a sign that she had feelings for *him*, wanted *him*, their eyes locked together.

'MANNY!'

It was the last thought Manny would have during the fight. With Prime about to throw in the towel, and the referee following orders, Alec, sensing a lapse in concentration, reared up from the ropes and threw a venomous right hook that connected with his brother's right temple splitting his skin and knocking him out cold. As he fell to the canvass with a sickening thud, a shower of blood and spittle arced through the air onto Vera spattering her face and splashing onto her virginal white blouse. The brutally violent conclusion to the bout snapped Doreen out of her trancelike state just in time to catch her fainting daughter.

Fred and Danny, smelling salts to hand, clambered into the ring to attend to Manny while Alec looked across at Vera who was being comforted by her mother.

'What the fuck happened?' bellowed Nick Hill, grabbing at the bottom rope, his normally sallow face crimson with rage. Sweat beading on his brow as he hauled himself onto the canvass.

'He took his fucking eyes off his opponent.' Despite Nick's anger, Fred looked more irate than worried as he helped Danny bring Manny round. 'I've told 'em both time and time again.'

'Well *he* must be a deaf cunt then.' Nick jabbed a finger at Manny's motionless body.

'Leave off, you saw what happened.'

'That's cost me… and it's going to cost you.'

'You okay my boy?' Fred ignored Hill's belligerence and continued tending to his son, cradling his head as Danny mopped the blood away from the cut on his temple. 'Need a couple of stiches that, but you'll live to fight another day.'

Manny blinked slowly as consciousness returned. Dad, Danny, Nick, he could see all their faces as his vision cleared.

'Fight another day. What happened to fighting today?' Nick continued to gripe as Fred stood up, pulling Manny to his feet as he did so.

'Sorry.' Manny shook his head in protest at the noxious odour of ammonia as Danny ran the smelling salts under his nose one last time. 'I've let everyone down.'

'You're not wrong there.' Nick wrung his hands in frustration as he glowered at Alec who was stood in the centre of the ring with his gloved fists down by his sides. 'Pair of useless wankers!'

Scowling with resentment at his perceived humiliation, Manny pushed Nick away, as he did so a ripple of applause circulated around the hall as Alec walked slowly across to him. Now was not the time for platitudes. Alec knew that. All eyes were on the brothers. The audience half-expected the fight, which had ended in the first round, to start again. Face-to-face, no words were exchanged. Alec shrugged his shoulders and smiled as Manny glared at him.

Sensing trouble, Fred made his way over and put his arms around his sons. 'Come on boys, that's enough. Shake hands.'

Manny ignored him, turning his attention first to Nick who was being accosted ringside by a group of men and then scanning the hall for Vera. Her look of love had been unmistakable. The thought of it dissipated the anger he felt at the apparent injustice of what had just occurred. It was a conspiracy. Hill, Prime, his father and brother… they were all in on it. But it didn't matter because he was sure he'd won the greatest prize of all… Vera's heart.

Fred never served with the British Army, his father had got him an apprenticeship with the London Power Company at Battersea Power Station and he'd started work at sixteen, two years before Chamberlain declared war on Germany. An only child, life moved fast. His girlfriend Avis fell pregnant quickly, too quickly. A first wage packet, a drunken fumble. He never thought it would happen, but drink made them careless. Avis was sweet, an elfin beauty with almond eyes, chestnut hair and perfect skin... they'd been inseparable since infant school. Marriage was expected, but not in these circumstances. Her family were furious.

"Oh the shame of it". Chapman had laughed as he'd quoted their comment about the situation. 'Don't worry, she can come and live with us. The old place could do with a woman's touch,' he'd said wistfully, patting Fred on the back as they'd supped pints of Watney's in the Duchess of York on Battersea Park Road. The pub stood in the shadows of the nearby power station's tall chimneys, and the landlord never questioned the age of his younger patrons most of whom were employed over the road by the LPC.

The day Fred started work was the day his mother Elsie left home to go and care for her sister Maisie who lived nearby in Stanley Grove. That's what she'd told Chapman, and that's what he'd told his son. The truth was, she'd had enough of her husband's drunkenness. Far from encouraging Chapman to consider sobriety, Elsie's departure saw him spend more time in the 'Duch' which subsequently became his home-from-home. Avis moved in with Fred, they married at the local registry office, and before both had reached the age of seventeen they were parents to Alec. Elsie often came round to help, it wasn't easy, but they managed. The house was clean, there was food to eat and there was love. Too much love. Avis fell pregnant again.

It was exactly a mile from the house where they lived on Queenstown Road to the power station. On that ill-fated day when he'd received news of his father's accident, Fred had cycled there in a matter of minutes. Chapman shouldn't have been working... it wasn't his shift. He was covering for a friend who'd taken ill. An early Sunday start. Too much gin the previous evening maybe affected his judgement. "I'm sorry, there's nothing we could do". He had questions but couldn't ask them. Numb with grief, he'd returned home on foot, walking slowly, dragging his feet, kicking at the cobbles... the image of his father's blistered, seared and blackened body imprinted indelibly on his retinas.

Standing at the front gate, Elsie was waiting. A double-tragedy. Fred sank to his knees. "I'm sorry son, nothing could be done for her". His wife's narrow frame had resulted in internal damage as the midwife was delivering the baby. Bleeding... convulsions... a heart attack... death. It was too much to take in sober. Nobody could find the right words to comfort him. Solace was found in the bottles of bootleg brandy his father kept in the roof space of the outside toilet... and then there was the 'Duch'. When the time came, it seemed like the whole of Battersea had turned out for the joint funeral service held at St Mary's. Young Father Slattery spoke about resurrection and eternal life. But to comprehend what he was saying you had to believe, you had to have faith in the words of Jesus Christ. *"And whosoever liveth and beleiveth in me shall never die. Believest thou this?"* (John 11:26)

Fred shook his head as he contemplated the priest's words. He wanted to stand up and shout, 'No Father Slattery. I don't believe,' but he didn't. Stoically, he bit his cracked lips in a valiant bid to fight back the tears. His father and wife were dead. What was the use in pretending otherwise? Father Slattery wasn't much older than him. What did he know? Fred was finished with religion. He would never set foot in a church again.

Following the deaths of Chapman and Avis, Elsie came back to live at her old family home in Queenstown Road to look after her son and her two grandchildren Alec and Chapman. Naming the new-born, a healthy baby boy, after his grandfather had been Fred's idea, but she'd shortened it to Manny. She felt more comfortable with that, and Fred went along with it. He went along with everything now… it was easier that way.

The outbreak of war saw Parliament rush through the National Service (Armed Forces) Act which enforced full conscription on all fit men aged between twenty and twenty-three, and required them to register to serve in one of the armed services. The following month, the British government announced that all men aged between eighteen and forty-one who were not employed in what were deemed to be 'reserved occupations', which included utility workers like Fred, could be called up. London needed electricity. The London Power Company provided it. Fred stayed at home and worked slavishly at the power station while his mother reared his sons.

When the war ended, young Alec and Manny would often find themselves playing army games with their friends in the school playground and on rubble-strewn bombsites. Boastful kids would tell of the heroic deeds of their fathers. Of courage displayed, of battles won, of medals awarded, of death and glory. The brothers were taunted. The brothers were envious. They questioned their father. They wanted to do what he had in their eyes failed to do. They wanted to serve their country.

★ ★ ★

Two weeks after becoming Junior Champion of Caius Boxing Club, Alec joined the British Army Airborne Forces, enlisting in the Parachute Regiment. Prior to 1953, direct enlistment into the Paras hadn't been possible, but having watched a war film released that year called *'The Red Beret'* in which Alan Ladd portrayed an American who pretended to be Canadian in order to become a paratrooper, Alec decided this was where his future lay. Fortunately for him, by 1955 the enlistment rules had changed and he found himself part of 40 Platoon stationed at Maida Barracks Aldershot. The training was rigorous and intense but he had the physique, stamina and mentality to cope with it.

Still smouldering with bitter resentment, Manny soon followed Alec to the Army recruitment office. Spurned by Vera who'd rejected his advances and made it clear she was his brother's girl, he'd taken the view that the two had conspired to distract him, to cause him to lose concentration and with it the bout. Sleepless night had followed sleepless night as he replayed the events in his head. He had to get even and then he had to get in front. The only way he could do this was to commit himself to the Army and be better than Alec at soldiering, at being a man, at loving Vera… at everything. But there was an unforeseen problem. Alec's knockout punch had been forceful enough to tear the retina of Manny's right eye. The black dots, specks and streaks that had floated across his field of view he'd kept to himself but the symptoms worsened. By the time he went to undertake the Army medical, the vision in his right eye had deteriorated and he failed the basic sight tests.

Forced to admit he'd falsified his application, and requiring an operation to repair the damaged retina, Manny was deselected from the Army recruitment process. The decision he viewed as a further injustice. Whatever he tried to do, there were obstacles placed in his path to prevent progress. Everything appeared deliberate. Treachery and collusion precipitated frustration and anger. Reluctantly, he went to work at Battersea Power Station with his father, but in his mind he was plotting ahead, planning for the future, waiting for an opportunity. Patience replaced intolerance. Persistence would pay off… he was certain of it.

TILL DEATH US DO PART

1 December 1962

H aving completed parachute training at RAF Abingdon at
the start of 1956, Private Alec Jones was sent to 3 Para.
His first two years in the Regiment were extremely active
and included deployments to Cyprus and Suez. In November
1956, at the height of the Suez Crisis, 3 Para had conducted
the first battalion parachute assault since the end of World War
Two when it attacked El Gamil airfield west of Port Said. The
drop took place under fire and Alec was part of the third wave
of troops who parachuted in from a height of three hundred
metres. Up to this point, he'd shared all the details of his life as
a soldier with Vera, but the fifteen adrenalin-filled seconds it
took from jumping out of the aircraft to landing on the ground
changed that. The roar of engines, acrid smell of fuel, rush of
air, sound of automatic gunfire and sight of the ground coming
to meet him he summarised in one word. Fear. It was a new
and raw emotion. Feeling scared and helpless… mortal not
immortal. He wondered if his comrades felt the same way. He
didn't ask though. That might be seen as a sign of weakness.

Promoted to Corporal the following year, in the summer
of 1958 Alec had been a part of the 16th Parachute Brigade's
intervention force that air-landed at Amman in Jordan.
During this time he considered leaving the Army. The love he
shared with Vera, and the opportunity to earn more money in
civilian life were compelling enough reasons, but every time
he returned home for a period of leave he soon found himself

missing the camaraderie and sense of belonging that came with being a part of the Parachute Regiment. The Army also provided him with an escape route from confrontations with Manny. Apart from pleasantries, the brothers had exchanged little dialogue since the fateful bout at Caius. Despite Fred doing his best to reconcile his sons, Manny remained surly and had become increasingly insular. His flattery of Vera however continued unabated, right up to the moment Fred pulled him to one side and told him that she and Alec were going to get married.

Alec being away for long periods of time had enabled Manny to continue his pursuit of Vera unhindered. When his shifts permitted, he would follow her. Always at a distance, always unnoticed. He noted every last detail about her. The way she wore her hair. Her clothes. Her shoes. The way she walked. If she looked happy, sad or indifferent. He didn't view it as an unhealthy obsession, nor did he consider his weekly visit to a prostitute who bore an uncanny resemblance to her as unnatural.

It had been his father, following a drunken session in the Duchess, who had inadvertently introduced him to the seamier side of London. Soho had been the port of call... and here, for the first time, amidst the market stalls, amusement arcades, pubs, bars, restaurants, cafes, illegal drinking dens, hole-and-corner spielers, nightclubs, jazz clubs, billiard halls and brothels, Manny found something, apart from Vera, that was genuinely interesting to him. Even during the day, the area had a life of its own. A distinct personality flavoured by exotic herbs and spices... fragranced by Italian coffee, French cigarettes and fake perfume, and serenaded by the sounds of Bobby Vee, Helen Shapiro and Adam Faith. From Leicester Square along Wardour Street to Brewer Street and Berwick Street, and in the warren of dimly lit alleyways that crisscrossed in-between, people were hustling for a living... the dynamic and economics of this newfound society fascinated him.

Glamorous were the gangsters and showgirls. Cockney criminals, Maltese villains. Blondes, brunettes and redheads… especially the redheads. Repellent were the drug addicts and drunks. Sleazy were the pimps, prostitutes and perverts. Intertwined with all of them were the artists, musicians, dancers, waiters, spivs, touts, card players, refugees, runaways, tourists and the occasional policeman trying to keep some sort of order. Bourgeois or bohemian? Heterosexual or homosexual? Tolerant or xenophobic? Honest or corrupt? From his seat by the window of the Top Ten coffee bar on Berwick Street, Manny played guessing games with all the passers-by. He didn't know anybody who belonged to this cosmopolitan subculture, but he wanted to because he sensed that there was money to be made. The London Power Company paid well, but here he recognised there were better ways to make a living. Criminality was everywhere. It held an appeal for him beyond the obvious financial potential.

'We need somebody who knows Nicholas Hill.'

Recognising the name, Manny turned round and saw two men deep in conversation sat at the table behind him. Identically attired in navy blue single-breasted suits worn over white shirts with rounded collars and French cuffs, the men looked as sharp as the razors they were probably carrying. Suspecting they were being spied on, both looked up at the same time, eyes narrowing, stares menacing. Manny had a fraction of a second to decide whether to grin inanely and hope they just marked him down as a gormless beatnik, or to make a play and potentially risk being disfigured for life.

'I know Nicholas Hill.' Surprised by his self-confidence, he stood up as he spoke.

'Yes, but we don't know you.'

The brass knuckle duster across the right hand of the man who replied should have been a visible enough deterrent to curb Manny's interest but he persisted. 'Likewise. It's just I heard you say you needed someone who knows Nicholas Hill. I know a Nick Hill if that's who you are talking about.'

'And you are?'

'Manny Jones.'

'We don't work with Jew boys.'

'I'm not Jewish.'

'What's Manny if it isn't a Jewish name?'

'It's short for Chapman.'

'Chapman eh. What sort of moniker is that?'

'It was my grandfather's name. He was killed in accident at work the day I was born.'

'Chapman Jones from?'

'Battersea.'

Silent until now, the second man pushed an empty chair out from under the table and beckoned Manny to sit down. 'What brings you to Soho today then? I've seen your face in here a few times. Narking for the filth are we?'

The first man leaned across the table and clenched his right hand into a fist. Manny wondered how much damage the knuckle duster could do if he took a punch. The doctor at Moorfields Eye Hospital who'd repaired his damaged retina had told him he needed to be careful. Figuring the closer he was, the less room there was to size him up, he sat forward. 'No. I'm looking to make some extra money. There's this girl...'

'You should've been more careful.'

'No. It's not like that.'

'Of course it isn't dear boy.' The second man laughed and pulled the first man back. Manny shrugged his shoulders and smiled. The men spoke in a polished manner that suggested they were well informed, that they understood the importance of knowledge. He had a little, and if he imparted it correctly, it might go a long way. 'Look, if it's Nick Hill the bookmaker from Battersea you're talking about... maybe I can help.'

'Why would you do that?' The first man removed the knuckle duster from his hand and placed it on the table.

'As I said, I need to make a few bob.'

'How well do you know Hill?'

'My father owes him money.'

The second man drummed his neatly manicured fingernails on the table slowly. 'A lot of people owe Hill money. The trouble is, Hill owes a lot of money to a few people.'

Manny digested the meaning of what he was hearing swiftly. 'And you're collecting on behalf of the few?'

The first man nodded. 'I might sound like Winston Churchill here, but never in the field of human conflict is so much owed by so many to so few… and the few are getting pissed off.'

'Was.' The second man wagged his finger at his associate who jerked his head forward irately. 'Was, what?'

'You said, "Never in the field of human conflict is so much by so many to so few". Churchill said, "was".

Manny laughed. Educated enforcers with cut glass accents. If he was going to start somewhere, it might as well be at the upper end of the criminal social scale.

'Don't laugh unless I laugh. The difference between past tense and present tense is no joke.'

Manny put his hand over his mouth. He'd wanted to laugh even louder, but the two men scowling at him, the thought of a knuckle duster smashing into his face, and the possibility of missing out on a chance to get his foot on the bottom rung of the same gilt-edged ladder they were on, swiftly enabled him to regain composure.

'The tense is correct,' said the first man smugly. 'We are talking about money still owed. I was quoting Churchill for illustrative purposes. So tell me young man, how much does your father owe Mr Hill?'

'At least two hundred pounds.'

The second man tutted. 'Gambling is a growing evil.'

Manny frowned. He wanted to explain about his father's tragic circumstances, but there was little point. He sat back in his chair, folded his arms and waited for the one-sided conversation to continue.

The first man picked up the brass knuckle duster and breathed on it before taking a blue silk handkerchief from his jacket pocket and polishing it. 'So Chapman Jones...' he said, speaking slowly and with great deliberation. 'If... If you can follow instructions... Fred Jones' debt to Nicholas Hill will be written off.'

Manny looked puzzled. He didn't recall mentioning his father's name.

The second man winked at him. 'Clever aren't we,' he said, looking at his watch. 'So... Would you be able to follow our instructions today?'

Manny nodded. For the first time in his life he was genuinely impressed. What a set up. Who were these men working for? What were their names? What else did they know? Would he ever find out? Settling his father's debt would be a notable thing to do, especially on a day when he'd probably increased it.

'Is that a yes then?'

'Yes. My brother is getting married at St Mary's at four o'clock this afternoon. There's a reception afterwards, upstairs at the Duchess. Hill is certain to come along after he's been to the football.'

'We know,' said the first man continuing to polish the knuckle duster. 'We want you to meet him when he's on his way back from the football. Before he gets to the party.'

'He'll be watching either Chelsea or Fulham, whoever's at home today. He supports Chelsea, but also takes bets at Fulham.'

'We know that as well.' The second man reached across to an adjacent empty table and picked up a copy of the previous day's *'Evening Standard'* lying on it. He opened the inside back page. 'Fulham are away at Liverpool. Now let me see. Second Division Chelsea eh. Home to Plymouth Argyle.'

Manny resisted the urge to smile. The men knew a lot, but they didn't know everything.

'Just checking in case you're wondering.' The second man winked. 'Your father will be at the wedding today. So Hill will be making his way home from the football alone.'

Manny shook his head in disbelief as the first man spoke. If he was going to be good at his new career, he had a lot to learn.

★ ★ ★

'First, I am required to ask anyone present who knows a reason why these persons my not lawfully marry, to declare it now.'

Manny clasped his hands together tightly and swallowed hard as he listened to Father Slattery address the congregation. The dryness in his mouth and throat felt as uncomfortable as the knot in the pit of his stomach. He wanted to shout, to scream, to cry. 'Reason. You want a reason. I'll tell you a reason, because I love Vera more than my brother ever could.'

'The vows you are about to take are in the presence of God, who is judge of all and knows all the secrets of our hearts; therefore if either of you knows of a reason why you may not lawfully marry, you must declare it now.'

The church was silent. Manny was tongue-tied. The time had finally come to let go. Except he couldn't... and had no intention of doing so. Vera looked beautiful, virginal. Resplendent in white. Doreen would have ensured her daughter's chastity, and now Alec was going to fucking ruin her. Manny felt his penis stiffening. A hard-on in church. He thought about Susan the French prostitute who had taken his virginity in Soho. He could smell the musky aroma of her perfume mingling with that of her sex. He could see her red hair and hear her husky voice when he'd asked her, 'Can I call you Vera?'

"For an extra ten shillings cherie, you can call me anything you want". He'd paid Susan the extra money. Beyond an uncanny resemblance to Vera, there were other things he liked about her. She was educated. She listened to classical music. She told him about the great composers. He appreciated the benefits having such comprehension could bring, and it pleased him how easily he absorbed the knowledge she imparted.

'In the presence of God, and before this congregation, Alec and Vera have given their consent and made their marriage vows to each other. They have declared their marriage by the joining of hands and by the giving and receiving of rings. I therefore proclaim that they are husband and wife.' Father Slattery joined Alec and Vera's hands together. 'Those whom God has joined together let no one put asunder.'

Manny cursed silently. 'Fuck it!' His vision of Susan, naked, was replaced by the reality of his brother and new sister-in-law kissing, the congregation cheering, and the sound of the church organist playing Felix Mendelssohn's wedding march. Now the difficulty of the challenge he faced had increased. 'Fuck it!' He bowed his head and thought about Nick Hill and how his father said they always took the same route home when walking back to Battersea after watching Chelsea play at Stamford Bridge. He only had a passing interest in football. He'd been along a few times, but was uncomfortable with the social experience and being in a crowd. More importantly, it took up too much of his precious free time.

After Alec had joined the Army, Fred had started going along to games with Nick when he wasn't working. He made sure he never had a shift when Chelsea played… he could take or leave Fulham. He talked often in the Duchess about his match-day routine, about how he lined Nick's pockets placing useless bets. "He knows I'm good for it". Manny learned his father had borrowed money to pay for the wedding. "Poor Doreen's a widow. She's on her own. Got nothing". It had crossed his mind on more than one occasion that his father was as obsessed with Doreen as he was with her daughter. He wondered if the coincidence stretched as far as their taste in prostitutes. Doreen and Vera shared the same hair colouring, complexion and figure. Perhaps his father had also fucked Susan and paid her an extra ten shillings so he could call her Doreen.

The organ sounded louder. Felix Mendelssohn was a cunt for having composed the piece that Susan had told him was originally a part of the suite of incidental music to Shakespeare's play 'A Midsummer Night's Dream.' Shakespeare was a cunt as well. Fuck them both. As he watched Alec and Vera walking down the aisle, Manny checked his watch. 4.30 p.m. Another fifteen minutes or so and Nick Hill would be traipsing out of Stamford Bridge. His father had bored him with the details often enough.

After leaving the ground they'd walk down Holmead Road and turn left onto the New Kings Road tarrying for a pint of Young's Special London Ale in the Nell Gwynne where Nick would hold court for twenty minutes and settle winning bets. Outside the pub, a taxi would be hailed and ridden in to Battersea Bridge. No matter how inclement the weather, Nick always insisted on walking across the bridge so the driver would be instructed to stop along Cheyne Walk by Lindsey House. His father laughed when he described Nick's obsessive single mindedness, secretly Manny found it admirable. He also admired the way Nick knew how to make money, but the admiration stopped there abruptly because Nick Hill was also a cunt of the highest order, right up there with Mendelssohn and Shakespeare. A first class cunt whom he was convinced had played an active role in rigging the fight he'd lost to his brother... the opportunity to contribute to his demise was intoxicating.

The two men Manny had met earlier in the Top Ten had eventually introduced themselves as Tim Rolls and David Chidgey. They could have been made up names, probably were. It didn't matter, nor did it matter whom they worked for. What mattered was what they knew, and how they knew it. He was sure he'd find out, but he could wait. Resonating loudly with him was the timescale. It was all about today. No time to think, no time to back out. Rolls and Chidgey had it all mapped out. What if he hadn't gone to the Top Ten? He always did though. Why had he never seen them before? Maybe he had. But he hadn't, he was certain. The questions added to the headiness he was experiencing. It felt sexual.

★ ★ ★

"Those whom God has joined together let no one put asunder". Manny muttered Father Slattery's words under his breath as he stood on the pavement on the south side of Battersea Bridge waiting for Nick. Alec wearing a ceremonial army uniform, Vera a traditional wedding dress, the perfect couple... that's how everybody described them. Mr and Mrs Jones were going to move to Doreen's house in Cedars Mews at the far end of Queenstown Road. Out of sight, but not out of mind. Who was God to say that no one could put those he had joined together asunder? Marriage was a commitment. Commitments were made to be broken. It was just a matter of time. He checked his watch. 6.11 p.m. It didn't matter. He'd slipped away from the wedding party unnoticed. It wasn't hard. Nobody had paid much attention to him this afternoon. 'That will change when I put those whom God had joined together asunder. Make no mistake Father Slattery.'

A thick November fog shrouded the Thames. It may have been December now, but the lingering mist had a mind of its own. Descending stealthily, rolling along the river, billowing onto its banks, blanketing the bridge, wrapping itself around every pillar and every post. Cold, unfeeling, heartless, soulless… only the lonely welcomed weather like this. The forlorn and the friendless, veiled in hazy anonymity, could walk inconspicuously along the paths and pavements that led to the water's edge where the creeping, cruel current beckoned. Depression and drunkenness were a deadly combination. Away from the pavement on the bridge, any cry for help that accompanied a change of mind would go unheard. Theirs was a silent suicide.

Manny's mind ticked over as he watched his breath condense in the cold air. Humiliated and lovelorn, he'd contemplated killing himself in the past… but not recently, not since he'd started scheming. His father was a consideration also. He wouldn't be able to handle it, not after all the grief he'd been through. A double-decker bus trundled slowly past. He looked at the passengers and imagined them giving him a round of applause for not being selfish. It made him smile. As the bus disappeared into the gloominess, he saw a figure sauntering towards him along the pavement. His heart began to pound rapidly in his chest in anticipation. Yes. Unmistakably, it was Nick Hill.

'Hello Nick.'

'Manny! What are you doing here? Shouldn't you be at the wedding?'

'I've been at the wedding. I forgot to get a present so I…'

'Present? Here?'

'Yeah. Well I thought I'd go to the Kings Road. But I didn't reckon on this pea souper. There's nothing. No buses or taxis.'

'A bit late though eh.'

'What time is it?'

'Near enough half six.'

'Blimey! Never mind. It's the thought and all that. I'll get 'em something on Monday. So how did Chelsea get on?'

'Drew one each. Frankie Blunstone put us ahead, but they equalised right at the end. Shit result for the team, but good for me.' Nick patted his coat and clenched his fist. 'Now then, are you going to walk with me?'

'It's a bit far to the Duch.'

'Fair point.'

'Look. There's a car coming. Let's see if we can hitch a lift down to Battersea Park Road. Be easier from there.'

'Good idea. Better still, I'll pay 'em to take us to the Duch.'

Manny stepped out into the road and waved his arms. The car, a pale blue Ford Zephyr, pulled over to the kerb and slowed to a halt. He could see David Chidgey behind the wheel and Tim Rolls sat next to him.

Rolls wound down his window. 'What seems to be the problem gentlemen?'

Nick tilted his head to one side admiring the flowing lines of the car as he approached it. 'We're stuck in the fog. Got a wedding reception to get to at the Duchess on Battersea Park Road. Make it worth your while if you can give us a lift.' He reached for his wallet and waved it. 'Lovely motor by the way.'

'Keep your money. But a favour for a favour. Got something heavy in the boot we need to move. Can you help?'

'What is it? A body?' Nick laughed as he spoke, stepping away from the car as Rolls opened the passenger door and got out. 'Hey! What the fuck's going on?'

The pistol Rolls pulled from his coat wiped the smile off Nick's face immediately. Concerned, he looked at Manny and then at Chidgey who had swiftly slid along the Zepyhr's bench-style front seat to join Rolls on the pavement.

'I've got money. Here look.' Nick opened his wallet.

As he did so, Chidgey linked arms with him. 'We know you have. The problem is… it's other peoples money.'

'Who are you? There was an air of desperation in Nick's voice. 'Manny! Help me out.'

'Shut it dear boy. You're coming with us.' Rolls jabbed the barrel of his pistol firmly into Nick's chest as Chidgey pulled him close and began walking away from the car towards the end of the bridge and the stairwell that led down to the riverbank.

Manny could sense Nick looking back him so he stared at the pavement and studied the cracked grey concrete slabs beneath his feet. Why hadn't he tried to make a run for it? Why hadn't he tried to take the men on? Was it a fear of being shot? It was the first time he'd seen a gun and witnessed the power that could be wielded by the person holding it. Gun law. The defenceless were incapable of fighting back. Jury, judge and executioner in the palm of your hand. Perfect! The sound of footsteps had faded quickly. He walked purposefully to the parapet of the bridge and glanced over. Through the mist he could see Nick stood on the riverbank with his hands raised. He knew what was coming. Rolls and Chidgey hadn't told him, but he knew all the same.

There was no gunshot. No cry for help. Not yet anyway. All that Manny heard was the muffled sound of Nick Hill falling into the icy river and being pulled beneath its surface by the surging tidal flow. Gasping for air, hands scrabbling at an imaginary ladder, his head bobbed up only to submerge again. Blindly panicking in the darkness, the struggle was rapidly exhausting him. Holding his breath and praying for the rescue that would never come quickly became impossible tasks. If only he hadn't been such a greedy bastard. 'Help!' A cry… pitiful, hopeless. And again, 'HELP!' If only he'd learned to swim. Spluttering and coughing, he inhaled water. The pain and pressure on his chest were beyond compare though only momentary. Lungs filled with Old Father Thames, brain deprived of oxygen, consciousness all but lost, he experienced a fleeting moment of tranquil peace before dying and descending deep into his watery grave.

★ ★ ★

An open verdict was given at the inquest into Nick Hill's death. His bloated body, battered by barges and boats and savaged by seabirds, had been washed up near the Isle of Dogs where the Thames meandered in a U-bend. Manny had made a point of going to the library and reading up on how pathologists unravelled the fate of the dead. In the case of an alleged drowning, they could ascertain if the person was alive or dead when they entered the water by examining the liver and kidneys. If algae were found in these organs, it meant the heart was beating when the body went in. If they were only found in the lungs and stomach, it pointed to a suspicious death.

Suspicious or not, it didn't matter. The coroner listened to witness statements that painted a portrait of a man who lived life to the full but went home to an empty house at night. A gambling man who took bets, but made bigger ones. It might have been suicide, but it was of no consequence because nobody cared.

Manny had lain awake the night of Nick's death replaying the events of the day. It had proved a welcome distraction from thoughts of Vera being deflowered by Alec. He'd often asked his brother how far she'd let him go.

'She won't stand for it till we're married.'

'Is that a reason to marry her though?'

'I love her.'

'What if she's no good at it.'

'She will be. I'll teach her.'

The discourse was always tinged with fractiousness. Alec was smug about Vera's devotion to him. It didn't matter that his brother was still smitten by her. That he was away often. She'd told him she'd made her decision and he believed her. "And remember… no sex before marriage". He imagined Doreen lecturing her daughter every time she got ready to go out on a date. Vera's strict religious upbringing was a source of frustration, but it meant he could trust her while he was away.

'Trust! What a fucking joke.' Manny was certain Alec was going with other girls. There was no way he was still a virgin. How could he say he would teach Vera about sex? He probably visited prostitutes as well. Being married would make no difference. Scrubbers and slappers were a hard habit to break.

Despite the Army making accommodation available to service families close to a soldier's duty station, Vera refused to leave Battersea. Aldershot wasn't far. Alec returned home most weekends. Post operational tour leave was reasonable, as were the number of working days off. Manny had almost convinced himself that the reason Vera didn't want to leave home was because she was unsure about Alec. About being with him. About being married. Maybe it was a mistake. Maybe she really was with the wrong brother. Who was the more polite, attentive, kind? Manny. The roses? Who arranged for those to be left by her front door? Manny. A white and coral bouquet on the fourth Monday of April every year. Vera no doubt admired their colour and fragrance, but did she understand the significance of their pairing and the day they were delivered? Surely she must wonder who sent them? Everything he did had meaning to it. Why do it otherwise? It was a sound, self-taught philosophy that he worked diligently at developing every day, and witnessing Nick Hill's murder had extended his thought process. The meaning of life and the way people lived it could only be truly evaluated in death. The ramifications of this were important.

Had anybody questioned Hill's absence at the wedding reception? No. Manny had wanted to tell his father that he didn't have to worry about his gambling debt anymore, but there was little point because his father wasn't worried about it anyway... he was a gambler. Gambling was for fools. Hill was dead. He thought the odds were in his favour, but in reality they were stacked against him. How much did he owe the connections of Rolls and Chidgey? Enough for it to cost him his life! How was that equation balanced? You can't just kill somebody for the sake of it, or can you? If you have the money, the authority and the need, you can do anything. You are *the* MAN. That muffled conversation by the riverbank. What would Hill have been saying as Rolls pointed the gun at him? "Look. I admit I've been a cunt, but I don't deserve to die". Purposeless pleading. "Take my wallet. Take my house keys. Take everything. But please don't take my life". Did *the* MAN exist though? Maybe Rolls and Chidgey were working alone. They weren't like the run-of-the-mill henchmen that frequented Soho. The more Manny thought about it, the less he realised he knew. The less he realised he knew, the more he thought about it and wanted to find out more.

More sleepless nights followed. He'd never done anything dishonest in his life, but there was a psychological aspect of the criminality he was considering that was compelling. Supposing he was in a position to have other people commit crimes for him, that wouldn't be so bad. Who would suspect anything? The police? His family? His friends and associates? Vera? Manny's self-analysis was persuasive. The police could be corrupted. His family amounted to a father who was an inveterate drunk and a brother who had taken away the only thing he'd ever loved. Friends and associates? The truth was he didn't have any. But that didn't matter. You could buy friends and associates. Vera? Her mother appeared suspicious of everything and everybody, all the local women were. Vera no doubt was the same too. That being the case, providing he was disciplined and meticulous, she would simply view him as a clever man who'd made the most of his abilities and established himself in business. "Look at Manny. Hasn't he done well". The attrition would be gradual as would be the realisation. Sitting there admiring the roses. His roses. "Manny has money. Manny is stable. Manny is single. Manny doesn't drink". Going teetotal. That wouldn't be a problem. He'd pretend. It would take time, but he could wait. Eventually, the day would dawn. Vera would be crestfallen at finding out the truth. Her husband was a worthless philanderer, a drunk like his father.

'Don't worry. Everyone makes mistakes. I'm here for you now, just as I always have been.' As he lay there on his bed in the small hours of the morning, Manny pictured Vera in his arms and began to masturbate vigorously. He'd done it countless times before, but this time, his orgasm was more intense. Buttocks clenched, body rigid, the pleasurable sensations that coursed through his body as he ejaculated onto his bare stomach were incomparable to anything he had previously experienced. Finally, he had a plan.

THE FIGHT OF THE CENTURY

13 June 1971

Richmond Park was peaceful for a Sunday afternoon, Vera liked it that way. Sitting on a blue-striped Witney Point blanket with her knees up to her chin and her hands clasped around her legs, she let her head fall back and looked up at the gnarled, knotted branches and dense green foliage of the old oak tree that had been rooted in the ground behind her for centuries. The tree knew everything. At the base of the trunk, Alec had carved her initials alongside his and encircled them with a heart. *'VC AJ'* Teenaged sweethearts for whom love had blossomed and so far stood the test of time.

The saccharine sound of Lynn Anderson singing *'Rose Garden'* warbled from the portable transistor radio by her feet. The sentiment of the song was simple. If you take hold of your life, you can make something out of nothing. Vera however had developed her own interpretation based on what she had experienced to date. In her mind, you couldn't expect to cultivate beautiful, fragrant roses without getting snagged by thorns along the way. She often dreamed of having her own rose garden. A colourful, walled floral retreat where she could steal a few hours for herself and be at peace with the world. Failing that, a job at the new flower market that was under construction close to home at Nine Elms would allow her to indulge her passion. Alec brought her roses on many occasions. Valentines Day. Wedding anniversary. When he returned home from leave. When he'd done something to upset her. They were always the same red roses that he

40

knew symbolised romantic love. Sometimes she wished he'd be more imaginative. Roses had a language that shared the sentiment of a knowledgeable sender. White spelt purity and innocence. A mixed bouquet of red and white blooms, unity. Yellow, friendship and caring. Orange, fascination. Lavender, enchantment. Light pink, joy. Regular pink, happiness. Dark pink, thankfulness. Peach, sympathy. Blue, mystery... and the biggest mystery of all were the coral and white roses that had been delivered without an accompanying note on every fourth Monday of April since her seventeenth birthday, which had fallen on a Monday.

Coral and white roses when mixed together implied heavenly looks and desire. At first she thought it might have been Manny, but the following year, the roses arrived on the 28th, the date of her mother's birthday. Maybe it was Fred, but he'd never made a secret of his affection for her. As the pattern emerged, the fourth Monday in April had coincided twice with her birthday, 1963 and 1968, and once with her mother's, 1969. Her seventeenth birthday had fallen on an Easter Monday, leading Vera to consider if there was a religious significance to the date. A study of the Bible provided no clues. Chapter and verse recalled nothing about what happened the day after the resurrection of Jesus Christ, and besides, the feast of Easter varied from year to year according to the date of the Paschal Full Moon.

'I beg your pardon, I never knew you was from Covent Garden.'

Vera jolted forward to see Alec careering clumsily into view. She was used to his drunken caterwauling, and yes there was humour in his re-wording of the song lyrics, but it *was* Sunday. It *was* the day of rest. It *was* too much. And... it *was* particularly annoying because the parakeets flocking in the branches above her head had taken flight screeching with indignation at the disturbance. 'Give it up Alec! You're spoiling the moment.' Rose-tinted harmony fractured by the chaotic cacophony, Vera frowned as she spoke. Why was she always so polite about things? Tousling her strawberry blonde locks nervously, she glimpsed the hip flask in her husband's right hand and looked beyond him at her son Kennedy pirouetting playfully on the verdant grass adjacent to the knoll upon which his grandfather Fred was slumped in a deckchair.

'What moment's that then?' The inflection in Alec's voice was tinged with sarcasm.

'A peaceful moment,' retorted Vera brusquely. 'It's the Lord's day. We're meant to be having a quiet family picnic.'

Alec, swigged from the hip flask as he dropped to his haunches. 'We are having a quiet family picnic my love.'

Vera smiled as he reached out to stroke her face. She couldn't help smiling. Alec was her world... always had been, always would be. He wasn't perfect, what man was? Besides she had no real comparison. She'd never sought out the company of other men and, while she was never short of admirers, her involvement with Alec had, from the outset, served as a deterrent to any aspiring suitors, and that included his brother Manny.

'Love you gorgeous.' Alec eased himself to his feet and stretched out his arms.

Vera squinted as rays of sunshine reflecting off the highly polished surface of his hipflask caught her eyes as he took another swig.

'Are you talking to me... or the whisky?' she enquired after some hesitation, but the double meaning of her words was lost on her husband who was now expertly shadow-boxing his way across to Kennedy and Fred.

'Come on son, stop nancying about with Granddad. Let's see what you've learned at school.' Alec crouched in front of his son holding the palms of his large shovel-like hands out in front of him.

'The fight of the century,' wheezed Fred, puffing on the navy-cut Capstan Full Strength fixed at the corner of his mouth.

'Joe Frazier v Muhammad Ali, Madison Square Garden.' The unfiltered cigarette bobbed up and down enthusiastically as he spoke, its fiery tip glowing with each short breath. Grey-white ash of burned tobacco would occasionally flake onto his bare chest causing him to curse, but he did that silently out of respect for Vera. Just like her mother Doreen, she was a fine woman and he often wondered what might have happened had he been successful in wooing her. Vera would have become a stepsister to Alec and Manny and he wouldn't have stood for any horseplay between them. It would have been nice to have that problem to think about, to have been a proper family man again, but unlike his wife Avis, Doreen Coyne hadn't been interested in his detailed knowledge of the noble art of boxing, nor had any other woman he'd met since the love of his life had passed away.

Soon they'd be together again. The doctor had told him that his persistent coughing and breathlessness were symptoms of the incurable lung disease emphysema and that he should give up smoking to slow its progress. He couldn't do it. A forty-a-day habit from the age of sixteen was unbreakable. Tests and a full diagnosis had followed. Fred kept the news to himself. Death was inescapable. Everyone died sooner or later. At least he knew the end was coming and could prepare for it. Now he could take pleasure from enjoying the company of his only grandchild. He smiled as he watched Kennedy throw a right punch and then a left. The kid sparred well. He looked a natural. Better than his Dad. Better than his Uncle. Better than him. Better maybe than Frazier and Ali. Right, left, up, down, faster and faster. Kennedy's tightly clenched fists thudded repeatedly into Alec's hands. He just needed guidance and encouragement. 'Go on boy! Pretend it's the fight of the century.'

Vera looked on disapprovingly, waiting for her husband to say 'don't pretend', but he was more interested in discussing the Frazier / Ali fight.

'I never thought they'd go the distance.' Alec pushed his arms out locking his elbows to provide more resistance.

'Right result though.' Fred coughed as he spoke. 'Frazier winning and putting that cowardly nigger Ali on his arse. If… if…'

Alec shook his head but said nothing, waiting for his father to catch his breath so he could finish the point he was making.

'If… if you can't fight for your country, you shouldn't be allowed to fight for anything let alone the World Heavyweight Boxing Championship and the millions of dollars that goes with it.'

'You never fought for your country.' Alec smiled as Kennedy continued to pummel his hands relentlessly. 'And besides, they're *both* black men. What have you got against Ali?'

Fred coughed and wheezed, eyes watering in protest at the billowing smoke. 'Does it matter?' He leaned forward and shrugged his shoulders taking the almost spent Capstan from his lips and flicking it towards his son, nodding as Alec instinctively reached out his left foot to tread on the stub.

'It matters because you make it sound like Frazier is white… and he ain't. That's part of the problem. Ignorance.'

'Problem? Ignorance?' Fred laughed as he patted the Capstan-holding breast pocket of the lemon paisley shirt he was wearing that was undone to his waist. 'Since when did you join the Civil Rights movement?'

Alec frowned as watched his chain-smoking father tap out another cigarette. 'Civil Rights movement! Ha ha. I'm surprised you've even heard of it.'

Fred coughed as he lit up. 'It ain't that long since Martin Luther King got shot.' Wheezes and gasps punctuated his words as he made his point. 'He might have had a dream… but it didn't get him very far… anyway that Frazier / Ali fight… showed the Septics up for what they are… hypocrites.'

Alec laughed. 'Whatever you say Dad. You'll be telling me Vietnam is a white man's war next. At least get your facts right.'

Fred weighed up his options. He could smoke or he could talk, but these days he couldn't smoke and talk. Better to enjoy the cigarette than exhaust himself arguing.

Alec pointed at the sky with the index finger of his right hand. 'See that up there?' Fred, Vera and Kennedy looked upwards and as they did so Alec slapped his son across the face with the palm of his left hand.

'What did you do that for?' said Vera, hurriedly getting to her feet.

Kennedy stood motionless, left cheek reddening, eyes moistening, battling to hold back the tears he would never shed... not for that. Not in front of Dad, not in front of Granddad.

'He's got to learn.' Fred and Alec's response was simultaneous.

'Just like his Uncle Manny,' added Alec, his eyes narrowing as he watched Vera put a comforting arm around Kennedy. Fred nodded in agreement, puffing on the Capstan that was now settled characteristically at the corner of his mouth.

'What's that then?' Vera glared at Alec. 'How... how to be... how to be... a... b... b... bully?' Stammering wasn't a trait of her manner of speaking. Difficulty asking the question was attributable to recalling the conclusion of the boxing match between her husband and brother in law which still had the capacity to trouble her in circumstances her subconscious deemed similar.

Alec appeared unsympathetic as he ruffled Kennedy's hair. 'Tell her son.'

Vera knew what Kennedy was going to say and sighed as he whispered. 'Never take your eyes off your opponent.'

'Again. So I can hear.'

Kennedy responded immediately to his father's authoritarian voice.

'Never take your eyes off your opponent.'

'Again. So Granddad can hear.'

Kennedy smiled as the stinging sensation of the slap he'd received abated. 'Never take your eyes off your opponent.'

Vera shut her eyes tightly. *"Never take your eyes off your opponent"*. Her son's words reverberated around her head as she protectively embraced him. *"Never take your eyes off your opponent"*. The memory of that first time she'd heard the Jones family mantra was still with her… it made her shudder.

FLOWERS AND FOOTBALL

24 August 1977

'The Brotherhood of Man! Ha ha.' Manny laughed as he held the telephone receiver away from his ear for a moment and looked out of the window onto the street below. It was still raining. He had a few minutes to spare, he'd continue the conversation. 'The Brotherhood of fucking Man. A song about a Mexican shepherd called Angelo who lives on a mountain. Fuck off! I thought you said the music of today was relevant. That the kids weren't buying this kind of shit anymore.'

Every Wednesday, without fail, Tony Cook would call Manny and try to convince him to invest in one of his music-related projects. He always said no, but found Cook entertaining enough to give him a nickname, Jester, because he made him laugh. 'Listen son, Elvis Presley died last week. Did that bit of news not filter up to the cloud you are floating on? People will be buying all things Elvis.' He checked the time. 7.35 p.m. Five more minutes of Jester's bollocks and it would be time to leave. 'The Floaters. No I haven't heard of them. Are they on that fucking cloud with you? Float, float on. Fuck, fuck off!' It was the same every week. He always hung up on Jester. Bang! He slammed the receiver into the cradle. 'One day Jester. One day.'

Despite the ceaseless downpour, Wardour Street was busy. Morning, noon and night, it was always busy. Fifteen years ago when Manny had started out in business, he'd rented an office on the top floor at number 105. Now he owned the building and was eyeing a further acquisition, number 76, located at the nearby junction with Meard Street. Chapman Security, the company he'd founded, was thriving. Installing and maintaining burglar alarm systems was a cash cow and he still afforded himself a wry smile when he valued his assets and recalled how he'd got started. All those lonely nights tossing and turning, plotting and scheming had proved beneficial in the long run… in business anyway.

Completing his apprenticeship with the London Power Company had meant Manny was a fully qualified electrician. From his regular vantage point sitting by the window in the Top Ten he could see the shop front of Hillier's, the large electrical hardware store across the street. Along with televisions, radios, kettles and toasters, the store also sold burglar alarms. Following on from his first encounter with mysterious enforcers Rolls and Chidgey, Manny had highlighted once more his desire to make extra money advising them of his technical skillsets. Chidgey mentioned that one of their associates required an alarm system fitting at his home in Knightsbridge but needed someone trustworthy to install it. Having scoped out and accepted the job, his plan was simple. Buy the system, fit the system and maintain the system.

One customer was not enough and there was plenty of competition. Discreet referrals helped him get started, but other companies employed sales staff to cold call, knock on doors and generate leads. It was a traditional route to business expansion that Chapman Security embraced at a later stage in its development, principally to avoid suspicion. At the outset however, he'd determined that the best time to contact a prospect about alarm systems was during the aftermath of a burglary or attempted burglary, all he needed was the knowledge of where and when. From that point on, closing the deal was easy.

Robberies were frequent in the West End. Department stores, jewellers and boutiques were compromised on a daily basis. For a small percentage of the quoted installation price, Rolls and Chidgey provided Manny with the information he needed. A personal sales pitch was made the day before a robbery went ahead, and in every case there would be no sale.

A walk-in-call a day or so after goods to the value of tens of thousands of pounds had been stolen was always received more favourably. It was an easy discussion. "You need the latest technology, fitted and maintained correctly. These are my clients in the area. Of course you know them. Feel free to contact them for a reference". It was a soft sell. Simple. In fact Manny couldn't believe how simple it was. Sabotage and vandalism of existing systems represented a further opportunity, and then there was bribery and corruption. That was the ultimate goal. To be powerful and well connected enough to win multiple site contracts. He had it all figured out.

Increased cash flow allowed him to contemplate other enterprises, but he wasn't frivolous with his money. Generosity had brought with it respect. He'd ensured that his father's final years had been as comfortable as possible. Medical care. Holidays. Fine dining. Whatever the old boy wanted. His final wish had been to see Muhammad Ali box. Fred had changed his opinion about Ali. It was his prerogative and he wouldn't be drawn into any debates that he was a hypocrite. In his eyes, Ali really was 'the greatest'. 30 October 1974. Undisputed World Heavyweight Champion George Foreman v challenger and former champion Ali. 'The Rumble in the Jungle' Kinshasa, Zaire. Manny and Fred had been ringside to witness the spectacle.

It had taken some organising and considerable expense, but it had been worth it. As well as Fred getting to realise a dream, Manny knew his charitable deed would not go unnoticed. Alec was offered the opportunity to attend but had insufficient leave left. It had been a source of great disappointment to Vera that he hadn't gone and that was gratifying news to him. Alec had remained in the Parachute Regiment and risen to the rank of Sergeant. Despite seeing the progress his brother was making and being offered the opportunity to join the business, it was clear he had no intention of leaving the Army. In a way, Manny was glad. Vera was bringing up young Kennedy virtually single-handed. He couldn't figure out if Alec was just being stubborn, whether he was just plain foolish, or if he was leading some kind of double life. It didn't cross his mind that he simply loved soldiering.

Fred and Manny enjoyed the fight for very different reasons. Ali secured victory when referee Zack Clayton stopped the bout with seconds remaining in the eighth round. Fred managed to stand up to cheer as Ali boxed his way off the ropes and delivered a five punch combination that culminated in a left hook to serve up Foreman's head and a right cross to knock him to the canvass. Foreman got to his feet at the count of nine but Clayton deemed he had taken enough punishment. Fred was elated. Manny was reminded of the time Alec had humiliated him in the boxing ring at Caius. *"Never take your eyes off your opponent"*. Foreman was beaten fair and square, but he'd been cheated. It still made his blood boil. It kept him motivated to continue his pursuit for personal justice and Vera.

Fred Jones finally succumbed to his illness later the same year on Christmas Day. It was a blessed release. At the wake, Manny and Alec talked, but not for long, and not about the business. He didn't have to raise the subject anymore because he knew that Doreen and Vera would be watching the news. The 'Troubles' in Northern Ireland were never far away from the headlines. Graphic imagery of civil unrest, riots and demonstrations coupled with the aftermath of bombings and shootings were a constant reminder of the risks involved for British troops tasked with keeping the peace.

3 Para had been deployed to the Province for the first time in January 1971. At face value, Alec seemed to take it in his stride. Descriptions of routine foot patrols, manning vehicle checkpoints and observation point surveillance were low key, there was never any detail added to any discussion. When he came home, he may have left the mean streets of Belfast and Londonderry behind, but the violence continued.

"Why doesn't that husband of yours leave the Army and work with his brother?" Manny envisaged the conversations being had between mother and daughter. "He's selfish. What about young Kennedy?" Doreen and Vera, bloody women... all talk. He'd occasionally thought of getting at Doreen. Speaking to her and seeing if he could find out what it would take, what he needed to do? What Vera wanted? He didn't though. She'd been impervious to his father's flattery. "Till death us do part". Even as a widow she'd remained true to her wedding vows, but she was sick now, frail, dying... not of a broken heart, but kidney failure. Maybe when she finally passed, her influence over her daughter would wane. 'Vera, Vera, Vera.' Every free moment was spent thinking about her being at home alone. Neglected.

Kennedy's birth had given him the opportunity to visit Vera occasionally without being viewed as a pest. "Uncle Manny's here my little lamb". Kind Uncle Manny. Toys for Kennedy. Flowers for Vera, not roses... up until now the roses had been a secret, but tonight that was going to change. He wasn't going to give the game away about the fourth Monday of April roses, nor was he going to stop the tradition. 'Oh and before I go love, here's a few quid to help with the bills. I know it can't be easy.' She'd be grateful, she always was. But she always kept herself at arms length... apart from when it was time to say goodbye. He would hold her firmly, but fleetingly, enjoying the way her body tensed. He'd practised it to perfection with Susan who never questioned what he was doing. A kiss on the cheek and a deep slow sniff as he breathed in her scent. After three or four repetitions, Susan would drop to her knees and deep throat him. Unfortunately, Vera pushed him back after that first kiss. Still, it made his groin tingle.

As he left the office, Manny thought about what he was going to say to Vera. 'Have you ever thought about your situation. What if Alec didn't come back?' Kennedy was older now. He still needed a father figure. He'd soon need a job. 'If anything ever happened to Alec, you know I'd be here for you. I'd take care of you. No, honestly I mean it. You know how I feel about you and Kennedy. He's a good lad. A credit to you. He can come and work for me. No, no... he can come and work *with* me.' Manny imagined Vera's reaction. Her facial expression would reflect relief, happiness, love.

"What can I say Manny?"

'You don't have to say anything now.'

Stepping out onto the pavement he remembered Father Slattery's words at the wedding service. "Those whom God has joined together let no one put asunder". Slattery's warning... if that's what it was, had been heeded for over fifteen years. Fifteen long fucking years.

Most days the flower seller at the stall by the Marquee Club just along the street from Manny's office would have gone home early because of the rain, but this evening she was waiting for him. The roses were going to be red tonight. Just red... no coral in the spray. Yes red, but not just any red. The flower seller had told him that amaranth red signified long-standing desire. These were the most expensive roses money could buy. He'd leave them outside, hidden in the front garden. Bring them to her before he left. Before Alec and Kennedy got home from the football.

'She ain't worth it.'

'Wanker!'

Manny heard two voices and turned to see a group of five dishevelled-looking youths stood outside the Marquee

52

laughing. He glanced at the billposter by the entrance door adjacent to them. *EDDIE AND THE HOT RODS* The name was familiar. They were one of the groups Jester had mentioned when he'd first telephoned him. Earlier today the saucy bastard had delighted in telling him that their single *'Do Anything You Wanna Do'* had made the Top 30 and was set to go higher. "I told you Mr Jones". Maybe Jester was onto something. Perhaps he'd invite him over to the office next week when he called.

Holding the roses in the crook of his left arm Manny approached the youths. Their laughter hastily turned to silence as he eyed each of them in turn. A contorted, teeth-baring facial expression he'd perfected in the mirror during his teens was enough to loosen the bowels of anyone whose bravado didn't match the words that invoked it.

'So which one of you gentlemen reckons she ain't worth it? And which one called me a wanker?'

'It was a joke.' The tallest of the youths raised his right hand, and stammered a nervous apology. 'Se Se Se Sorry.'

'Why was it a joke? What's so funny about a man buying flowers from a flower stall? What the fuck is the flower stall here for? So wankers like me can buy flowers. That's what wankers do right? If you buy flowers you're a wanker. Have you ever bought flowers?'

'Ye... y... yes.'

'So you're a wanker as well then.'

'Y... yes.'

'Except you're more than just a wanker. You're a cunt. What are you?'

'A c... cunt.'

'I need you to say it louder.'

'I'm a c... cunt.'

'I can't hear you.'

'I'M A CUNT!'

'Good. You won't forget now will you?

★ ★ ★

'Come on Chelsea!' Kennedy looked at Alec and leaned back against the stanchion. *'Come on Chelsea!'* The first home game of the season was always special. Having just won promotion back to the top flight, the Blues had been beaten convincingly by West Bromwich Albion at The Hawthorns on Saturday, so a good result at home against Birmingham City was imperative.

'I thought there'd have been more here.' Fletch bit into the hamburger he was holding squeezing grease and ketchup out of the bun and onto his cheeks.

'Half empty. No wonder we're skint.' Bertie reached out his arm and embraced Fletch, pulling him close and licking his face.

'Oi fuck off! Get your own.'

'I'm saving myself for half-time.'

'Might not get to half-time if it carries on raining like this.'

Kennedy chuckled as he listened to his friends banter. Fletch had a point. The pitch was sodden and the heavens showed no sign of closing as the deluge continued unabated. Water was everywhere. Pouring through the gaps and holes of the dilapidated roof of the Shed terrace. Forming huge puddles on the track by the perimeter wall. 'Rain, rain go away. Come again another day. Fuck off!'

'You all right son?' Alec had his eyes on the pitch as he spoke.

Kennedy didn't bother replying. His father knew he was all right. He was always all right. Thirteen years old. Being a teenager was great, especially as he was almost fourteen years old. He'd fingered his girlfriend Nicky for the first time at a party at the weekend. Chelsea were back in the First Division, and he'd decided he was going to join the Parachute Regiment when he left school. He'd told Fletch and Bertie and they were

54

impressed. He'd tell his father at Christmas. *'Come on Chelsea!'*

John Phillips, Gary Locke, John Sparrow, Garry Stanley, Steve Wicks, Ron Harris, Ian Britton, Ray Wilkins, Steve Finnieston, Ray Lewington, Tommy Langley. They were good enough to play for the Blues. It was a dream for Kennedy, but he knew he didn't have the skills. You need to be playing all the time, be encouraged. 'Our kid will play for Chelsea.' Nicky had been awe-struck by his words. Commitment. Maybe she'd open her legs for the first time for him. He meant it though. He wanted to make the effort.

'What a ball.' Bertie shouted, grabbing his arm and snapping him out of his daydream. Sparrow had just split the Birmingham City defence open with a precision pass to Langley.

'Go on Tommy.' Langley rounded City keeper Jim Montgomery and shot at goal.

'Bastard!' Gary Pendrey somehow managed to nudge the ball out. 'Shoot!' Stanley rifled home.

'YESSSS!'

The Shed erupted as Chelsea took the lead. Kennedy, Bertie and Fletch bounced down the terrace. Elated faces. Cheering voices. Alec clenched his fist. 'COME ON!'

Kennedy pulled Bertie and Fletch back from the stanchion they'd bounded into that had prevented further progress down the crumbling concrete terracing. Fletch raised his arms aloft and clapped his hands. As he did so, the satin scarves he had tied to each wrist swayed to and fro. Kennedy laughed. He and Bertie had stopped wearing scarves the previous season when his father had taken them to an away game against Bolton Wanderers. That afternoon he'd asked a simple question. 'Why do you never wear a scarf Dad?'

'A small badge is enough. Why advertise? This way I can walk where I want, stand where I want and avoid the attention of idiots. You'll soon see what I mean.'

They'd arrived late at Bolton's old ground Burden Park,

and the queue to get into the visitors entrance at the Railway End was long enough to suggest that those at the rear might not get in. Alec had motioned them to remove the blue and white Chelsea bar scarves they had knotted around their necks before they walked round a line of policemen and down the side of the ground.

LEVER END

HOME SUPPORTERS ONLY

Kennedy felt a surge of adrenalin course through his body as he read the sign above the turnstile they'd just clicked through.

'Wanderers, Wanderers.' The home crowd chanted their support. As kick-off time approached the end began to fill up. The accents, the faces, the colours, the clothes... everything was different.

'You're gonna get your fucking heads kicked in.'

Alec had a swig from his hip flask and passed it to the man stood next to him. Kennedy recognised him and nudged Bertie.

'Wanderers, Wanderers.'

Chelsea supporters congregated in the Railway End vaulted the perimeter wall and ran towards them. As they did so, the man stood next to Alec bellowed 'CHELSEA!' and several others joined in the repetitive chant. *'Chelsea, Chelsea, Chelsea.'* It was a biblical moment. Like Moses parting the Red Sea, a gap in the terrace opened up around them.

'Are you watching the game or thinking about that bird?'

Kennedy laughed as Fletch flicked his wrist and whiplashed him with a scarf. 'I wasn't thinking about her.'

'Course you were.'

He did momentarily and felt his cock stiffen. It happened a lot these days without much prompting. Fortunately, a fierce drive from Britton that brought the best out of Montgomery had the denizens of The Shed leaping in the air. It was a welcome distraction from potential embarrassment. He was surprised how often he got random erections… now was not the time for one.

The match was absorbing. Finnieston and Langley might have scored, but again Montgomery was equal to their efforts. Alec spent half-time explaining that Montgomery was the reason that his former club Sunderland beat Dirty Leeds in the 1973 FA Cup Final. 'He done a double save. First Cherry then Lorimer. Never seen anything like it. Not as good as Bonetti mind. No one will ever be as good as Catty. Wish he was playing tonight.'

'Penalty!' Kennedy, Fletch and Bertie punched the air in unison.

'No chance.' Alec shook his head. 'Langers was looking for it.'

'Penalty Dad!'

Referee Mike Taylor pointed to the spot. Finnieston stepped up and Montgomery pulled off a stunning save. Alec clapped and cheered. Kennedy, Fletch and Bertie looked puzzled. It had to be a grown-up thing.

'Come on Chelsea. Come on Chelsea.'

Alec looked at his watch. 9.20 p.m. 'Let's go home. You know I've got an early start tomorrow.'

'Oh Dad.' Kennedy protested, pulling himself up on the stanchion in front of him.

'Hit it Ray! HIT IT! Ha ha. Yes! YES! YES!'

Ray Wilkins had hit a mistimed shot which unbalanced Montgomery and Lewington was lurking to drill the ball home. 2-0. The Shed roared its approval, steam rising from the happy heaving throng of humanity. Alec clapped his hands, shrugged his shoulders and turned to walk up the steps. 'Come on boys. Let's go.'

Kennedy followed, turning once to check that Fletch and

Bertie were in tow and joining in the chant, *We are the famous, the famous Chelsea.'* As they reached the top of the terrace he thought about his father having an early start, going back to barracks. That would be him one day… and Fletch and Bertie. It felt good to have an idea about what he was going to do with his life, but most of all it felt good that Chelsea had won.

★ ★ ★

'Wardour Street mate.' Manny climbed into the black taxi and slumped into the back seat looking out of the rear window as the cabby did a U-turn on Queenstown Road and drove past Cedars Mews. Nothing ever went quite to plan where Vera was concerned.

'Shocking weather for the time of year guv.' The cabby's neck ticked forwards repeatedly as he spoke. Manny ignored him. Catching his eyes in the rear view mirror with the same menacing glare he'd used earlier in the evening was enough to ensure the journey would be free of the type of idle chitchat that infuriated him and a reminder that he'd planned to employ a permanent driver.

So what about Vera? 'Vera, Vera, Vera.' He toyed with her name in his mind. He'd known Alec would be at the Chelsea game with Kennedy. He had a copy of the fixture list. Summer was a nuisance because if his brother was home on leave there was no guarantee when he would be with his family or when he'd be in the pub. Variations of the routine were well rehearsed and free from suspicion. Why would anyone be suspicious anyway? It was obvious his love for Vera was a thing of the past. It interested him though that nobody ever questioned why he wasn't in a relationship. Maybe they did behind his back, but so what? He didn't care.

'I didn't realise their was a game tonight. I wanted to

catch Alec before he left.'

Vera's smile had been beguiling. Manny closed his eyes and visualised her. 'Oh… yes. These are for you.'

'Roses!'

The roses were well received.

'Here's some money for young Kennedy. Tell him Uncle Manny was asking after him.'

Vera's beautiful green eyes had widened and rolled as he'd pushed the notes across the table. Three hundred pounds was more than a month's wages. 'He's a bright kid. There's a job for him at Chapman Security when he's ready.' Vera's sad face had made Manny want to reach out and hold her. Take her in his arms. Tell her everything was going to be fine. He knew Kennedy had every intention of joining the Paras. He knew how concerned Vera was about it. 'The door's always open for Alec.' Vera's furrowed brow had told him all he needed to know.

Since Fred's death the brothers had become distant. Their father was the glue that bound them together. Rivalry or no rivalry, Manny knew that Alec was jealous of his success and Fred would constantly remind the family how they should be grateful for his generosity.

"Why not work with your brother? Imagine what you could achieve together". Gone now. Poor Dad. What a terrible way to die. Gasping for air. Manny thought briefly about Nick Hill drowning and about how the event had changed his life. What about the fight though? What if he'd beaten Alec? What if it was Alec whose sight had been damaged? What if he'd joined the Army instead of Alec? So many what ifs? And the biggest one of all was what if he had Vera? What if? What if nothing? He didn't go through with it all. What he'd wanted to say. The words of reassurance. He couldn't. Still. Why? It was infuriating. He needed to go and see Susan immediately.

'What number guv?' The taxi driver smiled as he turned

into Wardour Street. Another fare soon. Somebody with a bit more chat. A decent looking sort maybe. Soho was always swinging whatever the weather.

Manny opened his eyes. 'Here will do.'

'Sorry about earlier.'

'Don't be.' As Manny looked at the driver he noticed a British Karate Association sticker which was neatly positioned in the centre of the glass safety partition that was a feature of London taxis. 'You some kind of martial artist then?'

'Fifth Dan, Black Belt.'

Manny rubbed his chin. He didn't want to appear ignorant and ask what a Dan was. Being a Black Belt was enough to convince him the driver could take care of himself. Thickset. Short haired. Neatly dressed. Not like a lot of the scruffy younger herberts who drove taxis for a living, maybe he'd be worth employing. 'How long you been a cabby then?'

'Eight years. Done the Knowledge and bought my old man's cab off him so he could retire. Best job in the world.'

'I've got the best job in world.'

'Okay guv. Second best job in the world.'

Manny laughed. 'I need a driver, someone who knows London like the back of both their hands. Someone who can pack punches with those hands if they have to.'

'What's the pay?'

'How much do you make?'

'Depends how hard I work?'

'How hard do you work?'

'Well I'll be grafting all night. No missus or kids to worry about getting home for.'

Manny reached in his pocket and pulled out a silver money clip wedged with twenty pound notes. 'That's your daily rate, take it for the fare,' he said, winking as he picked a note out and handed it to the cabby whose eyes sparkled at the sight of the cash. 'Double for weekends. What's your name?'

'Harry. Harry Craven.'

'Well have a think about it Harry Craven. Here's my card. Call me tomorrow and let me know when you can start. If you can't start, don't call me.'

BE THE BEST

25 December 1978

"What an incredible year for those two, *'You're The One That I Want'*, the longest running Number One in 1978. But the most successful group in 1978 has to be Boney M". Watching the Christmas Day edition of *'Top of the Pops'* was a custom in the Jones' household and despite her circumstances Vera had no intention of breaking with tradition. Radio One DJ Noel Edmonds hosting the show was better than most, and she wondered how many millions of living rooms he was looking into from television sets tuned into BBC1 the length and breadth of the country.

'Everything neat, tidy and cosy as usual eh Noel.' Vera sighed as she spoke, unfolding her arms and averting her gaze from the television to the burning coals glowing on the grate of the newly tiled fireplace. The warmth radiating from the fire augmented by the yellow and orange flock wallpaper gave the recently decorated room an inviting ambience. It felt like home. It was home, her family home. *'Mary's Boy Child'* Vera swayed in time with the music. The flickering flames had a hypnotic effect that soothed her, but the pull of the photograph of her husband hanging above the mantelpiece was always too strong. She looked up and tugged gently at the Rosary necklace she was wearing.

'Ready for the Queen at 3 p.m. love?' As Vera locked eyes with Alec, the sound of loud music from upstairs disturbed her inner peace. 'Kennedy!' The volume increased. 'Kennedy! Turn it down.' Louder still. Irate, she clasped at the back of her neck in frustration ruffling her russet hair as she walked into the hall. 'Kennedy! I won't tell you again,' she shouted, but it was hopeless. The combined efforts of Boney M and her voice were no match for The Jam track 'David Watts' which was thundering from the speakers of the HMV Radiogram in her son's bedroom.

Kennedy had heard his mother's request, but pretended not to. He knew the next track on the album 'All Mod Cons' was the altogether mellower 'English Rose', a song that he thought she might like because it was soft, sentimental and mentioned her favourite flower. By the time she came upstairs Bruce Foxton would have stopped wishing he could be like David Watts and Paul Weller would be back on vocal duties.

Why were The Jam covering a Kinks song anyway? Did they know someone like David Watts? Kennedy preened himself in front of the mirror pondering the meaning of the song and why Foxton was singing it. Maybe it wasn't in the right key for Weller. It could be something as simple as that. He could reach the same notes when he sang along with other Jam songs the guitarist had lead vocal duties on, but he always struggled with this one. As the repetitive refrain 'David Watts' faded, he pulled the blue Fred Perry polo shirt he was holding over his lean frame and puffed out his chest. 'Just like Fletch's. Mustard!'

'And it will go back to the shop next week if you don't behave yourself.' Vera stood by the bedroom door with her arms folded and a vexed expression on her face. 'How many times do I have do tell you to keep the noise down?'

Kennedy's cheeks flushed with embarrassment as he turned around. 'Sorry Mum,' he replied sheepishly, scanning the room for anything else his mother might disapprove of. The 'Shoot' magazine colour page featuring Ray Wilkins of Chelsea. No. What mum didn't want Ray as a son? The posters. Blondie singer Debbie Harry in a leopard print catsuit always drew a frown and *'Charlie's Angels'* had been removed from the wall on several occasions including last night. Why though? Farah Fawcett-Majors wearing a boring white dress and Kate Jackson in a check shirt and trousers looked like schoolteachers. Okay, Jaclyn Smith was in a white bikini, but she was hardly X-rated.

X-rated! Shit! In the same split second Kennedy's thoughts panicked him, he heaved a sigh of relief. Fortunately, the album sleeve for *All Mod Cons'*, which was lying on his bed, was covering the dog-eared copy of *'Whitehouse'* Fletch had lent him. Now that would cause his mother some serious consternation. Fletch was gynaecologically obsessed with cover star, pneumatic blonde bombshell Mary Millington, but a forensic examination of the seventy-five pence top-shelf porn mag would show that it was the pages featuring lush brunette Rosemarie England that were curiously stuck together with something other than glue.

"Wanking is a sin. You will go to hell for wanking".

Why did he have to have a religious mother? 'Thing is though Mum, Fletch says there's nothing in the Bible about wanking. So it can't be a sin can it?' Kennedy was suddenly conscious of his mother staring at him with moistening eyes. Was it the *'Charlie's Angels'* poster? Maybe hearing *'English Rose'* was making her feel sentimental. The acoustic ballad was about a travelling man always returning home to his true love. Dad always said nothing would ever keep him from her. 'What's up Mum?'

Vera stared at Kennedy, taking in his features slowly as he walked towards her. Eyes, nose, ears, mouth... it was as if she were trying to memorise each in turn. 'You know what it is.'

Kennedy felt naïve. He somehow knew that the two and two he'd decided to put together were probably going to add up wrong. 'I'm sorry. I'll take the poster down.'

Vera smiled, brushing the tears from her face before holding her arms out. 'Don't be silly, you know what it is.' She ruffled her son's hair before embracing him. 'I just wish you could find something else to do when you leave school, even if it means working with Uncle Manny.'

'I could get a job with him any time.' Kennedy pulled himself away from his mother and looked at her. 'Dad could have as well. But he never did.'

'I know that. But look what happened.'

'Well if Uncle Manny had been concentrating when him and Dad boxed, he'd have got into the Army as well wouldn't he. I know the story.'

Vera reached for the crucifix at the end of her Rosary necklace and sighed. She could sense the frustration in her son's words. Maybe he was right. If she hadn't called out Manny's name and caught his eye that night he might have gone on to beat her future husband and maybe he and not Alec would have joined the Army. 'If you know the story, why are you asking me?'

'*English Rose*' ended and the more up-tempo '*In The Crowd*' started. Kennedy tapped his foot and thought about the significance of the discussion he was having with his mother. It was difficult to focus on two things at the same time. The urge to accompany Weller singing the song was strong, but the need to get his point across to his mother was stronger.

'I'm not asking you. I'm telling you. Uncle Manny lost the fight. Dad knocked him out. That's what happened. Dad told me, Granddad told me... even Manny told me. Three different versions of the same story... each with the same outcome. Dad joined the Army.'

'And died because of it.' Vera gripped the crucifix tightly with her right hand so the points dug into the flesh of her skin causing her to wince in pain. It was un-Christian of her to think this way, but she felt guilty. Everything was her fault. Alec's death was her punishment. Divine retribution. *"An eye for an eye, and a tooth for a tooth"*. (Matthew 5:38) Yes, Alec was dead. Dead, dead, dead. Murdered in the back of a Belfast taxi by an unknown assassin. The Troubles in Northern Ireland still raged, and now her only son was about to follow in his footsteps.

Kennedy walked across to the Radiogram and bent over so he could watch the needle in the run-out groove. 'In The Crowd' was the last track on side one. He liked the way the stylus would click and automatically lift away from the vinyl. Sometimes if there was a scratch or a flaw, the needle would stick. If this happened during a track, words would be repeated. His mother sounded like a stuck record. It didn't matter what she said or what she wanted him to do, when he turned sixteen he was going to join the Army, end of story.

Alec Jones. 3rd Battalion, Parachute Regiment. Kennedy Jones. 3rd Battalion, Parachute Regiment. Like father, like son. Kennedy stood to attention and faced his mother. The Jam were no distraction now. 'Utrinque Paratus.' His voice was resolute, authoritative and direct.

Vera shook her head. Reasoning was pointless. Arguing was futile. She knew the meaning of the Latin expression well enough. How could a boy of sixteen be… ready for anything? How could a boy of sixteen make an informed choice? She could refuse to sign the parental consent forms. He could end up resenting her. He was all she had left. Her mother had finally passed away in the summer to be reunited in heaven with her beloved Jimmy. One day she would be reunited with her beloved Alec, until that day she would stay true to him… and she would stay true to their son and let him follow his own path in life. That way she hoped she would never be forsaken. One day Kennedy would marry and have children of his own and the family circle would be complete again.

PART TWO

PART TWO

MORNING

1 June 2007

'Did you watch that Falklands programme on the Beeb last night Vee?'

The sound of Bertie's voice coming from the kitchen distracted Vera from her reminiscences. His was a welcome presence in the house, like another son, a good son. She'd fallen asleep in the rocking chair thinking about the past and was still thinking about it now, wide-awake, but at least she had company. 'Yes. Er yes love,' she replied somewhat hesitantly. 'You obviously didn't want to.'

Bertie eased his wheelchair forward to the kitchen doorway. 'Something like that,' he said, shaking his head. 'It annoys me. Because it's some kind of silver jubilee anniversary they decide to make a documentary about the war. So now the nation will be aware of what we went through. I don't need reminding, I was there.' As he spoke, he tapped the hooked end of his prosthetic right arm against his chest. The fibres of the threadbare maroon sweatshirt he was wearing protested but offered little resistance as the metal brushing against them snagged and tore a hole in the material by his heart.

Bertie was the living embodiment of the horror and futility of war. His once handsome, chiselled, youthful features were broken, blotchy, beaten and blemished. The mop of curly blonde hair that had crowned his head was now close cropped, and his piercing blue eyes faded by years of pain. The anti-personnel mine had destroyed his body. Evacuated from the battlefield by helicopter, by the time he arrived at the Advanced Surgical Centre 'field hospital' that had been set up in a disused slaughterhouse at Ajax Bay on East Falkland, he had no discernable pulse or blood pressure and was in desperate need of a blood transfusion. Stabilised by immediate intensive care, the Army surgeon had performed a trans-femoral amputation of both his legs and a shoulder disarticulation of his right arm. Against all odds, he'd survived. Consciousness returned following a transfer to the hospital ship SS Uganda. There he would learn that shrapnel had severed his spinal cord. In addition to the other injuries he had to contend with, he was irrevocably paralysed from the waist down.

Back in Britain, following months in hospital and then the Defence Medical Rehabilitation Unit at Headley Court in Surrey, Bertie was invalided out of the Army. Without immediate family to tend to his needs, Kennedy had made the suggestion that he move into his mother's house. His thought process may have been influenced by guilt, but the alternatives made grim reading. Cedars Mews became his home, and Vera his carer who willingly devoted her time to nursing him back to some semblance of health.

The shocking imagery associated with the battle for Mount Longdon was etched indelibly in his memory, seared into his soul like the burning phosphorus that had scarred his skin. A correct diagnosis that the chronic anxiety and hyper-alertness that shrouded his waking hours was Post Traumatic Stress Disorder had taken too long. Until recently, there had been a general lack of public awareness about the condition, and Bertie had been angered and disillusioned by the lack of psychiatric help that was available.

Through all the nightmares, flashbacks, depression, and sleepless nights, Vera had been his lifeline. She'd always been there for him, his own compassionate Florence Nightingale. He knew she loved him as if he were her own flesh and blood, and in his darkest bleakest hours, when the temptation to end his torment with a bullet to the head had been at its greatest, the thought of her overwhelming sadness at his suicide had brought him back from the brink time and again. The severity and nature of his injuries combined with the associated mental anguish made coming to terms with his circumstances a challenging task. What he had managed to do in the past couple of years was learn to cope. To focus on what he could do, who he could be, and what that might lead to.

Bertie wheeled his chair slowly into the living room and parked next to Vera. 'Tell me love, did you learn something you didn't already know?'

Vera frowned. 'Sadly, no. Unless people are directly touched by the tragedy of war, the only occasion they really stop and think about it for a couple of minutes is Remembrance Day.'

'You know what Vee,' replied Bertie, reaching out his left hand to pat her shoulder. 'You're right. But sadly that's human nature. I guess you could say the same for any situation that results in loss of life, injury or mental illness.'

Vera gripped at the Rosary necklace, tears welling in her eyes. 'I'm sorry Bertie,' she sobbed. 'It's all my fault.'

'What is Vee?'

'You, Fletch, Kennedy. Your lives have been ruined. If I'd been stronger, I would have put a stop to Kennedy following in his father's footsteps. And look at Jack now.'

Bertie bit his bottom lip hard fighting back emotions that had got the better of him so many times in the past. If he was able-bodied, he would be giving Vera a reassuring hug right now, just like any loving son would, but he couldn't... all he could provide were words of reassurance. 'Don't think that way Vee,' he replied calmly. 'You must never think that. Alec getting killed made Kennedy even more determined to do what he was always going to do, and the three musketeers of Battersea were always going to stick together. All for one and one for all.'

The doorbell chimed. Vera reached for the handkerchief she kept tucked in the top of her blouse and dabbed her eyes. Bertie looked relieved. It was too early to be sentimental, especially on a day like this. 'I'll get it,' he said, expertly spinning his chair through one hundred and eighty degrees. 'It'll be my man Fletcher.'

★ ★ ★

Kennedy stood by the broken window looking out across the city. Though it wasn't yet 9 a.m. there was already a comforting warmth to the morning sun that permeated his skin and stopped him shivering. The familiar London skyline melded to an azure blue, cloudless sky was a portrait of peaceful serenity, a celestial heaven compared to the hellish visions of the night before. A clear foreground vista... old Father Thames, Imperial Park, North Thames Gas Works, Battersea Bridge, Chelsea Embankment... beautiful. He wouldn't allow himself to be deceived though. Experience told him that he could simply be in the eye of the storm, a pitiable pouch of passivity ensnared by turbulence and turmoil, trepidation and terror. His mind remained a vortex of everything that had gone before. A whirling maelstrom of bloody madness, bloody murder... blood, blood and more blood.

He stretched his arms out and turned his hands over so he could see the cuts, scratches and bruising to his skin. The shards of broken glass scattered across the floor provided sobering clues to their origin, while the stale scars from the past that radiated out from fresh wounds told their own story. The sound of his mobile phone ringing distracted him, a shrill reminder that he wasn't alone in the world. He made his way across to the table taking care where he placed his feet. The bull terrier watched him intently, sniffing the air as he passed but keeping a sensible distance.

'Hello Fletch.' As he answered the call, Kennedy stared at the wall in front of him, his eyes drawn to three tatty photographs Blu-Tacked haphazardly to the yellowing woodchip paper. The first, him with his mother and father. The second, him with his wife and kids. The third, him with Fletch and Bertie. Life suddenly felt precious. Fletch was rambling on about football, he had to cut him short. 'Shit line mate. Listen I've gotta meet Jack. I'll see you down the Monty later.' He switched the phone off and looked from the wall to the vomit-stained lino tiled floor and the labels peeled off countless vodka bottles that were stuck to it. He clicked his fingers at the Staffy and smiled as the dog ambled across to him mewling with restored content. As he bent down and the dog licked his face, he could sense the animal's genuine affection for him. Now he wanted to feel the same affection from his family.

* * *

'Kennedy's gonna meet us later.' Fletch whistled a continuous high to low note as he pocketed his phone and turned to Vera and Bertie who were sat at the kitchen table.

'How did he sound? Vera's voice trembled with anxiety. Did he seem okay?'

Fletch looked directly at Bertie and rubbed at the stubble on his chin. 'As good as Vee, as good as. He's gonna meet Jack and then come down the Monty and watch the England Brazil game with us.'

'I wish he could be more like you two.' Vera sighed and fed the beads of her Rosary through her fingers. 'Our Father which art in heaven...' She continued mouthing the Lord's Prayer, but no sound came from her lips.

Fletch shrugged his shoulders and grimaced as he looked across at wheelchair-bound Bertie and then at the stainless steel

73

kettle on the kitchen table whose polished surface provided a mirror-like reflection of his own image. Caught in a hail of machine gun and artillery fire as the battle for Mount Longdon had raged, a bullet had smashed his cheekbone and taken out his left eye. Countless craniofacial operations had followed as surgeons sought to rebuild his face. The final result was hailed as remarkable, but he found his looks hard to live with. Hooded tops, a patch and looking at the ground were the order of every day, and self-consciousness haunted him still. 'I think I know what you mean Vee,' he said, affectionately putting his arm round her. People get what they see with guys like Bertie and me. They can tell there's a story behind our appearance. Kennedy just looks like any other man in the street.'

Vera smiled. 'I understand that,' she replied softly. 'What I meant though was that you two have slowly but surely moved on.'

'Don't be disheartened,' said Bertie. 'I've a feeling a lot of good will come from him being able to sort out his relationship with Jack.'

'Exactly,' added Fletch. 'That's one thing we've never had as a motivating factor… kith and kin.'

'I hope you're both right.' Vera appeared distant and more troubled than usual. 'Before… before it's too late,' she continued, clasping her hands tightly and closing her eyes to audibly complete the prayer she was saying for her son. 'But deliver us from evil. For thine is the kingdom, and the power, and the glory, forever and ever. Amen.'

★ ★ ★

Kennedy had a genuine sense of purpose as he strode along the road that led from Sheen Gate into Richmond Park. Last night's storm had cleared the air and the lush verdant grass smelt sweet as he flared his nostrils and breathed in deeply through his nose so he could fully appreciate it. The park never changed, only the seasons. Autumn, Winter, Spring and now Summer. Bathed in a deep pool of golden sunlight with myriad trees casting shadows and fallow deer frolicking in the distance, the timeless quality appealed to him. Lazy summer days spent here with family and friends. Conversation and laughter. The innocence of a childhood lost. A canvass painting of life hanging in the corner of his mind with the artist stood before it brush in hand, ready to add the final detail.

Straying from the tarmac, he traversed the sports pitches making a beeline for the familiar old oak tree at the edge of Duchess Wood. Jack was already there. Kennedy paused for a moment. He could see his track-suited son playing keepy-uppy with a football. Instep, thigh, chest, head…repeat. Jack kept the ball moving while retaining a balletic sense of poise and balance that was a joy to watch. 'Go on my son,' he hollered, raising his hands above his head to applaud him.

Jack looked across at his father's position as he headed the ball in the air and allowed it to drop sweetly onto his right foot. With perfect timing, he delivered an inch-perfect pass that would have had any crowd cheering. Kennedy picked the ball up and walked across to his son who was stood adroitly, arms folded, looking straight at him. His defensive body language told him all he needed to know. This was going to be a difficult conversation. Father and son… two men bonded by blood, separated by circumstance, brought together again by fate. Last night he'd stared into the abyss… had come within seconds of ending his years of torment. Defenestration would have taken him out of the frame… literally, but somehow he'd fought off the alcohol-fuelled demons that were battling for possession of his living spirit. One last impassioned mother's plea as his life flashed before his eyes had made him hang back. "Kennedy! Kennedy! Kennedy! For your children, for your wife, for me… stay with us". One final thought that there was more to his situation than he knew had made him think again.

'Hello Dad. Long time no see.'

Jack's loud, dissonant voice cut through his contemplation. Toe-to-toe, face-to-face, eye-to-eye. A split second to say the right words. Kennedy reached out to embrace him, taking a deep breath as he did so. 'Sorry son,' he said slowly, accentuating each word that followed and exhaling as he spoke. 'I apologise for what's happened… I know I've got some explaining to do.'

Jack didn't reciprocate his father's affection, rocking his head to one side and flexing every muscle in his body as he took a step back to break away from the clinch. 'You'll have to speak up,' he replied tersely. 'I'd like to say I'm all ears… but obviously I'm not.'

Kennedy clasped his hands behind his back and looked at his son. He was the spitting image of his mother Nicky, but the dimpled Jones' chin and green eyes confirmed of the presence of his own DNA. Tall, broad-shouldered and handsome with perfect hair, skin and teeth… he was every inch a poster boy. But for what? He chewed at the inside of his mouth. It felt as dry as the desert-like Afghanistan province of Helmand where Jack had been deployed in April 2006 with 3 Para as part of Operation Herrick IV.

On foot patrol during the siege of the Taliban stronghold of Sangin, Jack had been in close proximity to a passing Snatch Land Rover that had detonated an Improvised Explosive Device as it had swerved to the roadside during a fire fight with insurgents. The vehicle had taken the full force of the blast, seriously injuring its occupants, and the violent change in air pressure had ruptured Jack's eardrums breaking delicate nearby bones and deadening essential nerves. The damage to his hearing was severe and permanent and accompanied by tinnitus that affected his ability to concentrate. The loud ringing provided a constant reminder of what had happened… and there was no known cure for the condition.

Jack placed the football on the ground by the tree and sat down on it resting his back against the trunk. Kennedy crouched down on his haunches in front of him resting his hands on the floor scrunching at the verdant grass with his fingers. He wasn't sure who was going to be the biggest beneficiary of the story he was about to tell his son, but at least he was ready to tell it.

CHAPMAN SECURITY

24 October 1986

'*et fresh at the weekend*'. Kennedy laughed as he watched Nicky preening herself and pirouetting in front of the mirror, singing along with the manufactured sound of pop princesses Mel and Kim trilling from the radio cassette player perched on top of the television set. 'You gonna be showing out tonight then?' he asked gruffly, sidling up behind his wife and clasping her breasts from behind while thrusting his groin into her stretch denim clad backside.

'Not if you don't let me finish getting ready.' As she replied, Nicky giggled. She pulled the neon blue scrunchie from her left wrist and shook her permed mane of bleached blonde hair before gathering it up and threading it through in a high loose ponytail.

'You look like you've got a pineapple on your head... OUCCCH!' Kennedy winced as Nicky reached behind her back, grabbed his balls tightly... and squeezed.

'Shush! You'll wake the baby lover boy.' The doorbell rang as she pulled away and walked across the room. 'Get that, it'll be Trina, I'm going to check on Aimee.'

Kennedy was still rubbing his groin as he opened the front door.

'Pleased to see me then Mr Jones?' Trina cocked her head from side-to-side and pulled at the chewing gum in her mouth.

Kennedy grinned. Trina was full of it for a seventeen year old. Just like all the other kids on the estate.

'Gonna let me in then? I can't babysit out here now can I?'

Opening the door wider, Trina brushed past him. As she did so, he drew a deep breath taking in a heady cocktail of scents. Wrigley's Juicy Fruit, Embassy Regal, fish and chips and a faint trace of a musky perfume that smelt familiar. What was it? *'My Sin'* by Lanvin. Yeah! That was it. The same as Nicky wore. Vera had bottles of the stuff she'd given her. Probably was Nicky's as well, the little tealeaf… another prick teaser in the making. He eyed up her skinny gait and slapped his face as she skanked down the hall. He knew it was wrong… well sort of. If only from the point of view that he was married to Nicky, the mother of his kids Aimee and Jack. Young Jack, the apple of his eye who he was going to kiss goodnight right now. He closed the front door and frowned as he went into his son's bedroom.

'Da-ad, who was that at the door?'

'Trina'

'Are you and Mum going out?'

'Yes.'

'Why?'

'We're gonna meet your Uncles Fletch and Bertie.' Kennedy crouched by Jack's bed and combed his son's hair with his fingers.

'Fletch and Bertie nearly died in the war didn't they Dad.'

'They did. But they were very brave and lived.'

'Where would they have gone if they'd died?'

'Heaven. Everyone goes to heaven when they die.'

'It must be very crowded up there.'

Kennedy smiled at the innocence of his son's observation. 'Yes I expect it is.'

'Will you go to heaven before me?'

'Definitely.'

'So if it's crowded… when I get to heaven… how will I find you?'

'I'll be waiting by the gates.'

'I love you Dad.'

'I love you too son.' Kennedy swallowed hard, clearing the lump that had formed in his throat. Kids eh. The best thing in the world.

★ ★ ★

The ground floor bar at Viola was its usual kaleidoscope of colour and cacophony of music and conversation. Kennedy knew why Nicky loved the place. It was an escape from the hi-rise council flat, baby-waking drudgery of day-to-day life. On a Friday night she could 'show out' in the bar and later strut her stuff upstairs where she might see George and Andy, the boys from Wham! Siobham, Sarah and Keren from Bananarama, Sade, the Fine Young Cannibals and the rest of pops glitterati who patronised Uncle Manny's club which was located at the junction of Wardour Street and Meard Street in the heart of Soho.

This wasn't the Soho of his youth though. The creepy, crawling, seedy, shady streets that he'd explored with Bertie and Fletch had been given a makeover. Many of the traditional boozers, and the blaggers that inhabited them, now had a wine bar air of respectability. The drug dealers and their dysfunctional dependents, the pimps, prostitutes and punters, the pansies, punks and hooligans were less obvious. After hours, the atmosphere still reeked of tainted love… but it was different, more sanitised, more sterile. The allure had gone. Sold out or vanished? It didn't matter. It was plain and simple, just like all those bands they'd seen at the Marquee before they'd joined the Regiment. The Stukas, Count Bishops, The Slits, Generation X, Hi-Fi, The Boys, Bethnal, The Jam, Suburban Studs, UK Subs, Adam and the Ants… Eddie and the Hot Rods. Somebody had decided there was money to be made. Prime Minister Thatcher's 'yuppy' greed culture had been fully embraced by people such as Uncle Manny and it was being propagated by the teeming assortment of clubbers mixing without prejudice tonight in Viola. Fuck the lot of them.

'What's up mate?' Stan Roper sensed Kennedy's air of consternation. 'Seen something you don't like?'

'Ha ha... Maybe.' Kennedy shrugged his shoulders and smiled at Stan's ability to second-guess his thoughts.

'I know that look,' added Fletch, peeling the green foil away from the neck of the bottle of Holsten Pils he was holding.

'I don't want any trouble from you tonight.' Stan reached out and clasped Kennedy by both shoulders.

Kennedy flexed his arms and stepped backwards. 'Don't worry, I won't cause any grief.'

Stan Roper had done well for himself since leaving the Regiment. It had come as a surprise to hear that his old Company Sergeant Major was working for Manny but, having thought about it, it made sense. There was a military precision about everything his Uncle did, and employing a former soldier complemented his activities. Chapman Security had continued to flourish, and Manny's personal enterprise philosophy had seen him diversify his business interests. Viola appeared to be a hobby, an ego trip perhaps. But it was always full of people... and they were always spending money, lots of it. Somebody had to keep the place in order. Enter Stan 'the man' Roper. Tough, organised, and uncompromising, the ex CSM ran the place with an iron fist keeping the riff raff out on the street while the paying punters splashed out inside.

As far as career choices went, Chapman Security didn't appear to be a bad one. When Nicky complained about their cramped living conditions and asked for more housekeeping money, Kennedy would question his decision to avoid working for his Uncle. Maybe it was a genetic sixth sense. Maybe it was his mother's religion-muddled mawkishness. Maybe it was his father's ethereal influence. Maybe it was his inability to deal with the past. Since leaving the Army there'd been no real pressure to make a decision, to conform, to get real. He did what he did. He laboured on a building site. Turn up, work hard, get paid, go home. It was simple, but not secure.

'I went to see Bertie this morning.' Stan's voice stalled Kennedy's thoughts about work, and the sight of Nicky dancing provocatively in front of them on the small dancefloor that edged the bar banished them from his mind completely.

'My mum looks after him well,' he replied, winking and pointing at his wife.

'Like Mother Teresa... she's a proper saint,' added Fletch before taking a long swig of Holsten.

'Mother Teresa's still alive,' quipped Kennedy. 'But yeah! In among all those prayers... and the silent contemplation of Jesus Christ, she is the living embodiment of a saint.'

Fletch laughed and started singing along with the Furniture track *'Brilliant Mind'* that was pumping from the sound-system. The words were coincidental. Fancy having a brilliant mind to be out of... some of the stuff his friend came out with made him wonder about his intellect and sanity.

'Anyway... how was he?' Kennedy folded his arms and ignored Fletch who stopped singing immediately.

'Putting a brave face on things as you'd expect.' Stan frowned as he spoke.

'I do that every day,' said Fletch, shaking his head and tracing the fingers of his left hand across the scarred, pitted, pockmarked contours of his face.

'Sorry mate. I didn't mean nothing by it.' Stan looked crestfallen.

'I know you didn't.'

Nicky shimmied across to where the men were stood by the bar. Her effervescent presence lightened their mood immediately, stopping their morose conversation before it had a chance to develop further. 'All right for another drink?' She licked her plump pink lips lasciviously and fluttered her eyelashes at Stan.

'On the house gorgeous. Whatever you want.' Stan clapped his hands and looked beyond her.

'Looks like the guvnor might want you.' Fletch nodded at Stan and pointed waist high at the entrance door Manny Jones had just walked through with Harry Craven and Tony 'Jester' Cook.

'You're right,' said Stan, acknowledging Manny with a thumbs up signal. 'I'll catch you lads later.'

★ ★ ★

Manny was stood by the antique Victorian oak pedestal writing desk that dominated his office which was located on the fifth floor of Viola House. The surface of the desk had been beautifully re-trimmed in olive green leather. Keen to preserve its 'as new' appearance, he avoided placing anything on it that might create pressure marks or cause damage and publically admonished any member of staff who inadvertently did so. Tonight though, an exception had been made. The contents of three military-standard Pelican universal handgun cases lying on the desk were important enough to warrant a concession. The rule was his to break anyway.

'What's your expert opinion?' Manny opened one of the cases and turned it to face Stan who reached forward and withdrew an automatic pistol from the protective foam that cradled it.

'Glock 18. Nice piece.' Stan levelled the pistol at Harry Craven's head. 'On full-automatic fire mode, I could empty the thirty-three round extreme high-capacity magazine into H in seconds.'

Harry glared at Stan and didn't blink when he squeezed the trigger. The click was barely audible above the sound of music reverberating through the building from the main room of the club on the first floor.

Stan placed the pistol on the desk and drew another from the case. 'SIG-Sauer P226 mmm… and what else have we got in here? Beretta 93R… Browning BDA.'

Manny, Harry and Jester were noticeably impressed with Stan's knowledge of firearms and watched attentively as he arranged the pistols side-by-side.

Manny paced away slowly from the desk and folded his arms. 'If you had to go with one, which would you use?'

'I'd go with the G18. It can turn one man into an army.' Stan picked the Glock up once more and pointed it at the office door. 'A few words of caution though. Because it's so light, the recoil on this sexy little slut will render it useless to an untrained shooter… but then I guess that's not your problem is it?'

'You're right, it's not my problem.' Manny clenched his fists and raised them in front of his face staring at the ring he wore on the third finger of his left hand as he did so. The emerald stones fashioned into the initials C and J and set into gold appeared to have a special lustre tonight. A sign perhaps, an indication that what he was thinking was the right thing to do. Stan, Harry and Jester waited on his words. He shrugged his shoulders and lowered his arms. 'Hmmm. What is my problem though is keeping this expanding line of business running securely. You can't do everything Stan, and you two don't have the right background, knowhow or mentality.'

Manny knew the solution. Kennedy. It was part of his gameplan, but he needed Stan to figure it out and make the approach. His nephew continually resisted his advances, but he would listen to Stan. That was one half of the reason he'd employed him in the first place… the other half being to manage Chapman Security's illicit trade of small arms. Borne out of regular requests from private alarm system customers who wanted additional protection, over a period of time Manny had established relationships with key personnel who worked for Europe's leading firearm manufacturers. The margins to be made were significant. Few people knew the true value of guns, particularly in places like the United Kingdom where ownership was either illegal or restricted.

One client, Quique Di Santo, a Colombian national who owned a home in Kensington, had highlighted the scale of the opportunity. Di Santo fascinated Manny. He'd made his money in the clandestine world of emerald dealing, but his detailed knowledge and understanding of his country's criminal gangs, drug cartels, left-wing guerrillas, right wing paramilitary organisations, corrupt politicians, and the military and police aided by the United States government who tried to maintain order, was astonishing.

Di Santo had explained how the political conflicts in Colombia went unresolved often as a result of the direct and indirect actions of the cocaine cartels. Conflict was good, not only for the drug runners, but also the terrorists and people traffickers; it made the channelling of money easier. The security threat was intense. In the past five years, cartel death squads had murdered fifty Colombian judges and twelve Supreme Court Justices. Protection rackets, extortion and kidnappings were rife.

At the hub of this criminal insurgency were weapons and equipment imported by the cartels, and Di Santo had occasionally brokered arms deals when in Europe. Manny wasn't interested in trading guns for drugs, just hard currency. The British police had invested considerable resources in trying to stifle the influx of Class A narcotics into the country and he didn't want Chapman Security showing up on their radar. Part of Stan Roper's brief was to keep drugs out of Viola. It was a tough challenge, and Manny trumpeted his stance to the Met. From his early days sitting at the window of the Top Ten he'd seen the damage they could do to people. Joining the Persians party had never been on his agenda, and any employee he suspected of possession with intent to supply was dealt with ruthlessly. Di Santo had joked with him that he was a hypocrite; that in selling guns he was a part of the narcotics supply chain. It was a fair point, but he'd laughed it off. Not having a conscience helped.

★ ★ ★

'Look at her.' Kennedy slung his arm around Fletch and nodded at Nicky. 'She'd stay out all fucking night dancing if she could.'

'Plenty in here do,' replied Fletch, pointing at his good eye. 'Ecstasy, that's what they're all on, that or Percy.'

Kennedy shrugged his shoulders. 'It's a nightclub. People come here to enjoy themselves including us. Let's have another drink.'

Fletch nodded as they turned to face the bar. 'Stan reckons they have a zero-tolerance policy as far as drugs go. But someone's serving up.'

Nicky sashayed across the heaving dancefloor swaying slightly as she stepped in between Kennedy and Fletch. 'Come again,' she said breathing heavily. 'Come again.'

'I said someone's serving up.'

'What you on about Fletcher?'

'You said, "Come again".'

Nicky laughed. 'I'm on about the tune you donut. Proper ain't it,' she said coquettishly before continuing to sing along to the General Public track. 'Oh and a Southern Comfort and lemonade if you don't mind.'

Fletch shook his head as she clicked her fingers and winked at him.

'I'll get that doll face.' Stood next to Kennedy waving a twenty-pound note as he spoke was a tall, suntanned man with a shaggy mop of permed, blonde hair. A large hooked nose dominated his face that might otherwise have been considered handsome, and oversize gold-hooped earrings complemented by a Persil-white cap-sleeve T-shirt bearing the slogan 'CHOOSE LIFE' exaggerated the 'Boys from Wham!' look set off by stone-washed denim jeans and white loafers.

'Where the fuck did you come from, Club Tropicana?' Kennedy didn't wait for an answer to his questions. Reaching out with both hands he snatched at the man's earrings simultaneously splitting both his earlobes. The crowd gathered at the bar parted as he dropped to his knees howling in pain, blood spattering his T-shirt.

'For fucks sake what did you do that for?' Fletch grabbed Kennedy's arm and pulled him away as he was about to knee the hapless man in the face.

'Because he's a cunt!' Kennedy grinned, holding the earrings aloft like trophies as he allowed Fletch to police him.

'You've never seen him before.'

'And never will again I hope.'

'Fucking hooligan!' Nicky exclaimed, punching Kennedy squarely in the stomach. 'You couldn't wait for tomorrow could you? Gotta ruin my Friday night out.'

Kennedy puffed out his chest defiantly, throwing the earrings on the floor and bracing himself for more blows but Nicky dropped her arms to her side instead and scowled at him. 'All he did was offer to buy me a drink.'

'Well he won't be offering any more will he.'

To add insult to the man's injury, two burly members of Viola's security team were soon on hand to escort him to the door and eject him from the club.

★ ★ ★

'He's got worse if anything.' Fletch swirled a generous measure of Jack Daniels in the tumbler he was holding and looked up at the large screen above the video jukebox in Viola's basement bar that was now empty having closed at 2 a.m. 'The slightest provocation sets him off and he tears into anyone regardless of who they are and the consequences.'

Stan carefully pushed a slice of lime into the neck of the bottle of Sol standing on the bar in front of him before gently picking it up and admiring it. The club was still in full swing upstairs, but a break wouldn't do any harm at all. His staff knew the routine and he needed to sound Fletch out about Kennedy. 'That was naughty what he did tonight,' he said, licking his lips before taking a swig from the bottle. 'That aggression needs to be channelled.'

'You're not wrong.' Fletch necked the JD down in one. 'I seriously think he needs someone to help him get a grip before he does some real damage.' The fiery liquid passing down his throat made him gurn as he spoke. 'It's like he never left that fucking mountain. He hasn't been able to settle into a decent job since he left the Army.'

'Manny could help him get a grip.'

Fletch poured another generous measure of JD from the bottle on the bar and pointed at the screen. The Stranglers video for their single *Always the Sun'* was playing. 'Coincidence or what?'

'What, Manny?'

'No. Kennedy needing to get a grip.'

'Ha ha.' Stan laughed. He was a massive fan of the Stranglers, and his favourite track remained their first single *'(get A) Grip (on Yourself)'*. 'Exactly!'

'Actually mate. You'll know the answer to this.' Fletch paused to eye the JD in the tumbler in front of him. 'In *'Grip'* What was Cornwell on about when he said he didn't have the cash to buy a Morry Thou?'

Without hesitation, Stan replied. 'Morris Minor 1000.'

'Ha ha. The car. Of course. Fucking hell! That's been bugging me for years.' Fletch knocked back the JD and coughed. 'This is a decent track as well.'

Stan nodded in agreement.

'I like this bit coming up where Hugh shoots the Astec Sun Calendar wheel. I wonder what that means?'

Stan shrugged his shoulders. He wished he knew the answer, but he didn't. 'Fuck all probably. Just being random and hoping people wonder what he's on about.'

Both men laughed.

'Yeah. But why would a man with a gun always have fun?'

'Maybe he's just saying that because it rhymes.'

'Nah. Not Hugh Cornwell. '

Stan looked at Fletch and smiled before taking another swig from the bottle. 'If only you knew,' he thought to himself, silently contemplating the ramifications of what he had just seen in Manny's office and weighing up the pros and cons of Kennedy being involved in the business. 'Nicky's got a hot arse though, ain't she?' he said, deliberately changing the subject. 'She's a proper flirt. Everyone fancies her. I can see why Kennedy gets wound up.'

'It's a nice problem to have.' Fletch paused to light a cigarette. 'I wouldn't have the confidence to be with someone half as lively… well anyone really.'

'You'll be okay. There's someone out there for you.'

'Yeah! Maybe. I don't just want *someone* though.'

'Well you can't have Nicky. Despite all her front, she wouldn't have it from anyone else.'

'Ha ha yeah, I know that. Everyone wants to get their fingers in her fish mitten, but he got in there first. And the fact he's hung like a Christmas stocking helps.'

'What bigger than you?'

'Fuck off! No ones bigger than me, not even John Holmes.'
Fletch laughed, he could feel his sombre mood lifting, Stan
'the man' was always good company.

Stan checked his watch. 'Whoa well are you two big boys
going to the game later?'

'Does a rocking horse have a wooden cock?'

'Not if it's a filly. Anyway, who are we playing?'

Fletch smiled. "We". The expression used to rankle with
him. But he didn't care anymore. Stan was an armchair
Chelsea fan, not a proper supporter like him and Kennedy.
'We... are at Arsenal, or should I say *the* Arsenal.'

Stan swigged the last of the Sol and placed the bottle on
the bar. 'Well stay out of trouble and get Kennedy to ring me
as soon as you see him.'

★ ★ ★

The London Underground concourse at Victoria Station was
busier than usual. Saturday afternoon shoppers and tourists
scurrying to and from trains buses and tubes were bustling
through the ticket barriers with little care for the welfare
of their fellow passengers. The unexplained presence of
uniformed police officers with incessantly barking Alsatian
dogs created an atmosphere of apprehension in what was
already a claustrophobic environment, and the suspicious
stares of groups of smartly attired men frayed the nerves and
quickened the pace of those who sensed they were in the
wrong place at the wrong time.

'I'm gonna call Stan now.' Kennedy cupped his hands and
blew onto them. 'Any idea what he wanted?'

Fletch shook his head deliberately. He didn't want to get
involved.

'Might as well wait here and see what happens then. It
could get lively in a minute.'

90

Fletch shrugged his shoulders and yawned. Five hours sleep and a hangover were not ideal preparations for watching a football match, and standing on the Clock End at Highbury in the wind and rain wasn't going to improve matters. Neither of them had ever seen Chelsea win at Arsenal, and with the Blues hovering just above the relegation zone, the odds that they would be disappointed come 5 p.m. were shorter than those printed on the Ladbrokes Long List betting coupon he had just pulled from his pocket to study.

Kennedy leaned against the public telephone box. As he waited for Stan to answer the phone he sniffed the fingers of his right hand. Sex! Nicky! God! She'd been good last night. So fucking horny. All that tetchiness at his aggressive behaviour was just a front. She loved it really. They all did. Women like a man to be protective. He wasn't the jealous type. The beeping sound from the receiver derailed his train of thought. He jammed a ten pence piece into the coin mechanism. 'Stan. Is that you?'

'Yes mate.'

'Fletch said you wanted a word. Listen, if it's about last night. I'm sorry for losing my rag with that bloke.'

'Nah. Not that. I'd forgotten about him already.'

'What then?'

'I'll get straight to the point. Manny has a job lined up for you.'

'Why can't he tell me himself?'

'He will.'

'Why are you telling me then?' Kennedy clenched the fist of his right hand and watched his knuckles whiten.

'I'm telling you because you keep knocking him back.'

'I've got my reasons.'

'Your reasons don't pay the bills though. Wouldn't you like to get out of that flat? I'm sure Nicky would.'

'Leave her out of this. I'll decide what's right for my family.' The background sound of dogs barking and raised voices couldn't mask the irritated tone of Kennedy's voice.

'Sorry mate, I didn't mean nothing by it. Just looking out for you...'

Suddenly, Kennedy lost interest in the call. Catching sight of a group of Pringle jumper-wearing, Adidas Trimm Trabb trainer-shod men in their early to mid-twenties stepping off the up escalator, he tuned out of Stan's sales patter about Manny. He'd heard it all before anyway. What was unfolding in front of his eyes was far more stimulating. Two, six, ten, twelve... and still they came. Who were they? Take your pick. Tottenham Hotspur away at Queens Park Rangers. Chelsea away at Arsenal. Different teams, same uniform... funny that. No scarves or colours. He remembered the Bolton game he'd gone to with his father. This was different though. Not some far-flung provincial outpost where you could be betrayed by your accent and manners, this was the London Underground... and today the Victoria Line was an unwitting conveyor belt carrying those who fancied a ruck the chance to prove themselves from station to station. Bandit country. Wathamstow Central, Blackhorse Road, Seven Sisters, Finsbury Park, Highbury and Islington, Kings Cross, Euston, Warren Street. God's country. Oxford Circus, Green Park, Victoria, Pimlico, Vauxhall, Stockwell, Brixton. The police would have their work cut out trying to maintain order.

'Are you still there?' Kennedy smiled at the sound of Stan's raised voice as he watched the group of men vault the ticket barriers.

'Where the fuck are you? Sounds like Piccadilly Station.

'Ha ha. Nah Victoria. Let's talk later.' Kennedy clunked the receiver down and looked across at Fletch who was still immersed in figuring out what would make a good bet for the day. Arsenal, Everton, Liverpool and Aston Villa were bankers for sure. A Yankee. Six doubles, four trebles and a four-fold accumulator. Tidy. He didn't like betting against his own team, but money was money.

'Fletch!' Kennedy shouted, stretching out his right arm towards the passageway that led to the District and Circle lines which was now partially obstructed by the Pringle Boys whose progress had been halted by the police.

Hearing his name, Fletch looked across at the phone kiosks and saw his friend's clenched fist, thumb extended downwards. He smiled at the fact that they still used the tactical field signals they had learned in the Regiment. The enemy were nearby. The fucking enemy, you had to laugh. Kennedy patted the top of his head signalling Fletch to join him, but his headway was hampered by a tide of impatient, neck-craning-curious civilians being slowed by the police bottleneck.

Kennedy's gimlet eyes scanned slowly from left to right. Football hooligans made him smile. The so-called 'Casual' look had been conceived partly to enable those who wanted to cause trouble to blend in with the average men in the average high street of the average town they happened to find themselves in. Old Bill used to have it easy. The terrace troublemakers of yesteryear could be spotted a mile off. Skinhead haircuts, button down Ben Sherman's, Levi's Sta-Prest, braces, Harrington jackets, Crombie overcoats and cherry red polished Dr. Martens boots. Mind you, the way it was going now, with wannabes up and down the country swathing themselves from head to foot in clobber featuring large green crocodiles, yellow flying eagles and rampant lions clutching golf clubs, the ability to vanish into the crowd had once again been lost.

Zipping up the front of his black MA-1 flight jacket to the collar so the orange lining wasn't visible, Kennedy folded his arms and smiled at the sight of Fletch jostling his way towards him. 'Right then, straight through this lot,' he muttered, just as the up escalator spewed forth another unruly mob of Rowdy likely lads whose presence immediately attracted the attention of both the Pringle Boys and the police. His surveillance had been of limited use. He didn't recognise anyone. They probably weren't Chelsea, however wankers were wankers irrespective of which football club they were affiliated to. It was fifteen metres to the ticket barriers that were now being illegally breached by the Rowdies, and a further five metres from there to the objective... the down escalator.

'Chelsea scum. Let's have it!'

The battle cry reverberated off the low ceiling. The enemy had declared war. Within seconds, the comparative if uneasy calm erupted into a noisy fracas. Kennedy lunged forward pitching himself into the middle of the affray. The command to 'CHARGE!' was in his head, just as it always had been since that night on Mount Longdon. This time there were no tracer rounds, no mortar shells, no mines, no automatic weapons and no fixed bayonets; this was hand-to-hand combat of a different kind.

'Shit! Cunt! Bastard! Twat! Fucking mug! Shit-cunt-bastard-FUCKING-MUG!' A fifteen metre expletive-riddled, Tourette-esque, you'll never take me alive, left hook, right upper cut, jab-jab journey to the down escalator followed. The station concourse was a tangle of flailing arms, legs and heads. This was a decent skirmish. Blood, gristle and crunching bone. Forehead and knuckles meeting little resistance. Kennedy felt giddy. His temples were pounding, his heart racing. Enveloped in a mist of rage, momentarily he looked up and saw Fletch grappling with two truncheon-wielding police officers and three Rowdies who were kicking and pummelling the body of a prostrate Pringle Boy.

'Urgent assistance required!'

One of the policemen radioed for help, they needed it. Fletch could hold Old Bill for the moment. The Pringle Boy required support. 'Leave him right out you cunts!' Kennedy lashed out with his right foot catching the first Rowdy on the side of his knee causing him to cry out in pain as his anterior cruciate ligament ruptured. A perfectly timed right hook caught the second Rowdy with such force that his head jolted sideways and smashed into the temple of the third, the jarring impact rendering both men senseless before they fell to the floor. Looking bemused, the Pringle Boy uncurled himself from the protective foetus position he had adopted.

'Never take your eyes off your opponent.' The words ricocheted around Kennedy's head. 'Never take your eyes off your opponent.' As he spat them out again, but more venomously this time, the sound of the panicking crowd flanged between his ears. 'Never take your eyes off your opponent.' The Pringle Boy got to his feet and assessed the damage to his clothes. Kennedy shook his head, but he couldn't clear the mist. 'CHARRRGE!' he screamed, tearing into the police officers attempting to apprehend Fletch. Speed and the venomous ferocity of his punching were the keys to being successful now. Kidney, liver, groin. Precision blows delivered with unerring accuracy dropped the policemen to their knees in seconds.

'Stay down,' he growled. An adrenalin-stimulated feeling of euphoria counterbalanced his anger as he caught his breath and glanced across at the foot of the steps to the main station concourse where the Pringle Boys and Rowdies were going toe-to-toe with each other and the police. Everywhere was crowded, more so now as many of the passers-by, having finally realised what the commotion was about, felt less threatened and were standing in their tracks compelled to watch the brawl reach its inevitable conclusion as police reinforcements arrived on the scene.

'Forget 'em. Let's go!' Kennedy nudged Fletch who was looking at the tangle of groaning bodies by his feet. 'Excuse us love,' he continued, resting his hands on the shoulders of a troubled looking mother whose young son was staring with wide-eyed incredulity at him.

'Are you Superman?' questioned the boy as Kennedy brushed past him.

Fletch laughed and patted the boy on the head. 'He ain't Superman son.'

'How do you know Mister?'

'Superman wears his underpants on the outside.'

The boy shook his head and smiled. Wanting to follow them, as he watched Kennedy and Fletch burrow their way into the heaving throng making for the Wilton Street exit, he tugged at his mother's hand, but she scolded sense into him. Oh well. Never mind. At least he'd be able to tell his friends at school on Monday about the new comic book hero he'd seen.

Outside, Fletch and Kennedy's utilitarian attire afforded them the anonymity required to avoid the attention of police officers spilling out of the back of two carriers that had just pulled up outside the station with sirens wailing and blue lights flashing. Kennedy looked up at the large clock that dominated its imposing Edwardian Baroque redbrick and Portland stone façade. 'Still early,' he said, reaching into his pocket for a packet of cigarettes. 'Let's have a drink in the Shakespeare. We can come back later when Old Bill have calmed things down.'

'Could easily have got nicked back there.' Fletch peeled off the balaclava he was wearing and using it to mop the perspiration forming on his brow. The headgear was perfect for hiding scars away from prying eyes. The changing of the seasons made it easier for him in winter, but the self-consciousness remained all the same.

'Yeah! Well we didn't.' Kennedy cupped his hands to shelter the flame of the match he'd just struck from the stiffening breeze.

'I didn't mean it like that.' Fletch frowned as he stooped down to light a cigarette. 'What I meant was, thanks. Thanks to you we didn't get nicked.'

Kennedy looked nonplussed. 'Come on,' he replied, talking as he smoked. 'Fuck this shit. Let's have a pint and go to the game.'

* * *

Manny Jones' Jaguar XJ12 Sovereign was an understated model of comfort and good design that elevated transportation to an art form. Its specially tuned 5.3 litre, V12 engine provided incredible warp-speed power and smooth acceleration that could leave standing other limousines such as the Bentleys and Rollers favoured by the upper echelons of Soho's criminal fraternity.

Sitting on the mushroom leather Chesterfield bench seat at the rear, gazing out of the dark-tinted window, Manny felt safe and secure in the knowledge that the customised car, which featured bulletproof glazing and armoured panels, could thwart all but the most determined of would-be assassins. If the Jag was compromised, he still had his driver and personal bodyguard Harry Craven to call on. If the need arose, Harry would die for him. It was written into his contract of employment.

Despite frequently operating outside the law, Manny didn't consider himself to be a villain. Viola was the respectable front of what was now a lucrative global business empire. While Chapman Security touched many bases, he particularly enjoyed matching buyers with sellers and vice versa. Tonight, the nation would be sitting in their collective armchairs laughing at the popular BBC television sitcom *'Only Fools and Horses'*. He had it recorded on VCR to watch tomorrow after Sunday lunch. The knockdown enterprise culture that Delboy and Rodney Trotter embraced on the streets of Peckham was a close approximation of how he'd started out... the difference was that whereas Del continued to live in hope that his maxim *'this time next year, we'll be millionaires'* would come true, he had made it a reality.

Classical music soothed Manny's soul. *'Pavane Op.50'* by Gabriel Faure oozed mellifluously from the speakers at just the right volume to provide a canvass for his thoughts without overriding them. It was less easy to get distracted by familiar changes in pitch and tempo but the harmonic and melodic climax of the haunting tune always snagged his attention as did Harry's weekly request which he anticipated would be made at any moment. He glanced at his Casio SDB digital watch, 5.58 p.m. It was a small concession he allowed his driver. Disturbing his peace. Funny that. 5.59 p.m. 'Go on then H,' he said, sparing Harry the embarrassment of asking.

Harry smiled and tapped the control panel of the car stereo. String instruments, flutes, oboes, clarinets, bassoons and horns were replaced by the voice of a BBC Radio 2 continuity announcer. 'And now a second reading of the football results with James Alexander Gordon.'

'Today League Division One... Arsenal 3 Chelsea 1.'

'Get in!'

'Aston Villa 2 Newcastle United 0. Everton 3 Watford 2. Leicester City 2 Southampton 3. Luton Town 4 Liverpool 1.'

'Go on you Hatters!' Harry cheered, feeding the steering wheel of the Jaguar through his leather-gloved hands as he turned into Wardour Street.

'Oxford United 2 Nottingham Forest 1. Queens Park Rangers 2 Tottenham Hospur 0.'

'Yes!' Harry clenched his fist but kept it in his lap. He checked the rear view mirror where his eyes met Manny's. His boss looked singularly unimpressed.

'Wimbledon 2 Norwich City 0.'

Harry frowned and tapped the control panel of the car stereo. String instruments, flutes, oboes, clarinets, bassoons and horns replaced the voice of James Alexander Gordon. He was only allowed the First Division results, but that was enough. Arsenal had won, Spurs had lost... happy days.

Manny looked at ease once more. He gazed out of the window and pondered briefly what had motivated James Alexander Gordon to deliberately alter the tone of his voice to indicate to the listener whether the result was a home win, an away win, or a draw. Maybe it was to alleviate the boredom of the job. What did he do for the rest of the week? It had begun to rain and the sight of two women, a fiery redhead and a peroxide blonde, leaning into each other and sharing an umbrella as they walked briskly along the pavement towards Viola caught his eye. Immediately, the mystery surrounding James Alexander Gordon's enunciation was forgotten.

'Ginger and Phoebe.' Manny sighed, cracking his knuckles one by one as Harry eased the car to a halt outside Viola's entrance.

'Ahh Phoebe.'

'You can have her.'

'I already did boss.' Harry chuckled as he cut the engine.

'Each to their own.'

'You like that Ginger don't you.'

'I like a lady with a finely turned ankle.'

'Maybe you should go to the ballet.'

'Maybe you should shut the fuck up, get out of the car... and open the door for me. Remember who pays your wages.'

★ ★ ★

Manny laid the palm of his left hand flat on the desk and spread out his fingers. It was no coincidence that the pigment of the leather that bound the wood matched the intense, radiant green of the emeralds set in the ring he wore. The colour symbolised life, love and beauty, and, carat-for-carat, these particular gemstones, whose provenance Di Santo had told him could be traced back to the ancient Inca mine at Chivor, some fifty miles to the northeast of Colombia's capital Bogota, were more valuable than diamonds.

Despite the positivity of the meaning they embodied, scrutinising the emeralds made him frown. Portrayed in his mind was Vera in the virginal splendour of her youth. Red hair scraped back into a severe bun. Freckle-flecked porcelain skin. Deep, meaningful green eyes sparkling like emeralds. Yes, to him, the emeralds also represented love… but his was a silent, soulless, dispiriting, disturbing, unrequited love. Originally set in a pendant and gifted to Vera the Christmas following Alec's murder, the gemstone jewellery had been returned without a note. For several years it had sat in the top drawer of his desk, there to be looked at… a lustrous example that money couldn't buy everything. The recollection angered him. He raised his hand above the table and slapped it down hard on the surface. 'Never take your eyes of your opponent,' he hissed, grimacing as he envisaged his blood spattering Vera's face.

'What was that?' Jester Cook, who was stood at the far end of the office, looked up from the sheaf of files he was holding.

'Never take your eyes off your opponent.' Manny repeated the words, standing up and walking across to Jester.

'Oh yeah! Well you'd be right there as far as that Colombian crook Di Santo is concerned.'

'Late again eh. Even with that bent copper Jacobsen on the firm. You'll have to remind me what exactly are we paying that cunt for?' Manny turned to face the large portrait of Queen Elizabeth I that dominated the wall opposite his desk and laid his hands on the gilt-edged frame. 'What would you do Gloriana?' he said, smiling as he slid the frame to the left to reveal a safe door.

'If you want my opinion, we have too many customers like Di Santo.'

'I wasn't asking you for an opinion, I was asking Good Queen Bess. You can never have too many customers. But you can have too many people taking a fucking liberty.'

Manny worked the combination dial on the safe door until he was able to pull it open. Neatly stacked banknotes occupied the rear of the safe. In front of the cash lay an A4 size green leather bound notebook. On top of the notebook was an emerald beaded Rosary necklace. 'I need to lean on Jacobsen a bit more.' He reached into the safe for the notebook taking care when moving the necklace. 'He needs to be brought under manners… so he understands the value of things.' As he opened the notebook he shook his head. 'And as for Di Santo, it's time to put the frighteners on. By the end of tonight, he'll be so scared he'll be sweating like a leper at a finger buffet.' Manny placed the notebook under his arm, swung the safe door shut, span the combination dial and slid the Queen Elizabeth portrait back to its customary position. 'You know what I mean… don't you my lovely.'

Jester ran his fingers slowly through his hair brushing his foppish fringe off his forehead. 'I expect he'll be downstairs now,' he said, holding his hands out and looking at his neatly manicured nails. 'I'll check with Franco.'

* * *

There were three public entrances to Viola. The restaurant and bar were accessed in Wardour Street whilst the club entrance was round the corner in Meard Street. It was a good idea as it meant the party people waiting in line did not dissuade clientele from frequenting the upmarket eatery and lounge bar. It hadn't been his idea, but Manny was pleased he had every angle covered and could exploit every square foot of the valuable property which had cost just under two million pounds to purchase and a further two hundred thousand to renovate and restyle.

Everyone who worked at Viola earned well above the going rate. No other establishment in the West End paid the sort of wages Manny offered. It meant the staff could be hand-picked. They were the cream of the crop, the best people. They worked hard and were rewarded accordingly... and with that came loyalty, respect and goodwill. It was a genius move. Customers didn't mind paying that little extra for the outstanding service they received. Viola gave Manny a cloak of respectability, and while rumours abounded in certain circles of shadowy underworld dealings, there was nothing to suggest he wasn't anything other than a slightly eccentric impresario who'd gentrified a run down corner of Soho and made it his own personal fiefdom.

Ginger Francisco was the cool, calm, calculating businesswoman who had been in the right place at the right time when Manny had acquired what was now Viola. Originally, she'd been plain old Vivian Francis, an agent for the commercial property firm tasked with selling 76 Wardour Street, but her keenly developed sense of female intuition had told her that Manny represented a once in a lifetime opportunity to make a serious amount of money.

It had taken almost a year for the transaction to be concluded in a manner that was satisfactory to all parties, and Vivian had invested time and effort figuring out how to piece together the complicated jigsaw puzzle that Manny represented. Her approach had been meticulous, finite detail worthy of a criminological investigation. From the brutal back streets of Battersea to the stucco-fronted Georgian splendour of Belgravia, he'd revelled in providing her with a step-by-step guide of his personal journey to glory. *'My Life'* by Chapman Jones. A fascinating autobiography of the nations best-loved entrepreneur. Of course it wouldn't be chapter and verse... it couldn't be, but if it was ever published, his compelling story would be a best seller in a day and age when huge swathes of the British public were having their heads turned by the upwardly mobile principles of Thatcherism.

Vivian Francis' metamorphosis to Ginger Francisco had been a gradual one. Rather than the obvious caterpillar, chrysalis, butterfly, evolutionary stages, she'd enhanced Manny's awareness of her stealthily. Directing her own development through careful choice and self selection of hair dye, her tresses had gone from mousey brown to reddish blonde, light copper and auburn with nuances of ginger before arriving at the flame-haired approximation of Goddessness that he clearly obsessed about. Contact lenses had completed a look enhanced by careful wardrobe management and thrice weekly, high-impact step aerobic classes.

"I've never noticed your green eyes before", he'd said over dinner after a planning meeting. She could sense him evaluating her, but never mentally undressing her. He knew she was strong-willed; it seemed to faze him. Women of power, he admired them. Talked about them, was scared of them... well that's what she thought. The change of name had been his idea, originating at the time he'd made the offer of a job at Viola. Ginger Francisco had a showgirl ring to it, a memorable name unlike plain old Vivian Francis. He said he hadn't thought about it much; that it had just come to him. She wasn't so sure. There was something odd about Manny, but she couldn't define precisely what it was.

The red hair fetish was strange, but could have been worse. Biblical and historical figures, Mary Magdalene, Boudicca, Queen of the Iceni and Queen Elizabeth I were his heroines. To him they represented strength and vigour. Then there were the actresses and singers he often spoke about. Natural redheads like Shirley MacLaine, Maureen O'Hara,

Judy Garland and Cilla Black. He never mentioned the fakes. Glamour pusses such as Lucille Ball and Rita Hayworth had, like her, dyed their hair red... maybe that went some way to explaining why in the past five years he'd never laid a finger on her. There had been no flirting, no innuendo... nothing.

It had been a source of frustration. A challenge. At the outset, she'd considered seduction. Route one. The tried and tested direct approach. But soon enough she'd realised it wouldn't work. He'd told her many things, but never once why he hadn't made a move on her. In the guise of Ginger Francisco, every man she'd met wanted to fuck her. She could see their piggy little faces. Eyes prying and widening as they imagined her naked. Pupils dilating at the sight of her perfectly sculpted breasts with their saucer sized areolae and prominent nipples. Lips licked at her flat stomach and the shaved mound of her sex.

Vivian/Ginger, Ginger/Vivian. She had been surprised at how easy the transition had been. At twenty-eight years of age she had everything she'd ever wanted and, despite having initially been willing to do so, hadn't compromised herself in getting it. As Ginger Francisco began settling into life as Viola's matriarch, Vivian Francis realised that Manny Jones and his lecherous, sweaty-palmed cohorts were of no use to her in the bedroom should they ever have got her there. It had been a voyage of self-discovery. If Manny was somehow androgynous, she was now certain of her sexuality, and Viola was a never-ending source of yielding, hard-bodied ladies. "Each to their own", as Manny often said. If only he knew the truth. If only she knew the truth, whatever that was. Maybe the truth didn't matter. After she'd banked her first hundred thousand pounds she'd stopped thinking about it.

★ ★ ★

Ginger believed that first impressions were of paramount importance. Manny had given her carte blanche with the restaurant designer, and she'd indulged her whim. The entrance to Viola's eatery, with it's black awning and unmarked double-fronted black doors, created a mood of anticipation and mystery for guests fortunate enough to have been able to secure a table or better still one of the private dining rooms. The doors were a portal to an understated realm of elegance where nouveau-riche celebrities, old money, and impatient upstarts could experience smells, tastes, sights and sounds diametrically opposed to the world outside.

The concept of private dining wasn't a new one, and when Ginger had explained her plans to Manny, he'd immediately thought of several ways he could profitably exploit their presence. The installation of Chapman Security's latest state-of-the-art permanent surveillance equipment had been a shrewd move, not only for demonstration purposes but also to source valuable information. Insider share dealing, match fixing, political chicanery, espionage... affairs of the heart... anything and everything that people spoke about in confidence and perceived secrecy had been piped into Manny's office, and if that wasn't enough to be going on with there were the Viola Girls.

Businessmen in town looking to party a little were encouraged to let their hair down, and their trousers. Underneath Viola's thin veneer of culture and sophistication was a sleazy layer of voyeuristic, five-fingered-knuckle-shuffling, Michelin-starred extortion, bribery and corruption that Manny positively thrived on. Tonight he was going to exploit its capabilities to the maximum. Quique Di Santo, Eddie Jacobsen, Derek Delaney and Jimmy Baker were booked into the fabled Emerald Room, the most expensive private dining room in London. Di Santo, the self-styled Colombian crown prince of arms dealing. Jacobsen, Chief Inspector in the City of London Police who served in the Economic Crime Directorate. Delaney, an affable Ulsterman who profited from The Troubles back home and Baker, the Cockney wide-boy son of Barry Baker, the man he'd found out was behind the nefarious activities of Tim Rolls and David Chidgey.

★ ★ ★

'Okay Franco. Thank you for letting me know.' Jester raised his clenched left fist. 'They're in the Emerald.'

Manny rubbed his hands together and contemplated having a scotch and soda, but it was too early. There was work to be done. 'Okay,' he replied, turning his attention to the television monitor on his desk and smiling at the grainy image of Ginger and Phoebe schmoozing with Di Santo, Jacobsen, Delaney and Baker. 'Let's see how things go downstairs. I doubt it'll take long before that corpulent cunt Jacobsen starts waxing his dolphin over Sir Christopher Wren.'

Jester smiled as he leaned across the desk to adjust the controls on the sound mixer next to the monitor so the conversation in the room was discernable from the music. 'Imagine if this room were bugged. The spies wouldn't have a fucking clue what you're talking about boss.'

'What's that shit?' Manny rubbed his eyes and looked closely at the monitor.

'*Rumors*' by Timex Social Club.'

'No! Not the music you prick. That shit on the wall?

'Ah the Andy Warhol self-portrait. It's got the latest microphone and RF transmitter technology from Audiotel built into the frame.'

'Andy fucking Warhol! Whose idea was that?'

'Ginger's. It's a talking piece. His latest work. What's wrong with it?'

'What's fucking right with it? She could've asked me first.'

As they watched the monitor and saw Jacobsen walk across the room to stand in front of the Warhol portrait, Jester managed to attenuate the sound perfectly.

'You see, it's all down to the numbers Quique and how far you can push your lines of credit.'

Manny gritted his teeth as he glared at the screen and listened to Jacobsen.

'Credit is a great way to expand your business.'

'Credit!' roared Manny. 'Who the fuck does Jacobsen think he is? The Chancellor of the fucking Exchequer? Credit is half our fucking problem. I prefer to keep things simple. Cash on delivery. Credit creates problems… I don't like IOU's.' He switched the screen off and looked at Jester in disgust. 'Right, enough of this! Set it to record, and let's go downstairs.'

★ ★ ★

Harry Craven enjoyed working for Manny. Being patronised came with the territory and was soon forgotten when he considered the perks of the job. Driving the best cars, getting hold of the best looking women and occasionally enforcing the rules and regulations of the organisation were compensation enough for the long hours and the put downs… and then of course there were the wages to consider. Fifteen grand a year was at least double what the average man in the street was earning, throw in the rent-free loft apartment in the Belgravia block where Manny lived and it was an unbeatable deal.

Saturday night was the best night of week. Without fail, Manny would be at Viola which meant he could loiter in the vicinity with sober intent keeping a hawkish eye on proceedings while chatting to the great and the good who wanted to see and be seen at the hottest ticket in town. Shortly after 8 p.m. the footballers would start rolling in… the day's winners and losers. It had taken a while to come to terms with the reality that it was just a job to them. But now it was crystal clear. This kiss-the-badge veneration that had become prevalent in the nascent live television era the game had entered was a charade. And the funniest thing about it? You'd see players from opposing teams, whose supporters were sworn enemies, rubbing shoulders like they were the best of friends. It was a different world, one that those who battled each other to uphold the reputation of their clubs on the rundown terraces of football grounds and avenues and alleyways nearby would be horrified to see.

Two Wimbledon footballers Harry recognised entered the main bar and he boldly stepped forward to greet them. Over a period of time he'd got on first name terms with many of the game's stars that were regulars at Viola. He wasn't pushy, just polite. They appreciated his enthusiasm, and as a consequence were always willing to sign shirts and other merchandise that subsequently he could sell on. 'All right John. Hello Vinnie. Good result for your lot today.'

As the men shook hands and exchanged pleasantries, Harry caught sight of Manny and Jester emerging from the lift and beckoned them over. Manny never displayed any interest in football, but he was convinced that he'd find Wimbledon's rags-to-riches story enthralling. Admitted to the football league in 1977, less than a decade later, having been promoted five times and relegated twice, the Dons were playing in the top flight and already making a reasonable fist of it having audaciously led the table last month. He'd save the yarn for the next car journey. A little follow up to the introduction he was about to make.

'Good evening Manny, I thought you'd be interested to meet John and Vinnie, they play for Wimbledon.'

'They don't look like tennis players to me.'

'I said *for* Wimbledon, not *at* Wimbledon.'

Everyone laughed, though Harry swiftly realised Manny had failed to see his joke. 'Sorry boss,' he added apologetically as Manny stood poker-faced shaking hands with the footballers.

'Don't worry about it now H…' As he spoke, he raised his eyebrows. The sight of Ginger Francisco, dressed to thrill, approaching the bar nearby to talk to Stan Roper, was distracting, but insufficient for him not to finish getting his message across to Harry. 'Worry about it on payday.' Everyone laughed again which pleased him this time. 'You'll have to excuse me now, I've got some business to attend to.'

'I didn't catch your name,' said Vinnie, firmly keeping hold of Manny's hand.

Manny smiled. He was used to it. His autobiography was imaginary. Unless you knew him, you didn't know him, and that was for the best. 'Jones. Manny Jones. I own this place.'

'Maybe we're related.' Vinnie joked, relaxing his grip.

'So you're a Jones as well. Did you know there's over three hundred thousand people with our surname living in the United Kingdom?'

'That many?'

'Yeah! And fourteen percent of them live in Wales.'

'Maybe I'm related to one of them.'

'Might be worth checking out,' interjected Harry as Manny stepped back. 'A Welsh cap or two would be nice to have.'

Jester caught Harry's eye and winked as he led Manny away towards the bar. 'Maybe you should be interested in those lads boss,' he said, flicking his fringe back and smiling. 'Four years ago, Wimbledon were playing at Rochdale in Division Four, next week they're away at Tottenham.'

'I know Spurs are poor, but I didn't know they were in Division Four as well?' Manny laughed, clasping his hands and rubbing them together. 'I'm kidding. Listen, I know what you're implying. It's something I've thought about a few times. The business angle is exciting if you know what I mean?'

Jester was ready for a discussion, but Manny's fleeting interest in football immediately dissipated as they approached Ginger who was swathed in a black Romeo Gigli dress that hugged the gym-honed contours of her svelte body like a second skin. He paused to drink the vision in. Majestic. A twentieth century Queen Elisabeth I with feline grace, fluidity… and six-inch killer heels.

'Looks amazing doesn't she.' Manny grabbed Jester by the arm and whispered in his ear. 'Shame she's as snide as that fake Rolex your wearing.'

Jester laughed nervously, looking at his watch as Manny released him and sidled up next to Ginger, engaging her in an mwah-mwah-style social kiss and embrace.

'Are my special guests enjoying themselves?' he whispered in her ear.

'Absolutely.'

'Are they talking freely?'

'Of course. The girls are looking after them. Large Mojito's a go-go.'

'I want each of them fixed up if you know what I mean?'

Ginger smiled and wrinkled her nose. 'Shouldn't be too difficult, though Baker is being greedy… and my sixth sense tells me that Delaney might prefer the company of men.'

'Men eh. Well it takes all sorts. Perhaps our friend here in the green prickly suit can take care of him.' Manny often liked to make jokes at Jester's expense, about his slightly effeminate style, about him playing gooseberry when women were around.

Jester heard the glib comment but chose to ignore it. Like Harry and Stan who had joined him, he was scanning the faces of the clientele in the bar. From a security perspective, when Manny was around, familiarity was important, particularly to Stan who was monitoring two men who kept looking across in their direction.

'Nine o'clock approaching.' Stan braced himself as the men began walking slowly towards them.

'Fuck me! It's Crockett and Tubbs,' joked Harry, checking out their attire. Jeans, Matching mauve pastel coloured T-shirts and jackets with the sleeves rolled up. 'Miami Vice comes to London,' he continued, catching Jester's eye and nodding at the door.

Stan stepped in their path. 'Looking for anyone in particular?'

'It's... it's about last night,' said 'Crockett' hesitantly. Raising his hands to point at his sticking plaster covered earlobes.

Stan studied 'Crockett's' face intently, focussing on his hooked nose and swiftly putting two and two together. 'Sorry beaky, if you're going to ask me if anyone handed in a pair of gold earrings, the answer's, NO!'

'Crockett' glanced at 'Tubbs' and then back at Stan, Jester, Harry and finally Manny who had linked arms with Ginger. Remembering what had happened the previous night, he decided against looking at Ginger.

'The door's that way,' said Stan, pointing at the exit. 'Close it on your way out.'

'Did I miss a couple of chapters in the book?' enquired Manny with a quizzical expression on his face.

'No just a paragraph boss,' replied Stan as they watched 'Crockett' and 'Tubbs' scurry away. 'Big nose had a little run-in with your nephew last night.'

'Kennedy?'

'Yeah! He tried to pull Nicky and got more than he'd bargained for.'

'Good... which reminds me... did you speak with him?'

★ ★ ★

'Shhh. Remember we've got kids.' Nicky raised her head from Kennedy's groin and grabbed the shaft of his erect penis tightly with her right hand. He winced in pleasurable protest, a sharp intake of breath helping control the urge to climax.

'I can't help it babe. You're just too good at that.'

'Well turn the music up a little if you're going to moan and groan.' Kennedy reached across to the cassette radio that was perched on the edge of the bedside table and slid the volume control sufficiently for Millie Scott's rendition of *'Prisoner of Love'* to fill the room.

'That's better,' breathed Nicky huskily, pushing Kennedy back down onto the bed. 'Now where were we? Oh yeah, you'd just told me that Vera wouldn't be impressed with you joining Uncle Manny's firm, and I was giving you the best blowjob of your life... again... while thinking about how I'm going to spend those fat wages he'll be paying you.'

Kennedy's eyes rolled back in his head as he bit his bottom lip. Not because he was thinking about his mother getting upset or berating his acquisitive wife. She was right. Working with Manny represented a chance to get off the estate, to make a better life for his family. His reactions were a response to Nicky expertly deep-throating him. How she had learned to control her gag reflex was a mystery he didn't want to unravel. He ran his fingers through her hair, arching his back as he felt sexual pressure building in the pit of his stomach. 'I'm coming babe.' It was a warning as much as anything, but it went unheeded. Nicky could have pulled away. He wasn't holding her head, forcing her to fellate him to completion. He sometimes wondered when they rowed if she ever thought about sinking her teeth into him. 'Oh... oh... Nicky... ohhhhh.' Writhing and bucking with the intensity of his orgasm, Kennedy lost himself in the moment and remained lost as sleep immediately claimed his spent body.

★ ★ ★

Harry drove slowly as he guided the Jaguar through the maze-like streets of Soho. Sunday morning after the night before was always the same. Pavements strewn with litter, beer bottles, cigarette ends and chewing gum. Random doorways occupied by rough sleepers comatose in filthy, flea-ridden sleeping bags. Cafes packed with dishevelled revellers curing hangovers with tea, toast and a full English breakfast.

Manny's classical music seemed appropriate enough as an accompaniment to the scenes. A relaxing melodic soundtrack featuring the flute and oboe, *'Peer Gynt – Suite No. 1'* by Edvard Grieg, which he'd known as *'Morning'* as a kid, felt delicate on the ears. As he looked and listened, he smiled at the apparent incongruity of it all. He'd never asked Manny where his love of these old composers had stemmed from.

'Music has charms to sooth a savage breast', was all he'd say.

Harry had gone to the British Library to look up the origins of the phrase that his boss attributed to Shakespeare. In fact it was another playwright William Congreve who'd written the line in his work *'The Mourning Bride'*. He'd yet to figure out a way to way to inform Manny of the error of his ways. It paid to be careful. He'd seen what could happen at a number of private parties at Viola. Culture vulture smartarses smugly belittling their generous host whose breast knew no limits when it came to the savagery meted out to those who intentionally patronised him.

Saul Thomson was a case in point. A crooked city financier, Old Harrovian Thomson had derived great pleasure from correcting Manny at every given opportunity during the course of several social events he'd been invited to. Mispronunciations, malapropisms, miscellaneous mistakes. It was a fool's errand considering who was lining his velvet pockets. Over a period of time, Thomson had wound Manny up like a watch spring. He'd been patient though, give him his due. Harry had been amazed at his tolerance. Perhaps he should have said something earlier, a few words of warning maybe. But he didn't, principally because he wanted to see what would happen.

There'd been a small gathering to celebrate the passing of a planning application to add a two-storey extension to Viola. Thomson had played his part, attracting straight money to bridge the funding required and get the project underway. His mission accomplished, the snooty duffer had outlived his usefulness. One more comment and Manny would surely snap back.

"What? Ha ha ha". Thomson had sneered condescendingly in his cut glass upper class English accent, berating Manny for asking for the "Hovis music" to be turned up. "You can take the boy out of Battersea, but you can't take Battersea out of the boy. Hey, hey ha ha", he'd brayed, striding across to the brand new Bang and Olufsen Beogram 4002 record player delivered earlier that day. "Antonin Dvorak. *'Symphony Number Nine in E minor'*, What? Hovis music... ha ha. Also known as the *'New World Symphony'*"... Thomson had been leaning over the turntable as he'd spoken, but he didn't get a chance to finish what he was saying. He had no idea Manny had crept up behind him and was about to smash his skull with an ornate glass paperweight.

As Thomson fell across the expensive stereo system, those present had gasped in shock and cupped their ears as the volume control slid to maximum and the needle dug into the vinyl, scratching across the surface of the record. Crimson blood and hissing static a visual-come-aural representation of the violence they had just witnessed. It was almost artistic.

"If anybody else has an opinion about not being able to take Battersea out of the boy, please share it now", Manny had said, turning to face his stunned audience. Nobody uttered a word. Thomson spent three months in hospital and the rest of his life in a wheelchair. Ah the savage breast. It was a source of personal amusement to Harry that from then on Manny had never asked for the "Hovis music" or any of Dvorak's other compositions to be played again.

★ ★ ★

'Are you going to drink that?' Stan asked, pointing at the mug of tea that had been sitting on the table in front of Kennedy long enough to go cold.

'Doesn't look like it does it?' Kennedy scowled. A mixture of cheers and groans from the patrons of the Montgomery Arms who were engrossed in the Manchester derby being screened live on television for the first time alerted him to the possibility a goal had been scored. 'United! Bollocks!' he exclaimed, looking around the bar to see who was cheering Frank Stapleton's opener for the Red Devils.

'Give it up mate,' replied Stan tersely. 'What are you going to do kick it off in here? I heard what happened yesterday. Not forgetting the night before. You'll get nicked if you're not careful.'

Kennedy shrugged his shoulders and folded his arms. 'Just a bit of milling, nothing serious.'

'You can forget that bullshit working for Chapman Security.'

'You're forgetting Manny's my Uncle.'

'Oh yeah, I forgot. Flesh and blood.'

'Cold blood.' Kennedy laughed, rocking himself back in his chair. As he did so, the entrance door to the bar opened and Manny walked in with Harry Craven. It wasn't a grand entrance of any sort, but as both men were attired in business suits it was enough for them to momentarily draw the attention of everyone present. 'Talk of the devil.'

Stan winked at Harry and got to his feet. 'Better the devil you know.'

Kennedy remained seated, placing his hands flat on the table and watching Manny as he walked towards him. For a moment, all that could be heard was the sound of football commentator Brian Moore... and then Mick McCarthy equalised for Manchester City. McCarthy's goal for City attracted more cheers than Stapleton's for United, Kennedy scanned the bar again and wondered why, but not for long.

'It still smells of poor people in here,' said Manny, sniffing the air as he motioned Stan to sit down again. 'Nothing's changed.'

Stan drummed his fingers on the table. 'I'd give it a go one day. Always fancied running a pub.'

'I haven't come here to talk about the Monty. I've come to talk business with my nephew here.' Manny leaned across the table, reached out his hands and placed them on Kennedy's. Narrowing his eyes, he scrutinised his features, frowning as he saw his brother Alec staring back at him, Vera too, especially Vera. A slight rush of adrenaline made the hairs on the back of his neck stand on-end as his mind was fleetingly consumed by a combination of rage and sexual arousal.

Kennedy's subconscious told him Manny was ill at ease. He wasn't sure why, maybe it was the surroundings. 'Shall we talk outside?'

'It's fine here ain't it?' Manny looked at Stan for confirmation. It came in the form of a nod. 'Good,' he continued, taking his jacket off and handing it to Harry before sitting down. 'Now let's see if finally we help each other out.'

'I'd rather we spoke alone... if that's all right?'

Manny bowed his head and clenched his fists. 'Stan. Harry, if you don't mind,' he said, a familiar ring of impatience creeping into his voice.

'We'll be over there watching the game,' said Stan, pointing at the television as he got up.

'Football on a Sunday, that's a fucking sin.'

Manny's words drew a smile from Kennedy.

'Now tell me son. How is that wonderful mother of yours?'

'Same old.'

'She's not that old.'

'She's my mother.'

'She must be very proud of you.'

'Proud?' Kennedy knew what Manny was alluding to but wanted to hear his opinion. This was the first time they had spoken together since he'd left the Regiment.

'Not many people would have had the courage to do what you did.'

'Perhaps.' Kennedy felt his hackles rising as he pictured his mother arguing with him. 'But she'd rather I hadn't gone there in the first place. And if I'd listened to her, my mates wouldn't have been there either.'

'You shouldn't feel bad about it. The Parachute Regiment is in your blood. In mine too, but I never got the chance to fight for Queen and Country like you and Alec did.'

Kennedy frowned. 'I know the story. My mother's told me often enough.'

Manny fidgeted with the gold ring on the third finger of his left hand. 'What else has your mother tell you?'

'Don't ask questions that you already know the answer to.'

'What's that supposed to mean?'

Kennedy rubbed his chin. 'You tell me. You've known her longer than I have.'

Manny glared at his nephew. He felt riled, but he wasn't going to allow his emotions to get in the way of business. 'Okay, listen to me. I've not come here to play games or talk about the past. You're family. Remember... your father was my brother. Don't you think he'd want the best for you?'

Kennedy nodded. He felt foolish. Embarrassed almost. There and then, he decided to give Manny the benefit of the doubt. 'Yeah. Well carry on.'

'We all have to make a living one way or another. I can help you make a better living than most. Speak to your missus. Look at your kids. Do you really want them brought up on the Yelverton? Look at this place. It's a fucking ruin. Look at these people. In twenty years time do you want to be sitting here skint like them? I'm giving you an opportunity, just like I gave Harry and Stan over there. Work for me and it's one less thing you have to worry about. Now shall I tell you about the job first... or the wages?'

MURDER

11 April 1987

'Fancy some of this later?' Kennedy squeezed his groin gently. It didn't take much to get a favourable response downstairs, and picturing Nicky lifting her T-shirt, cupping her pert breasts, and tracing the tip of her tongue slowly across her lips was encouragement enough, not that he needed it, to get the job done and get home.

Working for Manny hadn't turned out to be the chore he thought it was going to be. His mother, Bertie, Fletch, even Nicky, when she wasn't counting the cash, had their opinions, and he had his. At the end of the day, beggars couldn't be choosers, and once he'd got used to his uncle's egocentric manner and indirectly taking orders from Jester, he'd actually begun to appreciate and benefit from being a part of a disciplined regime once more.

Chapman Security was far from being a well-drilled military unit, but Kennedy had taken the approach that it was. Fitness was paramount, and the focus that came from physical training sharpened his mind, had a therapeutic effect on his troubled psyche, and increased his libido. A daily programme of ten sets of one hundred metre swims followed by a five hundred metres race against the clock formed the core of his routine. Ten minutes was a good time. Twelve minutes acceptable. Push-ups, sit-ups, pull-ups. Twenty-five, fifty, one hundred. Again and again. Repetition equalled order. Everything timed and noted. A punishing but picturesque five-mile run from the flat on Yelverton

119

Road, through Battersea Park, over Chelsea Bridge, along Chelsea Embankment and back over the Thames via Albert Bridge provided stunning visual reference points. From Big Ben and the Houses of Parliament to the old chimneys of the power station. This was London, the greatest city on earth. A willing, giving mistress. A muse who suppressed depressing memories of the bleak Falklands landscape that still haunted him. A lover who gave him hope and ideas for the future.

When she failed him, The Clash played loud on his Sony WM-109 Cassette Walkman drowned out the sounds of battle. *'Combat Rock'* versus gunfire, explosions and the screams of wounded and dying men.

Last, but not least, there his father, Alec. His invisible Physical Training Instructor, there with him every step of the way. They talked, but their conversations were always one way. What did he think of him working for his brother? There was no answer. There never was, just his personal thoughts and opinions. The day had passed quickly, the usual programme, the same discussion… apart from one thing, tonight's job. He couldn't bring himself to mention it.

"Son, you have to be honest with me. Tell me the truth, the whole truth and nothing but the truth".

'I'm sorry I can't… so help me God.'

'Unusual name that… Kennedy.'

Distracted from his 'discourse' with his father by Harry Craven's comment, Kennedy blinked slowly and glanced at his watch. 3.24 a.m. '22 November 1963,' he replied, looking out of the cab windscreen of the decommissioned Bedford MK truck they were sitting in. 'The day John F Kennedy was assassinated.'

'Imaginative, I'll give your parents that.'

'Give them nothing.'

'You must get tired explaining it.'

'Not really. Most people suppose it's my surname and don't take it any further if you get my drift.'

Harry's small talk irritated Kennedy. Perhaps the stillness outside had unnerved him. If there was a dead-of-night in London... it was at this time and it should be respected. Sensing his dialogue was superfluous, Harry gave up and stared straight ahead.

Tranquillity restored, Kennedy relaxed. Thinking time again. They'd arrived on site as planned at 3.00 a.m. and waited. In front of them, the gloomy steel and masonry edifice of Grosvenor Bridge arched across the Thames whose murky water lapped at its concrete-cased piers. Still and silent now, by daybreak trains would start rumbling along the ribbons of steel heading to and from Victoria station. Ten tracks... thousands of passengers. It didn't bare thinking about. There was no security. You'd never travel anywhere in the Capital if you were paranoid. The Houses of Parliament, Tower of London, Harrods, Selfridges, the Hilton, Earls Court, the House of Commons, Chelsea Barracks, Hyde Park, Regents Park, all had seen politically-driven violent incidents perpetrated by Irish Republican active service units that had resulted in loss of life and countless injuries. One bomb on the mainland was worth far more to the Provisional IRA than ten in Northern Ireland. In 1984 they'd bombed Brighton's Grand Hotel with the specific intention of killing Prime Minister Margaret Thatcher and her cabinet who were in residence for the Conservative Party conference. Thatcher escaped harm, but five people were murdered and thirty-one injured.

"Today we were unlucky, but remember we only have to be lucky once. You will have to be lucky always". The comments made by the IRA in a statement claiming responsibility for the Brighton bombing came to Kennedy's mind every time he thought about his father's murder. The night his luck ran out. There had been no public outrage about his killing. If it had happened here, in London, it would have been headline news. There, he was just another British soldier.

Thatcher and her politics did nothing for Kennedy. He could understand why she was despised by many sections of society, but failed to see why some wished the IRA had succeeded. Fortunately, like him, the majority of people appeared thankful that another attempt to destroy democracy had failed. Politicians were only really in it for themselves, and Thatcher was no different. They always seemed to make good currency out of conflict.

A year after the Falklands War, the Conservatives had been voted back into power. In a couple of months he had no doubt they'd be voted in again. You couldn't argue with the results of a General Election, though the dissenters always would. Domestic and foreign affairs, economy and taxation, industrial relations, privatisation. Did the average man-in-the-street have a grip on what went into a political manifesto? As Kennedy shrugged his shoulders, the sight of a yellow Sherpa box van turning off slowly off the approach to Chelsea Bridge and driving down the slip road towards the wharf buildings by the pier refocused his mind on the task ahead. He lifted the night vision monocular he was holding to his right eye and checked the vehicle's number plate. 'Delta One Five Seven Tango Whiskey Echo.'

'Confirmed.'

Kennedy could sense the relief in Harry's voice. Just one word, no conversation needed.

3.28 a.m. He looked at the LED clock display as he tugged on the heavy brass zipper of the black M65 regiment jacket he was wearing and snapped shut its storm flap. Preparation, planning, all of it meticulous and coming together now for this operation. Although he knew Stan was still the man and he'd retained faith in his own ability, he'd had his doubts about working with Harry and Jester. They came across as subservient wankers. Personalities aside though, he couldn't find a fault with their approach to the job.

3.29 a.m. So here he was, a part of Uncle Manny's private army. A mercenary. He hated the word because of what he felt it represented to others. Greed! The desire to take part in an armed conflict he wasn't directly a party to for private gain. Yes! The cash was in the bank. It needed more analysis, a discussion with his father. But that could wait.

3.30 a.m. This wasn't the time to wrestle with his conscience. This was the time for action. Kennedy opened the door of truck and jumped to the floor. There was something familiar about the cold damp air that filled his lungs. He knew the voices he could hear once more inside his head... the screams, the anguish... the horror. As he walked towards the van, the rubble strewn across the wasteland crunched under the rubber soles of his combat boots. A whisper, an echo, distant, repeated. 'Fix bayonets! Fix bayonets! Fix bayonets!' Would the battle ever fade away? He shook his head several times as he watched the mist swirling silently in off the river veil the ramshackle wharf buildings behind the Sherpa van. One of the van's occupants had got out from its rear doors further along the track and made a beeline for the wharf. Stan would have him in the telescopic sights of his rifle. A stray dog barked, and with it another. The sounds were reassuring, cries for help muffled by the sound of explosions faded.

'Never take your eyes off your opponent.' Kennedy stood in front of the van and stared intently at the man in civilian attire sitting in the passenger seat. Jimmy Baker. No mistake. Next to him sat a larger figure wearing a paramilitary jacket. If one man had been in the back, how many more were still in there? As Baker clambered out of the cab, he heard the van's rear doors open. Another accomplice similarly dressed to the driver but armed with a Glock 18 semi-automatic pistol emerged and began walking slowly towards him.

Expressionless, Baker scrutinised Kennedy's face and then looked beyond him at the Bedford. 'Where's Delaney?' he asked, raising his right hand and motioning forward the armed man.

'Derek had to fly to New York today for a meeting with The Family,' replied Kennedy in a pitch-perfect, blue-collar Belfast accent. His ability to master the nuances of the dialect to provide authenticity to the role Manny had required one of them to play for this job had taken him by surprise. It had started with a throwaway impersonation of high-profile Ulster politician Ian Paisley, and concluded with a well-rehearsed regurgitation of the leader of the Democratic Unionist Party's infamous diatribe against the 1985 Anglo-Irish agreement.

"Where do the terrorists operate from? From the Irish Republic! Where do the terrorists return to for sanctuary? To the Irish Republic! And yet Mrs Thatcher tells us that the Republic must have some say in our Province. We say never, never, never, never!"

Video clips watched obsessively day-after-day-after-day, amalgamated with his training regime had kept his mind occupied creating thoughts and feelings detached from the reality of his own personal emotions and memories.

'And you are?'

'Derek's brother Jackie. I'm sure he'll have mentioned me to you.'

Baker nodded. 'He called me yesterday and said you might be involved in the deal. Didn't mention anything about going to New York though.'

Kennedy resisted the urge to smile. He'd been the one who'd telephoned Baker not Derek Delaney. Di Santo as well, and Jacobsen. He'd felt in control. Manny had been suitably impressed.

'Good job the brief on your motor checked out or we wouldn't have been doing business here tonight.'

There was an assertive smugness about the way Baker spoke that annoyed Kennedy, but he kept calm. The training, all of it, was paying dividends. 'Aye and rightly so, though I don't think we have any concerns about being interrupted. Mr Jacobsen has taken care of that.'

'It's not the filth that worries me.'

'Who then?'

Baker ignored the question. 'Frisk him Davo. No tools or wires.'

'D'ya think I came up the Lagan in a bubble?'

'Do what? Frisk him. This ain't Christmas Day, I don't want any more surprises.'

'Surprises?'

'Meeting here for a start.'

Kennedy tensed his body and watched as Davo holstered his pistol. There was no technique to it. Clearly the man lacked military pedigree. He was tall though and broad in the shoulder… a giant who towered over him. As Davo's shovel-like hands patted him down he considered his size. Pound-for-pound he had an advantage, but this counted for little at close quarters.

'He's clean boss.'

'Good. Let's get this done quickly.'

As Kennedy followed Baker to the rear of the Sherpa he noticed the British Telecom livery. *'It's you we answer to'*. He smiled as the advertising slogan came to mind and continued smiling at the thought it was a good call. Day and night, BT vehicles were everywhere. A familiar sight on the streets of London that nobody, least of all the police, paid any attention to.

The rear doors of the van were open. From the middle

to the back, floor to ceiling, a large number of crushproof Pelican storage cases were secured by strapping. It was difficult to ascertain how many. It didn't matter. What mattered was the total quantity and condition of the goods they contained.

'Enough there to keep you all busy for a while.' As he spoke, Baker turned up the collar of his lightweight jacket and looked up at the sky. It was starting to spit fine raindrops.

'Meaning?' Kennedy clicked his heels, and screwed his eyes shut momentarily as he realised he'd dropped out of character.

'You having a giraffe or what?'

'So I am.'

'Keep both sides armed.'

'That's the deal right?'

'Right. The Troubles are good for business.'

'So they are.'

'They keep the security forces occupied which makes our life easier. Know what I mean?'

Kennedy nodded and bit his lip as he climbed into the van. Silence was the best policy. He prised one of the cases away from the strapping placed it on the floor and opened it. He knew what to expect. Glock 18's identical to Davo's, the full consignment, minus one. He went through the motions, handling the five pistols one-by-one, checking weight, balance and line of sight.

'Everything in good order?'

'Aye it is.' Kennedy dry-fired the last pistol before carefully placing it back in the case. 'Derek will be happy.'

Baker pointed at the wharf buildings. 'Okay let's get the vehicles lined up over there, do the exchange, sort the paperwork out... then we can all go home. You have got a home to haven't you?'

As he climbed out of the back of the Sherpa, Kennedy felt

the rain falling on his head. The breeze had stiffened clearing the mist. He didn't know Baker, but he hated him. Despised his arrogance. The feelings of anger toyed with his composure. He looked at Baker and saw the blood-spattered face of Sergeant Prime staring back at him. As he blinked, red and green tracer rounds crisscrossed his retinas. It was happening again. He had to keep his eyes open. He raised his left hand and signalled the Bedford to drive towards the wharf.

'Get back in the van,' growled Baker impatiently. 'We haven't got all night.'

'I'll walk if it's all the same to you.'

'You don't have a choice.' Baker pointed at Davo who drew his pistol. 'Non negotiable then?'

'You're learning fast. Didn't your brother tell you anything about me? Kennedy deliberately ignored the question, keeping his eyes fixed on Davo who motioned him to get into the back of the van and climbed in after him leaving the doors open. Baker meanwhile started walking towards the wharf, quickening his pace to reach the arches that provided shelter from the rain.

'Sly cunt,' thought Kennedy as he stared down the barrel of Davo's pistol. Davo smiled as if he had just read his mind. He had an air of confidence that suggested he'd been in similar situations before. The driver started the engine, dipped the clutch and allowed the Sherpa to inch forward slowly. Split-second decisions might be called for, but with Baker's firm only being four-handed, and the main man on the outside, he'd take his chances if he had to. His thought process was academic as it took less than a minute to drive to the wharf where the driver parked up directly behind the Bedford. Nevertheless, as situations could change in an instant, it was important to constantly assess and reassess the situation.

'Okay Paddy. Get outta the van.'

Kennedy's head ticked to one side. Davo was a cunt as well. He knew his 'name' was Jackie. He wasn't Irish, but now he could understand why an Irishman might be offended at being called Paddy. Accustomed to the natural darkness, he eased himself out of the back of the Sherpa squinting as the driver switched its headlamps on and the light reflected back off the rear doors of the Bedford as he turned and reversed up to it. Wanker! What was it with Baker's mob?

If there was one potential flaw in Manny's plan it was the fact that Harry Craven had met Jimmy Baker on several occasions. Amusingly, he'd gambled on the probability that Baker would have been far too self-obsessed to take any notice of anyone he viewed as lacking in importance, but he was taking no chances… and the anonymous latex rubber flesh tone mask he'd donned proved it. Kennedy looked on as Harry, who was carrying a large haversack got out of the Bedford.

'Everything all right Jackie?' asked Harry, slinging the sack across his back.

'Aye.'

As Harry walked to the rear of the truck, the man they'd seen leaving the Sherpa earlier emerged from the shadows. Until now, he'd been an unknown quantity. Not anymore. There he was, another sizable specimen like Davo also armed with a Glock that he waved from side-to-side as he joined them.

'Okay Macca, you check the merchandise.' Baker tapped him on the shoulder and then leaned into Harry and peered at his face. 'And who've you come as? Michael fucking Myers? This isn't a fancy dress party you cunt!'

Kennedy smiled. It was a good line. Baker obviously knew his films. 'Halloween' wasn't bad, but they'd spoiled the original by making too many sequels. 'He's got a skin allergy,' he said, taking the pressure off Harry to reply and coarsening his accent.

'I've got an allergy to cunts.'

Kennedy wondered if Baker understood the inference of what he had just said. Probably not. Would he be as cocky without his armed accomplices? Probably not. Was he a hard man? Probably not. Trading off his father's reputation. Living 'The Long Good Friday' dream. A plastic gangster who thought it was clever to use the word 'cunt' in every sentence. He needed a new scriptwriter. That or a hole in the head. He chose his reply carefully. 'I hope you're not allergic to money Mr Baker?'

Baker folded his arms as Harry unslung the haversack and unzipped it in front of him.

'The dope's come up short, so we'll balance the transaction with hard cash.' Kennedy reached into the haversack and produced a sleeve of fifty-pound notes. 'Bank of England Series D. The first notes to depict historical figures on he reverse.' He smiled as he handed the sleeve to Baker. He deserved to be patronised. 'Sir Christopher Wren has been with us on the Bullseye since 1981.'

'Are you sure you're fucking Irish?' Baker scowled as he flicked at the notes before putting the sleeve back in the haversack. 'How much?'

'Twenty.'

'Davo check it. Macca how are we looking?'

'Sound boss,' replied Macca in a distinctive nasal accent. I just need to get to the back cases.'

As Harry handed Davo the haversack, Kennedy checked his watch and walked to the rear of the Bedford. 3.42 a.m. Not long to go, but he was enjoying playing the game especially now.

'Red or Blue?' he enquired.

'You're joking me la.'

'I'm not fucking psychic.'

'Breck Road Red.'

'Shit result today.'

Macca stepped away from the back of the Bedford and turned to face him. 'How did we get on?'

'Lost by the odd goal in three at Norwich.' Kennedy smiled. 'Everton won again,' he added, staring Macca in the eyes. Football was a universal language that everyone understood. Well almost everyone. Macca looked dejected. 'You'd better get back to checking the inventory. We haven't got much time.'

Macca shook his head and returned to his task. Why Baker had agreed to conduct the transaction with Derek Delaney where Manny had suggested was beyond Kennedy, but then they'd done deals together before he'd been involved. To further his aims, Manny had bought Delaney's silence. He hadn't mentioned the price. Avarice was, as he was finding out himself, an influential beast. In the process, greedy grasping Baker had unwittingly allowed himself to be set up. The repercussions from the robbery that was to take place at 3.45 a.m. would not only make Manny a significant amount of money, but also play his debtors off against each other. It was all about knowing what was going to happen next? Baker, Davo, Macca and their driver didn't have a clue.

'Oi Macca. Want one of these?'

Surprised by the change of accent, Belfast to Battersea, Macca turned around, mouth open, ready to speak. As he did so, Kennedy lunged forward and delivered a right uppercut that caught him on the side of the jaw causing it to fracture and dislocate.

Simultaneously, Stan Roper, who was crouched in the roof of the Bedford, pounced on Davo cudgelling him unconscious with the butt of his rifle as they went to ground and then spinning round to kick Baker's legs from under him.

Baker's driver tried to get out of the Sherpa, but as he opened the door Harry, readied in a karate fighting stance, fists clenched, left foot one step forward, swung his body round and kicked it back with sufficient force to wind him. As the door rebounded open, the driver, doubled-up and groaning in pain, took a second kick to the groin and a third to the face.

Kennedy dropped to his haunches, picked up Macca's pistol and smashed it across his face breaking his nose. 'Fix bayonets!' Frightened Spanish voices blended in with the theme from the 'Liver Birds' television sitcom. "Madre de Dios! Yo no quiero morir por esto". He shook his head and looked at Macca's blood and spittle-covered face before grabbing him by the scruff of the neck with his free hand and dragging him round to the side of the truck where Stan had Baker secured in a headlock and Harry was stood over Davo and the driver.

'Who are you?' growled Baker, struggling to speak as Stan tightened his grip.

'Catch yourself on,' snarled Kennedy, reverting to the Belfast accent that had served him well so far. 'Jacobsen doesn't like the deal.' As he propped Macca against the truck, Stan threw Baker forward so he fell to the floor between Davo and the driver.

'Wha wha whadya mean Jacobsen doesn't like the deal?' There was an element of panic in Baker's voice as he pushed himself onto his knees. 'He's filth. Bent filth. He takes the money and does what he's told.'

'So he does Mr Baker.' Kennedy held out Macca's pistol so it was fully visible in the glare of the Sherpa's headlights. 'Glock 18. Nice piece so it is.'

'I don't... I don't understand,' stammered Baker. 'If this is about cash, we can work something out so everyone's a winner.'

'Yeah! But you don't play the game that way.' Kennedy held the pistol in both hands and pointed it at Baker's forehead.

'Come on. For fuck's sake, I don't understand. Please... tell me what this is all about?' The inflection in Baker's voice changed from panic to pleading fear.

'Going all milky on me now eh?'

Harry and Stan looked at Kennedy.

'Come on Jackie,' said Harry in a low voice. 'Let's tie 'em up, take what we came for and fuck off.'

'No. Wait a minute,' replied Kennedy, Belfast accent gone. 'I need this cunt to explain something to me.'

Stan contemplated taking control of the situation but did nothing. Kennedy had blown his cover, but as far as he could tell it was only with Baker and he clearly had no idea what was going on, or whom any of them were.

Harry looked on and wondered if Kennedy was still working to Manny's plan. It was possible. As he'd learned in the ten years he'd been employed by Chapman Security, anything was possible. Manny shared information on a need-to-know basis only, and employees who valued their jobs never questioned his policies.

'Eh eh explain wh… what?' Baker's confusion was evident.

'The Troubles.' Kennedy checked the Glock's magazine load, pulled the trigger to disengage the pistol's internal safety mechanism, and levelled the barrel at Baker's chin.

Baker wiped his upturned face. The falling rain made him look like he was crying. 'Whwhat ababout The T…Tro… Troubles?'

'You said they were good for business.'

'Th… that's bebecause I ththought you were De… Delaney.'

'And that makes it different does it?'

'C'mon. You know what I mmmean.' Resigned to his fate, and suddenly feeling the cold, Baker began to shiver.

'Yeah. I know what you mean all right.' Kennedy tensed his finger against the Glock's trigger. He stared at Baker and saw his father Alec. Bullets punching their way into his face, tearing through his skull. Five. Four. Three. Two. One.

'Tell m… me wh… who you are?' sobbed Baker.

'I am my father's son.' Gripping the handle of the Glock with both hands to minimise recoil, Kennedy squeezed the trigger.

STAY FREE

11 December 2006

'*Stay Free*'. The Clash song had buzzed around Kennedy's brain for the last eighteen years. He hadn't heard it as such. Not on the radio. He knew where to find it though. Track three, side two of their second studio album '*Give 'Em Enough Rope*' which had spawned the hit singles '*Tommy Gun*' and '*English Civil War*'. They still got occasional airplay on Golden Hour-type shows, but '*Stay Free*' had become neglected, remembered only by hard-core fans of the band and people like him for whom the lyrics had meaning.

Written and sung by guitarist Mick Jones, the song, about male bonding and friendship, was inspired by an old classmate of Jones' called Robin Crocker whose life had taken a slightly different direction to his... robbing banks. A trip to the Old Bailey and a stretch in jail had followed for Crocker, while Jones enjoyed stardom in one of the greatest rock bands of all time.

Kennedy and Fletch had been into the Clash and seen them play live a couple of times at the Music Machine in Camden during the summer of 1978, and Kennedy had hoped they could do so again if the band, which Jones was sacked from in 1983 and finally disbanded in 1986, ever reformed. That hope had been dashed when lead singer Joe Strummer had died four years ago.

Kennedy thought about death every day. Perish, pass, decease, expire... die. There was no escaping it. One day we would all be killed by death. And how? Old age? Natural causes? Illness? Accident? War? Murder? Suicide? Murder and suicide, suicide and murder. He wondered if the words, whose meanings had preoccupied him throughout the lengthy prison sentence he'd served, would still play on his mind on the other side of the gate the screws were about to open. Freedom was just a short walk away.

'*Stay Free*'. Mick Jones. Could he be a relative? Maybe. Except, as everyone in the family knew, Jones was the second most common surname in the country after Smith. Was it possible to find out? Bored, he'd started with a scrap of paper and good intentions but given up researching his family tree at the great, great grandfather stage.

'*Stay Free*'. Why didn't the Clash ever release that as a single? The record company probably thought Mick's vocal wasn't as strong as Joe's. If they'd released it as a single it would have got into the charts and then it would have made it onto one of those Golden Hour shows and he would have heard it on the radio. Eighteen years was enough time to feature it, even for the schedulers who put the playlists together.

'*Stay Free*'. Ha ha. He picked up the plain nylon prison discharge bag containing his possessions. He'd stayed free for a year after the Baker incident but that had been stage-managed by Manny. When the time came, he was sitting with Vera and Nicky at the family spot in Richmond Park watching Jack, resplendent in a shocking-looking, jade green Chelsea kit, doing keepy-ups with a football.

'*Stay Free*'. At first Nicky hadn't seen the two patrol cars and their flashing blue lights, she was busy rocking Aimee in her lap singing along to '*Son of My Father*' by Chicory Tip. Ironic really. 3 April 1988. Easter Sunday. Radio One DJ Mike Read's oldies show. Life was good. Manny's money had made a massive difference. Goodbye Battersea, hello

Barnes. These days, her style was more Chanel than Sharon. Clothes by Christian Lacroix, shoes by Fiamma Ferragamo, hair by John Freida, nails by Carmen Maria. Nicky had the look.

'Stay Free'. His mother Vera hadn't changed. Why should she? The same discussion. The same complex. *"For out of the heart proceed evil thoughts, murders, adulteries, fornications, thefts, false witness, blasphemies."* (Matthew 15:19) She'd made him feel culpable for what he had done.

"Why did you do it son?"

It was a question he couldn't answer, not to his mother.

"Tell me the truth".

What could he say? 'It was nothing to do with Manny. The voices in my head told me to do it. A vision. Vodka. The pain of Dad's murder… all the murders, all the injuries, Fletch, Bertie… and the rest. All the suffering. I had to take the bastard out. Those last few seconds thinking, do it, do it. Baker deserved to die!'

'Jack Jones here, Jack Jones there, Jack Jones every fucking where tra la la la, la la la, la la,' he'd chanted as he stood up, kissed Vera, Nicky, Jack and Aimee, and walked across the grass to the road where armed police were waiting to arrest him. There was no point running, because there was nowhere to run to. He couldn't escape from himself.

"I am arresting you on the suspicion of murdering Jimmy Baker".

The cuffs felt tight.

"You do not have to say anything. But it may harm your defence if you do not mention when questioned something you later rely on in court".

He'd resisted the temptation to look back at his family. To see Vera and Nicky in tears, to see Jack and Aimee. Visiting time would have to do.

"Anything you do say maybe given in evidence".

He didn't say a word. Nothing. A code of silence that resulted in him being sentenced to life in prison with the Judge recommending he serve a minimum of fifteen years.

'Stay Free'. A buzzer sounded and the door opened. He was half expecting the screw to say something along the lines of. "Go easy Jones". Or, "Step lightly Jones". Or even, "Stay free Jones". Nothing. Not a word.

★ ★ ★

Fletch stood across the road facing the imposing Wormwood Scrubs gatehouse. He'd been here often enough but never really noticed the arched wooden door and neatly pointed brickwork of the two towers that carried the emblems of two famous prison reformers John Howard and Elizabeth Fry. For the past twenty minutes he'd been racking his brain trying to figure out why it looked overtly familiar. Norman Stanley Fletcher, the habitual criminal from Muswell Hill. Ha ha, that was it! He always laughed at the fact he shared a nickname with main character in the old Ronnie Barker sitcom 'Porridge'. Set in the confines of fictitious nick HMP Slade, the Scrubs gatehouse had been remodelled and filmed for the show's opening credits. Fletch clicked his fingers. He should have realised sooner given the fact Barker had passed away last year and he'd religiously watched all the reruns the Beeb had screened as a tribute. The bit where the prison quack asked him if he'd ever been a practicing homosexual had to be one of the funniest moments.

'Eldritch, stop staring.'

Fletch was sidetracked from his recollections of the comedy genius 'Porridge' represented by an Indian woman tugging anxiously at the hand of a young boy who was stood gawking goggle-eyed at him.

'I'm sorry sir, my son's not learned his manners yet,' she

continued in a heavily accented voice, tilting her head from side to side as she spoke.

'Why's he wearing a patch over his eye?'

'Stop it Eldritch, come on now.'

'Are you a pirate?'

Fletch reached into his coat pocket and laughed. The kid was funny, and his mother, who was wearing an olive green puffer jacket over her sari, presumably to keep the winter chill out, was beautiful. Huge deep-set brown eyes, flawless make-up-free skin, perfect features. Mesmerising.

'Do you know Captain Jack Sparrow?' persisted Eldritch.

His mother frowned in embarrassment. 'I'm so sorry sir.'

Fletch bent down and held the upturned clasped fist of his right hand out. 'I've got this here jar of dirt,' he said in an unthreatening voice. 'And guess what's in it.'

Eldritch stepped back as Fletch opened his hand to reveal a one-pound coin.

'I'm sorry sir, I've told him not to accept money from strangers.'

'Strangers eh. Very wise. My name's Paul Fletcher, but you can call me Fletch. Everyone else does. So what's your name love?'

'Tara,' replied the woman coyly. 'And this is my son Eldritch.'

'Well now, there you go. We're not strangers anymore.' Fletch handed the coin to a grateful Eldritch and patted him on the head.

'What do you say?' said Tara looking relieved.

'Thank you Mr Pirate Fletch.'

'You are very kind.'

'It's only a pound.'

'It may only be a pound to you but it's a lot to my boy.'

Fletch looked at Tara's pained expression. He wanted to embrace her, comfort her and tell her everything was going to be all right. Tell her he was going to take care of things now. Look after her and Eldritch. He'd never had the chance to say those words to anyone. Sadly, he didn't have the confidence to say them now.

'Come on Eldritch, say goodbye.'

The boy held up the pound coin and Tara waved at Fletch. A brief moment of flickering smiles flashing perfect pearly white teeth and they were gone. As he watched them walk slowly down Du Cane Road towards Hammersmith Hospital he cursed himself for resisting the compelling temptation to run after them. 'Fuck it Fletch!'

'Taxi!'

Fletch turned to see Kennedy stood behind him. 'Ha ha you rascal, come here.'

The two men grappled each other in a friendly bear hug.

'Is that all your stuff?' Fletch pointed at the nylon discharge bag Kennedy had dropped on the floor by his feet.

'Course not. Let's go to baggage reclaim.'

'Eighteen years! It don't seem a lot.'

'I wasn't on fucking holiday.' Kennedy gripped Fletch by both arms and looked at him. 'I'm only joking. Thanks for coming. You got any decent salmon on you?'

Fletch smiled as he reached in his pocket for a packet of Benson. Kennedy released from prison on licence. How things had changed in London. A great city, a great solitude. He'd soon notice. People, places, science, technology, animals, plants, arts, entertainment, the earth, the universe, everything… but most of all, the word on the street oh, and the fact that nearly everyone was Polish. Not that he had a problem with the Poles. By and large they came here to work and put a shift in, and besides the women were proper sorts. 'Here you go.' Fletch unwrapped the cellophane from the packet, opened it, tapped out a cigarette and watched as Kennedy flicked it up to his mouth. He'd forgotten how cool it looked.

'Haven't smoked in almost fifteen years,' said Kennedy, Benson at the corner of his mouth wiggling up and down as he spoke. 'Useful currency though tobacco. Tobacco and tuna.'

'Salmon. I get that.' Fletch paused midsentence as he considered having a smoke himself. 'But tuna, what the fuck's that about?' he continued, deciding against it and putting the packet in his jacket pocket.

Kennedy grinned. Fletch was naïve, but then why would he know that paper money was worthless in prison? The currency behind bars comprised postage stamps, chocolate bars, cans of tuna, and cigarettes. These could be traded for anything ranging from sex, drugs, and gambling to bloody murder. He couldn't be bothered to explain the system. He tapped the side of the Benson and coughed. 'You got a light then?'

Fletch smiled. 'Tuna.' He thought to himself, spinning the word round in his mind a few times. He didn't want to ask. He knew the nick had its own language. 'Salmon and trout. Snout. Tuna though. Tuna what? Was it rhyming slang? Maybe it was an acronym. Fuck it! Who cared? Kennedy would soon learn Salmon, Trout and fucking Tuna wouldn't get him far with Jadwiga, the bottle-blonde battle maiden who ran the Polski Sklep convenience store on Queenstown Road.

The Indians might have refined the concept of the traditional corner shop with an 'open all hours' policy, but they sold the same old stuff you could get at a supermarket except it had a minimum ten percent mark-up. Jadwiga's shop on the other hand provided an opportunity for curious locals to sample international cuisine that stretched beyond the usual fried chicken from Kentucky, assorted Turkish kebabs and Chinese takeaways. White sausages, salted herrings, cucumbers in brine, Fletch had tried them all... more in a bid to impress the perfectly sculpted Jadwiga than out of any great desire to treat his palate. Indigestion was the inevitable outcome. Heartburn was the perfect partner for rejection, and of course Jadwiga sold a cure for that as well. Heartburn, not rejection. *'Manti Gastop'*. Great name. Did the job. Ahhh Jadwiga. Then for some reason, as he struck a Bryant and May for Kennedy, he randomly visualised Tara in his mind's eye. That was half his problem. He fell in love too easily.

'Let me guess. That's your motor.' Exhaling smoke as he spoke, Kennedy pointed at a scratched and scuffed navy blue Ford Mondeo that was parked proud of the kerb between two nondescript saloon cars.

'Good to see you've still got your psychic powers.' Fletch chuckled as they walked towards the car. 'Actually it's less of a shitter than it looks.'

'Doesn't look much of a fanny magnet to me.' Kennedy took several long drags before dropping the half-smoked Benson on the floor and stubbing it out.

'I don't need one.' Fletch grinned as he motioned Kennedy to get into the Mondeo.

As he opened the passenger door, Kennedy turned to look back up the road at the prison gatehouse. 'Fuck it!' He cursed as he got into the car sat down and rubbed his hand along the dust-free dashboard. 'I see what you mean about the inside of the motor.' He leaned back to look in the foot well and then glanced over his shoulder at the backseat. 'Very tidy. What's that all about then?'

Fletch turned the key in the ignition and revved the engine. 'It's been a while since you've been on the manor. It's not so much the thieving that goes on with skagheads trying to pinch anything they can sell to feed their filthy habits… it's the vandalism of anything that looks new. I can leave this parked up where I like and no one will touch it.'

Kennedy watched with interest as Fletch fastened his seatbelt, opened the Mondeo's central storage compartment, pulled out a Bluetooth headset and fitted it to his left ear. 'Are we going home or the outer reaches of the fucking galaxy Captain Kirk?'

Fletch smiled. 'Having the car look like a shitter from the outside is a double-edged sword. Old Bill are always looking for reasons to pull you over. Not wearing a seatbelt or talking on a hand-held mobile phone will get you nicked.'

Kennedy pursed his lips as he fastened his seatbelt. 'Dunno the exact conditions of my licence. But until I see my probation officer, I'm taking no chances.' He grimaced as Fletch drove past the Scrubs. 'One thing's for certain though, I'm never going back inside.' He closed his eyes and let his head fall back. The price of silence. How could you value that against spending half your life behind bars? The world of stamps, chocolate bars, oily rags and even oilier fish was behind him now. The exchange rate didn't matter. Money was once again hard currency, and Manny would tell him soon enough what his loyalty had been worth to him.

★ ★ ★

Despite the passage of time, he could still see the expression on his mother's face as the jury at the Old Bailey convicted him. *"Jesus said, Thou shalt do no murder, Thou shalt not commit adultery, Thou shalt not steal, Thou shalt not bear false witness."* (Matthew 19:18) How many times had she recited this verse of the Bible to him? Or the one that followed? *"Honour thy father and thy mother: and, Thou shalt love thy neighbour as thyself."* (Matthew 19:19) How many times had she prayed the Holy Rosary in the belief she had the power of God in her hands?

He'd considered religion. It was hard not to. It could have given him a sense of wellbeing as he contemplated his actions and their consequences, but he couldn't get past his personal viewpoint that organised religion was a cynical way of manipulating the masses. How many wars had been started because one grouping of people interpreted faith differently to another? How many acts of terror? How many murders? Why had his father met his death? Why? Why? Why? There were plenty of questions and there had been plenty of hours behind bars to determine the answers.

Deemed to be a Category A prisoner, dangerous to the public or national security, Kennedy had served the first five years of his sentence at HMP Frankland in County Durham. 270 miles from London, visiting Frankland represented an arduous journey for family and friends so he'd met the excuses head-on before they'd arisen and told them not to bother. The mood swings he experienced were misinterpreted by prison staff and, because of his background and the view held by the governor that he was influential amongst other prisoners, he was upgraded to 'exceptional escape risk' status and transferred to HMP Belmarsh in southeast London. Opened in 1991, with its high brick walls and razor wire fences, Belmarsh, which occupied sixty acres of the old Ministry of Defence Woolwich Arsenal site, was viewed as the most important prison in the country and Kennedy had soon found himself in the company of some of the most notorious criminals in the land. High profile gangsters, terrorists, drug barons and sex offenders were incarcerated in the High Security Unit, a prison within a prison that was split into four spurs across two floors. Each spur contained twelve single-occupancy cells. Each cell was about two metres wide and less than four metres long.

Throughout his trial, he'd clung to the belief that through his many corrupt tentacles Manny would find a way to get him acquitted. It hadn't happened. The case for his prosecution was too compelling. Murder, firearms, drugs and conspiracy when blended with silence were not a recipe for leniency, but there was always hope wasn't there. His mother prayed for him, had faith in his innocence. "God is on your side son", she'd said. Ah but God sees everything. The omnipotent one knew the score as well as he did, his mother didn't.

The bleak reality of his situation had finally dawned on him when the cell door slammed shut after he'd been taken down following sentencing. He had two choices. To accept guilt, deal with it and get on with life behind bars, or to wallow in a pit of resentment. He'd taken the decision to join Chapman Security, and that fact alone countered the lingering question marks he had against the judge, the jury, the prosecution witnesses, the police and Manny whose Godlike presence and power was as evident in jail as it was in the free world.

Prison routine provided plenty of thinking time. Twelve hours in the cell, twelve hours out. Twenty minutes for breakfast, an hour of exercise outdoors, one hour's access to the gym, half an hour cleaning the wing and five hours association time during which it was permissible to watch television, play pool or table football and chat to fellow convicts. Kennedy kept his own counsel and dedicated himself to maintaining fitness and keeping his body hard while his mind mulled things over.

Was it a figment of his imagination that Manny had rigged his transfers to Belmarsh and finally Wormwood Scrubs, where he'd spent the last six months of his sentence, so he could be nearer to his relatives? At Frankland, he'd been accused of attempting to corrupt a prison officer as part of an escape plot. His name had featured on a note that had been passed to the officer by one of the cucumbers segregated for their own protection on the 'vulnerable prisoners' wing. The note carried a threat to several members of his family along with their addresses. It was intimidating, but it made no sense as the whole story was a fabrication. The VP wing housed paedophiles and other despised beasts of the prison jungle not on normal courtyard exercise like bent coppers and grasses. Eddie Jacobsen was in there. Why? Was he part of some elaborate sub plot? Surely he had to have something to do with it. Cucumbers equalled numbers. Specifically, Prison Rule 43 that allowed inmates to apply to be isolated for their own protection. Was Jacobsen running scared of him? Four years earlier it had been his team who'd arrested him, yet he'd been on Manny's payroll.

Too much thought was both tortuous and academic. Protesting his innocence was pointless. At least he was back in London. Six months after being transferred to Belmarsh, Kennedy's escape risk was downgraded to high. Again there was no point questioning why the original information received had been discredited as unreliable. Things happened quickly, without the need for appeal. For a period of time he was moved from the maximum security unit to the normal prison. There he found an unwelcome surprise waiting for him.

At the age of forty-two, Sergeant Eric Prime had left the Parachute Regiment and joined Her Majesty's Prison Service. It was a logical move with a high proportion of staff being ex-military personnel and Prime found the regime suited him well. Comparatively poor management, lack of leadership and teamwork had been a shock to the system, but he'd got used to it in a short space of time and his no-nonsense approach to the job soon earned him the respect of colleagues and the ire of prisoners who viewed him as an intimidating bully. Having completed his probation and worked for several years at HMP Brixton, Prime had moved to Belmarsh shortly after it became operational.

Kennedy recognised him immediately. He was a part of his hellish memories that infused themselves with the noise and sickly, sweaty, shitty stench of prison life that sapped his spirit. Prime was always there. At association, during the twice-daily movements to education classes or work and, worst of all, at bang-up time back in his cell when the doors were locked. Night-after-night he lay awake on his bunk replaying different events of his life, threading common aspects together and drawing conclusions. It would have made a compelling film, but he kept changing the storyline. He knew what he knew, what he'd seen with his own eyes, but it was what he didn't know, what he hadn't seen, what he relied on others to tell him that gnawed away constantly at his sanity. Paranoia made for an unwelcome bedfellow in prison.

From the minute he'd arrived in House Block One, Kennedy sensed that Prime was watching him obsessively. Was he like that with other prisoners, or was it just him? His reputation at Brixton for being fond of planned cell interventions with 'Control and Restraint' teams had followed him to Belmarsh. Big Barry Churchhouse, a career criminal who'd progressed from breaking and entering to armed robbery, had spoken to him about Prime. Corrupt and violent were the two adjectives he'd used to describe him. Physical assaults of prisoners Prime disliked went hand-in-hand with spurious disciplinary charges. There was no escape from his life-wrecking, psychotic harassment.

It was a waiting game. Kennedy knew something was coming. Maybe Prime had harboured a jealous grudge against him for the recognition he'd received for his valorous actions during the battle for Mount Longdon. For his gallantry he'd been awarded the Military Medal. There'd been no medal and no mention in despatches for Prime. He'd led the heroic assault on that Argentine bunker, but it had become common knowledge that he'd repeatedly shot dying and dead enemy soldiers. Kennedy had seen him do it, but hadn't said a word. It was the heat of the battle. Combat stress. Prime had sworn him to silence anyway. Why? What was the point? He relived the horror of the bunker often and the final words of the dying Argentine were lodged in his brain. *"Madre de Dios! Yo no quiero morir por esto".* He'd heard them before, and he heard them again. He heard them still. Eventually, he'd learned what they meant. "Mother of God! I don't want to die for this". Was that really it, or was there more to it?

Seeing Prime again reminded him of discourse they'd had when he'd mentioned his father. Now, he was able to recall it word-by-word.

'What's your name Private?'
'Jones... Kennedy Jones.'
'Kennedy eh.'
'Yes Sergeant.'
'Alec Jones' boy?'
'Yes Sergeant.'
'I served with your father in Northern Ireland.'

In the end, Kennedy never got to Ulster, either as a soldier or a civilian. Having left the Regiment, there was little point. He'd never been able to uncover any additional information about his father's murder; all he had to go on was the official report. He'd served in the forces, seen first hand how men died. There was no way of softening the blow of a knock at the door that brought with it news dreaded by families and loved ones. The graphic minutiae of death were always distilled. Violence and suffering were omitted. The likelihood that those responsible for his father's murder would never be brought to justice still tormented him, and Prime's presence fanned flames of rage from embers that had glowed and burned since the day his mother broke the news to him.

23 April 1978. St. George's Day. Kennedy's father had been shot dead the previous night, and over twenty-four years later he would learn a version of the truth about what happened which would have dire consequences for him. He could still remember the exact time and date. 10.06 a.m. 9 June 2002.

In prison, physical training had helped dissipate his anger. It was the best way of passing the time and conditioning mind and body. Push-ups, sit-ups and even pull-ups could be undertaken anywhere, and with Prime taking closer order Kennedy had taken to exercising in his cell instead of the gym. Endless sets and repetitions were timed and noted. Twenty-five, fifty, one hundred, fifty, twenty-five. Stripped to the waist, wearing prison-issue maroon jogging bottoms, he was at push-up forty-three and enjoying his exertions, counting out the numbers and testing his stamina by adding an additional ten repetitions into each cycle. Today was an important day, he had an oral hearing before the Parole Board fixed for 2 p.m. Having served over half his sentence, in line with the 1991 Criminal Justice Act, it was common knowledge that the Secretary of State was obliged, if recommended to do so by the Parole Board, to release him on licence.

'Your old man was good at press-ups Jones.'

Kennedy heard Prime speak but chose to ignore him.

'Did you hear me?' Prime was stood just inside the open cell door, the highly polished toecaps of his anti-slip boots inches from Kennedy's chin as he touched the ground.

'Forty-four, forty-five, forty-six.'

'He never could say no.'

'Forty-seven, forty-eight, forty-nine.'

'Is there something wrong with your hearing this morning Jones?'

'Fifty.'

At the fiftieth repetition, Kennedy pushed himself up and locked his arms, regulating his breathing as he waited for Prime to speak again.

'He always said yes.'

'To what?' Kennedy eased himself back onto his haunches and stood up slowly flexing his muscles as he glared at Prime who curiously appeared relaxed and smug. 'Say nothing else, just listen,' he thought to himself. Come on you can do it

Kennedy. If the Parole Board hearing went in his favour as expected, he would soon be waving goodbye to Prime.

'To a slapper.'

Largely self-taught from information gleaned from prison library books, Kennedy had harnessed the principles of Cognitive Behavioural Therapy to manage his anger. It was a slow process, but eventually he'd found an ally in a National Health Service psychiatrist who worked several days a week in the Mental Health Unit at Belmarsh. The unit had been set up in 1999 after four inmates had committed suicide over a period of seven months in 1997.

'A real ladies man was Alec.'

Kennedy envisaged the CBT schematic diagram that linked its key components. *'Feeling' 'Thought' 'Behaviour'*. He'd focussed mainly on past experiences and how they impacted the way he interpreted the world and reacted in certain situations. Negative thinking patterns had dominated his life with cataclysmic behavioural effects, but now he'd learned how to isolate them and change his perception of them.

'Cost him his life.'

Kennedy clenched his fists and felt his neck tick to one side and then back again the motion sending beads of perspiration dripping down his face. Like an anaesthetic wearing off, the schematic diagram explaining CBT had been replaced by Prime's face.

'What did?'

'As you well know, those official reports never tell the full story. That night Alec was murdered. He'd left the pub with a slutty barmaid.'

'Fuck off! My old man wouldn't do that. He only had eyes for mum.'

'That may have been the case when he was home on leave.'

'Fuck off!' Kennedy stepped forward and eyeballed Prime as he spoke. There was a metre or so between the men.

'A classic honey trap.'

Kennedy wrestled with the compelling urge to lash out. The CBT diagram faded back into his vision. Deep breathing. In out, in out. Try and relax. Try and harness the power of silence.

'That slag got three more of our lads murdered before she was found out.'

Momentarily, Kennedy wondered if he'd misinterpreted the situation. Maybe Prime was just passing the time of day, sharing information about what had happened to his father. Was he such a bad judge of character? Prime was sneering as he spoke. Was that just the way he was? He wanted to know the truth, but was this it, or was it Prime's twisted version of events? Had his father really chased other women? It wasn't something he'd been aware of as a kid or a teenager. Why would he be? Back then it was outside his frame of reference. He knew what he was like with women. Nicky was his wife. He loved her, cherished her, in sickness and in health, till death us do part... but he'd also played away whenever the opportunity had presented itself. If that wasn't what all men did, he had to have inherited that personality trait from somebody... and that somebody was certainly not his mother. Like father, like son. It was the same with the drink. Whatever the truth, his father had been unfortunate. In the wrong place at the wrong time.

'Dad was unlucky.'

'He was a chancer who got what he had coming to him.' Prime jutted his chin out and squared up to Kennedy. 'I always remember what my brother Danny said about your dad.'

'What the fuck are you talking about?' Kennedy tensed again as the CBT diagram faded from view for the last time.

'He was the boxing trainer at Caius.'

'So what?'

'That was a honey trap too. A reverse one though eh. Started at an early age didn't he, and with his brother's girlfriend. Sound's like a manipulative woman your mother.'

Kennedy's head swam. As he heard the command to 'Fix Bayonets!' the shouting voices and clanging sound of prison life fell silent.

'Come on Jones.'

'CHAAARGE!' Kennedy, a simmering, seething, coiled spring of rage sprang forward smashing his forehead against the bridge of Prime's nose fracturing it in a bloody explosion of bone, tissue and snot. The impact sent Prime reeling into the walkway outside the cell. Kennedy followed up the head-butt with a ferocious combination of punches that rendered him unconscious before he hit the floor with a resounding thud.

Kennedy retreated into his cell, kicked the door shut and pounded his fists in frustration against the wall as waited for the inevitable to happen. Now, the sound outside was deafening and riotous. Alarms braying. Doors banging. Screws shouting. Difficult and disruptive prisoners screaming abuse. Window warriors smashing tin cans against bars.

'Come on Jones... come on Jones... come on Jones.' Kennedy repeated Prime's words again and again. The wounds that had festered in his mind for years were opening up once more. Visions of diseased, decaying, charred, gangrenous, decomposing flesh melded with the maniacal camouflaged face of Prime and the grey steel of his own bloodied bayonet. Stinging tears ran down his cheeks, burning like acid.

'Come on Jones... come on Jones... come on Jones.'

Prime had lost the battle but won the war. There would be no Parole Board hearing. Now, there was no way out. No escape... or was there? He could sever the main artery in his arm. He'd be clinically dead before they had a chance to resuscitate him. The light in the cell went out, and with it so did fleeting thoughts of suicide. The screws had turned off the power and water supply. With the spur locked down, and the risk of being showered with a kettle-full of sugar-adulterated boiling water eliminated, a Control and Restraint team would be donning protective overalls, head and leg guards, padded gloves and reinforced boots readying themselves to take him out to the segregation unit. Kennedy looked at the photographs of his family stuck to the wall. As he waited for the inevitable to happen, he wondered what his father would make of his situation. "Just remember son, whatever happens, never take you eyes off your opponent". 'Cheers for the advice Dad, it's never let me down yet.'

★ ★ ★

'FUCK IT!' Kennedy screamed, his head whiplashing back and forth as Fletch slammed on the Mondeo's brakes in response to his outburst.

'You okay mate?'

Kennedy shivered and rubbed his face with both hands. 'Yeah. Sorry about that.'

'You sure?'

Kennedy nodded. 'Come on let's go.'

The irksome, repetitive sound of horns being sounded by impatient drivers stationary behind them piqued Fletch. 'Right! Enough of this!' he shouted, opening his door. 'You wait here, remember you're on licence.'

Kennedy smiled and shrugged his shoulders.

Fletch got out and walked briskly to the car immediately behind them. 'Is there something wrong with your horn?' he enquired sarcastically, slamming his hands on the roof of the customised Vauxhall Nova and then leaning in through the driver's window. 'Or are you just fucking stupid?' As he spoke, he checked out the car's occupants. Four nervous-looking, pimply-faced youths whose scrambled eyes were looking everywhere but at him.

The driver's face flushed with a combination of

embarrassment and fear. 'S sss sorry,' he stammered, hands gripping the steering wheel as he stared straight ahead.

'Sss sss something wrong with your vvvv voice?' Fletch didn't wait for a reply. The driver and his mates were little more than kids. This was a good example of 'all bluster, no bollocks'. As he turned to walk back to his car, the driver of a BMW directly behind the Nova sounded his horn. Fletch span round and glared at the driver who was leaning out of his window. 'Have you got a fucking problem with your horn as well?'

The BMW driver raised the middle finger of his right hand. 'Oi Ugly! Why don't you jog on back to your mobile skip.'

The abuse was too much for Fletch. Kids were one thing, but a grown man? As he sprinted towards the BMW, he noticed something familiar about the driver who was in his mid-forties. Tousled, blonde-streaked hair, gold earrings and a puffy face dominated by a large hooked nose. He was sure he'd seen him somewhere before but knew he wasn't a friend. There was no further pause for thought. On reaching the car, he delivered a rabbit punch through the open window forceful enough to knock the driver sideways into the passenger seat.

'So that's road rage,' quipped a recomposed Kennedy, rubbing his chin thoughtfully as Fletch got back into the Mondeo.

'No. That's anger management.' Fletch didn't waste any time in driving hastily away, but there was no dramatic squeal of tyres, no lurching forward like a scalded cat, and no cloud of exhaust smoke. Just smooth acceleration and a smile. 'I'd swear on my mother's life I knew the bloke in that Beamer back there.' Relaxed, he lit a Benson, took a couple of puffs, and handed it to Kennedy who shook his head as he put the cigarette to his lips.

'I could never do that,' he replied nonchalantly.

Fletch looked puzzled. 'Do what?'

'Swear on my mother's life.'

Fletch laughed. 'Missed you mate.'

Kennedy smiled and closed his eyes.

★ ★ ★

'When my time comes, I'd like this music to be played at my funeral.' As he spoke, Manny stretched out his hands and admired the neatness of his perfectly manicured fingernails. It annoyed him that he'd picked the habit up from Jester, but he did it all the same.

'I suppose I should know what it is by now,' replied Ginger Francisco zipping up her tracksuit top. 'I've heard it often enough. The military bands played it when we went to the Cenotaph on Remembrance Sunday last month.'

Manny looked across at Ginger and smiled. The ageing process had been kind to her. Flawless beauty was a perfect canvass for the artistry of a cosmetic surgeon. From tip to toe he couldn't fault the life portrait he sometimes perceived that he'd painted… except Ginger was real. Every strand of hair, the facial features, eyes, complexion, curves, limbs… every nuance was exactly as it should be. His very own Stepford Wife, except Vivian 'Ginger Francisco' Francis wasn't a submissive robot nor was she married to him.

'It's known as *'Nimrod'*. The ninth piece of the *'Enigma Variations'*. Manny twisted the emerald ring on his finger and looked forward to gauging Ginger's reaction to the profound words he was about to share with her. 'You're right about Remembrance Sunday,' he continued, gesticulating with his hands as if he were addressing an audience. 'Close your eyes and the pace of the music carries you in slow-motion across all the battlefields where brave British soldiers have fought and fallen… fighting to the last bullet to preserve the freedom of the people of our green and pleasant sceptered isle.'

Ginger stood with her lissom legs slightly apart. 'I've always had the impression you wish you'd fought for Queen and Country. Is that true?' As she spoke, she bent down with feline grace to touch her toes.

Manny sighed at the sight, but her comment and question angered him. 'That opportunity was taken away from me.' A familiar terseness returned to his voice as he clenched his fists and dropped his arms by his side. 'And besides, the Jones' family has never shirked playing its part in keeping Britain Great.'

Ginger sensed Manny's change of mood and steered a new path for their conversation. 'What other pieces of music would you like played when the time comes?' she enquired, continuing with her stretches.

'*Danse Macabre*' by Saint Saens.' He replied without hesitation, relaxing once more and smiling as he felt a familiar tingle in his groin. The office door buzzer sounded. It distracted him from the sordid thoughts pervading his mind, and arrested the flow of blood to his stiffening penis that would have forced him to sit down to spare his modesty.

Kennedy edged backwards when Ginger opened the door. Recognition was one thing, perception another.

'Hello stranger, long time no see,' she said huskily, tracing the tip of her tongue slowly across her top lip after speaking, fixing her eyes on Kennedy's while she waited for a response which wasn't forthcoming. 'We've been expecting you for some time,' she continued, flicking her fringe and smiling. 'Are you planning to come in? Or are you just going to stand there all afternoon?'

Kennedy shook his head and cleared his throat. 'You look... er. You look fantas... er fa familar,' he replied eventually, surprised at the weak-kneed, stuttering nervous schoolboy effect seeing Ginger was having on him. He couldn't be sure

155

he'd ever considered her as wanking material when he'd been in prison, and he was glad because she appeared to have taken on more than just a passing resemblance to his mother.

'Go on through,' she said, stepping aside as he entered the office. 'I'm going to the gym.' Her teasing manner as she brushed passed him on her way out suggested that she knew exactly what he was thinking. He shuddered at the unnatural aspect of this.

'Kennedy... Kennedy.' Manny repeated his nephew's name slowly before muting the stereo, picking up a pair of thick black-rimmed glasses from his desk and striding towards his him. 'How are you?' he asked donning the glasses and holding them in place momentarily.

Kennedy raised his eyebrows as he looked at his uncle. For a man in his mid-sixties he still carried himself well. His lean, lined face looked unseasonably tanned and with close-cropped hair a respectable silvery-grey he appeared a lot less menacing than he remembered. 'Well I'm free now, so I guess I feel okay,' he replied curtly, extending his right hand to meet Manny's. There had never been anything more than a handshake between them, and its vice-like firmness and the glaring intensity of their eye contact suggested it would be business as usual.

'You look fit.'

'You look prosperous.'

'Same old, same old.'

'Dunno about same old. There's a touch of the Peter Pan's about this place.'

'Ahh the march of time. We all do our best, especially Ginger.'

Kennedy loosened his grip on Manny's hand and stepped back. 'Time's hardly marched for me this past eighteen years.'

'That was a harsh sentence. We thought we had it covered. But you did yourself no favours.'

Kennedy walked across to the window and looked out

on the street below. 'Make's a change from wire mesh and a dismal view of a prison wall.'

'I expect it does. It's in the past now. You've served your time, kept your side of our bargain. Now it's time for me to keep mine. The deal we agreed remains in place right?'

Kennedy nodded.

Manny turned to his desk and picked up a set of keys. 'You'll find everything you need here,' he said, handing them to Kennedy who had followed him to the table. 'Oh, and you'll need this,' he continued, opening a drawer and producing a boxed mobile phone. 'I guess you haven't used one of these before so read the manual. It's pay-as-you-go. You'll be okay. We'll stay in touch by text message. Coded from me, you'll work it out! Oh, and when I tell you, get rid of it and get another one. Don't worry, we change the contact details every fortnight.'

'We?'

'Jester.'

'Still on the firm?'

'Yeah but more on the football side of the business these days.'

'I read about that. When did you become interested in football?'

'I didn't. I saw a commercial opportunity that if operated correctly would mean the filth wouldn't be able to get near us... so I took it. You know me.'

Kennedy resisted the urge to be sarcastic and remained silent. Manny would tell him as much as he felt he needed to know so he let him get on with it.

'It's a shame I didn't have the club when Jack was younger. I remember you saying he could play a bit.'

'He still can,' countered Kennedy, a rueful expression forming on his face. 'The biggest regret I had about battering that screw who coated Dad off was losing the chance to be there for my boy and give him the encouragement he needed to stick with the football rather than packing it in and joining the Army.'

Manny smiled wryly as he watched Kennedy make his way back to the window. 'Never give up on the dreams of your youth,' he said, unmuting the stereo and noting Kennedy's aggrieved expression as he walked to the oak bookcase that ran along the length of the opposite wall. 'I want you to take this,' he continued, reaching for an A5-size maroon leather-bound volume. 'Keep it with you at all times, everything you need and more is in here. There are only two copies. Remember I have the other one.'

Kennedy turned to look at the book Manny was holding up. *'Poetry, Verse and War.'* Poetry and classical music. It was puzzling. His uncle was hardly the archetypal villain. He'd met plenty of them in prison. As Manny handed him the book he studied his face and contemplated how his father would have aged. What would have interested him? Would his relationship with his brother have mellowed? Might they have finally worked together? He wanted to ask Manny his opinion, but intuition told him not to bother.

★ ★ ★

The first text message Kennedy received on his new mobile phone arrived as he pushed open Viola's double-fronted entrance door and walked out blinking into the winter sunshine.

Bleep Bleep Bleep 'RTFM'

'Read the fucking manual. Saucy bastard!' He stepped out on the pavement and paused for a minute as he held the handset out in front of him.

Bleep Bleep Bleep 'Don't lose the book'

Two women walked by, both were talking on mobile

phones. He wondered briefly if they were conversing with each other. Manny was right about the march of time. Progress eh. What else had changed? He tapped his jacket pockets to check he had the keys and the book and ambled slowly down Wardour Street admiring the expensive modern cars parked along the kerb. All of them waxed and polished, gleaming chrome and steel. Rolls Royce, Bentley, Ferrari, BMW, Mercedes, Audi, Jaguar, Porsche. He had to check the badges to see what the marques were as he recognised none of the models. Parked between the Jag and the Porsche was Fletch's Ford Mondeo. It may have looked anonymous on Du Cane Road or Battersea's back streets, but in Soho it appeared incongruous, a rusting, rotting relic from a bygone age. Good job it was taxed and tested.

'All sorted?' asked Fletch as Kennedy got into the car.

'I think so.'

'Good enough. Let's go to the old flat then. You can freshen up, get changed, and decide what you want to do. There's plenty of people who want to see you.'

Bleep Bleep Bleep Kennedy nodded and stared at the text message. *'Page 11 Word 14 Letter 6 Word 17 Letter 2 Page 3 Word 5 Letter 1 Word 7 Letter 1'* So that's what the poetry book was for. It wasn't the Enigma Code, but it was clever. Manny Jones, Battersea's Teflon Don, no wonder the police never got near him or made anything stick. Slippery fucker.

'You got a pen and a piece of paper?'

'In the glove compartment.'

Fletch kept his eyes on the road as Kennedy flicked through the pages of the book and decoded the text message.

'11SW3SL'

'Sounds like a postcode to me. What is this, the fucking *'Krypton Factor?'*

'Krypton what?'

'Could be SW11 3SL.'

'You're right. That's the Yelverton aint it.'

Bleep Bleep Bleep 'Simple eh'

'Clever bastard.'

Bleep Bleep Bleep 'Page 5 Word 9 Word 12 Word 22'

Kennedy deciphered. '5 Alley Blue Door.'

'Dunno about that.' Fletch looked puzzled. 'Alley? Is there a road round there called The Alley?'

'Nah. Tell you what there is though, a new cul-de-sac of lock-up garages. They're just off the Yelverton. A five minute walk from the old flat if that.'

Daylight was beginning to fade as Fletch parked the Mondeo in a bay by the entrance to Ridge House just off the Yelverton Road adjacent to the cul-de-sac. It was less than five miles from Manny's office in Wardour Street. Twenty years ago, Kennedy had regularly run the distance in under thirty minutes. Today, in heavy traffic, it had taken almost fifty minutes to make the short journey by car. He opened the door and gazed up slowly at the tower block he used to live in. The grim, grey slab of high-rise concrete still scarred the skyline, a testament to the hellish prison-like inner city living that he'd provided an escape route from for his family. If the sparkling, shiny, nouveau riche world of Soho they had just left had changed out of all proportion, this little part of London showed no signs of profitable progress. Nicky and the kids might have absconded, but all he'd managed to do was exchange one prison for several others. The dark shadows of crime and social alienation were probably the same here as they were behind bars. Adults condemned to a life of stress, mental health problems and marriage difficulties, juveniles hyperactive, hostile and delinquent. It was both satirical and depressing.

Kennedy clambered out of the car and shuddered as a chilling gust of wind blew down the deserted cul-de-sac. As he began walking, the dust and litter of urban decay tumbled past him bouncing along the pot-holed tarmac in the breeze and coming to rest against the graffiti-scrawled wall that blocked off the end of the street.

'Fifth garage, blue door. Here it is.' Kennedy shook the bunch of keys Manny had given him as he scanned the parapet of the garage roofs and carefully eyed the two lamp posts either side of the cul-de-sac's junction with Yelverton Road.

Fletch tapped him on the shoulder. 'Don't worry. Oddly enough, the council budget for twenty-four-hour CCTV didn't stretch far enough to get this lot under camera.' He turned his back on the wind momentarily and lit a cigarette as Kennedy unlocked the garage door and lifted it up and over. 'I'll wait here. Any drama, I'll knock.'

Kennedy entered the garage pulled the light switch cord and swung the door shut. The fluorescent tube mounted across the centre of the low ceiling flickered and buzzed before coming on and brightly illuminating the space cramped by what he assumed was a car draped in a protective cover. He squinted, accustoming his eyes to the yellowy neon glow. Cold and claustrophobic, the garage reminded him of the solitary cell he'd been confined to battered and bleeding by the Control and Restraint team at Belmarsh following the incident with Prime.

'Fuck you Prime. Fuck off!' Kennedy cursed Tourette-like at the memory as he pulled back the cover to reveal Manny's old Jaguar XJ12 Sovereign. De-chromed, and with paintwork looking like it had just been machine polished, the old bulletproof bomb was still in pristine condition. He opened the unlocked driver's door carefully and climbed inside. 'Beautiful.'

The cabin was a fresh-smelling cocoon of newness. He saw the key in the ignition and turned it once so the dashboard lit up and the stereo came on. There was no point firing up the engine, he knew the Jag would start first time. Music bubbled gently from the speakers. Manny's music. The tune he'd heard at his office earlier. In the centre-console compartment was the paperwork for the car. Registration document, MOT certificate, tax and insurance. He puzzled at the date he had been assigned as the registered keeper for a moment, 24 10 1986. It seemed familiar, but he couldn't recall its significance. In the passenger footwell was an unbranded black vinyl holdall. The Jag was a nice gesture, but hardly discreet. It would probably have to go, but that could wait. It was hard currency that interested him right now. The cash that had kept him motivated while behind bars was in the bag. Not all of it, he knew that. But there would be more than enough to tide him over. Manny had been true to his word so far, so there was no need to check the contents. Not yet anyway.

★ ★ ★

Kennedy emerged from the bathroom with a towel around his waist and looked around the stark living room. It redefined the word inhospitable. Living room defied the Trade Descriptions Act. Dying room would have been far more appropriate. There was no furniture or carpets. The only Spartan relics of previous inhabitation were a few faded photographs Blu-tacked to the paint-speckled woodchip wallpaper that was peeling from the walls.

'Sorry. I didn't bother much with the flat.' Fletch sounded rueful. 'I just made sure everything was in order once in a while and kept the rent paid like you wanted.'

'Don't worry about it, I'm not.' Kennedy glanced at the photos as he spoke, his eyes finally resting on a portrait of Nicky pouting. That's how he remembered her. He smiled in anticipation of what he hoped might happen later in the day.

Fletch grinned. 'I've bought you some new threads so at

least you'll look the bollocks when you go and see her.'

'Really?'

'Yeah! Expensive. Don't worry though, if you don't like 'em, I've kept the receipts.'

Kennedy laughed as he walked across to the holdall he'd retrieved from the Jag that was now lying in the middle of the floor. 'Will that cover it?' he enquired, crouching down, unzipping the bag, and showing Fletch the contents. 'There's a decent drink in there for you.'

'A drink!' exclaimed Fletch. 'Looks more like a fucking brewery.'

Kennedy reached into the holdall and handed Fletch a wad of fifty-pound notes.

'I can't take this, there's gotta be five bags here.'

'Ten actually.'

'Ten grand. Fuck me!'

'No thanks!' Kennedy raised his hand and smiled. 'Take it. I'd be offended if you didn't.'

'Offended? Ha ha! You haven't seen the clothes I've bought you yet.'

Within minutes, Kennedy was dressed and stood in front of the cracked wall mirror in his old bedroom. 'How did you manage it? Everything fits perfectly. Even the socks and boxer shorts.'

Resplendent in a white formal shirt with a cutaway collar, black V-neck pullover, black trousers and black brogues he stretched upwards and then dropped to his haunches just to double check. 'Mustard!'

'Check out the jacket in the wardrobe.'

'My old leather?'

'No a new one, same style. I took your old clothes to Hymie's in the High Street where Coxy gets his clobber made. Told him to copy them exactly.'

'That old goat still alive?'

'Which one?

'Both?'

'Yeah both of 'em still going… just about.'

Kennedy put on the jacket, stepped into the corridor and shook his limbs. 'Whaddya think?'

'Tidy mate. I reckon Nicky will be well impressed. Come on, I'll see you to the lock up.'

Fletch opened the door and looked up and down the walkway. Approaching were two hoodie-wearing men of indeterminate age. Heads hung down, faces partially obscured, one drew on a cigarette whilst the other spat on the floor as they shuffled aimlessly past. Behind them ambled a brindle-coloured Staffordshire bull terrier. Fletch sighed at the uncompromising, brutish reality of the all-to-familiar scene as Kennedy joined him at the door. The Staffy paused to look at them, sniffing the air. The dog, with its moody, menacing, mean face, muscular body and short bristly coat which bore the scars of many battles, added damning realism to the stereotypical statement made by its owners.

'Meet the neighbours.' Fletch rubbed his hands together and stepped out onto the walkway. 'Drug dealers, junkies, muggers, burglars, car thieves, bag snatchers. You can't tell 'em apart from the decent people. They all wear the same uniform and speak their own language. None of it makes sense… especially the language.'

The Staffy sat down and fixed his black eyes on Kennedy, watching him as he bolted the door shut, waiting for him to turn round. Instead of being piercing and spiteful they appeared to beseech compassion. Kennedy patted the dog on the head. A shrill whistle from one of the hoodies who had reached the end of the walkway was met with a cat-like meow from the Staffy who reluctantly got to his feet and sauntered slowly after them.

'It's always good to remind yourself of your roots.' As the

dog scuttled away, Kennedy smiled, stepping forward to lean on the walkway's concrete retaining wall and allowing his eyes to meander along the Thames. 'It still amazes me how close the West End is. The land of opportunity... so near and yet so far.'

Fletch shrugged his shoulders, there was nothing he could add to keep the conversation going. Somethings in life never changed.

'Enough said then.' Kennedy clapped his hands and changed the subject as they began walking to the lift. 'What you doing for a bird these days?'

Fletch grinned, winking his good eye and cracking his knuckles one-by-one. 'I've got this hard-bodied Thai brass called Blossom that sorts me out once a month for a Bullseye. I get the full works for that. Massage, blow job... even anal if I want it.'

As they reached the lift, Kennedy jabbed his finger at the illuminated call button. 'I'd never pay for it.'

'You've always paid for it.' Fletch put his ear to the lift door. 'You just never realised.'

'Poxy lift! Still on the blink after all these years.' Irately, Kennedy pushed the call button again.

Fletch ignored Kennedy's protests about the lift opting to lecture his friend sagely about the benefits of his monthly arrangement. 'All men really want to do is get their end away with a bird right? So why go to all that expense? My way there's no fancy dinner, no underwear, no engagement ring, no wedding, no honeymoon, no kids, no mother-in-law, no arguments and no affair.'

'I get it,' retorted Kennedy, snappy impatience giving way to a sigh of relief as a clunking whirring sound indicated the lift was finally on its way.

Fletch encircled his left arm as the door opened. 'And no divorce settlement. So... all-in-all, fifty quid a month is a fucking bargain.'

'Let me guess... she love you long time.' Kennedy's Thai

accent was poor enough to make Fletch laugh out loud.

'She's Thai not Welsh you wanker!'

* * *

'Sit down Mum, you're making me nervous.' Aimee flicked her long mane of blonde hair and patted the empty space next to her on the sofa. 'Come on it's still early.'

'I wish I still smoked,' replied Nicky, standing in front of the ornate fireplace that dominated her living room and studying her reflection in the large mirror that hung above it. Gently tanned, there was a delicate sheen to her skin, and her face, if you discounted the tattooed eyebrows and permanent eye and lip liner, was free of makeup. A vision of middle-aged beauty as her personal instructor at the gym had once called her. She blew a kiss at herself and sighed.

'I've got some Marlboro Lights if you're desperate,' offered her daughter-in-law Tess, cradling baby grandson Freddie in her arms as she walked to the window and looked out at the driveway.

'Nah. I'll leave it.' Nicky drummed the tips of her electric blue, bejewelled acrylic nail extensions on the mantelpiece. 'He'll be here soon enough.'

Freddie gurgled demanding attention from his mother.

'Yes my little lamb,' cooed Tess, turning to look at Nicky. 'Grandpa Kennedy is coming to see you today,' she continued, embellishing her words with girlish giggles.

Nicky frowned. 'Grandpa Kennedy! Stop it. You're making me feel old.'

'Give it up Nick. You look amazing.'

'Yeah Mum, you do. Let's hope Dad appreciates it.'

Nicky smiled, sashaying across to Tess and giving Freddie a kiss on the forehead.

'He's a proper little soldier ain't he Nick.'

'Let's hope not, poor mite. We don't want this little lamb becoming another Jones' sheep.'

A loud knock, knock, knock at the front door startled the women.

'Oh my God! Oh my God!' Nicky span on her heels and glanced in the mirror again ruffling her bobbed peroxide hair and pouting her lips.

'Dad!' exclaimed Aimee excitedly. 'I'll get it.'

Uniform or no uniform, Nicky knew a soldier when she saw one, and the colour drained from her cheeks when ashen-faced Aimee ushered a civilian-attired British Army Casualty Notification Officer into the living room.

'Mrs Jones... Captain Anthony Gilbert.'

There was a moment's silence.

"I regret to inform you..." No don't say it. Please. Nicky's mind whirled. "I'm sorry to inform you..." What was he going to say? She looked at the photograph of her son Jack on the wall and then at Freddie and Tess whose eyes had welled up with tears. "I have some bad news". She turned to face the sombrely-suited, grey-haired officer who appeared hesitant to speak. "I regret to inform you that your son has been killed". 'Please God! No no, don't say it,' she sobbed, clasping her brow.

Captain Gilbert cleared his throat. 'Mrs Jones. I'm here to inform you that your son has been injured ... er your son is injured but okay.'

'Thank God!' Nicky resisted the urge to fling her arms around the officer. 'What's happened to him? He's meant to be home on leave next week.'

'There was a serious incident yesterday evening while his unit was on foot patrol near Sangin in Helmand Province.'

'How serious?' asked Tess anxiously, cradling Freddie to her bosom as she spoke.

'There was an explosion. A roadside IED... that's an

Improvised Explosive Device. Four soldiers sustained life-threatening injuries. Jack suffered concussion and lacerations to the upper part of his body. He is fully conscious now and responding well to treatment… though there is some concern that his hearing may have been permanently damaged.'

'Lacerations?'

'Yes. Caused by shrapnel. There will be some scarring, but his eyesight and limbs are fine. He's in the field hospital at Camp Bastion. It's expected he should be able to fly home as planned.'

★ ★ ★

Kennedy had been parked across the road from Nicky's house for ten minutes. He'd said 6 p.m. and didn't want to be early in case she wasn't ready for him. He'd waited long enough, so a few more minutes wouldn't do any harm. His incarceration may have kept them apart, but they were still married. While Nicky had stood by him, he hoped she hadn't lain beside anyone else.

Prison visits had been few and far between, but that had been his decision. Sitting in his bare, naked, windowless, concrete Orwellian cell in Bellmarsh, he'd always been troubled by the thought of screws in the control room lusting after his wife as they'd watched her every move on CCTV as she made her way through the jail's fifteen gated security doors. Zooming in on her with remote cameras, finger printing her, body-searching her, checking the lining of her clothes, the soles of her feet, inside her mouth, inside anything else they chose to examine… and then wanking at the memory of her later. Filthy, dirty bastards!

Nicky could have provided the resources he needed to attempt an escape should he have had the motivation to do so, but he could see means and motive were always countered by surveillance. For a start, all correspondence and phone calls were monitored. The screws had their agenda, and he was always on it. And if he was on it, so was Nicky. To them he was just a number, A2311AA, on the National Offender Management Information System. To them she was real-life porn. Another tool with which to taunt him and fuck with his mind that apparently was brighter than he'd realised according to the prison psychologist who had analysed his numerous risk assessments.

"Jones has a university graduate level IQ of 118".

'Patronising cunt! Fuck off!'

"Jones is an anti-social criminal with extensive knowledge and experience of conflict and weapons".

Prime would have been reeling off the notes to the governor after he'd taken him down.

'Cunt!'

"Mr Jones is currently assessed as posing a high risk of harm to the public. The nature of this harm is that he will engage in threatening or actual violent and aggressive behaviour, which may result in serious psychological, emotional and physical harm".

'Bollocks! All of it!'

"Mr Jones is also currently assessed as posing a high risk of re-offending based on the nature and circumstance of his conviction, and the minimal work he has completed to date on his offending behaviour since sentence".

'Bastards!' If they wanted to keep you inside, they kept you inside, and the tests, statistics and percentages they produced were there to be manipulated. Throughout all the benching, crunching, squatting and stretching he'd done to sweat the emotional negativity out of his system, Kennedy couldn't help feeling he was somehow caught in the morass of a sinister conspiracy and he didn't want Nicky or any other member of his family to be drawn into it. Uncle Manny was enough to contend with.

Bleep Bleep Bleep 'Page 15 Letter A Word 17 Word 24'

'Talk of the devil.'

The text message refocused Kennedy, halting the downward spiral of his morale. He was a free man, but he didn't feel free. He picked up the poetry book on the passenger seat and decoded the message. An address. *15A Chivalry Road.* That was easy enough to remember, but he still scribbled it down in biro on the palm of his hand.

Bleep bleep bleep 'Never take your eyes off your opponent.'

No code. Not needed. Kennedy sighed. The expression was like a thin film of glue that bound the Jones family together. If only his father had paid more heed to it. He checked his watch, 6 p.m. As he readied himself to get out of the car, he glanced out of the window and saw a man leaving Nicky's house.

'Slag!' Kennedy rapped a clenched fist against the steering wheel. 'I fucking knew it!' He caught a glimpse of Nicky waving and perhaps blowing a kiss before closing the door. He couldn't be sure, but the way his mind had been working that's what he supposed. The temptation to confront the man as he made his way to the end of the drive where his car, a black Volkswagen Golf, was parked, was overridden by the information he'd received earlier. He still had work to do. He was on license. He had to stay out of trouble.

He studied the man's features briefly. There was something familiar about the thin pointed nose and hollowed cheeks, but he'd been too far away and in a matter of moments he'd got into his car and driven away.

'BD06THX' Kennedy texted the registration number of the VW to Manny. Throughout his sentence, he'd tormented himself with thoughts that Nicky was sleeping around. Not only was she stunningly attractive, she was also a very physical person. Sex was important to her. She'd said she hadn't. Occasionally his mother had convinced him that she wouldn't. Mother and her unwritten widow's vow of chastity, it was a nice sentiment. But mother and Nicky were at opposite ends of the spectrum when it came to relationships. Passive to passionate with nothing in between make no mistake.

Bleep bleep bleep. 'Info tomorrow'

Kennedy hadn't seen enough of the man's face, but a name would help. Names and faces, he was good at that. 'Who was that then Nicky? Your boyfriend?' Sarcasm wouldn't be the best way to start a conversation, to rekindle love... or at the most basic level to get laid, and that's what he wanted more than anything. Well almost. He stared at the address he'd written down on the palm of his hand. Payback, retribution, retaliation. Revenge in all its guises was a powerful emotion, more powerful than jealousy. Maybe Fletch had the right philosophy when it came to affairs of the heart. His hands felt clammy. He looked at his palms and saw beading sweat beginning to blur the biro ink. As he rubbed them together, the address he'd written down dissolved into an illegible smudge. It didn't matter. 15A Chivalry Road was mentally noted.

'Chivalry? Was that a fucking joke or what? Courteousness, courage, loyalty. That's what chivalry meant didn't it? Yes!' His mouth felt dry as he muttered to himself. Right now he needed that first drink and then another one and one more after that. Visiting Nicky could wait until tomorrow once he knew the identity of her boyfriend. He turned the key in the ignition and revved the Jag's engine. The crooked path that was his life had taken another turn and he had no idea where it was heading.

★ ★ ★

'Perfect!' Kennedy couldn't have asked for better. He could have been more patient... maybe. Got to see Nicky, all of her... maybe. He could have waited... maybe. He could even have gone with Fletch to the massage parlour... maybe.

But this was a result... no maybes about it. The woman's pale skin glistened with sweat as he lifted himself up and paused to catch his breath.

'Don't stop you dirty fucker,' she said gutturally, bucking her hips.

He held her down and admired her small perfectly formed breasts and large nipples that were crimson from being suckled, chewed, bitten and tweaked. Every inch of her flesh was firm yet silky. Slim, slender limbs easy to overpower and dominate. Her face was still freckled, soft hair still a mousy brown, blue eyes wide open... sparkling with lust.

'Come on Kennedy. Harder this time. I want you to come for me.'

The woman opened her mouth and jutted out her pierced tongue. That had been a new experience for him. How she loved playing the dirty slut. Life was still full of surprises, not all of them bad. He'd thought about fucking her years ago. But she'd been lost to his memory... until last night. In the Duchess, having a drink with Fletch. Vodka might have got the better of him, but as far as he was concerned he'd had a right touch. Instant karma.

'You don't remember me do you?'

'Should I?'

'You should.'

The woman had looked familiar. Familiar and horny, or was it just horny? 'I should. But I've been away for a while.'

'Trina.'

'Trina Jackson?'

The woman had smiled and winked at him.

'Trina Jackson! Well fuck me!'

'Maybe. If you play your cards right.'

Their embrace was immediate, warm, giving. Kennedy had breathed in her familiar tobacco-tainted musky aroma. She'd

cooed as she'd pressed herself against his groin. 'Mmm…
perhaps I've had one to many Pinot's tonight. You wouldn't
dare take advantage of me now would you?'

It would have been rude not to. Kennedy lowered
himself and met her mouth with his, grunting as he thrust
himself inside her. His fingers clawed their way down her
back, gripping at the cheeks of her arse, pulling her thighs
open. She lifted her legs to encircle him, to take him in
deep.

'Fuck me! Fuck me! Fuck me!'

Kennedy winced as Trina clawed his back with her
fingernails.

'Fuck me! Fuck me! Fuck me!'

He may have considered himself fit. But she was working
him hard. Panting from the exertion, he closed his eyes and
pumped her rhythmically, faster and faster.

'Fuck me! Fuck me! Fuck me!'

She writhed and quivered beneath him as his engorged,
sex-starved manhood stretched her moist vagina. Eighteen
years perfecting the art of masturbation proved one thing.
Fantasy was no substitute for reality. A five knuckle shuffle
and a vivid imagination were no substitute for a warm, wet,
velvety snatch pulsating with desire. The bulbous head of his
cock pressed against her cervix again and again.

'Fuck me! Fuck me! Fuck me!'

She felt every sinew of his body tense. He felt her
contractions begin.

'Argghhhhhh!'

Kennedy shuddered as he climaxed. Groaning as waves of
pleasure rippled through his body. Jerking his neck up as he
ejaculated repeatedly.

Trina closed her eyes and rocked her head back, tensing
her undulating stomach. 'Ohhhh!' Her orgasm was so
powerful, she felt herself blacking out. 'Ohhhh!' Losing

control. 'Fuck me! Fuck me! Fuck me! Ohhhh!' She was awash as Kennedy kept pounding her until he was spent. 'Ohhhh. Oh my God!'

Energy sapped, bathed in sweaty, sticky, sexy secretions, they lay there, limbs entwined, silent and satisfied.

DUBS OR B?

12 December 2006

'Shit! What time is it?' Kennedy cursed as he opened his eyes slowly, squinting at the sunlight beaming through the naked window. Easing himself out of Trina's embrace he got out of bed and made his way to the pile of clothes lying on the floor. Finding his trousers, he retrieved the wristwatch he'd put in his pocket. 9.20 a.m. 'Bollocks!'

'What is it babe?'

'I've got to get round to Nicky's.'

Trina arched her back and yawned. 'I thought you said she was with someone else.'

'Yeah! Well…'

'Yeah! Well what?'

'I need to see her.'

Trina sat up, crossed her legs, and slowly rubbed her hands down her body resting them on the insides of her thighs. 'After eighteen years, a few more hours ain't gonna make much difference.'

'You don't understand.' Kennedy eyed Trina's breasts navel and sex. The sap was rising in his loins again.

'I didn't hear you asking for understanding last night big boy.'

'You didn't hear nothing.'

Trina puckered up her lips and blew a kiss. 'There's plenty more where that came from love,' she drawled huskily.

Kennedy's little head was trying to rule his big head. The temptation to fuck Trina again, to spend all day fucking her, was raising his libido, but the 'love' word was castrating his thoughts.

'Don't call me love.'

'Why?' Trina grinned impudently, rapping the stud that pierced her tongue repeatedly against her teeth.

'I don't believe in love.'

Trina sat up and drew her knees up to her chin. 'Blimey! Listen to you Kennedy Jones. God's gift.'

'You know what I mean.'

'Don't worry Granddad... I'm not looking for a relationship.'

Trina lifted her legs over the side of the bed and stood up. Kennedy admired her lithe body and smiled at the bite marks, scratches and bruises forming on her skin. Suddenly, he felt bad. Guilty even. He wanted to hold her and kiss her nicely. A polite thank you. But then he caught sight of his back reflected in the mirror. The evidence of their sexual encounter was plain enough to see. Her talon-like nails had left scarlet welts from the nape of his neck to his backside. There was no point saying anything, plus he couldn't think of anything to say apart from 'fuck me' and she'd already done that.

★ ★ ★

By the time he'd finished showering and returned to the bedroom, Trina was gone. No ciao, no fond farewell, no lingering kiss, nothing. Not even a phone number hastily scrawled in lipstick on the mirror. Kennedy smiled, savouring the memory of her salty taste. He knew where to find her if he wanted her again. Shit, shower, shave. All done. Dressed now, and ready to go toe-to-toe with whatever the free world was going to throw at him. Money would help. He laughed at the fact he'd left the holdall containing the cash Manny had given him on the floor by the front door. Trina might have got nosey. But she hadn't, the money was still there, all of it. He placed the bag carefully under the false floor in the hall cupboard that housed the electricity and gas meters. Boxed and locked, the bank of Kennedy. Safe!

The walkway outside the flat seemed different in the daytime. Less threatening, less oppressive... even the lift worked properly. He hadn't paid much attention to it yesterday, but the graffiti that covered the drab grey concrete wall by the lock ups added a touch of colour, life and personality to the cul-de-sac that was otherwise lacking. He studied the wall as he unlocked the garage door and pushed it up and over. He had no idea what any of the gaudy images and slogans referred to with the exception of one comprised of three stark words that darkened his mood immediately.

FUCK THE ARMY

What was the relevance? Here of all places.

FUCK THE ARMY

The spray paint appeared fresh. Why now? He stepped forward and felt glass crunching underfoot. Looking down he saw a used syringe, cracked and broken. Next to it another, and there, one more. Adjacent to the wall, countless cigarette butts, foil wrappers, empty beer cans and used condoms littered the crumbling tarmac. The evidence was damning. Here, free from the prying eyes of CCTV, junkie whores plied their trade for one more fix.

FUCK THE ARMY

Kennedy swallowed hard. In his mind he pictured Jack marching along a sun-baked dusty track that snaked through a serene pastel-coloured poppy field. Courage and determination were etched into his face along with something else that he knew only too well... the pain of war. Is that what the graffiti related to? The poppy heartland, and the opium trade which resulted in cheap Afghan heroin being sold on streets of London?

FUCK THE ARMY

The British Army, bravely fighting the Taliban insurgents and terrorists funded by illicit crops of poppies? Poppies and insurgency were conjoined like evil Siamese twins, bastards at that! Eradicate one to starve the other and, as a consequence, stem the supply of smack to Britain. Kennedy bent down and ran the index finger of his right hand along each letter, spelling it out slowly.

FUCK THE ARMY

A smouldering landscape framed his mind. In it Jack and his platoon were coming under fire as a poppy field burned. He could see, hear, touch smell and taste the battle... and he could sense it was a lot nearer than at first it seemed.

'Fuck the Army Cuz ha ha.'

Kennedy stood up and span round on his heels. Two wiry-framed men, one slightly taller than the other, both similarly attired in grey hooded tops, baggy jeans and trainers faced him. Sat on the floor behind them sniffing the air inquisitively was the brindle Staffordshire bull terrier he'd seen on the walkway outside his flat the previous day.

'What did you say?'

'You lookin' for food bruv?'

Kennedy narrowed his eyes as he looked at the scabbed, scarred, pockmarked face of the taller man who had just spoken.

'Wha gwan?' asked his similarly featured associate, cracked lips moving to reveal nicotine-stained rotting teeth.

Simmering with contained rage, Kennedy thought quickly as he sized the two men up. 'I'm after some gear.'

'We've got the best food Cuz. Dubs or B?' The shorter man folded his arms as he reeled off his scant menu.

'Both.'

'You want four on four?'

'Yeah! That's exactly what I need.'

The taller man went to reach in his pocket.

'Not out here.' Kennedy marked time, pointing at the empty garage. The dealers winked at each other as he turned to walk towards it. Last night, he'd left the Jaguar parked in the NCP on Garratt Lane. Having witnessed Nicky's apparent deceit, drinking had been at the top of his agenda and Fletch had suggested parking the Jag there and forgetting about it for the evening. After several large vodkas and getting reacquainted with Trina, Fletch had taken the keys off him just to be sure. He hadn't been able to get hold of him this morning and was pleased Manny had told him there was a spare set in the large tool chest at the back of the lockup.

Sensing the men behind him, Kennedy pulled the wad of fifty-pound notes from his jacket pocket. It was all about timing now. A price for the drugs hadn't been agreed. He knew from prison that 'B' represented Brown... heroin. 'Dubs', like the street slang the dealers used, was lost on him. For now though, it didn't matter. He turned, held the money up and watched their hollow eyes widen.

'Will this cover it?'

'You been making serious paper blud.' The shorter man dropped his hands by his sides as he spoke.

Kennedy felt his hackles rising. The dealers were bracing themselves to mug him, he could see that, but he'd wait to react. Let them make the first move.

'Where are you from?'

'From right here cuz.'

'Why don't you speak fucking English then?'

The shorter man flicked out his right arm. In his hand was a lock knife.

'Man is gonna get dashed,' snarled his accomplice, raising his fists.

The knifeman lunged at Kennedy, but he was ready. Reflexes, hand to eye coordination, speed, strength and aggression. His mind whirred. 'CHAAARGE!' As the voice inside his head screamed the order, he burst forward grabbing the knifeman's wrist with his left hand while powerfully drilling his right fist into the side of his neck.

'CHAAARGE!' Louder and louder, over and over.

'CHAAARGE!' The man dropped the knife and collapsed to his knees. The targeted punch had struck the carotid sinus with such force he was already brain dead before Kennedy's knee connected with the point of his chin sending him reeling backwards. As he fell, his head smashed against the concrete floor fracturing his skull. It had taken a matter of seconds, but it was precious time the second dealer had failed to take advantage of. Perception and reactions dulled from using the drugs he was supposed to be selling meant the he was too slow in deciding what to do next.

Fight or flight? Fight! Too late! 'Never take your eyes off your opponent.' As the dealer pulled a knife from his pocket Kennedy's right foot connected with his groin rupturing his testicles. Pain and nausea were immediate. As he groaned in agony, Kennedy grabbed his knife-wielding arm and jerked it violently upwards snapping his collarbone.

'You say fuck the Army eh!'

One final anguished cry and the dealer was silenced by a right hook to the temple that rendered him unconscious. As he fell, Kennedy caught him in a side headlock snapping his neck back, breaking it, and severing his spinal cord.

'I say fuck you both!'

Kennedy flung the dealer's body to the floor. The only sounds he could hear now were his heart pounding in his chest and the Staffy lapping at the pool of crimson blood that was thickening on the floor by his first victim's head.

Bleep Bleep Bleep

'Shit!' The text message alert distracted him from the murderous scene he had just created with his bare hands. 'Fucking shit!' He didn't bother looking at his phone as he remembered he'd left the poetry book in the Jag's glove compartment. Quickly, he dragged the bodies of the two dead men to the rear of the garage and covered them with a tarpaulin. The Staffy sat on its haunches and watched intently licking the last traces of blood from its lips.

'Man's best friend eh.' Kennedy smiled as the dog followed him out of the garage. 'You're not going to bubble me up are you?' He reached up, swung the up and over door shut and locked it.

FUCK THE ARMY

He stared at the graffiti covered wall. The words seemed less prominent now. He'd paint them out later. He'd done his bit for the Queen and for the Country also. Who among the moral majority wouldn't applaud the courage of his actions? The Staffy looked at him apathetically and yawned, lolling his tongue out and shaking his head. Maybe he didn't get it. Probably just as well. He checked his watch. 10.15 a.m. It was a brisk twenty-minute walk to the NCP, if the dog was still with him when he got there he'd buy him a decent breakfast.

He needed one himself. Full English. Two fried eggs, sausage, bacon, beans, tomatoes, toast… the works. Handsome. At the end of the cul-de-sac, he paused to gaze up at the tower block. He'd been out of prison less than twenty-four hours, what would the next twenty-four bring? Fuck breakfast! What he really needed was another drink.

* * *

'Thought I would've heard from him by now.' Manny clicked his fingers impatiently and glanced at the mobile phone on his desk. 'Mind you, I heard he was busy last night… and not with the Missus.'

Jester looked up from the newspaper he was reading and flicked his fringe. 'Had some bird from the drinker wrapped around him.' His manner of speech betrayed a lack of interest. 'I see Jacobsen topped himself,' he continued, changing the subject, holding the paper up and pointing at a headline that read *CORRUPT FORMER POLICE OFFICER IN PRISON SUICIDE*.

'Elvis is dead.' Manny winked as he replied. 'And the Beatles have split up.'

'I know, I know. And…'

Manny interrupted Jester. 'And it's a shame it took so long to organise. The same goes for Kennedy. The fact he's ruled by his cock just like his father was doesn't help him, but it helps me.'

Jester walked across the office to the window, folded the newspaper and placed it on the sill. 'Not my thing, but apparently she's a right sort.'

'So's Nicky! She'd regret having kept her legs closed for the last eighteen years if she knew the score. He'll be hoping she never finds out.'

'Not sure what happened last night. According to the tracking device, he was at her house for thirty minutes or so and then came back to town. The Jag's still in the NCP where he parked it.'

'What time was that?'

'What?'

'When he was at Nicky's?'

'5.50 p.m. until 6.08 p.m.'

Manny picked up the mobile phone and scrolled through the text messages. 'That's when he asked for the brief on that motor registered to Anthony Gilbert. Did you find anything else out about him?'

'Yeah! He's fifty-two and a Captain in the Army.'

'An officer and a gentleman eh. Maybe Nicky's not so innocent after all.'

Manny turned his attention to the computer on his desk looking at the screen as he tapped the keys. 'I know it's not your thing, but have a butchers at this.' He beckoned Jester over. 'Dirty little slut.'

The images on the screen were grainy but clear enough to make out Trina Jackson lying on a bed with her legs apart masturbating.

★ ★ ★

'Have you managed to speak to him yet?' There was a hint of concern in Vera's voice, but busying herself preparing breakfast for Bertie was keeping her mind occupied as it did every morning.

'About Jack?' Bertie smiled as she placed a plate crammed with perfectly cooked rashers of bacon, scrambled eggs and baked beans onto the kitchen table in front of him.

'Er no Vee. Well not properly.' Bertie looked across the kitchen at Fletch and raised his eyebrows. 'He's on his mobile, it's a bad signal.'

Vera frowned, she had no idea what Bertie was talking about. Modern technology was a mystery to her. 'Hopefully he'll phone when he's off his mobile then.' She turned to the cooker and picked up the frying pan, shaking the sausages and sizzling them in their own juices. 'Plenty here for you Paul. Come on, have some. Don't pretend you're not hungry.'

Fletch laughed, nobody called him Paul anymore. Dear old Vera, bless her. She'd been through a lot. Never complained. Said everything that happened in life was God's will. Husband murdered? Son banged up for murder? Grandson blown up. He didn't do religion, but even if he did he knew he'd struggle with her reliance on the Bible to explain the meaning and purpose of life.

'Double fried egg? Cumberland sausage?'

Fletch didn't have to say yes. Licking his lips and smiling provided the approval Vera sought, and she swiftly cracked two eggs into the frying pan. Clearly there was nothing in the good book about the merits of eating a full English breakfast. God may have created the world and everything in it, but he couldn't take credit for the scrumptious nosebag Vera was preparing which was ready in a matter of seconds.

'Go on son.' Bertie paused to shovel a forkful of baked beans into his mouth. 'You can't beat Vee's fry-ups. Kennedy doesn't know what he's missing.'

'I expect he's forgotten.' Vera sighed as she dished up.

'He's forgotten nothing.' Fletch picked up a bottle of tomato ketchup from the table and tapped it in anticipation. 'Especially not you my love.'

'I don't understand though.' A wistful expression formed on Vera's face as she walked over to the far side of the kitchen table where Fletch was sat. 'Why didn't he come and see me last night. He never went to Nicky's. She rang wondering where he was and told me the news about Jack.'

'I know what you're thinking but...' Fletch paused to clear his throat. 'It's not like that. He was upset by something and a little edgy so it was the best he didn't see either of you yesterday. The world's changed since he last tasted freedom. A drink was what he needed.'

'Ah yes. He's a Jones boy isn't he? Silly me. Got a problem? Have a drink, and another… and another and then one more. Problem solved.' Vera wasn't noted for her use of sarcasm so her spiteful words confounded Fletch and Bertie in particular.

'That's a bit harsh. He's got…'

'I know what you're going to say. What happened to all of you was shocking and undeserved. But thanks to the Lord you have come through distressing times.' Vera spoke calmly and confidently before clasping the crucifix of the Rosary necklace she was wearing and closing her eyes. *"Peace I leave with you, my peace I give unto you: not as the world giveth, give I unto you. Let not your heart be troubled, neither let it be afraid."* (John 14:27)

Bertie let Vera finish her sermon. He always did. But her viewpoint angered him. 'If you, the Lord… and all his disciples had been Mount Longdon, you'd have a better understanding of our distressing times. Peace ha ha. I'm in pieces for fu…'

'Mind your ham.' Fletch rapped his plate with his knife and glared at Bertie. 'Not in front of Vee she don't deserve it. Not after everything she's done for you mate.'

'I'm so sorry. That was selfish of me.' As she walked across to Bertie, Vera's eyes welled up with tears. 'I wasn't thinking.' She bent down and put her arm around him. 'What I was trying to say is that you two seem to have found some kind of peace whereas my Kennedy, just like his father and his grandfather before him, still believes that solace is to be found at the bottom of a bottle… and all those years in prison have changed nothing.'

Bertie felt a lump forming in his throat. He wanted to apologise, but couldn't find the words.

Fletch, realising it had been a folly to mention Kennedy having a drink, thought about restoring normality with a bit of humour by asking for some 'Holy Ghost' but not wanting to offend Vera, he decided against the use of religion-slanted rhyming slang. He stared at his plate. There was merit in everything that had been said. Truth, understanding and compassion went together just like the sausage and eggs he was now smothering with ketchup. 'This looks lovely Vee. Any chance of some toast, I'm Hank Marvin.'

★ ★ ★

'What did they call you then?' Kennedy pulled the Jag's handbrake and looked across at the Staffy sat on the passenger seat. 'Something fucking stupid like Rambo or Rocky or Tyson?'

The dog sniffed the air nonchalantly.

'Oh I see, like that is it?'

Without a collar, identification was impossible. Orphaned by his previous owners, this was a new beginning for the mutt, and why not? Everyone deserves a fresh start in life, even a dog.

'How about Spot?' Kennedy glanced at his watch as he patted the Staffy's head. 1.17 p.m. 'As good a name as any eh?' The dog squealed in a meow-like fashion. 'Come on then Spot. Now's a time as good as any, let's face this together.'

The house was impressive from the outside. A sweeping in-and-out key block driveway cut through a verdant lawn bordered by tall manicured Leylandii hedgerows. Rosebushes climbed the neatly pointed brickwork, and a Wisteria vine snaked across the russet-tiled roof overhang of a wide-open porch that was supported by Romanesque columns. In the full blossom of summer it would look stunning. Spot cocked his leg against one of the columns in appreciation.

As he approached the oak panelled front door, Kennedy paused and stared at the identical stained glass side scree leaded lights that depicted a tree interwoven with poppies.

A sense of deja vu brushed his mind, but he couldn't put his finger on why and the thought soon passed as he wondered who was responsible for maintaining the property. Anthony Gilbert perhaps? Now he had the name, he'd placed the face. At the time he'd requested to be discharged from the Army, Gilbert had been the Regimental Administrative Officer, one of a number of people who had interviewed him as part of the leaving process. He'd seemed all right, an honest man doing an honest job. Trying to help. Fucking backdoor merchant more like. Kennedy cursed his lack of judgment and, ignoring the doorbell, rapped his knuckles firmly on the door. He was just about to knock again when it opened.

'BASTARD!' Nicky screamed, slapping him across the face catching him unawares. Spot barked his disapproval loudly, but she ignored him. 'I thought you got out yesterday,' she snarled, hand raised ready to strike again.

'I did.' Kennedy remained calm, catching her flailing arm and holding it firmly. 'I came round but you had company.'

Spot stopped barking and sat on his haunches gazing up at the two protagonists.

'Company? What fucking company?' Nicky rocked her head back slightly as she locked eyes with Kennedy, struggling in vain as he snatched her free hand with his.

He'd always been attracted to her feistiness, but the tone of her voice was more aggressive than the one he remembered chiding him for rucking at the football or staying out late drinking. Some welcome home considering he was the one who'd been wronged. Spot yelped, outwardly encouraging further dialogue from his new master.

'You always had a soft spot for a man in uniform.'

Nicky looked puzzled.

'It's a shame it wasn't a prison uniform.'

'What are you talking about?'

'Anthony Gilbert. How long have you been fucking him?'

'Gilbert… Anthony Gilbert! You mean, the Army officer who was here yesterday?'

'No the man on the fucking moon.'

'You idiot. He was here about Jack.'

'What about Jack?'

As Nicky began to sob, the realisation that he'd completely misinterpreted the situation dawned on Kennedy immediately. Face flushed with concern, he released her arms and embraced her.

* * *

'Remember this?' Nicky flicked the remote control at the stereo and turned the volume up.

Kennedy shook his head as she hummed the opening bars of *'I forgot to be your lover'* by William Bell. The sex would have been better if he'd saved himself. Nicky wanted it hard, just like he'd given it to Trina. There was nothing better than kiss-and-make-up fucking, channelling anger into passion. Fortunately, it hadn't taken long. There had been no slow seduction, no undressing, no foreplay and thankfully no chance for Nicky's mouth to wander, to lick and nip and suck and notice the legacy of Trina's sharp acrylic nails as she'd roamed across his body.

Shared tears at the explanation of Captain Anthony Gilbert's presence at the house the previous day had been followed by up-against-the-wall, tongue-in-mouth kissing, hand-up-skirt groping, belt-unbuckling, trousers-round-the-ankles, knickers-pulled-to-one-side, frantic coupling.

'I love you Kennedy, I've missed you so much.'

'Nicky… Nicky!'

'Kennedy… Kennedy!'

Heaving breaths, beating hearts, thrusting, grinding…

coming together quickly and with perfect timing. Spot, looking on, meowed like a cat. They both laughed. It had been an eventful day for the dog. Good job for Kennedy he couldn't speak. Nicky cozied into his arms as they lay on the hand-dyed navy blue leather sofa in the tastefully furnished living room. Centre table, side chairs, shelves, lamps, photos in frames, paintings, stereo system, television set. Nothing appeared out of place and everything looked expensive. It was a beautiful space in which to relax and enjoy the afterglow of great sex, and it made the Southern Comfort and lemonade he was sipping taste better than he'd ever remembered. Sweeter somehow. Vulgar vodka consumption wasn't on the agenda, just a decent drink and sharing a nice Benson and Hedges.

'I forgot to be your lover'. He remembered now. He hadn't completely forgotten. Just hadn't heard it in years. Not since their wedding day when it had been the first dance at their reception. It was an old erection section number from when they'd first courted at discos while still at school. The words weren't exactly matrimonial, but they were sung soulfully by a man who clearly understood what it took to make things better in a relationship. He looked at Nicky and ran the fingers of his free hand through her hair, frowning as he recalled his wedding vows and how he'd broken most of them.

"Will you love her, comfort her, honour and protect her, and, forsaking all others, be faithful to her as long as you both shall live?" His eyes moistened as feelings of guilt washed over him.

'You remember the tune now don't you?' Nicky squeezed his thigh.

'For better, for worse.' Kennedy nodded, kissing her on the side of her head. 'Till death us do part.'

'You missed a bit.'

'Yeah well, you know me Nick. I've never been that good

with words.' His self-reproach ebbed, and sentiment flowed. 'If I could find a way to change the past I would, but that ain't gonna happen now.'

Nicky sat up and looked at him, scrutinising his face for tell tale signs of sincerity. 'You'll be saying you're sorry next.'

Kennedy drained the contents of the tumbler he was holding and shook it so the ice rattled against the glass while he thought about what he was going to say. He didn't take long, placing the tumbler on the floor before he spoke. 'Sorry? Sorry for what?'

Regretting her words, Nicky remained silent. She knew Kennedy hated sarcasm but hoped he wouldn't spoil the moment.

'Sorry for fighting for Queen and Country? There was no anger in the inflection of his words, just pain. 'Sorry for wanting to give my family the best in life? Sorry for the consequences of that? Sorry for going to Prison?'

Nicky's mouth felt dry. She swallowed hard and bit her bottom lip in a vain attempt to stem the flow of tears she had begun to cry.

'I could say sorry for many things I've done in life that need an apology.' Kennedy paused and closed his eyes, overcome by the raw emotion of expressing his feelings with words rather than actions. The events of the past day flashed before him. He couldn't explain what had happened, let alone apologise for what he had done. There would be no understanding and no second chance. Third chance even, or was it a fourth or fifth. He considered saying more, but instead he embraced Nicky pulling her down onto him, seeking her mouth with his. Sex was inevitable. Slower this time. He opened his eyes and winced as she raked his back with her fingernails as he entered her. Trina's handiwork could be passed off as hers now. Thank heaven for small mercies.

SUICIDE

13 December 2006

leep Bleep Bleep The text message alert had failed to distract Kennedy from the morose train of thought that ensnared him as he'd driven away from Nicky's house. She'd seemed happy enough, but in a selfish way. Maybe he'd over analysed their situation. It was possible. He hadn't slept well, drifting in and out of consciousness, fretting, fidgeting, twitching, tossing and turning. Night-time hours passed the slowest of all when insomnia struck, and the news about Jack had heightened nocturnal anxiety stimulated by evaluating the consequences of neglecting his duty as a father. He'd resisted the temptation to get up and drink himself to sleep. He could do without Nicky nagging him about alcohol dependency. The funny thing was he hadn't touched a drop in prison despite it being readily available. Booze numbed the senses. Behind bars you needed your wits about you at all times, outside there was more control, less threat. Having said that, it was violence and death that preoccupied his mind which was still blighted by vivid flashbacks of battles and bloody murders.

The drug dealers. Had slaying them been necessary? Killing in the name of what? A throw away comment about the Army? His interpretation of the graffiti by the lockup? Kennedy Jones, urban vigilante. Was that his uncontrollable future? Maybe it was the change in routine, the vodka… a lack of self-esteem. He'd only been out for forty-eight hours, but already he felt remorseful and isolated. Eighteen years thinking about freedom… and when it finally arrived

191

it seemed pointless. The world had moved on, his family and friends had changed. They appeared more mature, well-rounded, capable. He'd been left behind in the past. Maybe he needed more time. Maybe he needed to sample again that euphoric feeling of release that he'd felt fucking Trina. Maybe he needed another drink. Maybe he needed to kill again. Maybe he needed to kill himself.

Feeling, thought, behaviour. He turned the Jag's stereo up to full volume. It was the only Cognitive Behavioural Therapy he could think of. Peter Coyne, The Godfathers lead singer, viscerally belting out *'This Damn Nation'*, the second track on their 1986 debut album *'Hit by Hit'*. Fletch had bought the compact disc for him. A surprise, he'd found it in the pocket of his new leather jacket. The Godfathers were probably the most underrated rock band in the world, they'd seen them play live plenty of times. It was always a great show.

'I'm tired of life. I am tired of this life. When I lay down on my bed, with a gun pressed to my head.' Coyne always had his feelings nailed. *'This Damn Nation. This frustration. This Damn Nation.'* 23 December 1986. Almost twenty years ago. A Godfathers gig at the Marquee, the last time he'd seen them live. *'All alone, I am all alone. I cry at night, so all alone.'* Life was less complicated then. They'd had a good drink. It was Christmas. *'This Damn Nation. This frustration. This Damn Nation.'* They always had a good drink. *'Five, four, three, two, one.'*

Kennedy parked up in Battersea Park Road and switched the engine off. Silence. *'This Damn Nation'*, he wondered if it had a double meaning? This Damnation would be equally appropriate. Could he be related to Peter Coyne? Coyne was his mother's maiden name. Maybe that's why he felt drawn to the band and their music. He looked at Spot the dog and then out of the passenger window. He could see the street sign for St Mary's church. Cognitive Behavioural Therapy hadn't worked for long. His head was filled with negative thoughts again. He got out of the car and waited for Spot to join him on the pavement before closing the door.

When he'd said goodbye to Nicky earlier, she'd asked him when she would see him again? That fresh start she spoke of, did she mean it? Were her tears genuine? Plus, she wanted to know everything.

"What are you going to do now? Where are you going? Who are you meeting?"

It felt like an interrogation. There were too many questions. There was too much to cope with. 'Take good care of yourself,' he'd said as he'd embraced her on the doorstep. 'Give my love to everyone.' It sounded like a last farewell.

"You are coming back aren't you?"

He repeated Nicky's last words and pictured her as he'd seen her waving goodbye when he'd turned to walk away. Was it a question that highlighted her concern?

"You are coming back aren't you?"

Shiny blonde hair piled up on the top of her head. White towelling robe covering lithe, tanned limbs but showing just a little bit too much cleavage. That impudent smile betrayed her thoughts. It was a rhetorical question surely.

'What do you think Spot?'

Kennedy dropped to his haunches to stroke the dog. He knew he wasn't going to get a reply, and that was a relief because the last thing he needed right now was a second opinion.

It took longer than he thought it would to find his father's grave, though St Mary's was exactly as he remembered it. Weathered red and brown bricks, arched stained and enamel glass windows, decorative stone quoins, coves, cornices and columns and the distinctive octagonal wooden steeple. There was something comforting about its anachronistic presence, but the black painted wrought iron gates that led to the graveyard and the spearheaded railings that surrounded it appeared new. Disturbing. Ominous. Prison-like. A final sentence for the souls of the departed from which there would be no escape.

Kennedy shivered as he traversed the flagstone path that weaved between the weed encroached graves. Neglected for generations by mourners who had themselves long since passed away, the cracked, crumbling, mould-covered headstones with eroded inscriptions barely legible, jutted like rotten teeth at haphazard angles from the coarse grass. Eventually, as he reached the corner of the cemetery where the more recently departed were buried, the headstones straightened up, standing to attention, respecting the fresh floral tributes laid in memory of the precious ones that lay at peace in the soil below.

And suddenly, there he was. Dad.

IN LOVING MEMORY
ALEC JONES
THE PARACHUTE REGIMENT
DEARLY LOVED HUSBAND AND FATHER

His father's name engraved neatly in gold lettering into white marble. The fragrant flowers arranged neatly in three urns adjacent to the headstone were beautiful. Every Sunday Vera tended the grave. Red roses, yellow roses, nasturtium, forget-me-nots and poppies. Each in turn symbolised love, friendship, patriotism, memories and eternal sleep. Though she'd written often to tell him of this while he was in prison, Kennedy couldn't be certain which were the nasturtiums and which were the forget-me-nots. Another failing to add to the list of personal let-downs he'd been compiling that was lengthening like the shadow of the church tower across the graveyard as the winter sun began to dip over the horizon.

Bleep Bleep Bleep He'd forgotten to acknowledge the earlier text message from Manny. Now he had a reminder. *'Page 11'*

Was that it? A whole page, it had to be a mistake. He checked the previous message. *'Page 11'*

The poetry book was in his jacket pocket. He opened it and flicked to page eleven. Beyond deciphering the code, previously he hadn't paid any attention to the content, now he had to. The page was headed *'The Fallen'* by James Coyne. James Coyne his maternal grandfather? No. Surely it was just a coincidence. Or was it? He read the poem slowly.

> *'We, the fallen, lie here dead. We did not choose our fate. We wanted to live, to return to the land of our birth. Without knowing, we took life for granted for we were young. Without knowing, we let them take our lives. We, the fallen, lie here dead.'*

There was a haunting hopelessness about the sentences that summed up the futility of war and the tragedy of young men sent into battle. They say that only the good die young. Maybe he wasn't good enough. Maybe his life was a punishment just like his prison sentence had been. *'We, the fallen, lie here dead.'* He read the poem again and looked at his father's headstone.

DIED APRIL 22 1978 AGED 39 YEARS
WE WHO MISS YOU NEVER FORGET
REST IN PEACE

Thirty-nine was young. Any age was young if you suffered a brutal death in conflict. *'We did not choose our fate. We wanted to live, to return to the land of our birth.'* What about the survivors? *'Without knowing, we took life for granted for we were young.'* What about Fletch, Bertie, Jack and all the others? *'Without knowing, we let them take our lives.'* He read the poem a final time as he contemplated the meaning of life, and the permanence of death. Did the dead really rest in peace? Nobody knew the answer. He could find out, but he wouldn't be able to pass on his findings.

★ ★ ★

'Get in there my son!' exclaimed Bertie ebulliently; rapping his hand on the kitchen table hard enough to make the portable radio he was listening to fall on its side. *'Who let the Drog out?'* he continued, chanting loudly. *'Who? Who?'*

'Have they scored?' Vera looked up from the pot of tea she was making.

'Yeah! Sounded like a good move. Started by Robben, Sheva played Drogba in. Boom! Chelsea 1 Newcastle United 0. Fletch will be well pleased. He had a bullseye on Drogba to score first. Must have soiled himself when Mourinho only named him as a sub.'

'Sounds good love.' Vera placed a steaming mug of tea and a saucer of digestive biscuits in front of Bertie. 'If only I knew what you were talking about.'

'Actually, I was talking to your son.' Bertie smiled and pointed at Kennedy who was staring blankly at the screen of his mobile phone. 'Oi Oi. Penny for your thoughts mate.'

Kennedy looked up and frowned. 'You'd need more than a penny,' he said sullenly, cursing himself with his next thoughts for leaving the poetry book in the Jag. *'The Fallen'* by James Coyne. It was a short poem. He wanted to learn it quickly so he could recite it to his mother, to gauge her reaction. Had her father written the poem, surely she would have known of it. If she knew of it, why had she never brought it to his attention?

'Would you like a cup of tea as well love?' Vera asked him hopefully.

'No thanks, I have to go.'

'What for?' Crestfallen, she put her hands together as if about to pray. 'I thought you would stay here tonight.'

Kennedy pocketed the phone and stood up. 'There's something I need to do.'

Staring at the transistor radio, hearing honed in on the football commentary, Bertie didn't catch Kennedy's words or see the sombre look on his face as he walked across to Vera and embraced her. 'I'm sorry if I've let you down Mum.'

Vera hugged him tightly. 'You don't need to apologise to me. What's done is done. Remember, I never stopped praying for you.'

'Thanks for that. Don't worry. I'll see you all right. All of you.'

'Can't you see I don't want anything. After all these years I don't need anything... just my family.'

'I know. And you'll be all right with Nicky, Aimee, Jack, Tess, baby Freddie and laughing boy over there.' Kennedy kissed his mother on the forehead and eased himself out of their clinch.

'What do you mean?'

'You've got your family.'

Vera put her hands together once more, but Kennedy placed the index finger of his left hand against her lips before she could speak.

'Tell me one thing before I go. Something's puzzled me for years. What did you have against that *'Charlie's Angels'* poster I used to have on the wall in my bedroom?'

Vera shook her head. 'The three women? The Jezebels who looked like they were praying? Blasphemers trying to lead you into temptation. To spill your seed.'

'Madre de Dios! I should have known.' Kennedy grinned half-heartedly, hoping his Spanish would fall on deaf ears. Vera looked perplexed as he kissed her again and walked towards the back door tapping Bertie on the shoulder as passed by.

197

Bertie glanced up. 'You off out?'

'Yeah! I need to get some fresh air. I ain't had much recently.'

'You should have gone to the game with Fletch.'

'Nah. That's not my Chelsea anymore. Anyway… take care.'

As he opened the door, Kennedy looked around the kitchen. Everything was the same as he remembered it before he went inside. Mum fidgeting with her Rosary necklace, Bertie sipping tea. He sensed his friend had long since taken his place. A doting, grateful, loving son who'd replaced the miscreant black sheep of the family that had been led astray. She'd laid it on him with a Bible lesson the minute he'd arrived. *"Watch and pray, that ye enter not into temptation: the spirit indeed is willing, but the flesh is weak".* (Matthew 26:41)

He'd smiled. He'd entered into temptation. His flesh was weak. But that wasn't all. "You don't need to apologise to me. What's done is done". If only she knew what he had done and, more importantly, why? The world he inhabited was different to hers. There was no point trying to explain his troubles, not now. It was too late. Soon it would be over.

★ ★ ★

A body weight of fourteen-stones would require a drop of around five-feet to break the neck and spinal cord. With a clearance of around ten-feet between the landing and the hall, the rope needed to be tied short. It wouldn't be easy, but then immediate death was a privilege that wasn't really deserved.

The handwritten note Kennedy placed on the table in the hall said little. *'I've had it with everything. I can't do this anymore. Sorry.'*

Dropping to his haunches he pulled a three-quarter-inch diameter, ten-foot length of rope from the rucksack on his back and laid it out on the floor. Swiftly, he made a backward 'S' shape about eighteen-inches wide at one end leaving a trailing tail of similar length. It was dark, but he'd practised tying the knot so often he could do it with gloved hands and his eyes shut. Wrapping the tail around and under the 'S', he made a coil and methodically repeated the process six times leaving a loop at each end before passing the reminder of the tail through the loop at the top and pulling it tight into a slip knot. There it was, the perfect, life-ending hangman's noose.

Walking slowly up the darkened stairway, he placed the noose on the right side of the top step and continued to the landing where he secured the loose end of the rope to the bannister rail with a swing hitch knot that allowed a play of approximately five-feet. Everything felt as tight as it should. There was little margin for error, but as he made his way to the landing window he felt confident. The sodium glow of the streetlamp outside illuminated his balaclava-clad face. He glanced at his watch.

10.05 p.m. It was a waiting game now. The element of surprise would be augmented by darkness. The power supply to the house had been disconnected at the main fuse box located in the landing cupboard between the top of the stairs and the bathroom.

10.06 p.m. You could learn a lot in prison if you put your mind to it. Viewed by many as a route to self-respect, Kennedy hadn't been interested in furthering his education. What was the point? He didn't need to learn a trade or get qualifications because he wouldn't need to find a job. Money was waiting for him on the outside. He just had to serve his sentence, all of it. Prime had seen to that.

10.07 p.m. What he had learned was a self-taught skill for copying handwriting. He didn't view it as forgery. The word 'forgery' had criminal connotations and, in his mind, when linked to this plan, his purpose wasn't illicit. It had taken time to refine his ability, but he'd had plenty of that.

10.08 p.m. He glanced at the rope tied around the bannister and smiled. *'I've had it with everything. I can't do this anymore. Sorry'*. If he was being honest, a suicide note wasn't required. It didn't even have to look like suicide, but the pursuit of obsessive detail had become compulsive. The note was self-explanatory. It left nothing open to question.

10.09 p.m. He'd started with letters from members of his family and then notes fellow prisoners had written. Copying words over and over, creating a master alphabet of different writing styles so eventually he could create original sentences. Eventually, he wrote a letter to Nicky in her handwriting style. She didn't notice. He did the same with Jack, Aimee and his mother. The process had kept him entertained but it served a purpose. The prisoner report written by Prime following the assault at Belmarsh had been a priceless acquisition though it remained a mystery how easily it had come into his possession so soon after the event.

10.10 p.m. Kennedy heard a key turn in the front door lock and made his way stealthily back along the landing.

'Shit!'

It was only one word but he recognised Prime's voice immediately. The hall light switch flicked several times without effect.

'Shit!'

The open door slammed shut.

'Shit!'

Kennedy drew the Glock 18 from the inside pocket of the M65 regiment jacket he was wearing. It was the same gun he'd used to shoot Jimmy Baker and the same jacket he'd worn that night. The symmetry appealed to him. The clumping sound of footsteps and smell of beer and cigarettes heralded Prime's arrival at the top of the stairs.

'Don't move another inch or I'll blow your fucking head off.'

Prime stopped in his tracks. In the shadows he could make out the barrel of a gun levelled at his head. He rolled his eyes and tried to focus on the man behind it.

'Is this a fucking joke?'

'Can you hear anyone laughing?'

'Are you sure you've got the correct address?'

'This is 15A Chivalry Road right?'

Four pints of strong lager and several glasses of whisky had clouded his senses, but the reality that his situation was more perilous than he'd initially considered it to be dawned as he put a face to the voice. 'Jones. Kennedy fucking Jones.'

'On your knees.'

Sobriety was instantaneous. Prime dropped to the floor and considered his options. What did Jones want? Revenge for Belmarsh? Why bother with the surprise greeting? He'd obviously come for something. Information perhaps. Yes, that was it. There was plenty of information he could share to buy some time. He wasn't as young or as fit as he once was, but he was still a man of war. Jones' head wasn't in the right place. It hadn't been since that night on Mount Longdon. He'd played him before, and he could play him again.

'Fix bayonets!' Kennedy's mind flashed. A photograph. It's night-time. His father is stood outside a Belfast pub with a woman. A group of men are looking on. One of them is Sergeant Eric Prime.

'What are you talking about Jones?'

'Fix bayonets!' Kennedy's mind flashed again. Another photograph. The group of men are waving their arms and appear to be cheering. His father is stood further along the road facing them. He has his right forearm in the crook of his left arm. The woman is hailing a black taxi. In the background, he can just make out Prime talking to another

201

man. They have edged to the mouth of an alleyway that flanks the pub. That had to be where the money changed hands.

'Is this about Belmarsh?'

'Fix bayonets!' Kennedy's mind flashed once more. The photograph depicts his father in the back of the taxi. The woman has her head buried in his groin. The driver is pointing a gun at his head.

'Come on Jones. We haven't got bayonets. That was a long time ago. You need help.' Prime's rasping voice was tinged with patronising arrogance.

'Charrrrge!'

Prime flinched as Kennedy growled and jabbed the barrel of the Glock in his temple. Now he was concerned. No. Now, for the first time in his life, he was scared. He'd never stammered. But now the words he wanted to say wouldn't form properly. His pulse was racing, his mouth dry. He swallowed hard. 'Wha w-w-w-w wha-wha-ddd'ya www-want?'

'You know what I want.' Kennedy dropped to his knees, snatched the noose from the bannister rail, slipped it over Prime's head and pushed him down the stairs.

There was barely a split-second for Prime to think about what was wanted of him, and no time to react. As he fell forward, the noose stretched his neck, jerking his spinning body upwards. Legs flailing wildly, he swung beneath the bannister, feet kicking out at the wall. How had he let himself be caught out? He hated himself for this, but he hated Kennedy Jones more.

These were his final thoughts and a matter of moments separated hatred from pain… and panic from eye-bulging terror. 'Jones, Jo…' Strangulated mid-cry, unable to breathe… as the tightening noose compressed the arteries in his neck, consciousness faded fast. Chest heaving, body shivering, brain overwhelmed, as Prime swung like a pendulum, he lost control of his functions… convulsing, urinating, soiling, ejaculating… a degrading end to contemplate briefly as death claimed him.

Kennedy looked on intently as Prime's reflex muscular spasms ebbed, hypnotic motion slowing, creaking sound of the rope pulling against the bannister fading. Back-and-forth. Back-and-forth. Back-and-forth. Back-and-forth. Back-and-forth. Back-and-forth.

> *'Where is death's sting? Where grave thy victory? I triumph still if thou abide with me.'*

The eighth and final verse of the hymn *'Abide With me.'* Father Slattery leading the singing from the pulpit at his father's funeral service held at St Mary's. Kennedy, heartbroken, angry, fighting back tears, stood in the front row of pews flanked by his mother and Manny. Everyone he knew and plenty more he didn't were congregated in the church to pay their final respects.

Back-and-forth. Back-and-forth. Back-and-forth. Back-and-forth. Back-and-forth. Back-and-forth.

> *'Hold thou thy cross before my closing eyes, shine through the gloom and point me to the skies.'*

Back-and-forth. Back-and-forth. Back-and-forth. Back-back. Forth-forth. Stop. Prime was still, silent, dead.

Kennedy opened the landing cupboard and restored electrical power to 15A Chivalry Road, as he did so the light came on in the hall.

'Heaven's morning breaks, and earth's vain shadows flee…' Father Slattery singing louder than the rest. His mother mouthing the words to the hymn in an exaggerated manner that reminded him of the times she'd made him watch *'Songs of Praise'* on television as a kid. When the camera panned around, as soon

as members of the church or cathedral's congregation realised they might be on screen they always opened their mouths wider as they sang, a look-at-me-plea that weirdly worked as the camera paused and zoomed in. He smiled at the memory.

Descending the stairs hurriedly, he passed three framed photographs; Her Majesty the Queen at her coronation. Prime and his elder brother Danny as boys. The Tottenham Hotspur side that won the Football League First Division and FA Cup double in 1961.

'In life, in death, O Lord, abide with me.'

Kennedy switched off the hall light and opened the front door. As he removed the balaclava he was still wearing, the cold night air pinched at his face. He took a deep breath, stepped outside, closed the door and checked his watch. 10.30 p.m. It was time for a drink.

PART THREE

PART THREE

AFTERNOON

1 June 2007

'And you ain't stopped drinking since.'

Jack's sarcasm was harsh but fair. Kennedy smiled but, sensing there was more to follow, said nothing. His son was right about the drink. After the story he'd just told him, he could have said any number of things. Called him a murderer, a madman, a philanderer, a cheat, a drunk. He might even have turned his back on him and walked away. Who would have blamed him?

'I hated Prime as much as you did. Every day when I was on foot patrol in the desert, I cursed the cunt.'

Kennedy looked bewildered but remained silent.

'I blamed him for not making the grade at Chelsea.'

His puzzlement was complete. Now he needed some answers. 'Why would you do that? It was my fault, I wasn't there for you.'

'Remember that time I came to visit? The day Beckham scored that penalty to beat the Argies?'

'Yeah! The 2002 World Cup.'

'7 June. It was a Friday. That was the day I told you Chelsea were releasing me 'cos I was too small.'

'I know. That old screw Jocky Sanford started banging on about Wee Pat Nevin being only five-foot-six and how he started out at Celtic, but they let him go because he wasn't tall enough.'

'Yeah! And how he signed for Clyde and then Chelsea came in for him. It's ironic. Hardly front page news that the people who run football clubs are hypocrites though, and anyway, what's that got to do with Prime?'

'He said "shit club, no history" when Jocky mentioned Chelsea the first time. I could see him deliberately winding you up. Fucking chicken kisser. Now it all makes sense. Stitching you up the following Monday when you were due before the Parole Board. Making sure you wouldn't be free to help me.'

Kennedy shook his head and frowned as he pointed at the road and the black Bentley Arnage that was driving slowly towards them. 'Well maybe I can now.'

The Bentley braked some fifty metres away where the tarmac met the grass and Spot the Staffy was still sat waiting patiently for his master. Oblivious to the car and his father's final words, Jack turned away. Scooping the ball up with his right foot, he chipped it into the air and caught it in the crook of his neck cradling it momentarily before flicking it up and heading it continuously.

'He's got some skill, I'll give him that.' Mark Parry sucked air in between his clenched teeth and rubbed his hands together as he watched Jack freestyle. 'Juggling's for the circus though.'

Manny cocked his head to one side and glared at Parry who was sat beside him in the rear of the Bentley. 'You'd know all about that wouldn't you.' he exclaimed, reaching out and grabbing his thigh with his left hand. 'Billy fucking Smart.'

'W W Whaddya m mean by that?' Parry stammered.

'Well it looked like we had eleven clowns on the pitch when we shipped five at home to Orient. That was some way to end the season.'

Sat in the Bentley's driver's seat, Harry Craven folded his arms and coughed to stifle a laugh. Manny didn't know much about the game of football, but he had a point. Cheam Athletic had been struggling in the lower reaches of Division One

South in what is traditionally known as the Isthmian League when he'd purchased the debt-ridden north Surrey club for one hundred pounds in 1997. He could have paid one pound, but didn't want to be compared with the former Chelsea FC supremo Ken Bates who'd paid that token amount in 1982 to secure ownership of the then virtually destitute London outfit. He didn't know Bates personally, but had taken an instant dislike to him when Harry had explained how, during his Chairmanship, he'd completely redesigned Chelsea's club crest and regularly changed their kit to capitalise on the marketing opportunities this presented. Despite loving a pound note, Manny was a stickler for heritage and tradition. The Cheam Athletic crest featured a pocket watch displaying the time as three o'clock, the standard kick-off time for football games played on a Saturday. It looked as old fashioned as the blue and gold quartered shirts it was embroidered onto, but he retained both. The only change he'd made was the addition of a Latin motto beneath the crest.

TOLLE ADVERSARIUM OCULOS DE ISTO NUSQUAM

Founded in 1919 by Parry's great grandfather George Parry, Cheam Athletic, nicknamed the Watchmakers after the family business, had initially competed in the Southern Suburban League before gaining election to the Athenian League in 1931. There they remained until 1977, when a run to the FA Amateur Cup semifinals for a third consecutive season enabled them to canvass sufficient votes to be elected to the Second Division of the Isthmian League.

The club had remained in the proprietorship of the Parry's throughout its history and was unique in the world of football having been managed solely by family members. A noble concept in amateur days, but one that had often been found wanting in the modern era. Mark 'Paz' Parry had made a record 1006 competitive appearances playing in goal for the Watchmakers before hanging up his gloves in 1998. It was an outstanding achievement, surpassing by one that of his hero Peter Shilton. Shilts though, as Paz would always highlight when the topic was raised, had played for eleven different league clubs winning a cabinet full of silverware in the process including the European Cup twice with Nottingham Forest. He also had 125 England caps to his name. Notwithstanding these facts, once Manny Jones had raised Cheam's profile, the media had taken a keen interest in mild-mannered, bespectacled Parry who had succeeded his father Roy as manager in 1999 and was now living the dream with a glamour model girlfriend, enjoying the trappings that success brought.

While Manny was smitten with the egotistical yet romantic notion of being the saviour of Cheam Athletic and becoming a pillar of the local community, his motives for buying the club were far more sinister. Principally, they involved money laundering and tax evasion. The sums of cash involved in the higher echelons of the game were astronomical. Television and image rights, sponsorship, transfer payments, agent fees, illegal betting syndicates; all these things could be leveraged, and he'd already used his ownership of the club to strengthen Chapman Security's presence in the area and secure a multi-million pound construction contract to convert an office block in Cheam into luxury flats.

At the outset, despite being in financial dire straits with average gates dwindling below five hundred, Athletic's crumbling ground at Peaches Close was still a cash cow. Hard-core supporters continued to click through the turnstiles and buy a programme a pie and a few pints and cheer on Parry's team. Behind the scenes, Jester Cook, who'd been instrumental in brokering the deal for Manny to buy Cheam, set about implementing the seven-year plan he'd devised to get the club into the Football League

Ahead of schedule, the ground had been redeveloped into a 10,000 capacity all-seated stadium and community centre. Experienced players like former England internationals Jim Jackson and Max Gardner had been brought in, and successive promotions through football's pyramid to the Isthmian Premier, Conference South, Conference Premier and Football League Two had followed. It was like a *'Boys Own'* comic-book story, and, despite a shocking end to the 2005/2006 season which had seen the Watchmakers fail to register a single victory since Christmas, Manny insisted on retaining the services of Mark Parry as manager.

"I know Jester wants me to sack him. But sometimes he forgets why we're doing this". Harry mulled over what Manny had told him as they'd waited for Parry to finish taking the end of season training session a couple of weeks previously. "HM revenue and Customs are starting to take money laundering and tax evasion very seriously. We need everyone associated with the football club to be loyal and trusted, that way no questions get asked. Change can create problems. The Cheam Athletic tradition is perfect for the serious part of the business".

While Harry smiled as he continued to watch Jack Jones juggling with the ball, Manny's mind was working overtime. 'We could get a tremendous amount of publicity out of signing the lad given what happened to him,' he said, finally relaxing his grip of Parry's thigh. 'And if he can play a bit, well that's a bonus. What do you think Paz?'

'He could play in Ben Richardson's testimonial against Crystal Palace on Monday.'

'That's the spirit. Get it organised. I'll tell Kennedy.'

Clearly relieved, Parry nodded as Manny caught Harry's eyes in the rearview mirror. 'How far is it to Peaches Close from here H?'

'Six miles boss.'

'Right then. You can jog along Paz. You look like you could do with some exercise. What was it those Orient fans were singing H?'

Harry chuckled before bursting into song. *'He's rich, he's fat, he's gonna get the sack, Mark Parry, Mark Parry.'*

Parry frowned as he looked out of the passenger window and caught sight of the heavy leaden sky. If it rained, he'd get wet. He thought about saying something, a token protest about the Orient chant, but decided against it.

Manny second-guessed him anyway. 'I know what you're thinking,' he sneered. 'Just remember why you're rich and fat... and still in a job... and go and pay some attention to that dolly bird of yours before someone else does.'

Parry said nothing as he got out of the car. He knew he was in no position to argue.

Manny chuckled as he watched Parry walk slowly towards the park gates. 'Well that wasn't too difficult,' he said, glancing at his watch. Suddenly, his confident smile was replaced by a look of nervous apprehension. 'Shit! Let's go. I'm late for my appointment with Clara.'

MISTRESS CLARA

To Mistress Clara, being a professional dominatrix was just like having any other job. The fact she made her living from fulfilling men's perverted fantasies about being dominated meant she earned significant amounts of money. Intelligent, articulate, cultured and graceful, Clara's approach to bondage, discipline, sadism and masochism was creative and tailored to the specific needs of her clients. Nobles, politicians, religious leaders, captains of industry, judges, lawyers, actors, sportsmen... and criminals could be found amongst the men who crossed her threshold. From all walks of life, they had one thing in common... all of them were addicted to Clara's superior understanding of their psyche, and her ability to satiate their deepest most degrading desires.

Physical and verbal humiliation, electrical play, human ashtray, edging, milking, face-slapping, spanking, cock-and-ball torture, corporal and judicial punishment, domination, slave and obedience training, trampling, bondage, foot worship, face-sitting, sensory deprivation, golden showers, anal play, asphyxiation, nipple torture, interrogation, kidnapping, imprisonment, bribery, infantilism, forced chastity, castration, cross-dressing, feminisation, maid training, voyeurism, mummification, hot wax, medical scenarios, punishment enemas, sounding, catheters, rubber, forced orgasms, PVC, drugs, gas-play, butt plugs, poppers, role-play and strap-on training... all these specialist fetishes were available, at a price, in a safe, hygienic and consensual environment.

For a minimum of five hundred pounds per session, Clara would rapidly propel her clients into their own tailor-made, humiliating subspace and inflict the most exquisite pain imaginable. The goal was the intense head-rush of a perfect orgasm... but there was no guarantee. Servitude coupled with endurance were the keys to pleasing Mistress, but few succeeded... and even fewer were fortunate enough to be granted a merciful release.

The one 'service' that Clara didn't offer as a part of any repertoire was full sex, and this made her all the more alluring and unattainable. It didn't stop men trying to inveigle her into parting with her 'virginity'. Gold, trinkets, jewels... hard cash, nothing had persuaded her yet. She'd been offered a king's ransom, literally, by an Arab prince, but had resisted the temptation. Money was a lot of things, but it wasn't everything.

Men were powerless in her presence. She was the ultimate aphrodisiac. Obsessive, compulsive, unrequited. "I think I'm in love with you Clara". She'd heard the same men say it a thousand times. Back they came, time and again. Submissive and willing partners... a habit-forming relationship that led to moral, spiritual and, in some cases, financial bankruptcy. Their quest was futile, Clara was an unreachable object of desire, a woman who could be worshipped and adored but never owned.

A true lifestyle dominatrix, in the guise of 'Mistress', Clara was a consummate professional who never allowed her personal feelings about deviant clients get in the way of business. An initial meeting was always recommended in order to provide the optimum surreal sensory experience. It was important to delve deep into the perverted minds of these often-complex characters. The better her understanding, the more rewarding the session. Sexually for the client, financially for her. Equally, it was imperative to set boundaries, list health problems, clarify physical limitations, and define pain thresholds. Being charged with assault, grievous bodily harm or manslaughter was not on her wish list, and so the intensity of the aching, discomfort, and agony she would administer was managed with prescribed safe words or signals.

"No Mistress please stop", was more often than not a request to increase punishment, whereas a simple 'Green', 'Amber', 'Red', traffic light system left no room for interpretation and was perfect for novices. The more experienced submissive might be given a single word to remember, but it was wise not to be too scheming. No matter how much she might despise a particular individual, 'deleterious', 'enervating' or 'perfidious' might prove difficult to recall if blood sugar levels were starting to drop, bondage ropes were too tight, or autoerotic asphyxiation felt more like choking.

Beauty she knew was most definitely in the eye of the beholder. While the majority of her clients bought into the concept of Mistress Clara and satisfied their fantasies via her 'natural' dominatrix look, a small percentage needed more than the pale-skinned, blue-eyed, red-lipped, razor-haired, peroxide-blonde, glamorous bitch-queen vision of superiority that would dress to request in anything from Victorian whalebone corsetry and lace, country riding attire, gothic or punk leathers and chains, to rubber and PVC. Uniforms were popular. Military, prison, hospital… Clara had them all, but none of these looks appealed to the client who was visiting her this afternoon, his tastes were very specific and to cater for them meant booking out the whole day to ready herself, prepare and perform the session and to wind down afterwards. The tribute she demanded for her time and effort was two thousand pounds, but she knew that to him she was worth every last penny.

Sitting in front of the mirror in her dressing room and working from a photograph provided by her client, she commenced her transformation. Flawless skin was essential and only premium cosmetics were used. First a primer was applied that formed a velvety second skin. Then came the custom foundation and balm that yielded a freakishly pale pallor. A concealer ensured that any blemishes or dark under-eye circles were obscured. Pink blusher enhanced her cheekbones, and eyes were made up with a trace of waterproof black mascara and liner with lashes teased out but not over emphasised. A modest pink lip-gloss complemented the look which overall gave her the appearance of a malnourished waif. Her metamorphosis was completed with green contact lenses and a strawberry blonde wig, and a final dash of realism was achieved by adding an auburn tint to the perfectly shaped triangle of pubic hair just below her bikini line.

She enjoyed the intricacy of the two-hour process, but the end result, and the effect she had on her client alarmed her to the point that she had used what free time she had to research who he was and, more importantly, who the object of his fantasy was. Manny Jones had been visiting her once a month for the past ten years. Chapman Security, Cheam Athletic, he'd kept no secrets from her about the public side of his business interests. But who was the real woman behind the character she transformed herself into for him? The woman he addressed as Vera? She didn't want to compromise her lucrative relationship with Manny by asking him directly even though it was the obvious thing to do. If he'd wanted to tell her, he would have done so by now.

Initially a challenging game for her to play, establishing the real identity of 'Vera' had become something of a fixation for Clara to the point that she had considered hiring the services of a private detective. 'Vera' was a relatively unusual name and the photograph provided further clues to work with.

To perfect the look for Manny, Clara had commissioned her wigmaker Eva Goodwin to make a bouffant updo hairpiece to replicate Vera's style. Without hesitation, Eva had said, "ahh Holly Golightly". With hindsight it was obvious, but Clara had never seen *'Breakfast at Tiffany's'* nor did she have any great appreciation of the actress Audrey Hepburn who played socialite Miss Golightly in the film that had first screened in October 1961.

'Vera' was wearing an engagement ring, meaning that at the time the photograph had been taken she was still unmarried but was clearly planning to get wed. Supposing the photo also dated back to 1961? Estimating 'Vera's' age at somewhere between eighteen and twenty-four narrowed her possible year of birth to the range 1937-1943. Just to be certain, Clara added two years either side of that range, consequentially she had ten years worth of birth records to sift through online.

It was painstaking work, but it passed the time between appointments. Making the assumption that 'Vera' had been born in London, Clara slowly but surely narrowed the field down. One of thirty-eight 'Vera's' Clara found was a Vera Coyne who had been born on 22 April 1940 to Doreen and James Coyne in Battersea. Further research uncovered the fact that on 1 December 1962, Vera Coyne had married a man called Alec Jones. Jones was a common enough surname, but the coincidence that it was Manny's as well merited further investigation.

Alec Jones, born 15 October 1938 deceased 22 April 1978, had a brother called Chapman, born 3 September 1939. CJ were the initials fashioned from emeralds set into the ring that Manny always wore. Chapman? What a strange Christian name that was… the diminutive Manny was now easy to comprehend. It had been relatively simple to trace Vera's address, and Clara had made a point of parking her car directly outside her house in Cedars Mews one day and patiently watching and waiting. When Vera had finally emerged to go shopping, Clara knew she had unravelled Manny's dark secret. She wanted to find out more. She wanted to understand why his obsession with his sister-in-law manifested itself in such a perverted way. In the same way she wanted to question

Manny, she also wanted to hear Vera's side of the story, but that hadn't been possible. It was a source of frustration that always vexed her prior to a session. By the time Trina Jackson, her maid and apprentice dominatrix, knocked on her dressing room door signalling it was time to 'go to work', she only ever had one thing on her mind... punishment. Today, Manny had been late arriving. 'Vera' hated tardiness more than Clara. This evening, his punishment would be more severe than usual.

★ ★ ★

Having got undressed in the changing room provided for clients, Manny had allowed Trina to place a dog collar around his neck, attach a chain link leash to it, and make him crawl slowly on all fours to the chamber where he hoped his depraved desires would eventually be satisfied. Unlike Clara who had a permanent aura of inaccessibility and appeared emotionally empty, Trina was spirited, warm and funny.

'Dirty little doggy', she'd said, wiggling her hips as she spoke in an accent that was pure unadulterated old-school London. 'I bet you're looking at my perfect arse aren't you?'

It had been difficult not too. From the ground up, Trina's six-inch white stilettos and perfectly sculpted white fishnet-stocking-clad legs led to a pair of white regulation gym knickers that covered the two peachy-skinned globes of her backside. Heaven!

'You'd like to bury your nose in there wouldn't you dirty doggy?'

'Oh yes Mistress Trina'. Manny had grunted excitedly. The Viagra tablet he'd taken half an hour previously was kicking in, and his previously flaccid cock was responding to Trina's visual and verbal stimulation.

'That will cost extra dirty doggy, and we mustn't tell Mistress Clara must we?' Trina had tugged sharply on the leash jerking his head forward.

'No Mistress Trina. It will be our secret'.

'On your back then doggy'. Manny had closed his eyes tightly shut as he rolled onto his back. The concrete floor was cold but it didn't matter. Trina squatted down onto his face and he breathed in her musky scent as she pulled aside the gusset of her knickers.

'Lick my arse doggy'. Manny slavered hungrily, licking, biting and burying his tongue as Trina ground her hips. He could feel the skin on the back of his head tearing against the floor but he didn't care.

'Now service my cunt'. Manny didn't need asking twice. His perspiration mingled with her juices. Trina squirmed and bucked feverishly as she reached orgasm quickly. 'Clever doggy', she'd squealed.

She could be faking, but it seemed real enough. Whatever the case maybe, it was well worth the one hundred pounds tip he'd pay her at the end of the session. Trina was a cool lady. She loved money as much as he did. He'd paid her five hundred pounds to fuck Kennedy so he could film it. Her presence at the Duchess the night he'd been released from prison had been no coincidence, and the footage of his nephew's subsequent infidelity, that was meant to be insurance policy to ensure full cooperation, he'd found himself masturbating over regularly. It was better than doing the real thing. Reality spoiled fantasy, that's why he visited Mistress Clara.

Trina had done a good job of securing him to the custom-made, leather-covered, stainless steel bondage wheel that was the centrepiece of Clara's dungeon. Two metres in diameter, the wheel was an unforgiving piece of equipment that could be rotated fully through 360 degrees and locked in any position by means of a spring-loaded footbrake. Leather restraining straps at the bicep, elbow, wrist, thigh, knee and calf, coupled with a chest harness and adjustable footplate allowed no freedom of movement when fully secured as they were now. He was completely at Clara's mercy.

'See you later doggy.' Trina grabbed him by the throat and slapped him hard across the face before leaving the room. Manny caught his breath, he knew from past experience that he now had almost seven minutes to contemplate his fate before Clara would arrive. Six minutes forty-three seconds to be exact. The length of time the orchestral piece of music Trina had cued up on the sound system took to play in its entirety.

'*Danse Macabre*' by Saint Saens. This was the reason he'd chosen the French composer's masterwork for his funeral when Vivian had asked. The irony was delicious. As the sepulchral silence was broken by gentle chords from the string section accompanied by a harp supposedly calling forth the dead to dance at midnight on Halloween, Manny looked around the dungeon.

Low-level, purple neon strip lighting illuminated the room whose black velvet-swathed walls had numerous shelves upon which Clara had neatly arranged her implements of torture. Canes, whips, floggers, tawses, paddles, straps, belts... and her personal favourite the cat-o-nine-tails. Genital-harming devices included crusher bars, weights, parachutes and stretchers... the eye-watering display was completed by variously sized vibrators, dildos, strap-ons and butt plugs, and a barbarous assortment of nipple clamps.

Manny flexed his muscles as he hummed along with the solo violin and absorbed the dungeon's devilish yet peaceful atmosphere, which was augmented by the calming soporific aroma of Frankincense resin burning on two smouldering charcoal pucks either side of the door. Over the years he'd allowed Clara to fiendishly experiment with him and push his limits, but these days, at almost sixty-eight years of age, having been diagnosed with coronary heart disease that would require bypass surgery to remedy, he had to be careful.

The hoods, gags and anaesthetic masks his eyes had now settled on were out of the equation, as was the use of nitrous oxide, amyl nitrate and the forty-piece electronic violet wand kit which he'd bought for Clara. The black and silver instrument case was open and he could see the mushroom, rake, curved, ball-tip and saturator electrodes along with numerous bulbs and lightning rods. He rocked his head in time with the descending and rising scales of the music and wondered if he could have 'that' discussion with his consultant heart surgeon. Being tormented by the violet wand was his personal favourite. Maybe he could make a joke of it. It wouldn't surprise him if his surgeon was one of Clara's punters. Maybe he should ask her.

Woodwind, brass, percussion, strings… the xylophone imitating the rattling sound of skeletal bones, Saint Saens had it all worked out… just like he did. He'd had the time. Countless hours of *'Danse Macabre'* in the dungeon, waiting for his Mistress to arrive. Waiting for 'Vera'. Today he was strapped to the bondage wheel, but he'd also sampled the perverse delights of everything else the room could offer. The corporal punishment bench, isolation chamber, St Andrew's cross, metal cage, suspension frame, fucking machine and bondage chair… he had exquisitely painful memories of them all, but it was the revolving wheel that provided him with the most memorable experiences.

He closed his eyes and listened to the delicate strains of the oboe that represented the crow of a cockerel heralding the dawn… and the dancing skeletons returning to their graves. As *'Danse Macabre'* concluded, Manny heard the metal tips of Clara's heels clicking on the floor and getting louder. The dungeon door opened behind him. He couldn't see 'Vera' yet, but his artificially erect penis began to quiver with anticipation.

★ ★ ★

221

Manny knew the routine. He had to abide by the rules. Failure to do so would displease Clara, and the scars that marked his old, leathery skin were a permanent reminder of the punishment she had meted out when he had invoked her wrath. Restrained, head bowed, eyes closed, he tensed his body against the bondage wheel as the dungeon door creaked open. At every session, at this very moment, the same thought fleetingly crossed his mind. What if it wasn't Clara or Trina? What if it was the filth finally bringing him to justice? Or Harry Craven, bored with sitting outside in the car waiting for him. Did he really believe that Clara was just a hired spy who passed on valuable information gleaned from the clients she tortured who held positions of privilege?

It would have mattered more in the past, but now he cared less. He realised his body could no longer withstand the rigours of bondage, discipline, sadism and masochism. Soon he would have to 'retire' from the scene. That's what he'd been telling himself since his heart condition had been diagnosed, but here he was again.

He shuddered as the dungeon door slammed shut. Beads of cold sweat began to trickle from his armpits as he heard the sound of approaching footsteps. He sniffed the air; the aroma of burning Frankincense was now suffused with the unmistakable scent of 'My Sin'. Created in 1925 by an enigmatic Russian lady known as Madame Zed, the perfume had subsequently been marketed worldwide by fashion mogul Jeanne Lanvin. Manny had first been intoxicated by the seductive, provocative and feminine fragrance of 'Mon Peché', as it was known to the French, during his sordid encounters with Soho whore Susan. He'd given his brother Alec a case of the eau du toilette knowing that it would be gifted to Vera. Prior to Lanvin discontinuing 'My Sin' in 1988, Manny had bought sufficient stock to ensure that for years to come he could propagate the essence of the woman he desired amongst the chosen few that helped him blur fantasy with reality.

'You kept me waiting today, I don't like to be kept waiting.'

Manny felt a shiver run down his spine as Clara spoke. Her clipped vowel enunciation and sensuous yet severe manner of speaking had more in keeping with Belgravia than Battersea, but it created atmosphere and tension that complemented perfectly her visual recreation of Vera.

'Did you hear me?'

Manny flinched as Clara slapped him across the face.

'Yes, I heard you,' he replied apologetically. 'I'm sorry.'

He opened his eyes and sighed. The hairstyle, the makeup, the emerald Rosary necklace, the clothes. Her attention to detail was astonishing. The night Alec had beaten him in the fight at Caius, Vera had worn a white, ruffle-neck, short-sleeve, button-down blouse embroidered with doves of peace over a green knee-length pleated skirt that had a banded waist. Her feet had been shod in a pair of low-heeled green and white shoes. Clara had recreated her look perfectly.

'I'm sorry Vera.'

Clara spat in Manny's face as he spoke. 'Sorry isn't good enough.'

She reached out both hands to pinch, squeeze and twist his nipples.

'N N No. Sss sorry VVVera,' he stammered, wincing in pain as she applied more pressure.

'You need to suffer for me.'

Clara turned and walked slowly to shelves where the tools of her trade were arranged. Manny licked at the gobbets of her saliva dribbling down his face as he watched her. 'I want to suffer for you.'

If only he was younger, he could suffer more. The spring-loaded, alligator nipple clamps Clara had selected made him howl as she attached them and in turn tightened the adjustable screws. 'Ahh... ahh... ahh.'

'Oh dear! Does that hurt?'

The sudden softness in Clara's voice was reassuring, but it was all a part of her wicked game. Twenty lashes with the cat o' nine tails followed, and he had to count out and say 'thank you' each time the knotted thongs of braided leather lacerated his chest. The stinging sensation was acute, but all the while he kept his eyes open... drinking in the twisted vision of Vera.

Clara administered ophthalmic morphine to dull the pain he felt and slowly span the bondage wheel through 180 degrees before applying the brake. Locked down, immobilised and exposed... being the ultimate control freak, having his world suddenly turned upside down always unnerved him as did the rush of blood to the head which was a consequence of the action.

'You have sinned against me and now you must repent.'

The sinister timbre of Clara's voice and religious overtone of her words resonated deeply with Manny.

'I have sinned. I must repent.'

All he'd ever wanted was Vera, and because she'd continually spurned his advances his vengeance had been deliberate and prolonged. He hated himself for all the anguish he had caused the woman he loved, and it was only right that 'she' should punish him.

'Arghhh...' Pain distracted him as molten wax from the lit candle Clara was holding at right angles above his groin drizzled onto his testicles.

'Kiss my feet.' Clara raised her left foot and forced the tip of her shoe into his mouth. For now, the agony and humiliation was worth it. As she stood above him, Manny gazed longingly up her skirt.

'Sin is the transgression of the law and must be punished.' Clara raised her left foot higher, affording him a better view of her creamy white thighs and naked sex. But as she did so she repeatedly flicked the alligator clamps attached to his nipples and dripped more molten wax on his groin.

'Vera, I'm sorry. Arghhh!' Manny screamed as searing pain danced from his chest to his genitals and back again. Clara stepped back. He could feel his blood pounding through his temples. He thought about using the safe word. What was it?

'What does the Rosary begin with?' The topic of Clara's brusque question sidetracked him. He could see her holding the crucifix of the Rosary necklace away from her heaving chest with her free hand, the emerald beads brushing against her blouse picking out the firmness of her nipples in the fine material.

'Arghhh! Ahhhh!' Manny cried out repeatedly, as Clara's right foot brushing up and down against the alligator clamps reminded him she was waiting for an answer. 'The Apostles Creed… one Our Father and…' He caught his breath as Clara walked away to her shelves.

'And what?'

'Three Hail Mary's, a Glory Be and a Hail Holy Queen.'

The respite from pain and discomfort was all too brief. He knew what was coming next, Vera's sinister final gesture. He closed his eyes as he heard her footsteps approaching.

'And what are the three Hail Mary's offered for?'

Clara paused from her duties to anoint her ankles with *'My Sin'*. Opening his eyes, Manny surreptitiously looked once more at the forbidden fruit between her legs as she stood over him. The passionate scent was heightening his desire for release.

'You worthless wretch, you can't remember can you?'

The ominous manner in which Clara spoke, and the sight of her hands that were now gloved in white latex, motivated Manny to find the right words.

'Three Hail Mary's are offered for an increase in the virtues of faith, hope, and charity.'

Clara laughed as she walked back to her shelves and returned with a tube of water-based lubricant and an extra-large black silicone butt plug. 'You sacrificed those qualities for power. Prayer cannot help you now.'

★ ★ ★

Abandoned as a child, and having been taken into care by a group of nuns known as the Sisters of London, Clara did not wholly approve of the sacrilegious aspect of the blasphemy and desecration she engaged in with Manny, but then her morals and ethics had been corrupted behind the locked doors of Hammersmith House, the convent where she had been homed.

To the wider world, the Sisters were the epitome of compassion and kindness, but the harsh reality of life at Hammersmith was altogether different. The regime of cruelty began daily at 5 a.m. Scrubbing floors, cleaning windows, polishing shoes. School was an ordeal, and church provided an excuse to find fault with as many children as possible. Ruthless, sadistic thrashings for trivial misdemeanours were frequent.

Clara's undiagnosed dyslexia made her especially vulnerable and she had been punched, kicked, slapped and frequently locked in cupboards as punishment for the difficulties she experienced when asked to read from the Bible. Sexual molestation by male helpers was routine and, by the time she ran away at the age of sixteen, the mental scars of her ordeal had matched the physical marks left by cane, belt and fist.

Penniless, starving, socially isolated, lacking self confidence and unable to comprehend the meaning of love, Clara's waif-like appearance and shorn hair would be her ticket to a bizarre salvation. It was 1976. London's nascent punk scene had brought with it new sounds and styles, and the jobsworth conductor of the number 211 Bus from Hammersmith did her a favour when asking her to get off at Chelsea Old Town Hall on the fashionable Kings Road.

With nothing to her name but the denim rags she was standing in, the last thing she'd considered her appearance to be was cool, hip and trendy. As she'd trudged aimlessly along the pavement, she'd been approached by a heavily made-up, thin-lipped middle-aged woman with a bouffant peroxide hairdo wearing black motorcycle leathers and stiletto-heeled boots who had just emerged from the Great Gear market.

The woman, who'd introduced herself as Janie J, was a clothes designer catering specifically for the fetish scene. Within minutes of their meeting, on the back of a hot meal, the promise of a roof over her head and a decent wage, Clara had a job as a model. Her catwalks were clandestine and the magazines she featured in available by mail order only, but it mattered little. In a world she previously never knew existed, she had an audience that in part, as Janie would later elaborate on, had an innate desire to be exploited.

★ ★ ★

The lubrication felt as cold as Clara's probing fingers in his rectum felt uncomfortable.

'Wisdom, understanding, counsel, fortitude, knowledge, piety, fear of the Lord… the seven gifts of the Holy Spirit. All of them wasted on you.'

Manny shivered as she spoke. While his ordeal was nearly over, the worst was yet to come.

'And so you must suffer and repent for the hurt that you have caused me.'

Clara kicked at the nipple clamps with her foot. As Manny cried out with pain she forced the butt plug into his arsehole. The stretching sensation brought tears to his eyes which he screwed tightly shut as she span the bondage wheel back through 180 degrees. Returned to the upright position, he felt giddy with fear and excitement.

'Open your eyes!' Clara commanded, spitting in his face as he did so and slapping him with the open palm of her hand. 'Reap what you sow, you worthless bastard.'

Manny felt broken and humiliated. Stinging, throbbing, aching pain assaulted his senses. 'I'm sorry Vera,' he wailed. 'Please, please no more.' Head bowed in contrition, he sobbed as he awaited her next move.

'Saying sorry is not enough. It will never be enough.' Clara slowly undid the screws securing the alligator clamps and released them. 'That's why you keep coming to see me isn't it?'

Manny nodded, coughing as he cleared his throat to speak and then wincing once more in pain as Clara tweaked his nipples.

'Now what do you say?'

'Thank you Mistress. Thank you.' Manny bowed his head as if to supplicate. If he was fortunate, she would unshackle his arms from the wheel and allow him the opportunity to gratify himself while he looked at her.

'You have created this world of pain for yourself and only I can take it away.' Clara undid the straps restraining Manny's right arm and stood back from him cupping her ample breasts through her blouse and then running her hands slowly down her stomach onto her thighs. 'Soon you will be purified and freed from the temporal punishment of sin.'

Complete control. If only Manny's associates could see him now. The thought of blackmail had crossed her mind, as it had with a number of her clients whom she disliked. These were the type of people she associated with the horrors of her childhood, real-life lunatics who remained free to walk the streets. One day perhaps, but for now, the money that came with repeat appointments was adequate compensation, as was the opportunity to vengefully and sadistically torment those people whose arrogant and selfish demeanour she despised with a passion. Retribution, as Manny had learned once more this afternoon, could be cold calculating and painful even if it was all an elaborate game.

'Come for me now.' Clara demanded. She'd thought about calling Trina in to witness the final part of Manny's degradation but had changed her mind when she remembered the little minx was clandestinely lining her pockets providing 'extras' for clients.

There were only two people who knew about the CCTV system installed in her chambers and dungeons. Manny and herself. She was pleased with the security this afforded her, but what she didn't know was that the man wanking himself into a frenzy in front of her had recently upgraded the analogue set up with Internet Protocol capable digital cameras meaning he could tune in whenever he wanted, wherever he was, provided he had a suitable viewing device and a connection to the world wide web. The sophisticated system was also configured to record footage on a dedicated server that only he had access to.

Clara sat down on the wooden throne that faced the bondage wheel, raised her legs and parted them. 'Come now you filthy wretch.'

'Vera, Vera, Vera.' Manny groaned loudly as he glimpsed Clara's heavenly sex. The sight of 'Vera' touching herself gave him the climatic energy he needed to reach orgasm. The butt plug enhanced his contractions, pressing against his prostate, causing him to ejaculate vigorously. 'Veraaaaah!'

As Clara brought her legs together, Manny closed his eyes and waited for her to pull the soiled butt plug from his arse and make him lick it clean. One last submissive act, and his journey through purgatory would be over.

THE MONTGOMERY ARMS

When it came to describing public houses, the Montgomery Arms redefined spit and sawdust. From the outside, crooked walls, bulging brickwork, rotting timber and boarded up windows gave the impression it was a derelict building. Above the battered entrance door, a sign stating *'abandon all hope ye who enter here'* would have been more appropriate than *'licensed to sell intoxicating liquor for consumption on or off the premises'*. Taken from Italian poet Dante Alighieri's legendary opus the *'Divine Comedy'*, *'abandon all hope ye who enter here'*, is the supposed inscription at the gates of hell. Had he been around to tarry for a beer at the Monty, Alighieri would almost certainly have thought he'd stumbled on the netherworld.

If first impressions created a sense of hopelessness, inside, things got decidedly worse. Illuminated gaudily by constantly flickering archaic brass-fitted pendant lights, scorched, stained, sticky, stiletto-heel-pitted parquet flooring that welded itself to the soles of shoes played host to ramshackle stools, chairs and tables splintered from years of use as makeshift weapons in countless brawls. Peeling in more places than it appeared glued, maroon-painted woodchip wallpaper fractured by plasterwork cracking beneath, was complemented in drabness by an Artex-covered ceiling that had long since lost its whiteness to the yellowing effects of nicotine-tainted cigarette smoke.

Landlady Bonny Mills was a drunk who spent every waking hour on the wrong side of the bar abusing her own hospitality and the moral decency of anyone she took a fancy to. This didn't include her fifth husband Denis who pulled pints and peddled Percy to permanently–pissed punters for whom happy hour never ended.

Live music, karaoke, talent shows, stand-up, quiz nights, bingo and strippers; during a lifetime's work Bonny had tried everything to save the soul of the pub, but the Monty, like the majority of its patrons, was condemned. Simply speaking, it was the hostelry from hell, a no-go area for the sensible. At night, the pub was the preserve of the vermin of the manor, a place where squint-eyed, sallow-faced vagrants with life-threatening illnesses mingled with crack-head Hoodies solely interested in threatening life. The police kept a watchful eye on comings-and-goings from a safe distance.

Redemption for Bonny could have come in many forms. Getting pregnant by a millionaire, marrying a millionaire, divorcing a millionaire... but despite her best endeavours, and five marriages, that hadn't happened, nor was it ever likely to now. Then there was winning the lottery. Scratchcard, National, Euro, Postcode. Though she did them all, they'd yielded nothing!

As it transpired, Bonny's future had been secured, for the time being anyway, by technology. An oversize satellite dish mounted on the pub's leaky roof mated to an illegal decoder and projector beamed live football onto a large dropdown screen at the far end of the bar. Forget Sky, this was heaven. Every Premier League match and international fixture was fair game, and Denis took great pleasure chalking up the matches the Monty would be showing on a blackboard that was crudely nailed to the outside door.

'England v Brazil eh.' Bertie's voice was laden with sadness. 'That was the last time I walked into a football stadium.

Fletch sighed as he wheeled him along the pavement approach to the Monty. 'Wembley. 12th May 1981.'

'We were on leave, remember?'

'Hard to forget, though it should have been.' Fletch frowned as he recalled the game. 'Ron Greenwood was manager. Brazil won one zip. Zico scored.'

Bertie rocked his head to one side and closed his eyes. 'Clemence, Neal, Martin, Rix, Robson, McDermott, Coppell, Wilkins, Withe, Barnes.'

'How the fuck did you remember that?' Fletch sounded genuinely impressed as he turned and backed Bertie through the pub doors.

'I was reading through the match programme this morning.'

'Ha ha. Very good.' Fletch struggled with the chair as its wheels repeatedly stuck to the floor as they passed the toilets in the hallway. 'Fuck me! I don't think they've cleaned this gaff since the last time we came here.'

Bertie shrugged his shoulders. 'Be about right by the look of it. That was just over twenty-five years ago. The last drink off limits before we went to the Falklands.'

'We can go somewhere else if you want.'

'Nah. We're here now.'

Fletch pushed open the door to the main bar. 'Yeah! The three of us together again.'

Bertie tapped the side of his chair with his prosthetic arm. 'I'm not sure about that. More like two and a half.' He liked to humour himself occasionally. It was something he'd learned to do out of necessity.

The general chit-chat in the bar turned to silence as they entered. Like a couple of gnarled Western B-Movie gunslingers entering a saloon in a one-horse town everyone turned to stare. Fletch's reconnaissance was still instinctive. Quickly scanning the room he counted eighteen men ranging in age from mid-teens to late twenties. Clad in the ubiquitous local uniform of baseball caps, hoodies, tracksuit bottoms and trainers, they were sat around four tables grouped together in the centre of the room. Six men in England shirts were stood near the large screen. At the bar, sat on a high stool was a whorish-looking woman in a leopard print blouse and black pleated pencil skirt that looked two sizes too small. Next to her a thick-set, pasty-faced man with close-cropped carrot-coloured hair holding an England baseball cap in one hand and a full pint glass in the other. Finally, his eyes settled on a well-known local character, Tom 'Battersea Bugle' Cox, sat on a distressed red leather sofa reading the *'Racing Post'*. 'Blimey! I never thought Coxy would see this place as God's waiting room,' he muttered, nudging Bertie. As he manoeuvred the wheelchair towards the bar the man with carrot-coloured hair brushed past them.

'Fuck me!' he bellowed loudly, attracting the attention of his friends sat at the tables nearby. 'It's the Pirates of the Caribbean!' His comment was greeted with hysterical laughter.

'For fucks sake.' Fletch cursed as he quickly weighed up the odds. Carrot Top was obviously the ringleader of the men he was with, but could he back his ridicule up with his own fists or would he rely on theirs, and would they support him?

'Where's your parrot Captain Hook?' Carrot Top's abuse continued. 'Pieces of eight! Pieces of eight!'

Maybe Carrot Top thought they posed no threat. A man in a wheelchair and his partially sighted friend were easy to mock and to bully. Fletch knew he could knock him out, but then his friends would start and where would that leave Bertie? It wasn't worth the aggravation especially now Carrot Top and his associates had already turned their attention to the big screen and the sight of John Terry leading out the England team.

'I know you don't I? The brassy woman sat at the bar turned to face Fletch as he parked Bertie at a table nearby. 'I never forget a face.' Dyed black hair, heavy mascara, trowelled-on foundation and freshly applied blood-red lipstick that was smeared across her teeth couldn't hide the ravages of time but it could disguise familiarity.

Fletch shook his head. 'Well that's not hard is it?' he replied, self-consciously rubbing his right hand across his forehead. He'd fucked so many trashy whores in his time before meeting his Thai princess Blossom that it was possible he'd spent money with this old harridan as well. He frowned and hoped it was when she was younger.

'You're Paul Fletcher aren't you?'

Fletch swallowed hard as he waited for her next line. The problem was, the more he looked at her, the more he realised he did know her. Admittedly, he liked her look, but she was well past her sell by date. Overdone makeup and painted lips spelt 'fuck my face, my mouth is a pussy'... and she knew his name as well. Had he? He could see Bertie smiling. Tonight's carrot-topped bad dream was turning into a nightmare before it had really got started.

'Bonny Mills.' The woman puckered her lips and leaned into him. 'Or Bonny Roper as you'll remember me... Stan's old girl bless his soul.'

'Bonny!' Fletch exclaimed, relief washing over him. 'You're looking well.'

'God save our gracious Queen, long live our noble Queen, God save the Queen.'

Fletch turned to see Carrot Top and his motley rabble stood on their feet barking out the National Anthem that was being played at Wembley.

'La la la la... send her victorious, happy and glorious, lo-hohohong to reign over us... Go-hod save the Queen.'

Fletch shook his head. 'Still running this place then?'

'Just about.'

'Well I can see that.' He nudged Bonny and cocked his

head back in the direction of Carrot Top.

'Oh that lot. Yeah, well they spend money.'

'Stan would have barred them.'

'That's as maybe, but Stan's long gone.'

'Sorry love, I wasn't thinking.'

'Don't worry about it. Listen, I don't want you coming in here causing no trouble.'

'We won't.'

'I'm not worried about you two. It's that mate of yours Kennedy. I take it he'll be joining you soon. The three amigos and all that.'

Fletch smiled. 'Yeah. He'll be here.'

'I can tell from that cheeky grin of yours that you ain't gonna put my mind at rest by telling me he's a changed man. Anyway, there's no such thing as a changed man is there Den?' Bonny pointed at her husband who had been looking and listening with interest.

'Get Paul and his friend a drink.'

Paul, there it was again. 'It's Fletch.'

'What would you like Fletch?' Den grinned and thrust his hand across the bar, but his handshake was limp-wristed.

'Two light and lagers.' Fletch glanced at his watch. It was exactly 8 p.m. 'Actually make that three.'

★ ★ ★

Kennedy had decided to walk to the Monty. He needed thinking time. At a regular pace, the five-mile jaunt from Richmond Park to Battersea should probably have taken around eighty minutes, but Spot the Staffy, with his inquisitive nose and short legs, had slowed him down. Looking back at Jack one last time as he'd exited the park through Roehampton Gate and strolled slowly down Priory Lane, he'd realised that his son presented him with an opportunity for redemption. Selfishness didn't come into it.

Jack was a talented footballer, and Manny was a businessman who would exploit every ounce of his marketability.

Like any father, he felt duty-bound to ensure his son didn't get ripped off, and if that meant acting as his agent so be it. There was nothing unusual in that, the only problem he could foresee was staying sober. It would be a challenge. The overwhelming compulsion to drink to get drunk had crept up on him unawares since his release from prison. Maybe it was hereditary. His mother was an abstemious, temperate, teetotal woman who reminded him often enough that she had married a man who was also in a deepening relationship with alcohol.

Waking up earlier in the day lying naked in a puddle of his own piss, head resting on a pile of vomit, mouth dry, head pounding, kidneys kicking, it would have been easy to blame somebody else, to self pity, to seek out help.

'Hello my name's Kennedy Jones and I'm an alcoholic.'

He'd never speak those words, because it wasn't true. He didn't think of himself as an alcoholic. Alcohol was a sharp tool that cut out the reality of his situation, the parts of his life that had made no sense. His father's murder, the Falklands, Bertie, Fletch, Prime, Manny, Baker, the drug dealers. Day-by-day he'd started to piece things together. Night after night, vodka after vodka stopped him thinking. Blocking the truth. Blotting out the past. It was a destructive and vicious cycle of self-harm.

In prison he'd read that alcoholism was a disease of the emotions combined with a physical allergy to the demon drink. Clever words written by a doctor or psychiatrist, he couldn't remember which, but that didn't matter because as a free man he didn't want their help as they might lock him away again, section him, straitjacket him... throw away the key. There was one way out, the only way. The solution was at the bottom of the bottle. Not that one, the next one and the one after that. The age-old proverb was correct. The night, and what it represented, was always at its darkest before dawn. Hours, minutes… a split second from suicide, as he'd stood in the window frame, a swan dive from oblivion, the darkness had almost enveloped him for eternity.

The flashbacks and visions, were they a sign of madness? Was he a lunatic? The definition of insanity was doing the same thing over and over and expecting a different outcome. Nicky had wanted him to live with her, but he couldn't, not while he was still working things out and taking care of business. Don't get mad get even. Don't settle for even, play to win.

If you stare at the four walls of a prison cell long enough, you'll see what you're looking for. It had been there all along. A photograph of Jack… Blu-tacked to the brickwork. A young kid in a football kit. Blue shirt, blue shorts, white socks. Chelsea. That's what he'd wanted. Standing on the Shed together, father and son.

The last time Kennedy had been through Roehampton Gate had been in the back of a police car with his hands cuffed. He knew the filth were coming for him, he knew the exact date and time. Shooting Jimmy Baker hadn't been on Manny's agenda. The body had been disposed of, but Baker was too big a fish, too well connected to just disappear. Pressured on all sides, Eddie Jacobsen needed a result, and Manny put money on the table for Kennedy to take the rap and diffuse the situation.

"With my brief, you'll get a fifteen stretch and be out in eight", he'd said confidently. "Chapman Security will buy a house in Nicky's name for your family. When you get released there'll be two hundred grand in cash waiting for you and more work if you want it".

Eight years? He could do that. He was still only twenty-three. When he got out, he'd still have his whole life in front of him. He agreed without hesitation and spent the subsequent years wondering if cruel fate had conspired against him. The

238

day before he was arrested, he'd taken Jack to his first Chelsea game. Four years old wasn't a bad age to start, it was just about the age he'd been when his father had taken him, Bertie and Fletch to Stamford Bridge for the first time.

Saturday 11 November 1967

Chelsea v Sheffield Wednesday

You never forget your first match, the sights, the sounds, the smells. Clicking through the turnstiles, scrambling up the concrete steps, reaching the top of The Shed terrace, looking out on the green expanse below. All the people, so many people. Thirty thousand souls... jostling, shouting, cheering. *'Come on Chelsea! Come on Chelsea!'*

'Go on boys. Go down the front, you'll see better.'

Ninety minutes later after the Blues had won 3-0 with goals from John Hollins, John Boyle and Peter Osgood, his father had explained what winning meant. It was the first time new manager Dave Sexton had guided the team to victory, and their first triumph in ten games.

'Osgood is good, isn't he dad.'

'Too right my sunny son. Mustard goal!'

Ossie's goal was a peach. Waltzing through the Wednesday defence, evading three tackles, the Chelsea striker had played a neat one-two with Joe Fascione and, from fifteen yards out, volleyed the ball past Owls goalie Peter Springett. At the time, the players and names meant nothing. It was only when he was older and read a match report his dad had clipped from a newspaper that he was able to add such detail to his memories.

Almost twenty years later, it had been Jack's turn to be baptised at the Bridge. Sadly, their one game together was nothing to write home about, a portent perhaps of things to come and a place where writing home was one of the few pleasurable pastimes to be had.

Monday 20 April 1987

Chelsea v Southampton

The Shed terrace was now a barren crumbling edifice. There was no need to burrow through legs to get to the front to see the action. You could stand where you wanted with plenty of space around you. It was sad. Johnny Hollins, who'd rippled the net in that first game he'd been to, was the manager now, but his Chelsea side weren't box office any more. It may have been Easter Monday, a bank holiday, but where was everyone? "Today's attendance 11,512. Thank you for your support". Dreadful. Mind you, maybe the fair-weather fans had a crystal ball. The game was a dull-as-ditch-water one all draw.

Thinking about it now, the only thing that was interesting about the match was the fact the Blues goalscorer that day was Pat Nevin. Wee Pat, the player who'd been rejected by his boyhood heroes Celtic for being too small! The ironic coincidence that the same fate befell Jack at Chelsea still angered Kennedy, but he placated himself by visualising Eric Prime with a hangman's noose around his neck.

Bleep Bleep Bleep

Kennedy stopped walking and checked the text message. *'Page 23 Word 17 Word 28 Word 32'*

'What now?' Hurriedly, he checked the poetry book. *'Bring Jack Monday.'* What did that mean? The penny dropped quickly. 'Bring Jack Monday! Yes! Get in there!' Kennedy punched the air with delight. 'Come on Spot!' As he set off with a spring in his heel, he clapped his hands at Spot but the Staffy had other ideas. Having cocked his leg on a lamppost outside the Priory Clinic, he was now sitting down looking pensively at the building. His constant companion from the day he'd killed the dealers, Spot had been there throughout all his nightmare benders. Alert, attentive, watchful. Maybe he was trying to tell him something. The Priory Clinic. He could check himself in. Join one of their noted rehabilitation programmes. He could afford it now.

'Hello my name's Kennedy Jones and I'm an alcoholic.

240

Fuck right off!' Kennedy shook his head and began walking again. Safety, comfort and support came at a price, and he'd already paid dearly. He'd do the rehab his way. A shrill, finger-less whistle and Spot was soon following him faithfully once more.

★ ★ ★

Old Tom Cox was stood just inside the Monty's doorway when Kennedy walked in. Despite the passage of time, recognition was instant which wasn't hard to understand when it came to Coxy. In his heyday, 'Bugle' had been a renowned musician. The trumpet was his instrument of choice, and he'd played everything from jazz to reggae in a career spanning fifty years.

Kennedy smiled. The old goat had to be in his seventies now and the only thing that had noticeably changed about his appearance was the colour of his chest-length Rastafarian beard that was no longer a dirty shade of grey, but white as the pure driven snow. He was still wearing his trademark blue tweed jacket, but this was now threadbare on the sleeves and patched at the elbows. Like the yellow open-necked shirt worn underneath, it hung unhealthily loose on his rickety old frame that was verging on skeletal. Levi jeans, polished two-tone Gatsby lace-up brogues and a blue felt pork pie hat completed a look that hadn't evolved in decades. Coxy was still the epitome of cool! But would he remember him?

'Well, well. Bad bwoy Kennedy Jones. Waa gwann blud?' Coxy croaked, puffing on the thin reefer stuck at the corner of his mouth.

He did remember him. Amazing. Kennedy held his hands out. He wasn't sure what to do or say. All he could think of was the two drug dealers he'd dispatched a few months ago. At his heal, Spot sniffed the air. The odour was familiar, the memories bad. He yelped and rubbed himself against Kennedy's legs.

'Babylon fuck wit you.' Coxy pointed beyond Kennedy at the world outside the Monty. 'Bombaclot dig down life, dig up sin.'

Kennedy nodded. 'I expect so.' He dropped down to his haunches to pat Spot on the head. The Staffy yelped again as raucous chanting coming from the bar unsettled him further.

'Keep Saint George in my heart keep me English. Keep Saint George in my heart I pray. Keep Saint George keep me English. Keep me English till my dying day.'

Kennedy stood up and looked at Coxy, but the old man had his eyes closed. He could hear him mumbling about 'Hingland' and 'Babylon' but couldn't understand what he was trying to say. He took a fifty-pound note from his jacket pocket and clasped Coxy's still outstretched hand wrapping the old mans frail fingers around the money. Comfortably numb, Coxy opened his eyes in time to see Kennedy push the doors open to the main bar that increased the volume of the chanting he could hear.

'No surrender, no surrender, no surrender to the IRA. No surrender, no surrender, no surrender to the IRA.'

The singing ceased as the bar door closed and Coxy was soon back in his own little world. 'Stay blessed Kennedy Jones,' he muttered as he opened his hand to reveal the money he'd been gifted. 'Always stay blessed.'

'All right lads?' Kennedy stood behind the table, stretched out his arms and clasped Fletch and Bertie's shoulders. The England game had kicked off and his entrance to the bar had gone completely unnoticed.

'Maayyyte!' Bertie raised his pint glass.

'A cold one there for you.' Fletch turned to shake Kennedy's

242

hand as he dragged a free stool across and sat down. 'A bit warm for gloves aint it?'

'Oh yeah. Ha ha. Fair point. I cut my hands on some broken glass last night. Nothing serious.' Kennedy resisted the temptation to have a drink and looked up at the big screen. He could concoct a yarn about why he wasn't going to be getting drunk with his friends, or he could take his gloves off and tell the truth, either way it didn't matter, alcohol would not be crossing his lips tonight or any other night in future. He'd made his mind up. He pictured himself stood outside the Priory. "My name's Kennedy Jones and I'm an alcoholic". Bertie and Fletch would understand, he'd explain everything in the fullness of time.

'Anything happened?'

Fletch shook his head and reached down to pat Spot on the head.

'Not yet... apart from those lairy idiots over there pushing their luck.'

Bertie tapped his prosthetic hook on the side of his wheelchair and nodded. 'I've ended up like some kind of ice cream fighting for cunts like that.'

Kennedy looked over at the men gathered in the centre of the bar. He couldn't see their faces but he already knew he didn't like them. Like Fletch, his recce was swift. Four small groups, eighteen of them in total, all of them together, cut from the same tainted piece of cloth. The drug dealers might have been their friends, but that was abusing the definition of friendship. Mouthy chavs. Wankers. Cowards who sought safety in numbers and hid behind a leader. Who was their leader? Their top boy? It wasn't apparent, but there had to be one. There always was.

Bertie was watching Kennedy watching the men. He knew what he was thinking. 'It's the big guy with the red hair,' he said calmly, pausing to neck back his beer before continuing. 'Took the piss out of our disabilities when we came in. Reckons we look like pirates.'

Kennedy's eyes focused in on the back of the carrot-haired ringleader who was pointing at the screen. 'Pirates?'

'Yeah!' Fletch glowered with resentment. 'I should've slapped him.' He attempted to stand up, but Kennedy tugged his arm firmly.

'I thought we were meant to be having a quiet drink.'

'We were, but I didn't reckon on that lot being in here.'

'Maybe we should go.' Bertie placed his empty pint glass on the table.

'Maybe not.' Kennedy removed his jacket off, wrapped it around the back of Bertie's wheelchair and then picked up his pint placing it on the floor next to Spot. 'Remember this?' he said, sitting up and rolling the left sleeve of his shirt. The tattoo on his forearm had faded, but for him its meaning hadn't. Two flags interlinked. On the left the red cross of Saint George, on the right a blue lion rampant regardant holding a staff. Beneath, a scroll bearing the writing *THESE COLOURS DON'T RUN*

'I can't run anywhere.' Bertie shrugged his shoulders and tapped his empty glass.

Fletch smiled and rubbed his chin thoughtfully. He didn't know why he hadn't reacted when Carrot Top had insulted them. Six months ago he would have chinned him and suffered the consequences of being set on by the rest of his gang. Right now, he felt somehow deflated, as if he'd hidden behind Bertie and used his wheelchair-bound friend as an excuse not to provoke trouble. How long could he go on fighting for? He had to stop sooner or later.

'Same again then?' Kennedy drummed his fingers on the table.

'Thought you'd never ask.' Bertie pushed his glass across the table. 'Are you having one as well? Or is the dog doing your drinking for you these days?'

The three men laughed as they looked down at Spot lapping beer enthusiastically. Kennedy shrugged his shoulders. He'd already decided now wasn't the time to explain his Damacene moment. His mother would appreciate it. Put her religious spin on it. Tell him about Saul's conversion to Christianity. About him being surrounded by a bright light as he'd walked along the road to Damascus. About his epiphany. On the road to Damascus, Saul had a life-transforming encounter with the risen Christ who'd given him a new vocation in life. He'd become Paul, God's co-worker, one of the apostles of Jesus Christ. On the road to Battersea, there had been no bright lights and no meeting with Jesus Christ for Kennedy, just a stark realisation that he was now in the last chance saloon and to take that chance he needed his wits about him.

'You still have two lifelines,' joked Bertie, trying to elicit an answer from Kennedy. 'Do you want me to remove two wrong answers and go 50/50, or would you like to phone a friend?'

Fletch laughed while Kennedy looked puzzled.

'I asked you if you were going to have a drink?' continued Bertie, shaking his head.

Kennedy shrugged his shoulders. 'Sorry, I was miles away. Just soft drinks for me at the moment,' he said, waving his gloved hands. 'I'm on antibiotics.'

Fletch lightened up. 'You seen Bonny yet? She could do with being on antibiotics as well.'

Kennedy said nothing. Frowning, he stood up and walked to the bar. Usually he enjoyed Fletch's humour, but in this case he didn't find it funny. He knew about Bonny's problems with drink and could relate to them. She hadn't been the same since Stan Roper had been killed in an accident at a firing range in Switzerland where he'd been demonstrating some new weaponry to Quique Di Santo. A hermetically sealed pouch of hand grenades had exploded as Stan picked it up.

Despite wearing body armour, both men had died instantly. He'd heard about the incident from Manny while he was in prison. Bonny had been well looked after financially, but she'd soon squandered the money and had been on the long road to rack and ruin since.

As he sidled up next to her at the bar, she tapped the tip of her tongue against her top lip and swirled ice cubes around the empty tumbler she was holding.

'I've been expecting you,' she said, rolling her eyes and puckering her lips.

Kennedy put his arm around her and kissed her on the cheek. 'Well I hope you ain't been waiting too long. Can I get you a drink?'

'Get me a drink? Don't be silly... Denis... Denis.' Bonny hectored her husband. 'Are you working or watching the football?'

Denis shook his head and walked over to face his wife across the bar. 'Both my angel,' he replied sarcastically. 'It's called multi-tasking.'

'Good! So you can multi-task me another gin and tonic and get Kennedy here whatever he wants.'

Denis looked sheepishly at Bonny. There was no point saying anything else. The old dragon was pickling her liver again. He eyed her briefly, trying to recall what possessed him to take up with her. Then one by one, as he remembered all his little side-lines, a smile replaced his scowl.

'Two light and lagers, a pint of soda water with lime and three packets of cheese and onion crisps please.' Kennedy turned to look up at the screen and then across the room at Carrot Top and his cronies. Almost twenty minutes gone and still no score, they'd be getting restless soon no doubt.

'So why's it taken you so long to come and see me then?'

Bonny's words were slightly slurred and Kennedy couldn't tell if she was being suggestive. Her tongue was out again. God forbid.

'You know how it is love. I've been away a long time. It's nothing personal.'

Denis placed another gin and tonic on the bar in front of Bonny... it wasn't there for long. A chorus of groans and 'fucking hell's' drew Kennedy's attention back to the screen. Brazil had scored. But the jeers turned to cheers as the goal was ruled offside.

'He was never off then ref,' bellowed Denis, reaching under the bar for the crisps.

'Who d'you want to win then Den?' Carrot Top had appeared at the bar on the other side of Bonny. 'All all right Jonesy. Did... didn't see you there. Eng England of course.'

'Well dat Brazilian was well offside Den innit.' Carrot Top sneered, pinching the end of his nose and sniffing. 'Same again when you're ready. I'll be back in five minutes like.'

Kennedy glanced at the top left corner of the screen, ENG 0 BRA 0 23.02. Five minutes would mean the time elapsed would read 28.02. As Carrot Top walked away from the bar towards the door he made a mental note of the navy blue tracksuit bottoms and distinctive maroon and white Adidas Gazelle trainers he was wearing. There was something familiar about 'Jonesy' as Den had referred to him, but he couldn't put his finger on it.

'Two light and lagers, a pint of soda with lime and three packets of cheese and onion. There you go.' Dennis opened the bottles of light ale and placed them on a tray with the rest of the order. 'Anything else?' he enquired, winking at Kennedy. 'Something for the nose perhaps?'

Kennedy shook his head and frowned. 'No thanks.'

'Behave yourself.' Bonny tapped Kennedy's arm with her bony, gold be-ringed left hand.

'Are you talking to me or him?' Kennedy shrugged his shoulders as he spoke.

Bonny looked perplexed. 'You of course ha ha,' she cackled. 'Come and see me later we'll have a chat about the old times.'

Kennedy nodded as he picked up the tray. 'Course we will. Thanks for the drinks.' What would Stan 'the man' Roper make of the way his drinker had declined? His old woman a lush, her latest old man serving up to snipes from the gutter. No surrender! He'd have been across the bar with a baseball bat. No fucking surrender! What did these pricks know? As he placed the tray on the table in front of an appreciative Fletch and Bertie, he looked once more at the top left corner of the screen. *ENG 0 BRA 0 24.12.*

'Just going for a slash.' There was no acknowledgement. Like everyone else in the bar, Fletch and Bertie were absorbed in the game. ENG 0 BRA 0 24.48, as he walked to the doors Kennedy quickened his step. The combined stench of bleach, disinfectant, stale piss and blocked drains assaulted his nostrils as he pushed open the toilet door. The room was small. On one side, three yellowing chipped enamel urinals clung to a graffiti-covered concrete wall. Yeast and water scale had combined to form a brown crust on the tiled floor beneath them that reached out like a toxic lava flow. Adjacent, there were two cubicles, one open, one closed. There was a gap of four inches between the base of the closed wooden door and the floor.

Kennedy dropped to his haunches and bent his head down so he could see inside the cubicle. The occupant was wearing maroon and white Adidas Gazelle trainers. 'Izzit you in there bruv?' he said, standing up and mimicking the so-called Jafaican accent that he believed had infected half the population of London during his time in prison.

'Innit.' The reply was accompanied with a sniff. 'I've just gone one up.'

Kennedy paced back as far as he could and took a running jump at the door, striking it with sufficient force to splinter the wood and shear it from its hinges.

'What the...?'

Jonesy didn't have a chance to finish his question as Kennedy stormed the cubicle and smashed his right fist into his face. The first punch split his nose open, the second fractured his cheekbone and the third pummelled him backwards.

'Pirates eh? You mug.' Kennedy raged as Jonesy's head bounced off the back wall. 'No fucking surrender eh? You cunt!'

Jonesy's eyes rolled, his face a bloodied mask of panic. Kennedy grabbed him by the neck, kneeing him in the groin as he did so. Jonesy groaned in pain, free hands flailing, trying to protect himself, but he was powerless to prevent Kennedy from forcing his head into the toilet bowl.

'RULE BRITANNIA!' Kennedy shouted stepping back and pulling the chain hanging down from the overhead cistern. As the toilet flushed, Jonesy raised his head from the bowl. The last thing he saw before unconsciousness claimed him was a boot lunging towards his face.

Kennedy stood still momentarily, taking in the sights and sounds. Something felt strange, different somehow. The lighting was normal. The balance and hue of colours were as they should be. All he could hear was the sound of the water being replenished in the cistern and his own heavy breathing. Was the battle that had been raging in his head all these years finally over?

He looked at Jonesy's prostrate body. Sodden red hair matted across his shit-spattered, bloodied face. Crumpled clothes dirtied by the filthy floor that was littered with cigarette dog-ends, strips of burned tin foil, Origami-style folded lottery tickets, drinking straws and spent Clipper lighters.

'Fucking degenerate.' He dragged Jonesy by his feet into the adjacent cubicle, removed his trainers, pulled the door shut from the outside and clambered up so he could reach down and lock it. Yeah! Maybe the battle was over. But the war was just beginning.

★ ★ ★

'Fuck me! You've been gone a while.' Bertie raised his glass as Kennedy returned to the table. Spot's eaten all the crisps.'

Kennedy smiled as he patted the dog's head and sat down. 'I was chatting to the Battersea Bugle outside. Gave him a drink for old times sake.'

'You didn't buy those off him did you?' Bertie looked puzzled as he pointed at the pair of maroon and white Adidas Gazelle trainers Kennedy had placed on the table.

'Lucky he can chat at all.' Fletch bypassed Bertie's curiosity about the trainers and raised his hand as Coxy shuffled past and made his way slowly to the near edge of the bar where a pint of Guinness was waiting for him.

'Why's that?' Kennedy wondered if he should have made a point of going to talk to Coxy again after he'd dealt with Jonesy.

'He didn't tell you?'

'No mate.'

'Poor bloke's riddled with cancer. He's only got a few months.'

'Shit! That's terrible. He never said anything.'

Bertie shook his head. 'Poor sod. All those years playing the trumpet in smoky clubs, night-after-night sucking that polluted air into his lungs. Same thing happened to Roy Castle.'

Fletch laughed. 'Yeah! But I bet old Roy wasn't puffing an ounce of weed a week.'

'What the fuck is he doing?' Kennedy screwed his eyes shut and then blinked several times as he watched Coxy take a large plastic syringe from his jacket pocket, place the nozzle into the pint in front of him, draw up the plunger and fill the chamber with Guinness.

'He's nil by mouth now. Feeds himself through a tube

connected to his stomach.'

'Feeds?'

'Yeah! Guinness. He says it's a meal in a glass.'

As Kennedy watched Coxy unbutton the bottom of his shirt and connect the syringe to the feeding tube, Fletch and Bertie turned their attentions back to the football.

'Come on Beckham. One decent ball in the box.' Bertie gritted his teeth in anticipation as the Real Madrid midfielder teed up a free-kick some forty yards out from the Brazil goal.

'Get in there JT!' Fletch bellowed, jumping to his feet.

The bar erupted as Beckham's perfectly flighted ball was met by John Terry rising unchallenged at the far post to head home. 'Ha ha. A proper captain's goal. Know what I mean.'

Bertie drummed his left hand on the table. 'Terry fucking loves Wembley.'

'Why's that?' Kennedy glanced up at the screen to catch the action replay.

'He skippered Chelsea to victory when they beat Man U last month in the FA Cup Final. That was the first game to be played at Wembley since they reopened it. Now he's captain of England.'

'Didn't he play for us in the last FA Cup Final to be staged there before the redevelopment?' Kennedy sat back and folded his arms as he spoke.

Fletch shook his head. 'He was on the bench but never got a game. He was still a kid then, learning from Marcel Desailly and Frank Leboeuf.'

Bertie burst into song and Fletch joined in the chorus. *'He's here, he's there, he's every fucking where Frank Leboeuf, Frank Leboeuf.'*

Kennedy noted the time of the goal that was being displayed on the screen. 'Terry 68' Almost an hour had passed since he'd locked Jonesy in the toilet. It was surprising that none of his friends had noticed he was missing. Maybe he'd told them he was going on an errand. Maybe the football was more important. Maybe they didn't care.

'Well, well.' Bertie looked across at the entrance door to the bar that had just been slammed open. 'No-one likes to see that happen.'

Jonesy, looking unsteady on his bare feet, staggered slowly into the room.

'Looks like he's been ten rounds with Tyson?' said Fletch.

'Or Kennedy.' Bertie pointed at the pair of trainers on the table in front of them. Suddenly, the England game was of secondary interest to everyone in the bar.

'What the fuck happened?' One of Jonesy's acolytes got up to offer support by way of a shoulder to lean on and another soon joined him. Jonesy flinched as he tried to look around the room. It was a difficult task. His right eye was closed and swollen and his badly bruised left eye was weeping blood from a deep cut to the lid.

Kennedy picked the trainers up and tossed them across the floor to where he was stood. 'Unless you're making a fashion statement, I'd say they must be yours.'

A ripple of laughter punctuated the silence. Jonesy raised his head. 'Do you know who I am?'

Kennedy stood up. 'Are you talking to me?'

'Well it ain't the raspberry innit?'

Kennedy immediately gauged the reaction of Jonesy's mob. Despite having numbers in their favour, those looking in his direction had worried expressions on their faces. 'You look like you need an ambulance.'

Jonesy lurched forward. 'Are you taking the piss?'

Kennedy stood up and raised his gloved hands. 'Looks like someone's already done that.'

Jonesy looked at his friends and then at Kennedy. 'I'll be back.' He said, spitting blood and groaning as he bent down to pick up his trainers.

'Course you will Arnie.'

As Jonesy was helped out of the bar, several more of his friends also decided to leave. As they did so, an irate finger-wagging Bonny tottered across to confront Kennedy. 'I thought I told you to behave yourself,' she screeched. 'I can't afford to lose any customers.'

Kennedy reached for his jacket pocket. 'Well you can now.'

Bonny's mascara-ringed eyes widened owl-like at the wad of money he thrust into her hand. For the first time in her life she was lost for words.

★ ★ ★

'I reckon all those fans who left Wembley early still reckon England won.'

Fletch shook his head as Bertie spoke. 'Shouldn't have subbed Terry off. He'd have cleared that Silva cross Diego headed in.'

'Nothing like an injury time goal to take the jam out of your donut,' added Kennedy, making a mental note of the faces of each of Jonesy's friends as they began drinking up in readiness to leave. 'At least we didn't lose.'

'I remember back-in-the-day, we sometimes used to leave games early,' said Fletch, laughing at the surreal sight of Coxy injecting himself with more Guinness and Bonny accidentally laddering her stockings with the nail file she was holding as she pestered her old man for another G&T.

'Man U away. May 79. Last match of the season. Remember that?' Bertie's eyes twinkled with enthusiasm as he spoke.

'Yeah! Man U away ha ha.' Kennedy chuckled. Briefly, he thought about taking his gloves off so he could inspect his damaged hands that were stinging as a result of punching Jonesy, but wanting to keep the conversation about the old days going, he decided against it. 'Drew one all, but we were already relegated.'

Fletch sat back in his chair and rubbed his chin thoughtfully. 'It was a Wednesday night. There were about ten minutes left and we walked out of the Scoreboard End and marched into the Stretford. It's funny how you can suddenly recall all that shit. Every little detail. Who was there, what happened... but I'm fucked if I can recall who scored for Chelsea?'

Kennedy leaned forward. 'I know, and you'll never get it. I'll tell you the rest of the Blues team that played that night and you'll still never get it.'

'Go on then.' Fletch and Bertie laughed at the fact they'd spoken simultaneously.

'Petar Borota, Graham Wilkins, Ron Harris, Eamonn Bannon, John Sitton, Gary Chivers, Trevor Aylott, Tommy Langley and Clive Walker.'

'How the fuck did you remember that?' There was an incredulous tone to Fletch's voice.

'One of the things I did to pass the time when I was banged up in solitary was make lists. All kinds of lists. Everything from favourite films to favourite fucks.'

'That would have been a short list.' Fletch clapped his hands as he interrupted.

'You know that.' Kennedy smiled, placing his hands on the table. 'Anyway... one of the lists was favourite away games, and that Man U game was on it. Once I'd made the list then I'd elaborate on the details.'

'Better than spending your time wanking I suppose.' Fletch laughed at his joke, but Bertie failed to see the funny side, tapping his chair by way of making his displeasure known. As he scowled, Fletch felt his cheeks flush with shame and embarrassment.

Kennedy reached into his pocket for a fifty-pound note and placed it on the table. 'There's a bullseye. Tell me who the other player was in the team, the lad who scored.'

Fletch shook his head. 'I ain't got a Scooby.'

'Bertie, whaddya reckon?'

Bertie drew his bottom row of teeth back and forth along his top lip as he considered his answer. 'You know what... I reckon it was Lee Frost,' he said confidently.

'Good call.' Kennedy smiled as he snatched the note away from Bertie's outstretched hand and put it back in his pocket. 'But not good enough. Frosty was sub that night. The lad who scored was Gary Johnson.'

Fletch looked amazed. 'Fucking hell, Gary Johnson. I'd never have remembered that in a month of Sunday's.'

Bertie shook his head. 'Gary Johnson! Yeah! Yeah! It's coming back... slowly. He came through the youth team. It was only his second game for us. Funnily enough he'd made his debut at Old Trafford in the FA Cup that January. We got dicked three nought.'

Fletch's memory banks began working overtime. 'Now you mention that, I do remember the kid. He was quite promising. Scored a few goals in the Second Division when they weren't exactly ten a penny. Pony Geoff Hurst never fancied him, I wonder where he ended up?'

Bertie raised his prosthetic hook as if he were sat in a school classroom requesting permission to answer a question. 'He got loaned to Palace, sold to Brentford and wound up at Aldershot.'

'Just shows how luck plays a part in football.'

'You're not wrong there, look at what happened with Jack.'

Kennedy, who'd stayed silent as Fletch and Bertie reminisced about Gary Johnson, rubbed his hands together and smiled. 'Well maybe, there's another chapter to that story. Cheam Athletic.'

'Cheam! Fuck me!' Fletch looked as astounded as Kennedy appeared pleased.

'Yeah! I know... Uncle Manny. Let's just say he owes me a favour.'

'I'd say he owes you more than that.' Bertie shook his head. 'That set up at Cheam is mental. Knowing Manny, I expected him to get a big name manager in and keep investing in players once they got promoted to League Two, but for some weird reason he's stuck with that Mark Parry and they only avoided relegation back to the Conference on goal difference.'

Fletch drummed his fingers on the table. 'Misplaced loyalty maybe.'

'Manny ain't the sort of bloke to misplace anything. Where there's a rhyme for him, there's always a reason.'

'Rhyme and reason.' Kennedy laughed as he thought about Manny's cryptic text messages that were mated to the war poetry book. 'Have Cheam got a game on Monday?' he asked, changing the course of the conversation. 'I thought the season was finished.'

Fletch rubbed at the stubble on his head. 'I remember reading something in the *'Standard'* the other week about Palace playing them in a testimonial.'

'That'll be it then.' As he got to his feet, Kennedy looked elated. 'Jack's big chance. Right then, do you two want one for the frog?'

★ ★ ★

Manny felt uncomfortable as he sat forward and opened the leather-trimmed cocktail cabinet in the rear of the Bentley. The Diamond Series Arnage was the definition of luxury motoring, but even its quilted upholstery and specially tuned suspension could not cushion his backside sufficiently to prevent him being constantly reminded of the trauma it had recently been subjected to.

'Did the CCTV equipment get picked up from Prime's house?' He enquired, grimacing as he poured a generous glass of Dewars.

'Yeah. Sorted this afternoon.' Harry looked in the rearview mirror and smiled. 'Jester said the house goes on the market on Monday. I'm glad he's out of the way. Never liked him. Nobody did come to think of it.'

Manny arched his back and winced.

'You okay boss?' Harry sounded genuinely concerned.

'Yeah! Just my arthritis playing up.' Manny knocked back the whisky and cleared his throat. 'I know what you mean about Prime. I didn't care much for him much either... but he had his uses right up to the minute he outlived them.'

Manny enjoyed Harry Craven's company more than most of his long-serving employees. Trustworthy and unquestioning, Harry was quite content with being updated on a need-to-know basis. He was the only member of staff obligated to put his life on the line should the need arise, and for that reason he was content to share information with him that nobody else was privy to knowing that his ego would probably be flattered in return. Clara had reminded him that this was one of his failings when she'd punished him earlier. Despite this, he couldn't help himself. Right now he could use some praise.

'I'll tell you this much H. There are four reasons why the filth has never been able to lay one dirty little finger on me,' he said smugly. 'Planning. Meticulous detail. Covering all the bases.' He could sense Harry was impressed. Along with the whisky it helped anesthetise the pain.

'What's the fourth reason boss?'

'I'm glad you asked me that. I just wanted to check you were paying attention. What do you think it is H?'

'Because you never take your eyes off your opponent?'

'Exactly! I only ever did it once in my life, and it cost me dearly.'

'Why did you bother with a suicide note for Prime?'

'Why not? Jacobsen left one before Prime killed him. It allayed suspicion. The same went for Prime. Kennedy faked his suicide note after I provided him with the report he'd handwritten on the Belmarsh assault.'

'Did Kennedy fake Jacobsen's suicide note as well?'

'No. He wasn't in on that. I actually got Jacobsen to write his note himself. It was a double bluff. He thought he was going to be chloroformed, and the prison doctor was going to sign his death certificate. I told him we were going to spring him from the mortuary. Switch his 'body' with someone else and give him a new identity and a new life in Australia. I told him there'd be a couple of mill' in it for him. He believed it. His note was priceless. Three paragraphs of it, explaining his involvement with Di Santo, Delaney and Baker and the shame he felt he brought on his family and the police force.'

'Why did he agree to take the fall and get sent down?'

'I paid him. He'd become a liability on the outside. Better to have him off the streets.'

'Killing Prime the day he'd killed Jacobsen... you weren't kidding about wasting him as soon as he'd outlived his usefulness.'

'Yeah! But as you pointed out, Prime was a cunt. Kennedy didn't really need any financial encouragement! He'd have done him for free.'

Harry gripped the steering wheel and shrugged his shoulders. 'This is like *'The Godfather,'* he said without thinking about it.

Manny smiled and looked out of the black-tinted window. 'I am the fucking Godfather.'

Harry nodded in agreement, but on reflection he wondered if *'The Godfather'* was the right analogy. Don Corleone, the head of the fictitious New York crime family in the film was, well just that, the head of a family. The concept of family seemed anathema to Manny. No wife, no kids that he knew of. Just an unlucky nephew whose life he had manipulated beyond reason. Any reason why? Because families create problems... trouble and strife. Maybe there was a lot of truth in the old adage about not being able to choose your family. Manny's way worked. He was a megalomaniac, a fiendish genius, but weren't all the top people? They all loved having smoke blown up their arses. So what? At the end of the day, he'd earned a small fortune working for him and that was good enough. Let the madman say what he wanted to say. Agree with him. Tell him he's great. Let the money roll in... and spend it.

Manny coughed. A signal to Harry to pay attention again as he hadn't quite finished his soliloquy. 'It's true what many people say. Money *is* the root all evil. But the majority say it for the wrong reason. Why? Because they're jealous of those who have it. Why? Because they're skint. Because they've failed in life. Let me tell you why money *is* the root of all evil. It's because it makes people greedy and reckless. Prime, Jacobsen, Baker, Delaney, Di Santo, Stan Roper... all those cunts and a few more you don't know about. Didn't I line their pockets well enough? More than enough, you know that.'

Harry nodded in agreement. 'You're dead right.'

'Dead is about right.' Manny laughed and opened the cocktail cabinet again.

'One thing's always puzzled me boss. Did Prime really sell your brother out in Belfast like you eventually told Kennedy?' Harry paused for a moment, worried that he might be asking for too much information, but curiosity compelled him to continue anyway. 'Or was Prime's version of events, that he wound Kennedy up in Belmarsh with, the truth?'

Manny raised his eyebrows. 'Good question,' he said, pouring another whisky. 'Officially, it was just a series of coincidences that Prime served with Alec in Northern Ireland and Kennedy in the Falklands and that his older brother knew our father. When he left the Army he became a screw. As you know, Prime liked a punt. He racked up some serious debts with Rolls and Chidgey who'd taken over Nick Hill's book, and that's when he was brought to my attention. A screw with gambling debts is easy to get at. Prime had a connection with both Alec and Kennedy, so it was perfect. Given what happened in Belfast and the Falklands, it was easy to play both ends off the middle and later to deal with Jacobsen.'

Harry tapped his fingers on the steering wheel. 'What about the unofficial version?'

Manny's mobile rang. 'Don't take me for a cunt like the rest of them H,' he said matter-of-factly, the self-satisfied expression on his face turning to a scowl as he looked at the phone's display and saw who was calling him. 'Especially this cunt!'

★ ★ ★

'I can't believe it was twenty-five years ago.' Fletch looked up at the ceiling as he spoke. A lull in conversation had prompted him to remember the fact, and now, as he'd brought the topic of the Falklands up, he wished he hadn't. The war had changed the course of each of their lives forever when they were still young men. The physical and mental scars would always be with them, but in his mind, they'd all moved on. They'd had to, because to remain caught in a vortex of flashbacks in that cold, dark, unforgiving place only those with personal experience fully understood was akin to being condemned to hell. An unending nightmare of eternal torment that despite having a recognisable medical diagnosis, Post Traumatic Stress Disorder, remained challenging to treat.

'I can.' Bertie tapped the side of his wheelchair with his prosthetic arm. 'I'd believe it if you said it was one year ago, ten years ago or fifty years ago.'

'I just stopped believing.' Kennedy tossed a packet of crisps on the floor to Spot which he burst open enthusiastically. The loud bang caused all three men to bob their heads instinctively. 'I had plenty of time to think about it inside. About how my life might have been different if I hadn't enlisted. About how your lives would have been different if I hadn't enlisted. I cried plenty of tears in solitary over the milk I've spilt... and I still cry now.'

Fletch shook his head and nodded at Jonesy's friends leaving the bar. 'Was it worth it for that lot?'

Bertie smiled. 'Who's to say, we wouldn't have ended up like them? They're a product of the society we live in. Patriotic but misguided. If they knew what we'd been through with the Regiment, they'd have been buying us drinks. Instead, they probably think we're tramps.'

Kennedy folded his arms. He was enjoying the lucidity of being sober. He liked being able to articulate his opinion. 'They're the kids of the English working class, just like we are. The difference is, in our day, there was less confusion. Britain was easy to understand. People knew their place. The government had a ready resource of men willing to enlist to fight their wars.'

Fletch bowed his head and spoke slowly and deliberately. 'Back then wars had a beginning a middle and an end. The Falklands conflict was short, sharp... and fucking brutal. But we were fighting for Queen and Country against a recognisable enemy. Look at it now. Take Afghanistan. Whose war is that? Who exactly are the Taliban? It's an unwinnable situation. What was Jack fighting for? Who was he fighting? They kill our men with bombs buried at the roadside. We kill their men, but more are being trained to take their place. Who will take the place of our men?'

Fletch's profound opinion was met with reflective silence and his questions went unanswered as both of the double entrance doors to the main bar of the Monty were kicked open simultaneously. The remaining members of Jonesy's brigade who were planning on leaving stepped back from the doors as two muscle-bound security guards in black T-shirts and

261

jeans strode in followed by Jonesy. Fletch and Kennedy were as quick to their feet as the remainder of the Monty's patrons were to sit down.

'That's him.' Jonesy pointed at Kennedy, and, as he did so, the Monty's doors swung open again. Manny and Harry's entrance stopped Kennedy, already advancing towards the security guards, in his tracks.

'Enough!' Manny raised his arm. 'That's enough!' As he shouted a second time, Denis lowered the bar's security shutters.

'Manny!' exclaimed Kennedy, startled by his uncle's dramatic appearance. As he walked towards him, he glanced at the two security guards and noticed the Chapman Security logo on the T-shirts. 'What the fuck's going on?'

Sensing his problems were about to magnify, Jonesy made his way to where his friends were stood, but they edged away from him. Harry Craven smiled. He knew this wasn't in 'The Godfather's' plan. Looking at Jonesy, the 'cunt' reference in the Bentley made sense now. So he did have a family after all. He was a father, not a godfather. He tried not to laugh

As he spoke to Manny, Kennedy pointed at Fletch and Bertie and then at Jonesy.

Manny, face reddening with rage, stepped forward. 'You filthy fucking peasant come here,' he roared, directing his ire at Jonesy who flinched as he tried to open his bruised eyelids more so he could see better. 'No. Actually, don't waste what energy you've got. I'll come to you.'

Kennedy returned to his stool, sat down, patted Spot on the head and winked at Fletch and Bertie.

As he confronted Jonesy, Manny glared at him. 'If you disrespect these men, you disrespect this country and you disrespect me,' he shouted, raising his hand and slapping Jonesy's face with sufficient strength to send him reeling to the floor. Scuttling after him, he dropped to his haunches, grimacing at the discomfort this caused and mentally cursing Clara in the process. 'What do you say?' he growled. Jonesy recoiled in fear as Manny grabbed him by the scruff of the neck and slapped his face again.

'Th th thank you.' His reply was stammered and it betrayed the sobs he was trying to stifle. 'Th th Thank you Dad.'

THE WATCHMAKERS CREST

28 January 2008

The main room at Viola had been transformed for Manny's private party. Custom-made blue and gold linings and drapes tastefully masked the exposed brick walls that were a feature of the nightclub, and blue Chiavari chairs with gold cushions surrounded banqueting tables that featured a cloth throw emblazoned with the Cheam Athletic Football Club crest. The focal point for the two hundred guests, a five metre stage-mounted plasma screen arced by blue and gold balloons was about to screen the live draw for the Fifth Round of the FA Cup.

Manny's decision to retain Mark Parry as manager and sign Jack Jones had been vindicated. Cheam were on the up again, and Jack had been a revelation. Not only had the eighteen goals he'd scored since making his debut six month's previously fired the Watchmakers to the top of League Two and into the Fifth Round of the Cup, they had also drawn the attention of the media to the club who'd flocked to Peaches Close once more to cover this new evolving story.

Manny was basking in the glory. He was being portrayed as a latter-day saint. The saviour of Cheam, one of life's good guys who bucked the trend of shady businessmen buying their way into football to exploit the game for their own ends. Right now, he was the man. It was incredible. Sometimes he had to pinch himself to believe it was real. He was untouchable. He looked around the room at all the people sat around the tables. The players, their family members, club staff, his family, friends, associates… most of them were unwitting pawns in a corrupt game of chess where he was the Grandmaster.

Admittedly, some of them knew more than they should, but it would have been impossible to get this far without assistance. Cold hard cash was the key. With the notable exception of one person, everybody present had a specified price and had been inveigled into working directly or indirectly for him. It was human nature that some of them might whisper or gossip or try to further their own aims behind his back… but he got to them in the end, all of them. Sleepless hours spent watching live and recorded CCTV footage provided him with an element of control he not only needed but also craved. Chapman Security cameras were everywhere.

Manny had convinced himself he wasn't paranoid, he just needed to allay fears and suspicions about certain people… well all the people if the truth be told, but the truth was never told, just his approximation of it. Intelligence was key. It was a twenty-four hour job, but it was worth doing. Know your friends and know your enemies. Keep your friends close and your enemies closer still. 'Never take your eyes off your opponent.'

Vivian Francis was a prime example. As Vivian he'd trusted her, but she'd been a clever scheming bitch. That Ginger Francisco split personality of hers was a calculating charade. She'd duped him for years, taken him for a fool. He'd bought into her flame-haired, green-eyed transformation, what man wouldn't have? Cunning vixen. He'd given her everything. Opportunity, money… a lifestyle she could only ever have dreamed of. What had he asked for in return? Nothing. He'd never tried to lay a finger on her because he knew the truth. She was a fake. She also preferred the company of women. He'd watched plenty of CCTV footage featuring her engaged in girl-on-girl action, not for self-gratification, more out of curiosity. Her sexuality disgusted him, but he let it pass because she was a capable businesswoman who had done an excellent job in establishing Viola as *the* premium entertainment venue in London. As far as he knew, she hadn't stolen from him or plotted behind his back. What she had done was say the wrong thing. *"I've always had the impression you wish you'd fought for Queen and Country. Is that true?"* It was the day Kennedy had been released from prison. Kennedy Jones the war hero. He'd replayed her insolent question over and over, imagining her chiding him behind his back. Who the fuck was she to get impressions about what he wished for? She'd also taken far too keen an interest in the music he wanted played at his own funeral. What was she planning? He'd thought about it in detail that evening. He could have questioned her, tortured her maybe in Clara's dungeon. No. That was a waste of time he didn't have. She'd riled him enough to make him decide she had to go.

Ginger Francisco's sudden disappearance had initially caused a stir, but not for long. Manny had explained her chameleon-like persona to the police. He'd shown them company bank details highlighting a series of irregular transfers to several accounts linked to her that totalled several million pounds. The scale of her deception had made the headlines. With a consummate ability to transform her appearance, she could be anywhere in the world. Interpol had been alerted, but the chances of finding her were slim, slimmer still given the fact that she was dead. A lethal cocktail of Botulinum toxin, Jack Daniels and Coca Cola had ended her life.

"I've always had the impression you wish you'd fought for Queen and Country. Is that true?" What the fuck has it got to do with you Ginger Francisco? It was amusing and ironic that Botulinum toxin was used for the age-defying Botox injections she swore by. Paralysis of her muscles and respiratory system had been swift and the silence of her death a blessed relief from her whining opinions and questions. He'd taken care of everything

himself. She lay buried in the concrete-filled footings of the new Cheam Athletic indoor training facility that had recently opened at Peaches Close. 'You see my dear Ginger, that's what happens to people who get the wrong impression of Chapman Jones.'

He'd often contemplated seeking the opinion of a psychiatrist, but that would involve telling all as a means of explaining his obsessions, his anxieties and his anger. Such an avowal would have to be underwritten by an insurance policy. Footage of an outwardly respectable counsellor dressed in a French maid's outfit being sodomised by Mistress Clara with a strap-on dildo would have helped with his quest to find someone to talk to, but none existed. Was it more than just a strange coincidence that of all her clients, and he had them all listed, not one was a trick cyclist that needed a lifestyle dominatrix to disconnect his own head!

That aside, what was the point anyway? Complete veracity during an initial psychiatric evaluation would uncover the root cause of his depression that had manifested itself in such sinister ways. The detail would rapidly lead to a diagnosis that he was clinically insane. Imagine if this became common knowledge. To the people gathered in front of him he would be remembered as a psychopath, but that was because they didn't understand the true meaning of what was a complex condition. When he'd questioned himself about this, he'd done some research. Psychopath's were antisocial, impulsive, hasty, and had no moral code of ethics. They made mistakes, left clues, got caught out... he didn't. He wasn't a psychopath he was a sociopath, a well-organised manipulative charmer whose meticulous, methodical approach to crime left no clues, someone capable of understanding human emotions but unable to feel them. Self-diagnosis helped. He was capable of feeling remorse and guilt for what he had done, and Clara in the guise of Vera punished him without knowing the truth.

To her, he was just another kinky punter. What saddened him was the fact that because he'd covered his tracks so skilfully, nobody would ever get to find out what a supreme criminal mind he had. He was the best. Imagine standing up and sharing his story now. The thought made him smile.

Manny looked at his watch, it was 2.40 p.m. He got to his feet, raised his hands and clapped them three times. By the third clap, the people gathered at the tables had fallen silent, a captive audience ready to be addressed. His people, his world. Family members... Vera, Kennedy, Nicky, Jack, Aimee, Tess. Cheam Athletic... Manager Mark Parry, his staff. Max Gardner, Jim Jackson, Ben Richardson and the rest of the team. Business partners and associates... Jester Cook, Tim Rolls, David Chidgey. Great Britons... Fletch, Bertie and their ladies, not forgetting Clara Bristow and Trina Jackson. He'd even invited old Tom Cox the Battersea Bugle and Bonny whatever her surname was now from the Monty. Everyone he wanted to impress was here apart from Harry Craven who'd sent him a text message saying he had a severe headache. Harry had never had a day off sick in thirty years. There was always a first time. Nevertheless, given the occasion, it was a surprise.

'Ladies and gentlemen. Friends. In a few minutes we'll find who Cheam will play in the Fifth Round of the FA Cup. This is uncharted territory for the football club, and today is all about celebrating this notable achievement which is matched by being top of League Two...'

Cheers, whistles and applause fractured his speech. This felt better than he thought it would. The adulation was really for him, Chapman Jones, the man who had made it all possible. Benefactor, employer... none of this would have happened without his foresight, wisdom and generosity. 'Right then, let's see what's in store on the next part of our adventure together.' He stepped back to further applause that was curtailed by the thunderous rattle and hum of static as the speakers connected to the television system were amplified and the sound swiftly balanced.

The BBC continuity announcer spoke. 'Okay! Let's go live to Soho Square to bring you the draw for the Fifth Round of the FA Cup.'

Manny looked up at the screen shook his head and smiled. The FA Cup draw taking place a couple of streets away was probably one of the only things in life he couldn't influence the outcome of. Such uncertainty would ordinarily have made him nervous. Normally the odds were always stacked in his favour. Time and again he'd made sure of that. This though was different. He'd looked at all the teams left in the competition and at first had thought it would be good to draw Manchester United away. Forty-five percent of the gate receipts from 75,000 paying punters at Old Trafford would bring in well over one million pounds, and then there was the television money, the merchandising and everything in between. Last, but by no means least, was the considerable revenue to be reaped from the illegal betting syndicates. Football was a fantastic business to be in, and he'd often reprimanded himself for not having seized an opportunity earlier.

Everybody at the club wanted to draw Chelsea at home, not only because they were the local team, but also because they had rejected Jack when he was a kid. Cheam had boosted its attendance by being an affordable alternative to Blues supporters priced out of going to Stamford Bridge, and his nephew Jack was their new hero. Ahhh the romance of the FA Cup. Fuck that! Let's get the tills ringing. If Jack did well he could be sold for millions. He'd bank the money and bring over a few kids from the illegal football academies that proliferated in West Africa and were effectively trafficking footballers. It was a poorly kept secret, and a lot of the big clubs were at it.

Football, 'the beautiful game', that's what people called it. Never kid a kidder. Look what happened to the old boy who claimed to have coined the phrase. The television and radio presenter who ended up getting jailed for multiple sex offences. Damn, he couldn't remember his name. Every time they did his laundry in the nick, he must be praying nothing else came out in the wash. Football, just like everything else in life, was tainted, open to exploitation. Exploit or be exploited. The choice was simple and hadn't required much thought.

As Manny watched the draw commence he felt his personal mobile phone vibrate in his jacket pocket. It was a text message alert. Only his closest associates had this number and, apart from Harry, they were all in front of him. Who would be stupid enough to disturb him now?

'Number One. Arsenal.'

His phone continued to vibrate.

'Number Fifteen. Tottenham Hotspur.'

As gasps blended with laughter in the room, Manny checked to see who had sent the text. It was from Harry. *'220440030939'* 'What is this shit H? Your national fucking insurance number?' Puzzled, he slowly checked the digits again. As the stark realisation of their meaning dawned on him, he dialled Harry and hurriedly got to his feet.

Kennedy, sat at a table near the screen with his family, Fletch and Bertie, rocked his head back and smiled. It wasn't the fact his friends were accompanied by Thai brasses Blossom and her sister Petal that amused him, it was more to do with *"Number Fifteen. Tottenham Hotspur"*. The number fifteen reminded him of 15A Chivalry Road, Eric Prime's address. He imagined the police forcing the door open and barging past the photographs on the wall of the Queen's coronation, the Prime brothers in their youth, and the Spurs side that had won the Double. All the photos were black and white, he hadn't noticed that the night he'd rigged Prime's apparent suicide. It made sense though given their age.

The cup draw continued. *'Number Three. Bristol City.'*

A buxom, redheaded waitress held the door open for ashen-faced Manny who had his mobile phone pressed to his ear as he scanned the faces of everybody gathered in the room.

'Harry… Harry! One of the things I pay you for is to answer your fucking phone when I call.' Manny undid the top button of his shirt, and, as he spoke, a familiar cold, clammy feeling of trepidation swathed his soul.

'Number Thirteen. Southampton.'

Mistress Clara, unrecognisable from her many dominatrix guises, smirked as she heard the number called and noticed Manny leaving the room. Number thirteen might represent Southampton in the FA Cup draw, but to her number thirteen symbolised the terrifying thirteen-inch strap-on dildo which she'd buggered him with on occasions when his arrogance had irked her. 'Number thirteen. Unlucky for some.'

'Number Sixteen. Wolverhampton Wanderers.'

Kennedy looked at his watch. 2.50 p.m. Time didn't matter now. It had stopped mattering when he'd stopped drinking. He winked at Fletch and gave a thumbs-up signal to Bertie.

'Number Seven. Liverpool.'

Red or Blue? The Breck Road Red. Memories of the night he shot Jimmy Baker came back to him. They always did every time Liverpool was mentioned. A cold-blooded murder, but his mind-set had been reptilian then. Was he stony and inhuman just like Manny? He'd considered the possibility more than once… they shared the same gene pool after all.

Manny was short of breath as he reached the lift and jabbed a pudgy finger at the call button. 'Come on you cunt!'

A young, nervous-looking security guard approached him. 'S S Sorry Mr J J Jones. The lift doesn't seem to be working today.'

'Is any fucker working today?'

The guard cowered as Manny growled and paced his way past him to the fire escape door. 'Harry fucking Craven, where are you?'

'Number Four. Burnley.'

Jack Jones was sat between Nicky and Tess rubbing his hands in anticipation of what the cup draw might yet bring.

'Number Nine. Newcastle United.'

'Yes! It's still on!'

Nicky gave him a bewildered look and shrugged her shoulders. Tess ignored his comments, preferring to sip champagne. She'd heard it all before. He knew that she knew exactly what he was thinking. Reading, Queens Park Rangers, Swansea, Manchester United, Port Vale and Aston Villa were all still possibilities for Cheam... as was Chelsea. Maybe, just maybe, it was written in the stars.

'Bollocks!'

The picture on the television screen fragmented.

'I'm sorry we seem to have a problem with transmission.' The voice of the BBC continuity announcer was met with groans around the room. 'We'll return to Soho Square as soon as possible.'

Manny's face was reddening with exertion. As he paused to catch his breath at the top of the stairs, he felt his mobile phone vibrate in his hand.

'Harry!' Another text? No... it was a picture message. 'Oh my fucking God! No!'

Backing in through his office door, he stared at the photo displayed on the screen. The still, taken from CCTV footage that had been digitally enhanced, was a graphic image of Clara dressed as Vera with the notorious Number Thirteen strap-on dildo harnessed between her legs. As he scurried towards the wall on which the portrait of Queen Elizabeth I was hung, his phone vibrated again. Another picture message. He half knew what was coming, but the surprise and horror of what he saw

272

was enough to raise his blood pressure further. There he was, kneeling in front of 'Vera' performing fellatio on the dildo.

His mind reeled as he slid back the portrait. Fucking Harry. Why? Harry, his loyal right-hand man… deceitful cunt! He would die a horrible lingering death for this. He'd take care of it himself. The safe door was locked. Thank fuck for that. He caught his breath and wiped the perspiration from his forehead with the cuff of his shirt. He looked at Queen Elizabeth I and wondered what she had seen with her eyes? Why had Harry texted him the combination? *220440030939* When he'd first seen the numbers, they hadn't made any sense. He'd never seen them represented in any other way than in his mind's eye. They didn't need to be written down because they were easy to remember. 22 04 40 was Vera's date of birth and 03 09 39 was his. Harry was the only other person who knew the combination, but he'd never enquired about the significance of the numbers. That was the priceless thing about Harry… he'd never asked any questions. The mother's cunt! Manny twisted the dial, *220440030939,* but the combination failed to open the safe. 'Fuck!' Panicking, he tried once more… and then he tried calling Harry again.

'Apologies for that temporary break in coverage. Let's go back to the FA Cup draw. I'm being told they've waited for us while that little glitch was fixed.'

'The wankers are teasing us.' Fletch nudged Bertie as he poured Blossom and Petal a glass of champagne. 'Who you gonna support if Cheam draw the Chels?'

Bertie smiled as he looked across at Jack, then at Kennedy, then back at Fletch. 'You know what? I'm gonna support Jack.'

'Number Ten. Port Vale. Number Twelve. Reading.'

Vera had been absently minded fidgeting with her Rosary necklace as the draw had started. Manny's sudden departure had gone unnoticed by everyone else in the room. But she'd seen him leave. He appeared worried. Seeing all her family and friends gathered around the tables gave the event a sense of occasion for her… like a wedding… a christening… or a funeral.

If Manny was the corrupt, villainous man she'd supposed he was for all these years, why had he never been brought to justice? Maybe she was a terrible judge of character. He'd gallantly stepped aside when she'd declared her love for his brother Alec. He'd always been kind to her and Kennedy. After Alec's murder, he hadn't been hasty. He'd waited before trying to woo her. The money had come in handy. The gifts were tasteful, and the flowers and some of the jewellery beautiful. But 'no' meant 'no'.

'Number Fourteen. Swansea City. Number Eleven. Queens Park Rangers.'

Kennedy had decided of his own volition to go and work for Manny. The sequence of events that followed could have been related to combat stress. She fed the emerald beads of the Rosary through her fingers and looked at her grandson. Seeing Jack play football again had given her a new lease of life, a sense of fulfilment that had been lacking for years.

'Man United and Chelsea are still in Gran.'

She nodded at Jack and smiled as Kennedy added, 'So are Villa.'

They were a family at last, and all of this was thanks to Manny. She scanned the room looking for him but he still hadn't returned. As she turned her attention back to the television screen, she noticed a smartly dressed middle-aged woman she did not recognise sat three tables away looking intently at her. The woman pursed her lips and placed the tip of her right index finger on them. Was that a sign meant for her? A shiver ran down her spine as she noticed the woman was wearing an emerald Rosary necklace just like hers. Was that also a gift from Manny, or just a coincidence? Her positive thought process about him was suddenly reversed. She contemplated the Bible… but couldn't think of an appropriate verse.

'*Number Seven. Manchester United.*'

Distracted by the sound of expectant voices in the room, she saw Jack and Kennedy clench their fists in anticipation.

'*Number Two. Aston Villa.*'

'YES!' As the room erupted in a raucous orgy of champagne-cork-popping celebration, Jack and Kennedy leapt from their seats and embraced each other

Manny heard the commotion and made the connection, but the respite from his stress was all too brief. For the third time, and this time with great deliberation, he dialled the numbers *220440030939* but the safe door would not open.

Beads of perspiration rolled down his temples as he worked his way through the possibilities. The permutations were endless, but everything pointed to Harry and Clara. Clara had access to the CCTV footage. No doubt she also had a copy of her client list that she'd provided him with as part of the deal in which he'd bought the property she lived in and where her chambers and dungeons were located. Names, addresses, phone numbers, videos, photos, sound recordings. In the wrong hands there was enough material to extort millions, to bring the high and mighty of society grovelling to their knees, snivelling in submission as they all had at the feet of Mistress Clara… as he had. But Clara was downstairs in the hall. It didn't make sense. Or maybe she wasn't there now… or maybe she planned to replay a video of him being defiled by her dressed as Vera on the big television screen for everyone to see. Nobody would recognise her as plain old Clara Bristow. His heart was pounding, his shirt saturated with sweat. She had to be in it with Harry. There was no other explanation. Maybe their relationship had developed beyond the medical room she tormented him in. Had she finally fallen for a client? He'd watched the first of their sessions but hadn't enjoyed it.

Now he'd have to watch them all. He'd been wrong about Ginger. She could have helped him, just as she always had. But this was no time for regret.

'Come on… one more time.' Manny dialled the combination again. *220440030939* Nothing. He switched the birthdates just in case. He realised as he did it that it was a ridiculous thing to do. *030939220440* Nothing. 'Bastard! Harry!' All those times he'd driven him to his 'appointments' with Clara. Curiosity had obviously got the better of him. Perhaps he'd been a client first? Their sessions conducted in secret away from prying camera lenses. Was it just the two of them? Who else might be involved in their conspiracy? It was clever, brilliant even. But such a plot would be difficult to keep quiet. Only a genius of his criminal intellect could mastermind such a grand plan and execute it without his minions knowing all the details.

What about Jester Cook? He and Harry were thick as thieves. Or were they just thick and thieves? He reached for his mobile phone. As he did so, it vibrated. 'Bastards!' Another picture message. Him with Jacobsen. Then another. Him with Prime. And one more. Him with Alec.

Manny tried calling Jester, but there was no answer. He couldn't call any of the men in the photos because they were all dead. He could still hear the sound of cheering coming from downstairs. He'd speak to Jester first, then Clara. He had to find Harry. He had to stay calm. 'Fuck it!' As he walked hurriedly to the office door, his phone vibrated again. 'Fucking Harry! BASTARD! What now?'

It was a plain text message. *'151038'* A new combination for the safe? But what was the rest of the number? Manny stared at the phone. 'One, five, one, zero, three, eight. Come on, I'm not fucking psychic.'

He thought about how he'd use Clara's creamy white stomach as an ironing board to torture the truth from her.

Dominatrix she may be, but she wouldn't be able to take the pain. Her slut maid Trina would strap her to the bondage bench and take care of it. She'd do it if the money was right. They all did it for the money eventually, even Vera would come round now. He knew right now she'd be thinking how she'd got him all wrong, how maybe she could have loved him like she'd loved his brother. She still could, but not in that way. It wouldn't feel right.

'Alec! Fuck!' He looked at the phone again. '*151038* Fuck!' 15 October 1938. Alec's birthday! If the first six numbers of the combination that no longer worked had represented Vera's date of birth but now related to Alec's, what was the second date? Manny bared his teeth and glared at the safe. His mouth was dry, it was painful to swallow and difficult to breath, but the sole focus of his attention was his phone. Again it vibrated. Another text. Another sequence of numbers. '*2704*' 'Bastard! 27 April. Vera's birthday. What about the last two numbers? Must be four and zero.' He snatched at the dial and span the new sequence of numbers. *151038270440* The safe failed to open.

'Bastard! Fucking clever bastard!' Manny began to laugh. 'It's seven and seven ain't it?' 27 April was Vera's birthday and also the date Alec had been murdered. 27 April 1977... such a cruel coincidence. 'What the fuck has Alec got to do with this?' Manny hissed, and then he spat out the numbers. 'One, five, one, zero, three, eight, two, seven, zero, four, seven, seven.' Propelled by adrenalin and fury, he ignored the feeling of nausea and tightness in his chest as he dialled the combination.

151038270477 The safe door opened.

'Cunt!' Manny wheezed. With the exception of a large emerald green velvet bag that hadn't been there before, the safe was empty. Cash was replaceable. The fifty thousand pounds he kept there for personal expenses was a small sum. The theft of the contract and transaction files that predated the computerisation of all Chapman Security companies undertaken in 1995 was problematic. The laptop was a different matter. It wouldn't take the most sophisticated hacker to access the information it contained. The hard drive wasn't encrypted. What would Harry and Clara do? They'd have a crack at the password and give up. It wouldn't matter to them anyway. What mattered was having it in their possession so they could blackmail him.

'Vermin! Scum! Cowards!' Raging at the betrayal, Manny clenched his fists several times before reaching into the safe and snatching the velvet bag. That adage about keeping 'friends close and enemies closer' needed refining. He opened the bag.

'Argh! Argh! What the fuck?'

Manny retched. As he dropped the bag, its contents spilled onto the floor. Seven severed, bloody fingers. His phone vibrated. Indignant and perplexed he looked at Harry's message. *'The magnificent seven boss. I did my best but I couldn't take the pain no more.'*

Breathing heavily, he dropped to his haunches and looked at the fingers. One was still ringed tightly with a gold band which had the initial H fashioned from an emerald set in it.

'Harry… Harry… Harry.' Manny growled. As he stood up, the realisation that his trusted lieutenant was not behind this heinous plot dawned on him rapidly. Whoever it was had Harry's phone. The calls would be easy to trace. He had people who could do that. Right now, he needed to get to the room downstairs. Pretend nothing had happened. Look people in the eye. One by one, starting with Clara… if she was still there. He flinched as he picked up Harrys fingers and put them back in the bag. 'Seven fingers! Fair play to the cunt!' He smiled as he placed the bag back in the safe. How many fingers would he have given up before he revealed any information? They'd have had to kill him first… or would they? Clara had taken him to the edge many times, and only a 'safe' word had saved him. 'Butter' had been the last one they'd used. Cool, calm and collected she may be, but if she were connected to this plot in anyway he'd make sure the butter that wouldn't melt in her mouth would be dissolved with a blowtorch.

As he reprogrammed the combination with a sequence of numbers that represented his own birthdate and today's date, the smugness he felt that he could ride out this challenge to his omnipotence became curbed by a sharp pain in his chest that began radiating to his jaw and left arm. A couple of aspirin would see him all right. He paused to catch his breath, slid the portrait of Queen Elizabeth I back to its customary position obscuring the safe, and walked uneasily to the door of his office. If Harry was dead, how had the door's security mechanism been compromised overnight?

★ ★ ★

Bertie enjoyed the independence that being able to drive afforded him. At the wheel of his specially modified, short-wheelbase Volkswagen Transporter he was the master of his own destiny. He could drive where he wanted without people watching his every move and commenting on his disability. The Transporter, which featured remote and hard-wired rear-opening doors and a rear tail-lift, was fitted with push-pull ignition, the latest thirteen-way wireless keypad control, a soft-touch steering grip, lightened power-steering, cruise control, Bluetooth and satellite navigation. All these features made it easy to access, and easy to drive.

Discreetly finished in gloss black, with windows providing ninety percent privacy, the Transporter glided stealthily from A to B... on many occasions when B was a completely random destination like when he took Vera out for afternoon tea. Hampton Court, Kew Gardens, Richmond Park. Vera loved Richmond Park. Sometimes, if the weather was nice, he'd drive them down to the coast. Brighton was a favourite, but it got too busy in the summer. Chichester Harbour and the Witterings were beautiful. Unspoilt beaches, rolling sand dunes, salty sea air and fish and chips. Bertie didn't feel glad to be alive too often, but when he had the sun on his face, and only the squawking seagulls and Vera for company, he was able to forget about his situation.

Boredom, loneliness and frustration had proved callous foes in the past, and waving good riddance to them hadn't been easy. He'd had too much time to think. There could be no turning the clock back, but the way he viewed his situation now was different and had changed dramatically in the months since Kennedy's release from prison. Alongside Fletch, he'd felt part of something again. The camaraderie of youth that had been blown to smithereens in battle had been reassembled. All the King's horses and all the King's men might not have been able to put Humpty Dumpty together again, but the musketeers of Battersea were giving it a go and they would never give up. They had rediscovered their 'all for one, and one for all' friendship. He even had the confidence now to have a girlfriend. Fletch's Thai brass Blossom had suggested an introduction to her sister Petal.

Blossom and Petal, with names like that they should be working in a florists not a brothel. He'd never been kissed like that before. Petal was as fragrant as her name suggested. A delicate, sweet-scented Thai rose with a flawless face, beguiling smile, and perfect tits. He couldn't love her fully, but she moaned at the right times, did the right things, and told him he was the kindest, gentlest, most considerate man she had ever met.

All this attention and affection came at a price, but then so did everything. Fletch was right with his philosophy. For men like them this was therapy. Even Kennedy had been tempted on occasion, but he never had to try with women. Since he'd been on the wagon, Nicky had taken him back and he was a family man again. A proud grandfather whose son was a professional footballer. If that wasn't enough to keep you on the straight and narrow, nothing was… well apart from having a masterplan to right all the wrongs that he and his family had suffered. The story about how Manny had manipulated his life had seemed far-fetched at first… but the explanation had been simple, the theory precise, and the evidence damning. Now it was payback time.

Bertie looked at the digital clock mounted on the Transporter's dashboard. 3.36 a.m. He pushed the ignition button.

FIX BAYONETS!

He smiled as he read the fresh graffiti that had been sprayed onto the wall at the end of the deserted dead-end alley adjacent to Yelverton Road where Kennedy's lockup was located. The last thing he remembered before waking up in hospital was hearing that command. He imagined the rest. The clunk-click as he'd fixed his bayonet to his weapon. The clamour of battle. The sound of gunfire. Ricocheting rounds zipping through the air… cracking into rock, thudding into earth, tearing into flesh. Screams and distressed cries for help. Voices shouting under duress. The order given. 'CHARGE!' Giving up the protection of the crag he was backed up against. Strenuous breathing. Heart pumping. Lungs bursting. Leaden feet. A Doppler effect of sound. An explosion. White light. Blackness. Kennedy was right. It was always darkest before the dawn.

FUCK THE ARMY

That was the only statement that used to be legible on the wall… the gang tags and scrawls were a mish-mash of hieroglyphic nonsense.

281

Three words that had summed up how he'd felt. Bitter, neglected, ruined.

FIX BAYONETS! was a call to action, but with a different meaning. It was time once more to engage the enemy face-to-face.

'Oscar, Romeo, Papa. I repeat, Oscar, Romeo, Papa.' Bertie tapped the end of the boom microphone as he spoke. The single channel ground and airborne radio system that Fletch had fitted to the Transporter was sophisticated enough to provide voice and data encryption, and it had proved one hundred percent reliable in the field tests they had conducted over the past six months.

The blue door to the lockup garage that Bertie had parked outside swung open and Kennedy and Fletch emerged both dressed in black rapid-wear military overalls. Kennedy, carrying a tactical low-profile EDC hydration backpack, opened the side door to the Transporter and clambered inside while Fletch closed the garage door.

'So far so good.' Kennedy beckoned Fletch to get into the vehicle. 'We'll come back later as planned to clean up and debrief.'

'You sure about leaving Spot in there?' Bertie pushed the ignition button and engaged the throttle.

'He'll be fine. He's a dog. Food, water and a blanket to sleep on. That's all he needs and he's got them.'

Fletch stepped into the Transporter and activated the automatic door closure mechanism. 'Good job that mutt can't talk. He'd yelp for a bowl of Winalot. Drop us right in the shit.'

Bertie eased the Transporter slowly onto Yelverton Road, turned left onto Gwynne Road and then made a right onto Lombard Road. The streets were empty. 3.38 a.m. Sunday night. The chances of attracting the attention of a police patrol car were minimal. Nevertheless, Bertie drove with due care and attention as he passed the deserted workshops and warehouses that gave way to residential housing on the right and a view of the Thames on the left as Lombard Road morphed into Vicarage Crescent.

'Looks peaceful.' Kennedy clasped the EDC backpack to his chest as he picked out the shadowy buildings on the north side of the river.

As he drove from Vicarage Crescent into Westbridge Road, Bertie picked up speed. It was 4.7 miles from the lock up to Soho Square, taking no risks the journey would take less than fifteen minutes. Perfect timing. He felt calm and relaxed. 'Did you get what you needed?' I know we've got a lot of high tech equipment, but none of it's psychic.'

Fletch laughed at Bertie's joke. This was serious business, and a little humour was more than welcome. 'Yeah! Yeah! Sorry mate. I was looking at those new flats going up at Chelsea Harbour. Wouldn't mind one of them when they're finished. Just to have a view of my London. Know what I mean?'

Bertie nodded. 'Yeah. I know exactly what you mean. You could sit on the balcony and look at the landmarks of your life... well most of 'em.'

Fletch shrugged his shoulders and reached out to pat the bag that Kennedy was holding. 'I'm not sure I'd want a constant reminder.'

Bertie slowed down again as he drove through Battersea Park. 'How many?'

Kennedy smiled. 'Why do you want to know?'

'Just curious.'

'Eight!'

'All of them! Fuck me! That's loyalty for you.'

'Not enough though eh.' Kennedy grimaced at the memory. Harry Craven hanging by his feet from the gantry in the lock up. Hands cuffed behind his back, head swinging a matter of inches above the floor, Spot licking his face. The key element in capturing him had been surprise. The last thing he'd expect after a session with Mistress Clara was to be kidnapped. Served him right. Everyone knew what happened to curious cats. Harry had always wondered what line of business Clara was in. When he'd finally found out, he'd decided he had to meet her and had soon fallen under her spell.

During an initial 'consultation', Clara had established that the somewhat straight-laced right-hand man of her strategic client had an arousing interest in nurses that she had developed over a period of time into an addictive fetish for medical roleplays involving urethral sounds. The CCTV footage Kennedy had seen had made his eyes water. Harry strapped to a padded examination chair. Clara dressed in white rubber plunging a range of thin stainless steel probes with rosebud ends of varying sizes, some electrified, into the tip of his penis. She'd explained in great detail that the remedial purpose of this process was to unblock strictures by increasing the diameter of the urethra, and how sexually it was associated with stimulation of the prostate gland. Apparently, the pain associated with the pleasure was intense.

Kennedy didn't feel any malice towards Harry, so the fact that he knew the man he was about to torture and kill had just enjoyed a mind-blowing orgasm had made him feel better when he'd levelled a pistol at his head as he'd left Clara's the previous afternoon. He'd been tempted to use Clara to elicit the information he required, or at least her instruments of torment, but that introduced too many variables into what was a simple equation. A sharp blow to the base of the skull had rendered Harry unconscious and Duct-tape placed across the mouth had prevented any unnecessary conversation or embarrassing pleas for mercy when he came round.

'We need the combination to the safe in Manny's office.'

Fletch was on his haunches, head cocked to one side looking at Harry who was breathing heavily and grunting. He peeled the Duct-tape from his mouth.

'Fuck off you lunatic. Do you really think he'd tell me that?' Harry gasped for air as he spoke.

'He told you everything else.' Harry tried to wriggle round so he could see Kennedy who was stood behind him.

'W W W Whadya mean?'

'That Bentley you drive him, or should I say, the Godfather, to and from Clara's in… we put a wire in it.'

'I don't know the number.'

'I think you do.' As Fletch secured the Duct-tape back across Harry's mouth, Kennedy used a pair of secateurs to cut the index finger of his left hand off.

Harry squealed in pain, and Fletch and Kennedy sang to drown out his groans. *'One man went to mow, went to mow a meadow. One man and his dog, Spot, went to mow a meadow.'*

Spot cocked his leg against Harry's face and relieved himself.

'You enjoying that H? Kennedy chuckled. You like water sports don't you. Not quite the same as Clara gushing over you eh?'

'How's that memory of yours now?' Fletch put the severed finger in the backpack and peeled away the Duct-tape from Harry's mouth.

As dog piss, sweat and tears mingled as they dribbled off his forehead, Harry pleaded with his captors. 'Please no more. I don't know the fucking number.'

Fletch secured the Duct-tape and Kennedy sang as he readied the secateurs. *'Two man went to mow, went to mow a meadow. Two men, one man, and his dog, Spot, went to mow a meadow.'* All eight bloody fingers to get the combination. *220440030939* He'd cut Harry's thumbs off as well just because he'd been such a stubborn bastard. They were a treat for Spot. Harry had still been alive as he'd watched the dog eat them.

Kennedy glanced at his watch. 3.49 a.m. 'ETA still 3.53?'

Bertie checked the Transporter's satellite navigation system. 'Exactly.' Kennedy nodded and rubbed his gloved hands together. Everything was going to plan. Why shouldn't it? Manny was in his crosshairs now. Having fathomed out the truth about his lifelong obsession with his mother, the murder of his father and the control of his own life, he'd been tempted to kill him at the earliest opportunity, but that would be too easy, too nice. He deserved a dose of his own bad medicine.

Interrogating Jonesy, the lout from the Monty, had been central to him piecing together the jigsaw of deception. "Th th Thank you Dad". Those last words he'd mumbled after Manny had slapped him had lodged in Kennedy's brain. Jonesy's tongue had been loosened with a threat of sustained violence and a sweetener of five thousand pounds. Andrew Jones was Manny's illegitimate son by a French prostitute called Susan who'd worked in Soho in the sixties and seventies. Jonesy had photographs of her when she was younger. The resemblance to Vera was uncanny.

After meeting Jonesy, he'd followed Manny for a month. He knew he had to have an Achilles heel. All men had one. His had been drink. Manny's was Clara Bristow. At the outset, he'd gone through the pretence of an initial 'consultation' with Clara to gain trust. 'How much do you charge your kinkiest client?' "Two thousand pounds". 'I'll pay you double if you tell me exactly what he asks you to do.' She didn't have to name Manny, simply mentioning Vera was enough. Clara had confirmed his suspicions, and Fletch's comprehensive understanding of CCTV technology and ability to hack any system completed the puzzle. After that, it was just a matter of planning. In exacting revenge, was he descending into the same perverted abyss that Manny inhabited? Possibly, but

Fletch and Bertie didn't think so... and that was good enough for him. 'All for one and one for all.' He closed his eyes and relaxed his mind for the remainder of the journey.

Fletch looked through the privacy glass as they entered the Piccadilly underpass. After crossing the Thames at Chelsea Bridge for the remainder of the journey they would be under camera. There was no point taking detours to avoid possible surveillance, in the unlikely event the Transporter's movements were being consciously monitored, anything other than a direct route at this time of night would arouse suspicion.

Sloane Street, Knightsbridge, Hyde Park Corner, Piccadilly Circus, Shaftesbury Avenue, Dean Street, Carlisle Street, Soho Square. The whole of the West End of London was saturated with CCTV cameras many of which were linked to the transport system. Manny had been in the business from the outset and installation and maintenance contracts had been unsurprisingly easy to come by, even without his special kind of leverage. Safety, crime detection and protection of property were of vital importance to the police and public authorities in particular, added to this were the business and personal systems that had proliferated with next to no regulation. One camera for every ten people in the capital was his guess.

"We are living in a surveillance society Mr Fletcher. There is money to be made". He could still hear Manny's patronising words now, twenty years after he'd turned down the opportunity to work for Chapman Security. Manny had been right on both counts, but at the time Fletch knew he couldn't hold down a regular job. The industry interested him. Largely self-taught, he'd immersed himself in learning about the technology and over time become confident enough in his ability to seek work as a contractor with a specialist company called Real Time Security.

Being ex-military, through RTS he'd also occasionally

been engaged by Scotland Yard in the laborious process of CCTV recovery, trawling through hours and hours of jerky grainy footage analysing people's movements. The 7 July 2005 terrorist bombings in London had highlighted to the general public just how rich the environment was in CCTV. Clips and stills were frequently broadcast and shared by the media as the police distilled the footage that would eventually help them identify and trace the movements of the perpetrators. Big Brother was definitely watching, but maybe it wasn't such a bad thing.

'3.53 a.m. precisely.' He looked over at the dashboard and then out of the windscreen. Bertie had been able to park the Transporter in one of the five suitable bays they had identified. Sunday was the only night Viola closed early. The nightclub wasn't open, just the bar and restaurant. Customers were encouraged to be off the premises by midnight, and staff always left before 1.00 a.m. Other businesses of similar scale employed the services of security guards, but Manny had long since put his faith in technology. People could be got at, machines couldn't. Bribery and corruption were of little consequence to a circuit board, and to prove his point none of his premises had ever been compromised.

Harry's wallet had yielded the magnetic stripe smartcard that identified him to Viola's biometric fingerprint entry system, the severed index finger of his right hand when placed against the integrated reader would match his details and unlock any door in the building. Harry was the only employee besides Manny to have 'access all areas' status. As they'd devised the plan, the realisation that Manny hadn't considered such a gruesome eventuality was a source of some amusement. Maybe he wasn't paranoid enough.

Viola's state-of-the-art CCTV and alarm system used wireless technology to connect cameras to monitoring equipment and sensors to control panels. The hardware incorporated jamming detection, but the 2.4 GHz WiFi and switchable 850, 900, 1800 and 1900 MHz GSM frequencies that respectively carried the CCTV signals and triggered the auto-dialler to issue alarm alerts were vulnerable to attack. The Transporter was parked close enough to Viola for the future-proof eight-band jammer Bertie would employ to neutralize the building's security system to be in range of every camera and every sensor. External street-view CCTV cameras that belonged to Westminster City Council had been shut down earlier by Fletch for 'essential maintenance'. The primary use of the equipment was to enforce traffic regulations, so given Sunday was the quietest day of the week, with fewer vehicles on the road, and relaxed permitted parking hours, it was the ideal time to undertake such work.

Real Time Security were also contracted to provide mobile patrols of the area. All of the company vehicles were fitted with GPS receivers to enable tracking and GSM transmitters to broadcast location coordinates to the control room at head office. Fletch had cloned the monitoring software and installed it on a laptop that would enable Bertie to provide updates on the whereabouts of any security vans in the vicinity and the indicative route they were taking. With over two hundred miles of carriageway to patrol, and only two RTS vehicles operational, Soho Square would be circuited infrequently however, given the confined nature of the inner London borough, they would never be more than ten minutes away, so intelligence of this kind could prove invaluable. The police were the only variable in the equation. West End Central station was less than a mile away, but Soho Square was tucked away from the labyrinth of seedy, sleepless streets and muggers alleys where the detritus of society traditionally kept law enforcement officers busy.

'4.00 a.m. Active.' Kennedy smiled as he exited the Transporter. With one RTS patrol van in Lisson Grove, and the other in Pimlico, the conditions were perfect. He hadn't thought of the operation as a robbery until now, but suddenly it felt like they were doing a bank job or a jewel heist. The rush of adrenalin had felt good. Everything went precisely to plan. Fifteen minutes later they were back in the Transporter heading back to the lock up. The contents of Manny's safe had been removed and replaced with the bag containing seven of Harry's fingers. His right index digit had been retained to enable them to exit the doors and the building. The hard part of the job was done. All that remained was for Fletch to program his laptop to send a timed series of coded text messages from Harry's mobile phone to Manny's.

★ ★ ★

'We love you Manny, we do. We love you Manny, we do. We love you Manny, we do… Oh Manny, we love you.'

Cheam Athletic manager, Mark Parry was stood on the stage leading the chanting. With training cancelled for the day and drink flowing, his players needed little encouragement to join in.

Vera nudged Jack who was noticeably reluctant to participate in the celebrations. 'Where on earth is he? I thought he'd be in here milking this for all it's worth.'

Jack smiled and looked at Kennedy. 'Probably sulking because we didn't get drawn against Man U eh Dad.'

Kennedy winked and checked his watch. It was 2.59 p.m. 'I expect so son. No doubt he'll be here soon.'

Waves of nausea had washed over Manny as he'd descended the fire escape stairs and slammed the safety bar to open the ground floor corridor door. Short of breath and bathed in cold perspiration, he'd paused as the pressure on his chest intensified. The pain scorching down his left arm and to his jaw had become unbearable causing him to curse out loud.

'*Manny, Manny, Manny.*' He could hear his name being chanted. His people loved him, but not all of them. Who? Who? Who?

'*Manny, Manny, Manny.*'

A fucking heart attack. He wasn't going to die like this. He wasn't going to die. Not without gaining revenge for this betrayal. Manny's head swam as blind panic enveloped him. Clenching his right fist, face flushed with exertion and contorted in agony, he stumbled towards the main hall bundling into the security guard he'd encountered earlier.

'Are y y you o-okay sir?'

'Call an ambulance you cunt!' Gasping for air, he pushed the security guard out of the way and careered into the main door to the party room that opened as he fell against it. The cheers and applause that greeted his entrance were muted in an instant and replaced by anxious cries of concern. As he dropped to his knees vomit began bubbling volcanically from his mouth. Just before consciousness left him for the last time, he caught sight of Kennedy stood with Vera and Clara. He was holding their emerald Rosary necklaces in his left hand and pointing at the large plasma screen that was displaying Cheam Athletic's club crest, the distinctive gold pocket watch with the time set to three o'clock. Scrolling beneath it was the Latin motto he'd added when he'd bought the club:

TOLLE ADVERSARIUM OCULOS DE ISTO NUSQUAM

This was closely followed by its English translation:

NEVER TAKE YOUR EYES OFF YOUR OPPONENT